Andrew MacAllan liv
His previous novel
Diamond Hard and *Fanfare*, are all available from
Headline.

Also by Andrew MacAllan

Succession
Generation
Diamond Hard
Fanfare

Speculator

Andrew MacAllan

HEADLINE

First published in 1993
by HEADLINE BOOK PUBLISHING PLC

First published in paperback in 1993
by HEADLINE BOOK PUBLISHING PLC

10 9 8 7 6 5 4 3 2 1

ISBN 0 7472 4181 3

Typeset by
Letterpart Limited, Reigate, Surrey

Printed and bound in Great Britain by
HarperCollins Manufacturing, Glasgow

HEADLINE BOOK PUBLISHING PLC
Headline House
79 Great Titchfield Street
London W1P 7FN

Speculator

Prologue

Marco Polo was dying.

He lay on his hard narrow bed, half covered by sheepskin rugs, and all around he could see familiar faces peering at him. His priest, his family, even distant relations he had not met for years, had crowded into this upper room in Venice for this last farewell.

'I beg of you,' said his priest earnestly, 'while you have time, renounce the lies you have told about things you say you saw on your journeys, the strange adventures you claim to have experienced. While you still have time, admit you imagined them.

'Perhaps you were fevered or the sun had touched your brain. Our Lord is merciful. Only repent and cleanse your soul of this unrighteousness, so that you may go to heaven and eternal peace.'

For a moment, no one else spoke. They stood staring at the old man with such intensity that it seemed to him that he was surrounded not by people, or even by faces, but by eyes boring into his eyes, peering into his soul.

You fools, he thought. You have never left Venice. You have never travelled or seen the sights I have seen. You have never known how chances, mistakes, totally irrelevant happenings can change our lives and bring one man to wealth and another to ruin. How can I persuade you I have told the truth, that there are other countries and other peoples whose ways you cannot even begin to comprehend?

1

Suddenly, the irony of his position – the adventurer surrounded by timid stay-at-homes, incapable of believing anything beyond their own sheltered experience – overcame him.

Painfully, Marco Polo raised himself up on one elbow. Looking at them all, he damned them.

'You fools!' he cried bitterly. 'You cannot believe what you have not seen and what you will never know. I tell you, I have not lied. Indeed, I have not told the half of what I saw and did.'

For a moment he stayed thus, on one elbow, surveying them all with contempt. And then, smiling, Marco Polo fell back on his pillow, and died.

The little boy came into the huge room and stood for a moment awkwardly, framed in the doorway. High above and beyond him, out of sight, he heard the diminishing drone of aircraft; the old house stood under the flight path for Heathrow. Planes coming in from Europe began to lose height here, over the Kent coast, more than fifty miles from London.

The old man who had first told him this lay propped up in the wide bed on the far side of the room. He did not like to lie flat. He would say to the boy, 'I'll be flat enough for long enough and soon enough in my grave. So I like to sit up while I can. The brain works better in an upright position, you know.'

David liked the old man, who had told him so many odd facts and stories of a kind that no one else seemed to know. He called him Uncle Richard, though he was not his uncle, but his grandfather. Although Uncle Richard was older than some of the grandfathers of his friends at school, in some strange way he did not seem so. He might be old in years, but he was still young in heart and mind and outlook. They treated each other as equals. People at different ends of their life span can be honest with each other; they have no need for make-believe, no time for falseness. Sometimes, though, David was not quite certain whether Uncle Richard was speaking the truth or making a joke. Often, it was very difficult to tell with grown-ups. What you privately thought was funny, they meant to be serious. Then, when they made a joke and you did not laugh, they would look at you and ask huffily, 'What's the matter, then? Got the sulks today, have you?'

'I didn't know that,' said David carefully, meaning the remark about the brain working better when you sat up.

'It's true,' Uncle Richard insisted seriously – or was he only half-serious? 'And I'll tell you something else. Do you remember the Bible story, how when the Jews brought Christ before Pontius Pilate, and told them what He had done, and that was the truth of the matter, Pilate asked them all a question. "What is truth?" he asked. And no one could answer him. Because, you see, truth can vary, depending on what you think it is.'

David was silent. Uncle Richard sometimes talked like this – in riddles, he thought. He did not think he was required to answer him. In any case, he had no answer to give.

The old man also kept silent, looking out of the wide mullioned windows at the lawn and beyond that, the park. In the distance, he could see one of the four lodges of the great house. How odd to think he had been a baby when he had first seen this house from his pram. That was a long time ago, he thought, a very long time.

Something Emerson had written still stuck in his mind: 'A man only counts his years when he has nothing else to count.'

Did Marco Polo think that when he was dying? He kept reliving that scene, which he had first read years and years ago, how Marco Polo had died unable to

3

convince his closest relatives that his experiences were true.

The doctor's car was moving slowly away over the raked gravel towards the South Lodge. He came to see Richard once a week: not that he was ill, of course. The doctor called each visit 'just checking'.

'On what?' Richard would ask him. 'That I'm still alive? You're speculating that one day I won't be?'

'One day none of us will be. But surely you're the speculator, not me?'

'I don't think so, Doctor,' Richard replied. 'To me, a speculator is someone who builds houses as a gamble – a speculation – and hopes to sell them.'

'There is another definition,' said the doctor. 'To spy out and observe – from the Latin *speculari*. And I'd say you have observed people and propositions pretty closely. Then – and only then – you worked out your calculations regarding men and machines. Am I right?'

Of course Richard agreed that he was. And they both laughed. There was nothing wrong with him; only that he was getting on a bit. Growing old might not always be pleasant – Dean Swift had declared that every man desired to live long, but no man would be old. Even so, growing old seemed better than the only other alternative.

The drive was so long that its length intimidated some people and irritated others. Some felt they should not drive fast in case they sprayed the lawns with gravel. Others drove with excessive speed, simply to show they were not impressed. In fact, of course, their behaviour simply proved the opposite.

He remembered when that drive had been lined with family servants for his father's funeral. They employed thirty servants inside the house then, and almost as many outside; an army of men and women and boys. Woodmen, water bailiffs, gardeners, under-gardeners;

4

butler, cook, kitchen maids and housemaids, his mother's ladies' maid and in-between maids – tweenies, as they were called – all of them dependent on the fortunes of those in the big house. Each knew his or her place and, in a way that didn't seem to happen much now, accepted this hierarchy. As with oarsmen in a great galley, he often thought, they all had to row together, for if one fell out, the rhythm would be lost, and the vessel falter.

He leaned towards David, seeing himself in the boy's blue eyes.

'Have you come to tell me tea is ready?'

'Yes,' said David. 'Mother is bringing up a tray.'

'She is very kind to me,' said the old man. 'Very kind indeed.'

As he spoke, he remembered how his own mother would simply pull a tasselled rope beside the mantelpiece and a maid would come in, curtsy, take her instructions and within moments, it seemed, she would return pushing a trolley with silver cream jug, tea pot, cucumber sandwiches finely cut on lace doilies and tongs beautifully polished to grip each sugar lump.

Often his mother would pick up the tongs and examine crevices in their claws to make sure no traces of silver polish remained after cleaning. They did things differently then, of course. He remembered that trolley well. The wheels squeaked until he oiled them. Later, he removed them and fitted others with ball bearings which took much of the effort out of pushing the trolley. The maid had been very pleased.

'Was there anything else?' he asked David, bringing his mind back to the present. He thought there might be; it seemed unlikely that David would come up to his room simply to tell him tea was on its way.

'I was wondering,' said David tentatively. 'That old steam engine. I've a friend coming to tea. I told him about it. Could we borrow it? Only for an hour or so, until he's gone.'

'Of course,' said Richard. 'Who's your friend? Anyone I've met?'

'I don't think so, Uncle Richard. He's Australian. His father's got a farm there – he calls it a station – as big as Wales.'

'Lucky man. What's his name?'

'Tommy. Tommy Gardener. His grandpa was a pilot in the First World War. Won the MC. He'd be as old as you – if he'd lived.'

'When did he die, then?'

'Oh, in the Second World War. He was a test pilot. Did you ever come across him? He was not Tommy, but Tom Gardener.'

Richard paused before he replied. Of course he had known Tom Gardener: the name was a key that opened the door to a whole host of memories. But did he want to remember now? How extraordinary that Tom's grandson should now be in his house, under his roof.

'About the steam engine,' he said, again bringing his mind back to the present. 'Take it away. But be careful you don't hurt yourself if you fire it up. Steam can be a dangerous thing. And remember that engine is an antique – almost as old as I am.'

David crossed the room. On a side table, under a glass case, stood a toy steam engine. Polished legs supported a miniature brass boiler. A small burner, little more than a flat tin with a wick protruding from a hole, fitted beneath this. The exhaust pipe was painted with imitation bricks to simulate a factory chimney. At the side of the boiler was the brass cylinder with a connecting rod joined to a crimson fly-wheel. On the name plate an inscription was engraved on a small brass plate: 'The Spirit and the Speed.'

As a boy, Richard had never quite known what this

6

meant. You needed methylated spirit to heat the boiler; and with that spirit the engine gave you speed. That was one interpretation. Another was that if you personally possessed spirit – ambition, drive, determination – then you could speed to your destination or goal.

'You have methylated spirits for the burner?' Richard asked his grandson.

David nodded. 'Yes,' he said. 'A whole bottle.'

'You know how to start it?'

'Yes.'

'Of course you do. I was forgetting, I've taught you often enough.'

'One day, will you tell me the story of how you first got it and what happened then? You promised.'

'I know I promised. And I will tell you. One day . . .'

David lifted off the glass cover and picked up the engine with both hands, carefully as though it was a fragile relic, something that might easily crumble with rough treatment.

As David lifted it, Richard saw the birthmark on the back of the boy's right hand; he had a similar mark on his own hand. All male Rowlands had them. Viewed from a certain angle it seemed to be in the shape of the letters M.P. entwined together. Richard had been born on a Thursday, and Dorothy, his nursemaid, had told him often enough, 'Thursday's child has far to go. You're like Marco Polo, who was the first to travel from Europe to China. In those days you couldn't go further than that or you'd be coming home. That's what the initials stand for – Marco Polo. The great traveller.' The mark was on this engine, on every engineering artefact Richard had ever designed.

Now he watched his grandson carry the engine out of the door. That engine was more than a relic, as far as he was concerned; it was a kind of icon.

It had been a gift from his Aunt Hannah, his mother's

unmarried sister, when he was young. Everything important in his life had started from that moment; and, curiously, in the lives of others who had never seen the engine, had probably never even heard of it.

He sat back against the pillows, closed his eyes. When David's mother brought in the tea, he appeared to be sleeping. She looked at him for a moment, at his calm face, white hair. She put the tea tray down quietly on the bedside table. He's still good-looking, she thought. I wonder what he was like when he was young. I wonder whether he's sorry about what happened or whether, when you're old, you don't really care. She tiptoed out so as not to awake him.

But Richard Rowlands was not sleeping. He just did not want to speak, because to speak would scatter his thoughts. And his thoughts now reached back across more years than most people could count, back to the time when he was a boy, and life was only beginning.

Chapter One

A grown-up's recollections of childhood, so his mother used to tell him, are like a half-remembered country landscape seen in the early morning. Here and there small hills rise up above the mist; their peaks are your special memories. Richard had not thought about that remark then, but later on he thought about it often. His first memory – his first peak, if you like – was gentle; a friendly hill rather than a jagged point. Dorothy, his nursemaid, was pushing him in a wide pram. He remembered its spidery wheels and an awning of white cloth with scalloped edges like the fringe on a surrey cart.

He had always liked Dorothy. She was a warm person, the antithesis of his mother. Dorothy's fair hair was drawn back in a bun, and sometimes she would press his head against her breasts and he could smell her scent of rough carbolic soap, clean and fresh. She smiled a lot and laughed, played games with him. His mother never cuddled him, nor did she smile often.

Richard's first memory was of rain falling. Dorothy had taken him out for a walk along the drive, down to the South Lodge and back. When they set out, the sun had been shining. Then the sky grew dark and big drops of rain began to fall. He had cried then. He could not understand why he felt cold water on his face.

'Never mind, Richard,' Dorothy told him reassuringly, rocking the pram as nurses did, trying to quieten him and induce him to go to sleep. 'It won't hurt you. It's only rain – the tears angels shed for all the bad things in the world.'

He had not understood what she meant, of course, but she reminded him later, when he did understand. He hadn't believed her, but that was the first memory. The next memory was of his elder brother, Tobin. This was a jagged, sharp peak in the landscape of recollection, impossible to conquer and unwise to approach too closely.

Again, he was in his pram, and suddenly a face appeared over the side, above the buttoned Rexine upholstery, looking down at him. The face somehow seemed contorted, like one of the stone gargoyles on the corners of the old church in the village, which frightened him.

He heard Dorothy say, 'Your brother wants to talk to you.'

But Richard knew this was not so; he sensed Tobin would have harmed him if Dorothy had not been there. He remembered his expression still. His brother hated him.

As Richard grew older, Tobin became more spiteful. Sometimes he said he wanted to play on the lawn and would throw a soft ball across. Richard would kick it or throw it back. Then Tobin would pick up the ball and carry it up to him. He would look around to see whether Dorothy or anyone else was watching them. If they weren't, he would suddenly push the ball hard into Richard's face. Once this made his nose bleed.

'He's been very silly,' said Tobin, explaining to Dorothy. 'I know he's my younger brother, but I think he's an idiot. He banged his head against the ball. I saw him do it. Gave himself a nose-bleed.'

But Richard wasn't an idiot; he feared Tobin because Tobin was older and bigger and would pinch him hard with his nails until the flesh bled through his shirt. He once pushed a needle into his body through his jacket.

Richard tried to explain to Dorothy and to his mother what was happening, but they would not believe him.

'You're imagining it,' his mother told him sharply. 'You're a funny little boy. You dream a lot. You imagine things that don't happen. Why, Tobin's very fond of you. He's told me so himself. He loves you.'

'He doesn't,' said Richard. 'I know that. He doesn't like me, even.'

'Now you're being stupid. Why, there are lots of little boys would love an older brother. Two's company, you know. It can be lonely on your own.'

'I'm never lonely,' said Richard stoutly.

'Oh, who's talking! I saw you on your own crying the other day.'

'That's because of Tobin. He had a needle. He stuck it in me.'

'I can't believe it. Show me where.'

Richard raised his shirt and his vest. His mother could see the pale blue bruise and the tiny dot.

'It's only an insect bite or something. That woman Dorothy, she should be looking after you. I'll ask her to rub some ointment into it. Goodness knows, servants these days, there's no doing with them. But your brother would never stick a needle into you. Why ever should he?'

Before Richard could reply, Tobin came into the room.

'Have you dug a needle into your brother?' their mother asked him.

'A needle?' said Tobin, his face puckering with surprise. 'I haven't got a needle. Who says I have?'

'Well, he does.'

Tobin looked at him and his eyes were cold and baleful, like the eyes of a goat Richard had seen tethered on the village green. Looking at them was like looking into the windows of an empty house. Nothing lay behind them, no feelings, no warmth.

'He's making it up.'

'I told him as much. It's his imagination, you know, Tobin. Perhaps he'll grow up and be a writer or an artist. Who knows?'

Richard was good with his hands. When he was seven he discovered that the pram in which he had first been caught in the rain was still in a shed behind the coach house. No one wanted it now, so he removed the axles and wheels and fitted them on a trolley made of four lengths of wood nailed together. One axle pivoted on a bolt in its centre and he tied a string at each end so that he could sit on the trolley and steer it. The trolley didn't go very fast because there weren't many hills on the estate, but he could paddle himself along with his feet. Then Tobin saw him doing this and tripped him up.

Richard grazed his leg so badly that the doctor said he might get blood poisoning. His mother took the trolley away from him. That hurt him more than the pain of his grazed knee. He had made that trolley. He had worked out how it could be steered, and now it had gone – and Tobin was to blame.

Years passed without any memorable peaks. Then, in 1914, when he was thirteen years old, Aunt Hannah, his mother's younger sister, unmarried, and living in a London flat, gave him a steam engine.

'You've got a mechanical bent, so I thought you'd like this steam engine,' she explained. 'You fill the boiler with water here.' She indicated the filler cap on the boiler. 'You put methylated spirits in the burner, light it underneath, and when the water boils, steam comes through to the cylinder. You'll hear it start to hiss, then you spin the fly-wheel and, Bob's your uncle, it's running.'

Richard would never forget that first smell of warm oil and new paint, the tang of methylated spirits in the burner. He held the red base plate of the engine in his hands and admired it, absorbing every detail: the safety valve on the boiler, a tap to drain off the water; crimson fly-wheel, polished copper pipes to the boiler and out to the dummy chimney. The Spirit and the Speed. What a gift!

For a moment he could think of nothing to say that adequately reflected his feelings. Then he smiled at his aunt, put his face up as she bent down. They kissed.

'Thank you,' he said gravely. 'I never imagined a present like this.'

'That's what a present should be,' she replied, pleased at his pleasure. She had her own ideas about Tobin's feelings towards his younger brother, and felt sorry for Richard; she had an elder sister. 'Something you choose especially for someone special. Not just to give them anything, but something you think they would like.'

'I like this very much,' Richard assured her.

As his aunt left the room, he became aware of someone looking at him from the doorway. Tobin. And he saw in his brother's eyes a look of envy clouded with that familiar dislike.

'Look what Aunt Hannah has given me,' Richard said, holding out the engine for him to examine and admire. Tobin shook his head.

'I saw it,' he said. 'But I'm not really interested in that sort of thing. They're so smelly, dirty.'

'We can work this together,' said Richard.

'I don't want to,' said his brother. 'I've got other things to do. Better things.'

And then he walked up the stairs. Through the open doorway Richard saw him turn and look back. He had never understood why his brother disliked him. He had tried to be friendly. He shared everything he was given with him. With a dull misery in his stomach, as though he had swallowed a lead weight, he sensed this chasm between them would be there for the rest of his life. He would be on one side and his brother on the other, and although he might call to his brother, to try and bring him over, his brother would never come.

For reasons he was never told, he was not allowed to play with the engine the evening he received it although Aunt Hannah had asked if she could see it working, but he took it to bed with him, put it on the pillow and turned the fly-wheel with his thumb, imagining it racing away. Next morning he filled the boiler with warm water from the kettle in the kitchen, carried the engine to an outhouse, lit the burner, smelled that evocative amalgam of hot paint and oil and heard water bubble in the boiler.

He spun the wheel just as his aunt had said. Puffs of steam blew out of the chimney as the fly-wheel kept spinning, and the cylinder moved on its pivot with every stroke of the piston. He was happy just watching it. Then he saw someone at the door of the shed, also watching him – Eames, one of the under-gardeners. There were so many, nearly a dozen, under the head gardener who looked after the greenhouses and never hid his displeasure when his mother wanted to pick flowers or grapes. His mother said he seemed to grow them for his own enjoyment. He would let them wither away rather than have them picked or cut by someone else.

Eames was a different sort. He was young, and worked in the vegetable garden, learning. That meant he dug and weeded and hoed and then started to dig again.

'A new toy, Master Richard?' he asked now.

'Yes,' said Richard.

'Have you seen the traction engine down by the lake? It makes a noise just like that. Much louder, of course.'

Richard had heard that his father was irritated because the lake had silted up. He had engaged a contractor to pump it out.

'I'll come and see it,' Richard said at once.

The steam engine worked on the same principle as his toy, but it had a solid cylinder that did not move. Shining rods, working from cog wheels, opened and closed valves with a great hissing of steam. It pounded away stolidly, spinning a huge fly-wheel. A pulley was connected to a pump. Water gurgled and gushed through hosepipes thick as a man's thigh.

An engineer stood by, stoking the boiler, adjusting steam cocks to keep the speed as steady as possible. He nodded respectfully to Richard.

'I've got a steam engine, too,' Richard told him.

'You have?' said the man. He had a beard and a Scottish accent. There was something roguish about him, as though he was only there briefly and would soon be away, somewhere else. Richard recognised the signs of a gypsy, of a man who lived in a caravan and owned a spotted Dalmatian. At fairs, Richard had seen similar engines with bright green boilers, crimson wheels and ribbed metal tyres. Smoke would belch out of the black funnel from the scalloped brass top as a slapping belt drove the dynamo to light the sideshows.

'I'd like to see your engine,' the man told him.

'It's in an outhouse. Can you come now?'

'Yes. I can leave this to run on its own for five minutes.'

He followed Richard over gravel paths to the outhouse. The engineer picked up the toy.

'It's got no valves,' he said, examining it closely.

Richard did not know quite what the man meant.

The engineer undid the nut on the bolt on which the cylinder pivoted, held by a spring tightly against a smooth metal face. He removed the cylinder. Richard

15

could see that the metal plate had two holes, one larger than the other.

'Why are the holes different sizes?' he asked.

'For safety. The steam that drives the engine goes in through the smaller hole and out through the larger one. The makers usually fit a bigger exhaust hole than an inlet so that you won't have too much pressure building up inside the cylinder.'

'What happens if I switch the pipes, so that more steam goes in than comes out?'

'The engine speeds up.'

'Could I switch them?'

'If you want to, very easily. You just need to solder the inlet to the exhaust hole and the exhaust to the inlet. It wouldn't take ten minutes to do that.'

'Could you do that for me?'

'If you're asking me to, yes,' said the engineer, smiling at the boy's enthusiasm.

He changed the pipes that afternoon and when Richard started the engine it ran twice as quickly – so fast, indeed, that the whole mechanism began to shake as though with a life of its own. Richard released the safety valve and blew out the flame on the burner. The engineer smiled at him as the fly-wheel slowed and then stopped.

'You've learned something, you see. The more pressure you can get into any engine, the faster it will go. It has no option.'

'But there must be a limit?'

'Of course. You could blow the whole thing up if you tightened the safety valve. But I know you wouldn't do that. Never fool around with safety valves. They're set by the makers who know what steam pressures their products will stand. Overload them and, bang, they may explode.'

'I'll show this to my mother,' said Richard.

'If my experience is any guide, boy, the ladies aren't

16

interested in mechanical things. All this smell and steam, they don't like. They may say they do. But they don't. Although to be fair, I've a daughter who's the exception. She's as good with engines as any boy, is Carola. Well, I'd better be getting back to my own engine.'

Tobin moved away from outside the shed as soon as he heard the man walk towards the door. He had overheard the conversation, and although he did not quite understand exactly what he had heard, it seemed that here he might have a chance to get back at his younger brother.

He had been so happy until Richard had been born, because then he had been the only son. Of course, he was still the elder son and his father had told him that one day he would inherit everything. Still, he would have preferred to be on his own, not with a younger brother snapping at his heels like a dog.

So he waited, out of sight, until he saw Richard leave the shed. Then he went inside it, wrinkling his nose in distaste at the tang of methylated spirits. His brother understood mechanical things. He had abilities Tobin knew he lacked, and would never possess. Richard had made that trolley entirely on his own. Tobin had wanted a trolley like that but had not known how to begin to make one. He had only ridden on it once and then Richard was steering, not him. He wasn't sure whether he had the courage to steer it on his own, for the only means of stopping the trolley from going too fast was to put his feet on the ground and drag the soles of his shoes on the road until the trolley slowed and finally stopped. And if he did that, he might wrench an ankle.

Now this steam engine was another reason for contention and envy. He didn't want one himself – he hated getting his hands dirty and feeling grease beneath his fingernails. But regardless of his own feelings, this engine was something special, and he was the elder, so if anything special was going, he should have the first chance, maybe the only chance. But then Aunt Hannah had never liked him. Once he had overheard her describe him to his mother as a milksop. Well, he would show her, and everyone else, that Richard didn't know as much about mechanical things as they imagined. After listening to the engineer, that should be quite easy to do. He'd let Richard look a fool, and then come in and make the engine work perfectly.

Tobin touched the boiler cautiously; he did not want to scald his fingers. The metal was still warm, but not hot. He unscrewed the safety valve and examined it; a plunger was held tightly against the base of the valve by a spring. If the pressure in the boiler grew too high, the steam forced this plunger up against the spring and allowed excess steam to escape. It was easy to screw the plunger up as tightly as it could go. That would take the smile off his brother's face. He replaced the valve, went out of the shed and back into the house.

In the hall he met his mother who was wearing a coat and hat.

'I'm just going down to the village,' she said. 'Do you want to come for the ride?' She took him sometimes with her in their new Panhard car. He liked to sit on the buttoned leather seat behind their chauffeur. He had heard his father's friends say how the owner of a motor car always sat directly behind the chauffeur, with any companions sitting on the left. So he always sat as though he were the owner of the car. His mother thought this rather amusing. Tobin thought it simply fitting. He would be the owner one day. Then there would be some changes, permanent changes.

'No,' he replied. 'I'm looking for Richard.'

'I expect he's playing with that engine.'

'No, he's not. I've been looking for him there.'

'He's been messing about with it, I know. Eames told

me. Why, is there something wrong?'

'Well, you know what he's like. He's never satisfied.'

'I don't think that's true, Tobin. He was very pleased when Aunt Hannah gave it to him.'

'It's not working.'

'I'm surprised. It was. He told me he'd made it go faster.'

'Probably broken it, more likely.'

She looked at him sharply. Perhaps Tobin was slightly jealous of his brother, as Hannah had so often suggested. But surely not over this little toy gift? Why, the boy had everything he wanted.

'We'll find him together,' she said brightly. 'We'll both get him to start it and prove that it's all right. Then I'll go to the village and you can come with me.'

They found Richard cleaning his bicycle. He looked up at her enquiringly.

'We were wondering where you were,' she said.

'I've been in here for the past ten minutes. Why?'

'Your brother thought there was something wrong with that steam engine.'

'Nothing at all. Why should he think that?'

She shrugged. 'I don't know. Why don't you start it up again and I'll go and get your father. Then we can all see it run.'

Richard went into the downstairs wash room, carried a jug of hot water to the shed to fill the boiler. It was quicker to use hot water, otherwise the little burner took several minutes to boil the water. Tobin stood watching him, hands in his pockets, a supercilious smile on his face.

'What are you grinning at?' Richard asked him.

'Nothing,' he said. 'Just watching you.'

'But why? You weren't interested in this before.'

Tobin shrugged. His mother and father came in. His father glanced at his watch.

'I have someone coming to see me in ten minutes,' he said pompously. 'There's been a problem draining the lake. The pump doesn't seem to be drawing as much water as it should. I believe the man with the traction engine left it unattended today. You can't trust anyone to do a job these days.'

Rose Rowlands nodded. There always seemed to be problems with everything her husband undertook. He was a muddler. He almost appeared to like creating difficulties, or at least magnifying them, because then he could give the semblance of importance to an otherwise idle life. When you have nothing whatever to do, the tiniest activities – washing your hands, going to the lavatory, deciding whether to have an extra cup of coffee at breakfast – can become important milestones in an otherwise empty day.

'How long will this take?' she asked Richard.

'About three minutes,' he assured her. 'No more. The water's nearly boiling.'

He spun the fly-wheel. It jerked. Water dripped from the cylinder. They stood looking at each other over the engine as the smell of hot paint became stronger.

Richard spun the wheel again. This time it caught and began to turn.

'It's faster than before,' said his father dubiously.

'Yes,' Richard agreed. 'The man with the traction engine told me how I could improve its performance.'

'Really?'

The fly-wheel was now spinning so quickly it appeared to be a crimson blur surrounded by a haze of steam.

'Well, it's certainly got some speed in it,' said his father. 'It's shaking itself to pieces.' He glanced again at his watch. 'Glad you've got it going. Now, I must go myself.'

He went out of the door, stood for a moment, thumbs in his waistcoat pockets. It was a spring day, which

20

meant he had about another eight hours to fill before night. But then every day seemed long when you had nothing to do but fill in time.

His wife followed him, turned back to Tobin.

'Are you coming with me?' she asked him.

'No, Mama. I'll stay here. I still think there's something not quite right with this engine.'

The two boys, standing on either side of the bench, glanced at each other.

'You've made it go very fast,' said Tobin with reluctant admiration.

Richard nodded. He knew it was going far too fast. The steam pressure must be too high, but he did not want to touch the safety valve. It would be madness to interfere with that. He put out a hand to try and pull the burner away from under the boiler so that the water would cool and the engine stop. But the heat was so great he could not reach it, and he turned away for a pair of pliers to pull it out.

He had his back to the engine when suddenly it exploded with a noise like a bomb bursting. He heard a scream of agony from Tobin, and the tiny shed was instantly filled with steam.

And then, in a silence that sang in his ears, he realised that the engine had stopped. As the steam cleared, he saw that the boiler had disintegrated. And his brother Tobin was staggering away, both hands held up to his face.

'What's the matter?' he asked him, alarmed.

Tobin removed his hands from his head. His face was raw and blistered and grotesquely discoloured. His eyes were no more than slits in the puffy, weeping flesh. His mother had heard the explosion and came running back to the shed.

'What was that noise?' she cried. 'Are you all right?' Then she saw Tobin's face.

'Oh my God! Charles!' she called to her husband. '*Charles!*'

He was already thirty yards away and turned, irritated by the interruption.

'Get the doctor quickly. Tobin's been hurt. The engine has blown up. Hurry!'

Chapter Two

Richard stood uneasily in his father's study. Charles Rowlands sat behind his desk in a swivel chair, its curved arms padded with leather and edged by brass, dome-headed nails. His mother stood against the mantelpiece on which a marble clock ticked loudly, its heavy brass pendulum swinging from side to side behind a crystal window. Richard watched it because this was less painful than watching the anger and bewilderment on the faces of his parents.

'You *were* messing about with that engine,' said his father coldly. 'Tobin was right.'

'I altered it, yes. I told you.'

'With the result that it blew up and your brother has been horribly injured. I know these surgeon fellows are damned clever these days, but, my God, I've never seen anything like that poor boy's face. He'll be disfigured for life, all through your stupid folly.'

'It was not anything to do with what I did, Father.'

'What the devil do you mean by that? That was a perfectly safe little engine, though I must say I thought your aunt ill-advised in giving it to you. Potentially dangerous, I thought, and it turned out to be very dangerous. What makes you think you know more than the manufacturers and can alter the pipes in the wretched thing as you tell me you have done?'

'I was experimenting, Father.'

'Experimenting on your brother's face, more likely. I simply don't know what to say. And still you stand there, calmly denying you had anything to do with it. You will have to be punished.' He did not elaborate. The truth was, he could not think of a suitable punishment. He had been savouring this moment of brief authority but now he wanted to forget the whole thing. They could do nothing about Tobin's face. His sister-in-law was damned foolish to give the kid the engine in the first place. Charles had never liked her because he felt she did not like him. This incident would not draw them any closer.

Richard put his hand in his pocket, took out the safety valve, held it out to his father.

'What's that?'

'The safety valve, Father.'

'Well, it didn't live up to its name.'

'It couldn't.'

'Why not? Is it faulty?'

'You see this nut and the spring?'

'Of course. What about it?'

'Someone has tightened it right up, so it couldn't work.'

'You've been messing around with that, too, have you?'

'No. I'd never do that. The whole point of a safety valve is to leave it. Otherwise you get what's happened now.'

'So who do you suggest did it? Your brother?'

'He was in there,' Rose said in a conciliatory way. 'He told me so himself.'

There was silence for a moment, as the two grown-ups looked at each other, sharing the same thought. The door opened. Tobin came into the room.

His face was swathed in bandages, like a mummy. They could see only his eyes and his nostrils and a little slit for his mouth. A strong smell of ether and iodine hung in the air. Smears of yellow ointment seeped through the bandages on his forehead.

'You poor boy,' said his mother, and held him in her arms. 'Are you in terrible pain?'

'Not now. But I was. *Terrible*, Mama. The doctor says I'm lucky I wasn't blinded. He's writing out some instructions about how and when to change the dressing.'

He looked across the desk at his brother and saw the safety valve.

'What's that?' he asked innocently.

'The safety valve from Richard's engine. You didn't touch it, did you?'

'Me? Touch it? I've never seen it before. How does it work?'

'It didn't work, that's the point. Someone tightened it up,' said Richard. 'I didn't. I swear I didn't.'

'It's your engine,' said Tobin flatly.

'It was,' said his father. 'I've given orders for it to be thrown out into the dustbin. I never want to see it again. Now let this be a lesson to you, Richard. A very serious lesson I'm sorry you've had to learn, and even more sorry that your brother has had to bear the consequences. No more mechanical things for you. You just buckle down and get all this nonsense out of your head.'

'Someone altered the valve,' said Richard dully. 'It wasn't my fault.' He looked up at his brother and saw his eyes, hostile and mocking. In that moment he knew who had altered the valve.

'As a punishment,' his father said, having finally decided on one, 'you will be confined to your room for the rest of the week for all meals. They will be of a rather more meagre character than you normally enjoy. There will be toast and tea without milk or sugar for breakfast, toast and a scrape of butter for lunch, the same for supper. Now, I'd better have a word with the doctor before he leaves.'

He stood up abruptly and left the room. He was glad to get this business over and be away. He was not really cut out to be a father and become involved in these ridiculous incidents. He had so much more on his mind than the question of which brother had altered a valve on a toy engine. Often he wondered how he could stay so calm outwardly when his mind seethed with other concerns that sometimes he felt would totally overwhelm him.

'You'd better rest, darling,' Rose said to Tobin when her husband had gone.

Tobin nodded. 'That's what the doctor said. I have to take things easy.'

'I'll get some calf's foot jelly for you, and beef tea. Strengthen you up a bit. Now, come on. We'll go up to your room together.'

They turned away, leaving Richard on his own. He stood for a moment and saw the reflection of his face in the ormolu mirror on the far wall. It was very pale, and he looked ill.

He could not understand why his brother would interfere with that valve unless to embarrass him. But his attempt had produced a totally unexpected result. Then he remembered that his father had said the steam engine was in the dustbin. He hurried through the kitchen quarters, along the service corridor where bells hung on curved springs, and a big board displayed indicators to show where a bell was being rung – in the billiard room, a bedroom, a bathroom, the private suite. A bell clanged as he passed. He glanced up at the indicator automatically. It was Tobin's bedroom. Grover the butler appeared, glanced up at the indicator dancing on its spring, smoothed down his tail coat, started to move towards the door.

26

'Have you thrown my toy engine in the dustbin?' Richard asked him.

'Well, it's not in there yet actually, Master Richard. Your father told me to be rid of it. But I haven't had a moment. I've put it in the boot room for the time being.'

'I'll throw it away for you, then,' said Richard.

'Very well, Master Richard.'

Richard found the engine on a table in the boot room. The boy who cleaned the shoes was examining it. He immediately started to polish a shoe, embarrassed at being seen to be idle as Richard entered.

'I'll get rid of that for you,' Richard told him.

'Very good, sir,' said the boy.

Richard picked up the engine and a duster, draped this over the toy. He was going to smuggle it up to his bedroom, hide it at the back of his cupboard under old shoes, an unwanted cricket bat, tennis racquets with broken strings. He knew no one ever looked there. This engine was something too precious to be thrown away. No one would know he had kept it.

Dr Murgatroyd, the family doctor, was an old man who dressed as he imagined a successful actor of his age would dress in a play about a distinguished physician. He was not particularly prominent in his profession, but he meant well. He wore a frock coat, rather baggy salt-and-pepper trousers with loops that went under the soles of his shoes, a high stiff collar.

He stood now in the morning room.

'Would you like a drink, Dr Murgatroyd?' Charles asked mechanically. He drank a lot, although he would deny it. In his opinion, a sherry, a Madeira, a large whisky or a brandy and Seltzer were all essential lubricants when men met to discuss difficult or serious matters.

'No, thank you very much,' said the doctor. 'I have

several calls still to make. I think it is a bad thing for a professional man if a patient can smell alcohol on his breath.'

'Do you smell it on mine?' asked Charles, only partly joking.

'Of course not, sir. That was not meant as a personal comment. Just my own belief.'

'I admire you for it,' said Charles insincerely. 'Now, what about my son's face? The damage looked terrible to me when I saw it. Will it ever heal completely?'

'It will mend in time, but I'd like to have an opinion from a burns specialist. There's no doubt, there will be some scars remaining.'

'Bad scars?'

'It's impossible to say yet. He's young, and the young have great recuperative powers. Tissue heals. Skin grows again. The worst scars I think will be on his forehead. But by rearranging his hair slightly, they could largely be concealed.'

'I see. Please make an early appointment with the specialist. I would like to get this matter dealt with as soon as possible. You never know, complications can so easily set in with any medical condition.'

'Quite so. I will give the matter my immediate attention. I understand from your wife there is some odium attaching to his younger brother for this unfortunate accident.'

Charles nodded. 'He denies all blame, of course. But then I suppose he would, though I must say I have always found him entirely truthful before. When he was to blame for anything – a broken window, a glass cracked, that sort of thing – he always admitted what he had done. But not in this instance.

'He's a funny chap, always reading books about engines and mechanical things of that nature. He has a ticket for the local library, you know. Only the junior

28

section, but they pander to his foibles and he reads all manner of scientific books. Can't make head or tail of them myself. He thinks his brother must have altered the setting of the safety valve. Of course, Tobin denies that totally. And why should he interfere with Richard's toy in any case? But unless someone else fooled around with the valve, one or other of them isn't telling the truth.'

'I have chatted to young Richard from time to time,' said Dr Murgatroyd. 'He seemed a trustworthy boy to me. He always asks me all sorts of things about the size of the teeth on saws used by surgeons to cut bones, and the strength of ether and chloroform, and so forth. He has a strong scientific bent. Perhaps he'll be a physician himself.'

'He might well, eventually.'

'As for Tobin, do you think he's telling the truth?'

'It's difficult for a father to be asked a question like that about his own son, especially the eldest son. But I would value your opinion, as a professional man, Doctor.'

'I have always felt, on the few times I have met him, that Tobin is a very pleasant lad, but he often seems to be under some stress.'

'Stress? What sort of stress? He has everything he wants. His mother dotes on him.'

'Perhaps that's the reason. A child is like an animal, Mr Rowlands. Give an animal everything and it becomes torpid, lazy, out of condition. Give a horse nothing to do and it becomes useless. You make it work and it's happy, for it's achieving something.'

'So you think my son is like a horse?'

'In the sense that everything may come too easily to him, yes, and he may have too little reason to exert himself.'

'I see,' said Charles. 'Perhaps I've been a bit lax. Well, I'm much indebted to you for your frankness, Doctor,

29

and I wait to hear from you about the specialist. Good day to you.'

He pulled the bell tassel. The butler, Grover, who had been listening outside the double doors, now knocked briskly and entered.

'Please show Dr Murgatroyd to his motor,' Charles told him.

'Yes, sir.'

Charles had just reached his study when Grover reappeared. 'There is a gentleman to see you, sir,' he announced.

'About what? I have no appointments for this afternoon.'

'I told him that, sir, and he said he had come to visit you on a rather urgent matter, sir. He seemed serious, so I took the liberty of showing him into the morning room. I can easily tell him you are engaged and ask him to return at a more convenient time.'

Charles stroked his chin, lost in a fog of indecision.

'What's his name?' he asked at last.

The butler held out a silver salver, on which lay a card engraved in black: Mr Thos. Harper, Special Commissions, Sackville Street, London W.

'Never heard of the fellow. What sort of a man is he? Gentleman?'

'A man of the business class, I would say, sir. He arrived by motor.'

'What make of motor?'

'A Daimler, sir. With a driver.'

'In livery?'

'Yes, sir.'

'All right. I'll see him. I'm having quite a busy afternoon, eh?'

Charles looked out of the window. Two gardeners with green baize aprons were raking the gravel in front of the house to remove all marks of tyres or feet. They did this

30

twice every day, turning each piece of gravel so that the whole drive appeared uniform and dry and bright. It was like a strip of beach, thought Charles, a beach leading to the sea.

Incongruously, he felt uneasy at the thought. The sea could stretch into seemingly endless distance, cold and ruthless. His estate had boundaries, so why did he suddenly feel almost afraid? Of what? Was the feeling due to Tobin's accident, the fact that one of his sons must be lying? Or was it because his wife had recently been unusually acerbic? From time to time she returned to a theme never far from her mind: why didn't he do something with his life instead of simply filling in the hours, pretending to run an estate that others, more active and astute, managed for him?

But he had no need to do anything he did not wish to do. He had inherited thirty thousand acres, a dozen farms, this splendid house with its four lodges, its twenty-acre lake, and rows and rows of terraced properties in south-east London. He had started out with so much more than almost anyone else in the country owned at the end of their lives.

You could be a Member of Parliament, his wife would tell him sharply. You could sit on the boards of companies, have a say in events. Instead, you're like someone in an open boat without a sail or a paddle or even an oar, just drifting on the tide.

The fact was that Rose simply could not, or maybe would not, understand what it was like to be a landed gentleman. She had not been born into that state of life; her father had been a manufacturer, not interested in field sports or country activities. Somehow, he had lost money, fallen on evil days, as the saying was; gone bust. He had committed suicide, poor devil, rather than face his creditors. His widow and two daughters had faced a difficult time. Rose's mother remarried, largely to provide a home for them all. Then she died and Rose and her sister Hannah were on their own.

Rose had some ability as an actress and found a job with a touring theatrical company. When the tour ended, she joined another company which lasted for several months, until the manager went off with the leading lady, and all the takings.

Rose was reduced to serving in a dressmaker's shop, even modelling clothes. Then she met him – he and his then fiancée had been customers in the shop. Hannah had meanwhile branched out on her own, making hats: a modest enough living, but at least it removed any need for him to help her.

Charles preferred to put these unhappy facts behind him. Gentlemen did not dwell on such unpleasant episodes in other people's lives. It would embarrass him if they became public knowledge. People might think – or, even worse, say – that he had married beneath him. This would be unthinkable, unbearable, because in his own private view, it was the truth. After all, if a gentleman's wife was criticised in this way, how could he possibly hold up his own head in Society?

Charles sighed. He supposed he had better see this fellow Harper, whoever he might be.

He took a pace towards the door, and then paused, turned back to his desk. From his pocket he took a key on a golden chain. He unlocked one drawer, removed a bottle of brandy and a small glass. He filled the glass, drank the spirit neat, filled it a second time, drank that as quickly. Then he replaced the bottle, carried the glass to the cloakroom, washed it under the tap, wiped it on the hand towel, noting instinctively as he did so that the housekeeper had placed out two matching towels as he liked.

He required everything to be neat, in order, in its place; everyone to do exactly as he wished. And why shouldn't he feel like this? People were there to give meaning, colour to his life, not to theirs. He slipped the glass back into the drawer, locked it. He thought no one knew he kept this secret bottle that he filled carefully from other bottles on the table of drinks in the morning room. It never occurred to him that Grover marked the level on the labels each day with a tiny dot from a sharpened pencil point. Grover knew that his master drank heavily. What he wasn't quite sure about, however, was just how heavily. And although he had no clear idea why, he felt it his business to find out.

Charles went into the morning room. Mr Harper stood with his back to the window; the sun was shining full into Charles's eyes as he closed the door behind him.

'You wished to see me, I understand,' he said without any preamble. 'About what matter?'

'The butler did not give you my message?'

'What message?' he asked brusquely.

Charles noted mentally that the man had not addressed him as 'sir', a mark of respect which was surely due to someone in his position.

Harper glanced pointedly at the visiting card Charles was holding. He turned it over and read the name, BRUCE, written in a semi-literate hand with a dot between each of the capital letters. His lips tightened. If Grover had told him something was written on the back of the card and he had read the name, he would never have seen this fellow. But either Grover had forgotten to give him the message or, more likely, Harper had not told him. He had deliberately preferred to shock his victim, to gauge his reaction.

'The name Bruce is familiar to you?' said Harper now, watching his man.

'It's a very common name,' Charles said carelessly.

'Agreed. But it marks a rather uncommon liaison

between you and this young lad.'

'I've no idea what you mean, or what you're getting at.' Charles's voice was sharp and hard, but it was pitched too high.

'No? There is another matter which I must also bring to your attention, and which may mean something to you.'

As Harper spoke, he took an envelope from his pocket, removed a photograph and handed it to Charles, watching his reaction.

'You recognise the person, I trust?' he asked.

Charles's face blanched. He nodded slightly, unable to speak. His throat felt as though it was gripped by a tightening noose.

'I am glad, Mr Rowlands. So, as the lawyers say, let me refresh your memory about Bruce. You and the young lad have had an association that is against the laws of God, of nature and, more immediately important, the laws of this country. You paid for your pleasure with a ten pound note. And, of course, this photograph of your wife, another matter altogether, is not one you would wish others to see.'

'Get out!' Charles hissed, his face contorted with rage and shock.

'By all means, if that is your wish. I will then go at once to the police. Not the local station, of course, because as a landowner, a man of means, doubtless the highly regarded landlord of all the cottages in this village, you could perhaps exert some influence over local officers. I will therefore go to the Police Commissioner in Scotland Yard.'

'Why?'

'Because I feel it is quite wrong that a man like you should be allowed to live like a leech, a parasite, with a reputation of generosity and public spiritedness which is quite false, while all the time you are indulging your

34

perverted lusts with young and innocent boys.'

'That is rubbish, and you know it. Who are you, exactly?'

'An ordinary private citizen, a friend of this young man, who desires you to help him.'

'How?'

'He wishes to emigrate to one of the colonies, to learn a skill there. But he needs money in order to achieve this very modest but entirely laudable aim.'

'This is blackmail. A crude attempt at blackmail.'

'Not so, Mr Rowlands. I have not come to a gentleman's residence to attempt to blackmail him. Why, he might have servants listening outside the door. I am simply asking you for an extension of your well-known generosity towards this poor, unhappy orphan lad.'

'What does he need?'

'Five thousand sovereigns.'

'That is a large sum with which to establish himself in a colony. I've heard of people doing it on fifty pounds.'

'I have also heard of people spending five thousand pounds in a single evening, giving a ball. I believe I am now talking to one such person, who is giving a ball in honour of his wife's birthday within the next few days. Please correct me if I am wrong.'

Charles looked at him closely. He could not make out Harper's face clearly, for the sun was very bright. He turned to one side to get a better view. He wanted to be able to recognise the man again. This would not be the only price he demanded for his silence; it was merely the first instalment. Inevitably, there would be others – requests for gifts to charities or worthy individuals. But how could he be rid of the fellow? Not just from this interview, but for ever. The threat about the boy was totally false. The threat about his wife's photograph was more dangerous.

There were people who could deal with Harper, he felt

sure. He had the money and the will to engage their services, but not the contacts. He must find someone more knowledgeable in these matters. In view of the photograph, he felt this was absolutely essential. But how could he get the time necessary to do this?

'I want an answer now,' said Harper sharply as though he had read Charles's mind.

'If I give you an answer now, it will be in the negative,' replied Charles. 'I cannot donate a sum of this size to any charity without involving my financial advisers. You must give me time.'

'How much time will you require – with your financial advisers?'

'A week from today should suffice.'

'That is impossible. I need an answer by this time tomorrow. My address is on my card. Sackville Street. I will await your pleasure there. Good day.' Harper strode to the door, opened it, and came face to face with Grover. The butler bowed respectfully and showed him out of the house.

Charles stood, trembling with reaction, furious at his own weakness, yet powerless to proceed. There was no truth whatever in Harper's claims. Charles had spoken to the creature Bruce in a house in Jermyn Street. The fellow was a servant, a page; but being offered a drink by him, exchanging a few words, was not a criminal act. The trouble was, he could not admit to visiting this house, as Harper obviously knew. More importantly, he could not conceivably stand by and allow that photograph of his wife to be made public. It would ruin them both.

The photograph was on the side table where Harper had put it on his way out. Charles went over, picked it up and pushed it into the brown envelope. The envelope felt heavy, and then Charles noticed the words 'Twenty prints' on it. His stomach turned over sickeningly. He couldn't bear to look at them now. Later, perhaps, when he felt calmer. He tucked the envelope under his arm and hurried from the room.

Grover, the butler, waiting outside, bowed and led the way to the front door. Rowlands walked to the window; Mr Harper was climbing into his Daimler. A chauffeur busied himself tucking a tartan rug around him, then swung the engine, climbed up behind the wheel. The car shuddered away in a haze of blue exhaust smoke.

Out on the main road, beyond sight of the house, the chauffeur turned to his passenger.

'How did it go, Tom?'

'I think he'll pay,' said Harper slowly. 'That photograph really hurt him. That's evidence he can't deny. No one can, not even the cleverest lawyer. Yes, I think the bastard will pay all right.'

'And if he doesn't?'

'We'll deal with that if we have to. In the meantime, get this car back to whoever hired it to you, and let's have a couple of large whiskies. I never like these jobs. You never really know how the subject will react. He'd kill me if he could. But can he?'

Chapter Three

On the first of June every year, or on the nearest Saturday to the first of June, which was his wife's birthday, Charles Rowlands held what had become known throughout the county as the Rowlands' summer ball. He had marquees erected on the main lawn and engaged two orchestras, one to play in the marquee, the other in the ballroom of the house. Invitations, which had been sent out six weeks earlier, were invariably answered immediately, for this was one of the county's great social events and not to be missed.

Charles was proud of his reputation as a host of prodigal generosity. There would be buffets with cold lobster salad, salmon in aspic, trout, crayfish, oysters. Champagne was ordered by the hundred bottles, and red and white wine would flow like the fountains of Rome.

People who might personally think it a gross extravagance to give a dinner party for twelve guests and then serve the cheapest continental wine, would drink at least a bottle of his champagne each. It was known that on occasion several guests had gorged themselves on two lobsters each *and* half a salmon. Since their host obviously derived much pleasure from such flamboyant expenditure, why should they seek to deny him? Eat, drink as much as you could, and always more than you should. He was paying the bill.

For days before the ball, Richard watched an army of

workmen lay a wooden dance floor in the marquee, and organise special kerosene stoves that would blow hot air through metal vents in the canvas sides if the weather unexpectedly proved cold.

Big poles, painted in red and white stripes, like the poles that hung outside barbers' shops, were driven into the ground at intervals of several feet along the main driveway and round the lake and the ornamental waterfall. From their tops, tar torches would throw a smoky, trembling light on the lawns and the glittering water.

This year, however, there was a departure. A steam traction engine had been engaged with a dynamo to light hundreds of coloured bulbs in the trees, along the drive, in the bushes. A whole nest of bulbs had been arranged around the fountain with a special mechanical device which could switch the colours from red to green to blue, yellow, white and back to red, so that the fountains continually changed colour as they played.

This was a ball that in extravagance and expense far outmatched all previous ones his father had arranged. No one in the county possessed the means – and the willingness to spend their money – to anything like this extent. This, above all others, would be a night to remember.

Richard made his way to the steam engine and stood watching a fireman in blue dungarees and peaked cap shovelling coke into the wide square mouth of the fire box. The engineer sat on the driver's seat; he was the same man to whom Richard had shown his toy engine. Gone were his oily dungarees. Instead, he wore a smart uniform with black buttons and a peaked cap, like the driver of a train. The quality would be at this ball; several gentlemen were bound to stroll over and see the engine that provided the coloured lights. He hoped to get commissions from some of them, and no one would be keen to engage a gypsy-looking fellow in dirty clothes.

He watched the fingers on the pressure gauges creep

round the dials. Then he jumped down, and with a masterly heave born of years of experience he put all his weight against the fly-wheel. Steam hissed and gushed and then roared from a vent. The wheel turned slowly. The piston forced down the connecting rod, the fly-wheel forced it back – and the engine was running. He winked at Richard.

'Easy when you know how to do it, son. Bit different from your engine, ain't it?'

Richard agreed that it was. The man moved a lever. At once, a belt began to slap and then tightened as the drive to the dynamo was taken up. All around the great gardens, lights began to glimmer, dimly at first, like glow-worms, and then, as the dynamo gathered speed and fed more current through the heavy wires, they glittered brightly like fallen stars. Richard always remembered that moment as one of magic. Of course, he was not allowed to stay up for the ball; by rights he should have been in bed already, but he didn't want to miss all the excitement. Tobin had stayed in his room, his face still heavily bandaged.

The orchestra in the ballroom began to play, and then, more faintly, the orchestra in the marquee. Soon the house, and then the whole night came alive with music. It was a wonderful moment, to feel that his father was the prime mover behind all this gaiety.

Charles stood at the top of the marble staircase, surveying the scene, also feeling pride in this most agreeable situation. He drew enormous pleasure from his position as the host with the deepest pocket. What the devil did it matter what it cost? He could afford it – couldn't he?

On either side of the stairs, hothouse plants – orchids, tuberoses, bougainvillaea – provided cascades of colour. Their scent sweetened the air. On the black and white tiles of the entrance hall, footmen in Rowlands livery –

dark green with deep red lapels – stood holding silver trays with glasses of champagne. Charles thought they looked like pieces in a chess game; the squares made a splendid chequerboard. This was an amusing notion. It might be an idea, next time perhaps, to dress them as bishops and knights. The hall was large enough. He must give the matter some thought.

As his mind dwelt happily on this possibility, he suddenly remembered the visit of Thomas Harper two weeks previously, which until then he had resolutely tried to put out of his mind. He had consulted his lawyer, Peter Once-Hogg, of course; he told him he was being blackmailed on a most ridiculous charge but he did not elaborate and did not mention the photograph. That was too personal and painful a subject to discuss with anyone.

Once-Hogg immediately engaged a private detective who reported that the address in Sackville Street was an empty shop. The whole thing was a try-on, of course. Just because Charles was rich, he was not necessarily a fool – although he had been a fool even to visit that house in Jermyn Street.

On that warm, summer evening, he had dined at his club, and afterwards walked up St James's and along Jermyn Street. This always had an alluring air of mystery after dark, with gas lamps lit and windows covered by deep red curtains that gave an enticing glow. Charles heard laughter from some rooms, strains of music from others and, on his own, he suddenly felt lonely.

He paused outside what, before his marriage, he had known as Mrs Jones's house. He knocked on the front door, telling himself he had no intention of anything more than just having a chat with her. She was a plump, friendly woman, more like a cook or a retired nanny than the madam of London's most expensive and exclusive brothel. This was part of her attraction and much of her success.

Listening to her would be more lively than having to make conversation with dull fellow members of his club, all bores, living, like him, on inherited fortunes, drawing dividends from the work of other men.

The flap dropped behind the judas hole and then the door opened. An old soldier in splendid livery saluted him smartly.

'Good evening, sir,' he said with professional enthusiasm. 'Haven't seen you for a long time. What a pleasure to meet you again, if I may say so. Mrs Jones was asking about you only the other day. Not like the people we see too much of these days, sir. They may have money, but they're not what we'd call gentlemen. Not like you, sir.' He paused. He had no idea who Rowlands was, but such a speech invariably pleased the listener; everyone liked to be remembered.

Charles put his hand in his back pocket. A sovereign changed hands.

'Thank you very much indeed, sir. Most generous of you. And most typical of you, sir, if I may say so. Mrs Jones will be delighted to see you. Do come in.'

The man ushered him in, closed and bolted the door firmly behind him.

Charles entered the warm hall, scented by Indian joss sticks that burned with faint beards of smoke in the hands of a bronze Indian god. A tiny trap door, barely an inch across, opened in the ceiling. A woman looked down at him through it.

'Do you recognise him?' she asked her companion quietly.

She shook her head.

'Get Madam. He looks a rich fellow. Probably hasn't been here for some time. Maybe he got married in between and she'll want to welcome him back.'

Mrs Jones arrived and applied her eye to the hole. 'I recognise him. Charlie Rowlands. Loaded with money.

Spends it like water. Always so anxious to be accepted as an important social person. No brain, but not a bad fellow.'

'What's he good for?'

'A hundred guineas any time. Minimum.'

'What does he like – girls or boys?'

'Neither really. He just likes to sit and talk and look at the girls, and imagine he's a hell of a ladies' man. A bit of a wet character, really. Send Bruce in with a bottle of champagne. Whether he drinks it or not, we'll still charge him. He'll not complain. He never does. You call him sir. You bow, you curtsy. He loves all that. He'll pay anything.' The tiny shutter closed.

A page in livery came into the hall through a service door, bowed deeply to Charles.

'A drink, sir? I think you normally take champagne?'

'Well, a glass. One glass would do very nicely,' Charles agreed. Damned civil youngster. He didn't remember the fellow, but clearly he remembered him. Champagne. Of course. What else could a gentleman drink at Mrs Jones's?

It was so long since he had been there that he felt rather ill at ease. This really wasn't his habitat; it never had been. He had only come here in the first place because all the other young bloods patronised it – or said they did. He did not wish to be thought prudish or feeble.

The page led him into a side room. It was overfurnished in the late Victorian way; half a dozen chairs, upholstered in dark red velvet, a very thick carpet, prints on the wall of English scenes – Lords, Henley, Ascot. The page picked out a bottle from an ice bucket, began to undo its wire and foil.

'A lovely night outside, sir,' he said carefully. 'I don't think we've met. I'm Bruce, sir.'

'Yes, Bruce, you're right. Very pleasant, really.'

Suddenly Charles wished he had never come. He did not want to become involved with a strange girl. He had simply felt lonely and wanted someone of his own age to talk to, not this mincing pederast. He'd drink the champagne, then he'd go. The page was pouring two glasses.

'Who's the second one for?' asked Charles.

'I wanted to drink your health, sir,' said Bruce in an effeminate voice.

'Very civil of you. Then I'll drink yours.'

They clinked glasses and drank. The champagne was cheap, bitter stuff. Perhaps with a second glass he'd feel better, more in the mood for something other than talking to this nancy boy?

Mrs Jones came into the room. 'Why Mr Rowlands, sir!' she cried in extravagant welcome. 'What a pleasure to see you again. What a great pity you've neglected our little establishment. The girls *all* remember you.'

'I remember them,' said Charles gallantly, not wishing to be outdone in manners.

'Irene and Sophia. Robina. Who would you like to see tonight?'

'I don't think anyone,' he said.

'*No one?* Why, sir, you're not unwell, I hope?'

'No, no. Not at all. I just thought I'd call in.'

'And you're always welcome. Would you like, per-haps, Bruce,' she smiled towards the page, 'to entertain you?'

'No, I think not. It's very kind of you. I'll have a drink and, without in any way wishing to cause the slightest offence, I think, as a married man, I'd better go.'

'As you wish, sir.' She bowed and smiled and went out of the room. Silly bloody fool, she thought. He was good for a hundred any time. Now she'd be hard put to get thirty off him for the champagne. Men never quibbled, though. They were afraid their wives might get to know.

45

And there were ways of informing them. Still, thirty wasn't a hundred. She went upstairs again. A new arrival needed to be identified. She applied her eye to the peephole.

Downstairs, the page refilled his own glass. Close to, his face was blotchy. Charles saw veins around his nose, and powder on the skin. He was older than he looked. No innocent boy, this, but an ageing, depraved sodomite.

'I had better be going, I think. I've a train to catch,' said Charles weakly.

Bruce smiled, and when he smiled his teeth were yellow, green at the gums. Charles felt instant revulsion.

'I'll give you your coat, sir.' The page opened the door. 'I have an elderly relative, an aunt, a maiden lady, in Surrey who is awfully glad of any assistance I can give her,' he said pointedly.

'Of course,' said Charles and gave him a ten pound note. He wished it were a fiver, but he couldn't start changing it now, not under the fellow's eyes.

A girl was waiting in the hall with a leather folder.

'The reckoning, sir. I'm sorry to give it to such a nice gentleman as you but, as they say, sir, we all have to live.'

'Of course. We all have to live.'

Charles opened the folder. Thirty guineas for the champagne. That was steep enough. That bottle wouldn't cost more than a pound top whack, even from a London wine merchant. Forty pounds for a few words of conversation. He was a bloody fool. He took the notes from his wallet.

'And something for the old lady who cleans,' said the girl sharply.

Charles added a ten pound note. The girl curtsied and smiled, and behind his back winked at Bruce. She let

Charles out into the street. He hurried thankfully back to his club.

That was what had happened. In a word, nothing. He'd been a fool, wanting to talk to someone. But, he could not possibly explain to Rose what had happened, precisely because nothing had happened, and no woman would ever believe that, certainly not his wife.

Guests were arriving now, some in carriages, more in the new motor cars that were becoming increasingly fashionable. The women wore expensive dresses, with tiaras in their hair, jewels glittering on wrists and round their throats. The men wore white ties and tails, some with medals and sashes of British and foreign orders of chivalry. Charles and Rose stood at the top of the marble stairway to greet them, exchanging pleasantries with some, shaking hands with others, before they passed on into the main rooms.

'We shall be here for quite a time, my dear,' Charles remarked to his wife. 'We've invited four hundred guests, and only a fraction are here so far.'

'I will ask a footman to bring us some champagne,' said Rose and left his side.

Charles saw the Chief Constable Sir Bernard Warner and his wife enter the hall. A very decent fellow, Warner, who owed him a good turn. Charles had used his influence to help secure for him the post of Chief Constable, and Sir Bernard had often assured him how greatly he appreciated this act of friendship. Well, it did no harm to be on good terms with the constabulary, especially with villains like Harper about.

He smiled at the Lord Lieutenant of the county, a bachelor who brought his plain and unmarried sister. There were so many people, and he knew them all and they knew him. They were his kind of people, he told himself. They spoke the same language. But as he watched and smiled, he wondered how many also had secrets like his. What were they like when they were at home? What follies haunted them? What terrible photographs lay in some swine's possession ready to ruin them if made public?

Here were men masquerading as wealthy landowners who Charles knew had three mortgages on their property and yet were accepted at their own valuation as gentlemen of means. The moneylenders to whom they owed huge and undisclosed sums, and who probably possessed more wealth than any half-dozen people here, would not be admitted as guests, of course. They were not gentlemen. We are all actors and actresses, Charles thought. But hadn't someone – Shakespeare, probably – known this centuries ago? All the world's a stage and all the men and women merely players. And what part am I to play?

He was musing on this when Grover approached from a side door. The staff never used the main staircase; they had their own set of stairs to reach the upper floors.

'There are two gentlemen to see you, sir,' he said.

'There are dozens, scores here,' Charles replied expansively. 'They are *all* seeing me. Who are these two people?'

'It's a matter connected with the Chief Constable, so one told me. In confidence, of course, sir.'

'Sir Bernard has just arrived. He can see me himself.'

'I think possibly not, sir.'

'What do you mean?'

'I mean, sir, these people wish to see you on an important matter.'

'But *now*? In the middle of the ball? What about?'

'I do not know, sir. But I think it might be advisable to see them. They appear to be serious gentlemen.'

'When all the guests have arrived, I will see them.'

'As you wish, sir. I will give them that message.'

As the butler turned, Charles called after him. 'Offer each of them a glass of champagne. That should put

48

them in a better mood for whatever they've got to tell me.'

'I have already offered them some, sir. They said they were on duty. They do not drink on duty.'

'On *duty*? What are they, policemen?'

'I do not know, sir. But I will inform them you will be down.'

The magic of the moment had vanished, shattered like a burst balloon. Why hadn't Warner come across and said, 'Look, Charles, when you have a moment I would appreciate a word with you'? Something like that. They shot together. They had known each other for years. He'd ask Warner what this visit was about and not waste time with minions.

Then he thought again. No, he wouldn't. He'd go down and see these men first. There was some mistake, obviously.

'Something's come up,' he told Rose when she reappeared. 'I must see someone downstairs.'

'But who? In the middle of receiving our guests?'

'I'll be back in a moment. I'll tell you then.'

Before she could ask any more questions, Charles hurried down the stairs, smiling and waving to guests who came up slowly, ladies lifting the hems of their dresses above the crimson carpet. Grover was waiting for him.

'In the morning room, sir.'

Charles nodded. Then he realised the footman had not arrived with his champagne.

'Get me a drink,' he said curtly.

Grover flicked his fingers. A footman approached, holding a tray of glasses. Charles took one, drained it, went into the morning room. Two men were standing with their backs to the fireplace. The fire had not been laid, and instead of coals, washed and cut to matching size, a huge mass of dried flowers gave the surround and

49

mantelpiece the effect of a marble picture frame.

Charles looked from one man to the other. They looked back at him. They were tall men in dark suits and heavy, well-polished boots. They were not gentlemen, of course, but of a military cast of countenance. They might have been sergeants in a good regiment of foot wearing mufti.

'You wish to see me, I understand,' said Charles coldly.

'Yes, sir. It's rather embarrassing. It might be better if you would close the door.'

Charles did so.

'Now, what's this about? It's deuced inconvenient for me.'

'My card, sir,' said the first, and handed Charles a square of pasteboard. He read: 'Detective Sergeant B.C. Gonville, Special Investigation Branch.'

'Well, Sergeant, what brings you here at this hour? As I say, it's a most awkward time for me. I'm host to four hundred people including, I may say, the Chief Constable and his lady wife.'

'Yes, sir. Actually, it is on Sir Bernard's suggestion that we are here.'

'About what? Has there been an accident somewhere? A fire at a farm, someone injured?'

'No, sir. Something concerning you, Mr Rowlands. Information has been laid officially – and I hesitate to say these words, sir, but as you understand, I must – that you have had carnal knowledge and committed an act of gross indecency with a male minor.'

'Bloody rubbish,' said Charles instantly.

'There are witnesses to this who have given their sworn testimony. According to them, the incident took place in a house in Jermyn Street in London, sir. The abode of a foreign lady, Italian by birth, but who goes by the name of Mrs Jones, although she has never been married to Mr Jones who actually is the tenant.'

Charles frowned. This was Harper's doing, of course. He had underestimated the man. He should have dealt with him immediately in some way, but he could not think how.

'Do you know a man called Thomas Harper?' he asked the sergeant.

'No, sir. I am not acquainted with anyone of that name. You do not deny the charge, sir?'

'I most certainly deny it and will do so strenuously in a court of law if necessary.'

'That is what the Chief Constable was afraid of, sir. He does not wish your name to be sullied, or that of your lady wife, or your family.'

'So why have you come to see me?'

'He tells me, sir, that on the grounds of your friendship, and the very high regard in which he holds you, he is willing to take the very considerable risk of recommending all prosecution be abandoned, provided you leave the country. At once. Tonight.'

'Leave the country? That is utterly impossible. I have, as you say, a wife and family here and many commitments. I'll stay and fight this.'

'That is your prerogative, sir. But it might not be an easy or even a fair fight. Win or lose, mud will be thrown and will stick, sir. Therefore, in all the circumstances, and in view of his own lengthy experience of such cases, Sir Bernard most earnestly suggests you leave the country – at least temporarily. Then perhaps some intermediary might come to a financial accommodation with the young minor concerned to drop the matter.'

'Is this blackmail?'

'Oh no, sir. Most certainly not. It's simply, if I may say so, one gentleman trying to help another.'

Richard hurried through the darkening garden, carefully

keeping away from the lines of lights strung up in the trees. He wanted to reach his room before anyone knew he had disobeyed his parents' orders and left it.

The front hall and the main stairway were crowded. He could see dozens of people, and banks of flowers which had taken a team of florists all day to arrange. To use this door was asking to be discovered. Instead, he climbed the servants' stairs. These were uncarpeted. Walls on either side were painted with pale green distemper. A faint smell of disinfectant hung over all these back premises. He hurried along the corridor to his room, pushed open the door.

Standing there, looking at him, was a girl of his own age. He had never seen her before. He had no idea who she was.

'What are you doing here?' Richard asked her, his voice sharpened by surprise and edged with alarm. 'Who are you?'

'Carola Marsh,' she replied easily. 'I saw you looking at the traction engine. My father's the engineer. He said you'd been having a chat, asking him questions. You showed him your steam engine.'

'Well? What has that got to do with you coming into my room like this?'

'Nothing, really. I'm sorry. It's just that I'm interested in engines myself. That's odd for a girl, I know, but I wanted to talk to you. I asked a maid at the back where you were, and she said up here. So I came up the back stairs hoping you'd be here, like she said. And, well, here you are. Here we both are.'

'But why come up here? Why not talk to me downstairs?'

'You weren't there, for one thing. And for another, that wouldn't be right. My father told me you're the son of the house.'

'One of them,' Richard admitted.

'Well, that's what he said. So I came up here to see you. You're not angry, are you?'

Was he? Richard was not sure. He hesitated. 'No,' he said at last. 'But you surprised me. I've never had a girl visit me in my room before.'

'Well, now you have. Where is this engine?'

'In the cupboard. I'll show you.'

He opened the cupboard, picked up the odd shoes, old clothes, discarded sports gear he had piled over the toy.

'Why do you hide it away like that? I'd be proud of it if I owned it.'

'My father said it was to be thrown out. No one knows it's here – except you. The boiler exploded. You can see for yourself what happened. My elder brother got very badly burned. They say his face will be scarred for life.'

'The pressure was too high?'

'Yes. Someone tightened up the safety valve. Not me.'

'I should hope not. That was a mad thing to do.'

Richard picked up the valve. 'You see. It's as tight as you can turn it.'

'Do you know who did that?'

'No.'

'But you have your own thoughts on the matter, yes?'

'In a sense, yes.'

Richard was surprised at Carola's questions. He had never spoken to any girl about engines before, or indeed about anything that could be important to him. At the parties he went to, girls tended to cluster in one group and boys a little way apart, talking in louder voices than usual while the girls giggled and looked at them coyly over their shoulders.

For a moment he wondered if there were many girls who liked engines.

'Have you any brothers or sisters?' he asked her.

'No. I'm the only one. And my mother's gone off.'

'Where to?'

53

She shrugged. 'With another man. But she'll be back. She's done that before. Several times. She always comes back.'

'Where do you live?'

'We've a caravan. You didn't see it? It's in the trees. We tow it behind the traction engine. We work fairs mostly. It's a good living – well, fair, anyway. My father hires out the engine with the dynamo to light the sideshows. We go all over the country, my father and me.'

'Do you go to school?'

'When we stop long enough, yes. My father teaches me.'

'About what?'

'All sorts of things. Arithmetic. English. History. He has books. I'm reading about Marco Polo now. Do you know anything about him?'

'Nothing, except he was an explorer, and sailed to the East centuries ago.'

'Seven centuries ago, to be exact. And he was much more than just an explorer. He journeyed for years. Finally, he reached China – Cathay, as it was called then. The ruler asked him to go home and return with a hundred men of science and the arts to teach his people. Marco Polo went back but couldn't get enough interest in the project. People back home simply didn't believe his accounts of his experiences.'

'So he was a failure?'

'In that, yes. But in nothing else. He opened up trade routes to the East. He actually commanded a galley in a war and was captured. That's when he wrote his account of his journeys. Even in terrible adversity, he found time and place to rise above his setbacks. Reading him has given me the urge to try and do something right out of the ordinary myself.' She paused, as though she had said too much.

Richard held out his hand, palm downwards. 'You see that birthmark?' he asked her. 'If you look at it from a certain angle you can see the initials M.P. All of us in our family have it. We say they're the initials of Marco Polo. At least, so I'm told. I was born on Thursday and Thursday's child has far to go. So it's apt. And odd you mention Marco Polo now.'

'I'll tell you what I'll do,' Carola said. 'I'll ask my father to make a new boiler for your engine.'

'Could he do that?'

'If he has the time, yes. He's very good at anything mechanical. This will be an easy job for him. You only need a section of metal tube about two inches wide and four inches long. He can cut out two circular pieces of metal, braze them on at each end, put back the safety valve at the top, braze a copper pipe to connect it to the cylinder, and there you are.'

'You really do have a mechanical mind, don't you?' Richard said admiringly.

'So people tell me. Now can I take your engine away with me to get it repaired?'

Richard looked at her closely. She was quite pretty, he thought, not in an accepted sort of way, not pert, but full of life and character. She was slightly built, with large eyes set well apart. A pleasant person, he thought. He couldn't imagine her sniggering like the other girls he met. But to give her the engine . . .

'Will you bring it back?' he asked her seriously.

'Of course.'

'But how do I know? I've no address for you.'

'I haven't got an address to give you. My father's name is painted on the side of the traction engine roof: James Marsh. We go from town to town.'

'When will you be back here?'

'I don't know. Probably not until next year, if your father has another ball. But we're at a fair in Brendon village next week, five miles from here. He'll have it done by Saturday. You can come over and collect it.'

'Does he want paying? I haven't any money,' Richard admitted.

'That doesn't matter. I'll ask him to do it without payment. He likes working with his hands. Don't you believe me?'

Did he? Richard wanted to, but he could not be certain. Was this simply an ingenious way to steal a toy which was probably out of the girl's reach financially? he wondered. His natural caution told him to doubt her, and yet she seemed honest, and she was unusual in liking engines. There was another thing. He wasn't supposed to have kept the engine, so if she didn't bring it back, his parents would not pursue the matter. He made up his mind.

'All right,' he said. 'You take it. Here, cover it with this.'

He gave her an old shirt. She wrapped it round the boiler.

'Are you going to the ball?' she asked him.

'Oh, no. Grown-ups only.'

'I've been watching them arrive.'

'You like the dresses, I suppose.'

'Not especially,' she said. 'But they're coming in cars, most of them.'

'You like cars, too?'

'I like anything mechanical,' she said. '*Anything*. I often wish I'd been a boy. Girls think it's odd.'

'*I* think it's odd,' Richard told her bluntly.

'Well, maybe I am odd. Or maybe, as my father says, not odd but unique.'

'What else makes you unique?'

'I'll tell you.' She came very close to him, looked in his face. 'It's a secret, really. But you won't laugh, I hope, if I tell you.'

56

'No. I promise,' said Richard, mystified.

'Well, one day I'd like to fly.'

'*Fly?*'

'Yes. In an aeroplane. The last fair we were at, there was an air pilot who gave demonstrations. He spun the propeller to start the engine and then he took off.'

'Did he take anyone up with him?'

'No. It was only a single-seater. People thought it all very clever, but rather pointless. No future in it, one man said. But I'd read something in one of my father's books about Benjamin Franklin, the American.'

'What about him?'

'Well, he saw a balloon when he was just a young man, a hot-air balloon. Someone said to him, laughing at this, "What use is *that*?" And Franklin turned to him and said, "What use is a baby?" '

'Well, not much use, I should think,' said Richard.

'Maybe not. But babies grow up to become men and women. These little motor cars that go phut-phutting along with their clouds of smoke and dust, they'll become useful very soon. And so will aeroplanes. One day I mean to fly.'

'Then I expect you will. If you want anything hard enough you often get it, so my mother told me,' said Richard.

'And I want to fly more than anything. Not just like the man at the fair, a hop round a couple of hundred feet up, and then down again in the field with a cap held out for coppers to pay for the petrol. I want to fly from city to city, country to country. Like Marco Polo, only in the air, not on the ground. Maybe, one day, I'll fly right round the world.'

'You've got a hope,' said Richard shortly.

'No,' Carola replied seriously. 'I've got more than a hope. I've got a dream.'

★ ★ ★

Jim Marsh had drawn off a bucket of water from the boiler of the traction engine and was washing his hands and face outside his caravan when Carola returned. He picked up a towel, scrubbed his face and hands dry and regarded his daughter without enthusiasm.

'What did you get?' he asked her.

She shook her head. 'Nothing.'

'What do you mean, nothing? You followed the boy, didn't you, like I told you?'

'Yes.'

'And then?'

'I asked a servant where the bedrooms were.'

'There must be a fortune lying about in there. As many jewels on their dressing tables as they are wearing. Probably more. And so easy to get your hands on. Stuff just waiting to walk. What did you pick up?'

'I only went into one room and the boy found me. So I got nothing.'

'Nothing? Whose room was that?'

Carola paused, looking at the ground.

'His.'

'Why his room?'

She shrugged her shoulders.

'I had to start somewhere.'

'You started nowhere, you silly little bitch. You missed your chance.' He cuffed her sharply on her right ear.

'Don't hit me,' Carola pleaded. 'Don't.'

'I bloody well will. Think I want to go on working this traction engine round the country, stoking the bloody boiler, when with one simple move we could be free and on easy street?'

'He seemed a nice boy,' she said sullenly.

'A nice boy,' her father mimicked. 'He touch you up or anything?'

'No, no,' Carola replied, shocked. 'Nothing like that at

all. He talked about engines. He gave me this.' She unwrapped the shirt.

'Bloody toy,' said her father. 'Boiler's burst, I see. It was working when he showed it to me.'

'Can you mend it for him?'

'Mend it? What the hell for? So we can flog it?'

'No. I thought I could take it back, then.'

He looked at her, eyes narrowed. 'You mean you'll have another go?'

'I suppose so.'

'You suppose so, do you? You're not Lady Muck, you know. You're not living in the big house, you're living in a caravan with your old man. We don't have too many chances to do anything better. You had one and you lost it. Now, maybe we'll have another. If you foul it up again, don't bother to come back to me. I don't need a bloody useless mouth to feed.'

He picked up the engine and examined the remains of the boiler.

'Did you tell him I'd do it?'

'I said I'd ask you.'

'How do you mean to get it back to him? You can't go up the back stairs a second time. They won't have another ball like this until next year.'

'I'll find a way.'

'You'd better, if I mend this engine. Now get out of my sight. I've got a long night ahead. The fireman's gone and got himself drunk. Last thing I want to see is you hanging about and getting in my bloody way. So get out of it. D'you hear?'

'Yes, Father,' she said quietly. 'I hear.'

Chapter Four

As Charles went into the ballroom, a footman approached bearing a tray of glasses of champagne. He drank one glass quickly. The sparkling wine went down his throat like water. He took a second glass, then a third, and felt slightly more at ease. He glanced around the great room. Couples dancing past smiled at him, hoping to catch his eye. If he smiled in recognition they felt cheered, accepted.

He saw his wife in conversation with a handful of people, including the Chief Constable. Sir Bernard was the last person he wanted to see now; he must keep out of his way. What must he think of him? How could he possibly appear so relaxed when he knew what he knew, when his men were waiting downstairs to take the host away?

Charles walked round the edge of the room. People sitting out waved to him, greeted him.

'How kind of you to ask us.'

'The best party of the year.'

'*Always* the same at your place.'

He nodded. It was always the same at his place – but from now on, things would be different.

His wife saw him approach, excused himself from the guests, crossed over to him.

'Where have you been? I've been looking for you everywhere.'

'I told you I had two visitors.'

'Gatecrashers, people of that kind?'

'No. Business callers. I have to talk to you. On your own. It's important.'

'Business callers? *Now?*' Disbelief sharpened Rose's voice.

'Now. It's very important,' he told her. 'For both of us.'

They went into a small anteroom. French windows opened onto the grounds. Bright lights in the trees, the throb of distant music and, in the background, the fountain constantly changing colour gave the scene an atmosphere of total unreality. This was a glimpse of fairyland, paradise, Charles thought wretchedly; a view from the gates of Hell.

'Well?' asked Rose impatiently. 'What is this business that's so important?'

'I have to leave.'

'*Leave?* Where? When?'

'Now,' he said. 'A very important matter has just come up.'

'What on earth do you mean?'

Charles paused, dredging for reasons. Alcohol fumed in his mind. He could think of nothing convincing.

He said, vaguely, 'Business. I have to go abroad.'

'Are you all right? *Go abroad?* In the middle of our ball? Can't you go tomorrow?'

'It'll be tomorrow when I get there.'

'Where are you going, then?'

'France.'

'What sort of business in France demands your attention so urgently?'

'Relating to the estate. To our whole future.'

'I don't understand what you're saying. I don't think you're well.'

She looked at him closely.

'You're not drunk, are you?'

He shook his head.

'No. I wish I were, that this was all a dream, all imagination.'

'Who *are* these men?'

'I can't tell you now. It's all too complicated. Just believe me, I have to go. You must make my excuses to everybody, if they ask.'

'What can I say?'

'I've become unwell. Not been myself for some days.'

'Come to think of it, you haven't,' said his wife, looking at him shrewdly. 'Not since poor Tobin got his face burned. You're worried about him, aren't you?'

'I suppose I am, yes. You're right. I am.'

'Has this got to do with Tobin?'

'It's got to do with all of us. Just believe me. But please don't keep asking questions. I'll tell you everything as soon as I can. I promise.'

'I think you're ill. Dr Murgatroyd is here. He could help you.'

'I don't want a doctor. I just want you to understand.'

'But how can I when you won't tell me anything?'

Charles did not reply.

'How long will you be away?' she asked him.

'I don't know.'

'But you *must* know. A week? A month?'

'Possibly that. Maybe longer. I'll make arrangements with the bank so you can draw on my account for as much as you want any time. You won't be short of money, that's one thing,' he said bitterly.

Rose looked at him, bewildered. She had never really understood her husband. The ways of the rich were very strange. They could do virtually what they wished – as long as their money lasted. Until it ran out, as sometimes it did, they seemed to be totally above laws that governed the behaviour of other people. They made their own rules. They did what they wanted and answered no questions they wished to avoid. She had never been rich herself, but was being married to a rich man the next best thing?

'Well,' she said slowly, 'I can't understand what can have happened, but I suppose I have to believe what you say.'

'I've never let you down before, have I?' Charles asked her miserably.

'You look so ill, suddenly,' said Rose more gently.

'I don't feel well,' he admitted. 'But just don't ask me any more questions. I can't answer them.'

'How will you pack?'

'I'll tell the valet to pack just what I need. I can buy what else I need over there.'

'I have no address for you.'

'I have no address myself, yet,' he said. 'But I'll be in touch. That's all. The end of the matter.'

But he knew it was not the end; it was barely the beginning. He could not see where the end might be, and he had no idea where the road would lead him before he reached the end – if he ever did. That photograph of Rose was the key; the others in the envelope, when he brought himself to look at them, were relatively harmless. Apart from that one of Rose, he had nothing to fear. Well, not much, although it would be embarrassing to have to admit in court he had visited a brothel, and almost as bad to claim he had only drunk a couple of glasses of champagne and then left – after paying fifty pounds for the privilege. The jury might believe that or they might not. At best, he would become the butt of lewd jokes; he was impotent, finished, only half a man. He could bear those stories, but he could not bear the publicity that would surround the photograph of his wife. That was evidence no one could deny.

'You'd better get back to our guests,' he said.

'I suppose so,' she said flatly. 'I suppose so.'

She leaned across and kissed him on the cheek, a cool peck, not a kiss of love or passion. He inhaled expensive scent from her hair; diamonds and rubies in her necklace, her tiara, her earrings glittered like frozen tears just in front of his eyes. Then Rose was gone and he was on his own.

He did not go back to the ballroom; he walked out of the French windows, round the side of the house and in through another entrance. He could not bear to see any of his guests and become embroiled in banal conversation. He went upstairs. His valet was in his dressing room brushing a tweed suit to be laid out for the morning.

'I have to leave unexpectedly,' Charles told him brusquely. 'Pack me enough clothes for a fortnight's stay.'

'In this country, sir?'

'No. France.'

'Town or country, sir?'

'Town, I think. No evening clothes. I'll be staying in an hotel.'

'Very good, sir.'

Now he'd say goodbye to his children. He crossed the landing to Tobin's room. The boy was asleep. His bandaged face, lit by a shaft of light where the curtains had not been completely drawn, seemed white, ghostly. Charles stood looking at him for a moment and then bent down and kissed the bandage. Tobin stirred slightly, one hand went up automatically to his face as though to ward off a fly or a kiss. Charles did not want to wake him. He tiptoed out of the room, went into his daughter's room.

Cecily lay with one arm outside the coverlet round a teddy bear. She looked defenceless, and of course she was. He hardly knew her. She was virtually a stranger. Nursemaids had brought up all the children. They were

65

as much strangers to him as he must be a stranger to them. Perhaps this was just as well in view of what had happened? He could not bend to kiss his daughter. That seemed somehow too much of a betrayal, a Judas kiss, in view of the fact he was going away – running away. He went out of her room and into Richard's.

Richard was not asleep, but seeing his father framed in the doorway, he pretended to be sleeping. He was afraid his father had come to punish him for being out of the house earlier – perhaps one of the servants had informed on him. Or maybe someone had seen Carola in his room. Servants liked to spy on their employer's children when they could. They thought the employer would regard this as an instance of their loyalty. He heard his father clear his throat. To his amazement he began to speak. Was he talking to himself? Richard listened attentively.

'I have never understood you,' his father said softly.

So he *must* be talking to him. Did he guess he was awake? Surely not. Richard listened, holding his breath, for his father was speaking in a whisper.

'I have three children and you're the strangest, the odd one out. Tobin, I know, just wants to live as a gentleman of leisure. And no doubt he will when he inherits the estate. Your sister will marry someone easily enough, I expect, for she'll be quite rich, too.

'But you, my odd son out, what's going to happen to you? You're only keen on engines and nuts and bolts, making things. There won't be much money for you. A farm and some property, I expect, so you won't starve. But you won't be able to live on your brother's level, and there's no future in getting your hands dirty, in just being a mechanic.

'I can't understand you. I just hope you'll be all right. It's a harsh world out there. Here, my estate is like a world of its own. Everyone's cosseted, looked after. But things may change, for nothing lasts for ever. And what

66

will happen to you then? You and I have never spoken the same language. I don't think I ever tried much. You were different, and when you're older you don't want to adjust to young people who are different. You want them to adjust to you. So goodbye, Richard, and may God look after you, if I cannot.' Charles's voice broke. He left the room hurriedly and went into his study. He had a letter to write.

Richard lay awake, pondering what he had heard, whether he had really heard it, whether it was all a dream, and he'd just awoken. He turned on his side and tried to sleep, but the music of two orchestras kept him awake. Dawn was already lightening up the sky, making the fairy lights seem poor and tawdry, when finally he did fall asleep.

Sergeant Gonville and his companion were still standing in the morning room when Charles went downstairs. He had a sudden strange feeling that they had not moved; they could have been statues. They had not sat down, and presumably had not examined any of the books on the shelves. But what did it matter whether they had or not? What did anything matter now?

'I'm ready to go,' he told them quietly. 'Shall I order up a car for the station?'

'We have our own motor, sir,' the sergeant replied. 'I can drive.' He glanced at a German silver turnip watch.

'There's a train in twenty minutes. I have consulted the timetable.'

'We'd better leave, then,' said Charles.

'You are taking the wisest course, if I may say so, sir.'

'Am I?'

He followed them out to their car. A guest was coming in the front door, cigar in hand, monocle in place.

'Why, my dear fellow, deserting us so soon? Host leaving before the party ends? Disgraceful behaviour!

67

Conduct most unbecoming, if I may say so.'

'I agree,' said Charles as lightly as he was able. 'But I'll be back, I assure you.'

'You'd damn well better be, sir. This is a *splendid* do. I'm just looking for my lady wife.'

'I hope you find her.'

'I certainly will. I most certainly will.'

The air felt cool outside the house. The front was lit by flares, now smoky and dying down. A few chauffeurs slept at the wheels of their cars.

The two men led the way between rows of parked cars, down the drive. In a space under some trees an old-fashioned Mors was parked, pointing towards the gate.

'You get in the back, sir,' said the sergeant.

Charles did as he was told, and was followed by the other officer. How odd, he did not even know his name and he felt no reason to ask it. Sergeant Gonville strapped Charles's suitcase on the luggage carrier, went to the front of the car, spun the crank handle. The engine fired. The whole car trembled on its spidery wheels with each beat of the cylinders. Gonville lit the oil lamps and then they drove down the drive, past the lodge, out onto the road.

'Will you leave the car at the station?' Charles asked him, not caring, only wishing to break the silence.

'I shall take it back, sir,' said the other man. 'It's on loan to the force, for this evening only. Thought it better, more discreet like, to use a private motor, not a police one. Sergeant Gonville will accompany you on the train.'

The station platform was deserted.

'I've no ticket,' said Charles.

'I took the precaution of buying two Third Class tickets, sir,' the sergeant informed him. 'I will accompany you to Dover and see you safely on the ferry.'

At last the train arrived. Charles climbed into a Third

Class smoker, sat down. A whistle sounded, the engine blew off steam, the train began to move out into the darkness towards the coast. And beyond the coast, Charles thought, lay the sea, and beyond the sea was another country, another life, another future. But of what terrible kind he still could not begin to imagine.

Grover sat in his pantry, smoking one of Charles's cigars. He poured himself another brandy from the bottle he had removed from his master's cellar, and peered intently at a plain sheet of paper, puckering his face with the effort of his concentration. Then he picked up a pencil and began to sketch in the outline of a face.

His wife came into the room, also helped herself liberally to a brandy, and glanced at her husband's drawing.

'You've got him there, all right, the police sergeant,' she said admiringly. 'Proper gift you have for taking people off. Smooth talker, he looks like. Much the same as that other man Harper who called some time ago.'

'Policemen,' said Grover with contempt. 'They're all tarred with the same brush. Bullies. You want to keep away from them.'

'Which, from what you tell me, the master's doing his best to do.'

They smiled at each other, emptied their glasses, and then refilled them.

Richard awoke suddenly. He lay for a moment looking up at the ceiling and then turned his head towards the window to look at the sky – he never liked to have the curtains drawn. The first streaks of dawn were appearing.

He pulled the quilt and blanket up to his chin. For some reason he felt uneasy, and he could not think why. Then he remembered his father standing in the doorway, speaking to him in a low voice. He wished now he had not pretended to be asleep, but he was never sure of his father's temper.

Downstairs, Rose was saying goodbye to the last of her guests in the hall. A footman handed stoles and mink coats to the ladies, bowing obsequiously to each one, receiving half a sovereign, even a sovereign, under cover of the fur.

'You are very generous, my lady,' he said unctuously. 'Thank you very much indeed, Your Royal Highness.'

Chauffeurs held open the doors of cars, adjusted rugs round their occupants. The motors drove off, trailing fronds of blue exhaust smoke.

The Chief Constable bade farewell. 'My wife and I have so enjoyed the evening,' he said. 'I did want to have a word with Charles, but I missed him, although I saw him earlier on in the evening.'

'He had to leave unexpectedly,' said Rose slowly, looking into his eyes.

'Nothing serious, I hope? No illness in the family?'

'A business matter. He'll be returning soon. I can assure you, the last thing Charles wanted to do was to leave precipitately in the middle of his own ball.'

'So I would imagine. He is always such a generous host. Please convey to him my best wishes, and once more, my very warmest thanks.'

He climbed into his car, made sure that the glass division between the driver and the driven was firmly closed. He never liked servants to hear what was not for their ears. His wife sat looking at him quizzically.

'I thought you would ask about Charles. I saw him dash off earlier on. Rather odd, I thought.'

'I expect he had a very good reason for going.'

'What makes you expect that, Bernard? Do you know the reason?'

Her husband smiled, reached into his pocket for his

cigar case. 'If I did, my dear, I couldn't tell you, could I?'

'I don't see why not. Other husbands tell their wives everything.'

'Not husbands of my acquaintance,' replied the Chief Constable. 'And not concerning delicate matters with which I sometimes have to deal.' He lit his Havana, sat back against the buttoned leather cushion and exhaled a cloud of expensive smoke.

'You must know *something*, or you wouldn't be so confoundedly arch about it,' said his wife sharply. Bernard liked to pretend he could keep a secret, but she would find it out sooner or later. She always did – and sooner rather than later.

After a quick breakfast, Richard went out into the garden. Men in blue dungarees had already dismantled the lights, and were now rolling up hundreds of yards of rubber-covered electric cable. Others, wearing green aprons, were moving chairs from the marquee, folding curtains, unpinning the striped lining from their walls with the smoothness that came from years of practice. The party was over, but they had another job to which they were contracted twenty miles away. They had no time to hang about.

The foreman, wearing a bowler hat and carrying an ebony walking stick, waved a second truck into position as the first was filled, shaking his head irritably as people came up to him with queries.

'What shall we do with the broken chairs?'

'Can we have two more men to help us get the main roof poles down?'

Richard passed all this activity, hurried on towards the traction engine. Carola's father was working a handpump to fill the boiler. He nodded a greeting. 'Slept through it, did you?' he asked.

'Yes. Carola said you would mend my steam engine.'

'That's right. I've already examined it. She'll bring it back to you here directly it's done.'

'That won't be necessary. I can come and pick it up. I have a bicycle – I was given it for my last birthday.'

'Then you're a lucky young man. But when Jim Marsh says he will do something, he does it. Now, if you'll excuse me, we're late already. We're due at Brendon village.'

Richard did not know where Carola was and did not like to ask. It was obvious they were in a hurry; the caravan was already hitched up behind the traction engine.

He waited to watch the engine move off with a great shudder of steam and a grinding of iron tyres on the gravel. Then he walked back to the house. He felt somehow deflated. He would like to have seen Carola, talked to her, got to know her better. He didn't know her at all, of course. But he could easily cycle over to Brendon and see her. Cheered by the thought and the fact that his engine would soon be repaired, he went inside. When he received it back he must think of a really secure place to hide it.

Tobin was finishing breakfast when Richard came into the room. He did not really want to ask Tobin about his face, but he felt he had to. Not to show any interest seemed too callous.

'Up early?' he asked him, skating round the subject.

'Hardly slept a wink,' Tobin replied. 'I ache all over. I've a terrible headache from the noise of those two orchestras all night long. Apart from that, I'm perfectly well, no thanks to you.'

'I'm very sorry,' said Richard. 'I mean about what happened. But, honestly, it wasn't my fault.'

When the Calais train pulled into the Gare du Nord in Paris, Charles took down his valise from the luggage rack

72

and stepped out onto the platform.

He stood for a moment, irresolute, inhaling the pungent aromas of French cigarette tobacco, garlic, smoke from the locomotive. He always liked Paris, but he had never visited the city in such circumstances, and for such a fearful reason.

He usually stayed at the Crillon, but now was not the occasion to go where he was well known. In a small and unfashionable hotel he would be more difficult to discover should a newspaper send a penny-a-liner to seek him out. The last thing he wanted was any publicity, or any public discussion as to why he had so precipitately travelled to France.

Charles walked along the platform slowly, wondering where he should go. The problem was that he did not know any small hotels in Paris. He had never visited a small hotel anywhere in his life. His usual custom was to find the best hotel and then engage not just one room, but a suite, sometimes an entire floor.

A porter saw the Englishman wearing an expensive overcoat, highly polished shoes, a loose scarf, a trilby hat, and instantly recognised the signs of English wealth. He hurried towards him.

'Carry your bag, monsieur, to a taxi?' he asked him politely in English, touching his cap in respectful salute.

Charles nodded and surrendered his valise. The porter opened the taxi door.

'Where to, monsieur?' he asked.

'Tell the driver, a small hotel. Quiet and discreet. Not anywhere well known.'

'Ah!' the porter nodded understandingly. These wealthy Englishmen. No doubt he was planning an assignation. He spoke rapidly to the driver.

'He suggests one in the Place Saint Sulpice, monsieur.'

Charles nodded; he had no idea where this was, but assumed the driver knew the sort of hotel he required.

He handed the porter half a sovereign, and sank back on faded cushions that smelt faintly of tobacco, scent and petrol.

The hotel seemed little more than an ungainly private house wedged between a shop selling crucifixes and brass candlesticks for altars on the one side and, on the other, an establishment that dealt with kneelers and altar cloths. The whole square seemed to be given up to the manufacture or sale of religious artefacts.

The hotel manager spoke English, which was a bonus.

'You are staying long, monsieur?' he asked.

'I am not sure,' Charles replied. He would see how comfortable the hotel was before he committed himself.

'I ask because we usually like a week's money in advance from people who have not booked. No offence, monsieur, I hope?'

'None.'

Charles took out his wallet. It contained only four five pound notes. What a damn fool he was to come without more money, but then he never carried money in England. His name was always good enough for credit anywhere. When he went shopping, a footman would accompany him to carry a chequebook and any purchases he made. But here in France he was not known, and he did not want to become known.

'I will have to telegraph my bank in London,' he explained.

'What you have would be more than sufficient for a week, monsieur,' the hotel manager assured him quickly. If this Englishman left to go to a bank, he might not return, and guests who stayed longer than one night were not too common.

'Possibly. But I will need some for myself.'

'You can telegraph from here, monsieur.' The man took a form from a drawer, pushed it across the top of the desk, with a pen and an inkwell.

'What is the name of the nearest bank?'

'Credit Lyonnais. On the corner, monsieur.'

Charles wrote on the porous form with a spluttering pen: 'Please telegraph five thousand pounds immediately to me c/o Credit Lyonnais'. He added the addresses of the bank and the hotel, signed it and handed it to the manager, together with a week's payment in advance.

Up in his room, Charles took off his shoes, his coat and suit, loosened his tie, and lay down thankfully on top of the bed. He had not realised how tired he was. When he awoke, it was late afternoon. Birds were gathering in the trees outside, filling the air with shrill twittering.

He swung himself off the bed, washed in cold water in the basin because there was no hot, rinsed out his mouth and dressed. He brushed and combed his hair carefully. Simply because he was in exile, there was no need to become slovenly.

Seeing his reflection for the first time in the streaky, yellowed mirror above the basin, a sudden feeling of horror engulfed him. He looked pale, drawn, worried – and of course he was all three; a man on the run. What was he to do about that photograph? Even if he gained possession of the negative, Harper would doubtless have dozens of prints. That photograph represented an income for him.

Charles sat down in a lumpy armchair, took out the hip flask of brandy he always carried in his valise, and gulped down two mouthfuls. The spirit had as little effect on him as the champagne the previous evening. Had the ball been only last night? It all seemed so distant now; it might have taken place in another era, another world – and in a sense it had. He had left that world, only temporarily, he assured himself, but it still belonged to the past.

He emptied the remains of the hip flask into a tooth glass and drank it neat. This made him feel slightly better. He must not allow himself to become melancholic. He would find a way out somehow. He was rich, and when you had enough money, you could buy your way out of almost any difficulty. Of course, he could have bought his way out for five thousand pounds – so Harper had told him. But that would not have been the final demand. That would only have been a down payment on a debt from which he would never be allowed to break free.

He went downstairs. The manager was behind the reception desk examining a ledger. He looked up as Charles approached.

'I have telephoned the bank, monsieur. Your money is already there for collection.'

'That's quick. Is the bank still open?'

The manager glanced at his watch. 'Not for usual transactions, but there is a bell at the side door for after hours. I am certain they will accommodate you. You are exchanging a very substantial sum.'

'I suppose so. In the meantime, could I have a brandy?'

The man produced a bottle of Courvoisier, and a huge balloon glass. He poured out three fingers of spirit.

'Put it on the bill,' Charles told him and drank greedily. Then he poured himself another glass. This stuff was good, far better than the brandy he had brought out from England. But then you would expect that; they made it over here.

He nodded to the manager, went out into the square. The weather felt colder than he imagined. The hotel must be centrally heated. These foreigners went in for such soft ideas. He set out at a good pace towards the main road. The brandy, much stronger than he usually drank, fumed in his blood like liquid fire. He felt vaguely disorientated, as though he was watching himself walk and not really personally involved.

He paused at an intersection, and glanced across the road, looking for the bank. Then his flesh tightened on his skull like a drumskin.

Standing on the opposite pavement, smiling at him, was Thomas Harper. Had he seen him? Had he recognised him? Of course he had. That was why the bastard was smiling.

Charles glanced behind him. The street was empty, except for a man walking slowly towards him and still forty yards away: Harper's chauffeur, who had driven the Daimler to his house. He was not wearing livery now, but a lounge suit. So was he simply a chauffeur, or an accomplice? And how could they both be here in Paris, just yards away from him? This could not conceivably be chance; they must have followed him here. But surely only the police knew he was coming here? He felt confused, trapped.

He must get out – fast. He would go to the bank, collect the money, take a taxi or hire a motor, anything, as long as he could escape. The hotel would not bother about him; he had already paid for his room. He would lose his clothes, agreed, but that was a small price compared with losing his freedom. He had money, much more than Harper was likely to command. He would use it all to purchase the fastest possible means of escape.

Charles hurried on, pretending he could not see Harper keeping pace with him on the opposite pavement. He reached the corner. Glancing out of the corner of his eye, he saw that Harper appeared to have fallen back a few feet. He was looking in a shop window. Of course, he could be watching Charles's reflection in the glass. Not that it mattered what he was doing. Charles knew he must now only be a few yards from the bank, and within minutes he would have five thousand pounds in his pocket.

Curiously enough, he thought, this was exactly the

same sum that Harper had demanded. No matter. He would leave the bank by a back entrance, if it had one, and be away to another city, maybe even to another country before these swine knew he had gone. But where the devil was this bank? It was not where the manager had said – or where he imagined it should be. Then he saw it was actually just across the road.

The traffic was heavier than he had anticipated. He glanced to the right. For a moment, the street was empty of motor cars and carts. He stepped out boldly across the street.

The Renault delivery van coming from the left hit him head on. The force of the blow carried him thirty yards up the road before the driver could stop. By then, Charles was dead. People started to scream. A woman fainted. The accident had been so unexpected, they could scarcely believe what they had seen. A gendarme came running, blowing his whistle. The van driver climbed out of his cab and stood staring down at the dead man in disbelief.

'He stepped right out in front of me,' he said hoarsely. 'Looked the other way. I can't understand it. He hadn't a chance.'

A crowd had gathered. A priest made the sign of the cross as the gendarme bent over the body. He felt for Charles's pulse; there was none.

'He is dead,' he pronounced solemnly.

'But why didn't he look?' asked the driver, staring at all the faces crowded round, trying to find anyone who could answer his question. The gendarme slipped a hand expertly into Charles's pocket, drew out his passport, his wallet.

'I will tell you why,' he replied, thumbing through the passport. 'He is English. They drive on the other side of the road in that country. An easy mistake for an English-man to make in France.'

'And one he will never make again, God rest his soul,' said Harper unctuously.

The gendarme looked up at him. 'You are English? You know this gentleman, then?'

'Yes. I had just seen him across the road. I was coming to meet him. A very tragic affair.'

Another gendarme appeared.

'A fatality,' said the first one. 'Please call an ambulance so we can get the traffic moving again.'

He turned to Harper.

'Now, monsieur. You saw the whole thing?'

'Everything.'

'And your name, monsieur?'

'Brown. Jack Brown. I was standing only feet away, and the driver was not to blame.'

'Perhaps you could accompany me to the station and sign a statement to that effect, Monsieur Brown.'

'Gladly. I will be pleased to be of any assistance.'

'Then, monsieur,' announced the gendarme, 'I think that should be the end of the matter.'

In fact, it was only the beginning.

Chapter Five

The maid came into Rose Rowlands' bedroom, crossed the white Aubusson carpet to the window, drew the wide brocaded curtains. It was a cold, wet morning. Rose, lying in bed, could see spears of rain being thrown against the panes by the force of the wind. They rattled in an irritating and somehow disconcerting way, like dice, she thought, or dead men's teeth in a skull.

'Will you have breakfast in bed, ma'am?' the maid asked her.

Rose nodded.

'Yes. Just toast and marmalade and black coffee. No butter.'

The girl hesitated for a moment. She was new, and awkward in the presence of her mistress.

'What's the matter?' Rose asked her sharply.

'There's a gentleman downstairs to see you, ma'am.'

'At this hour?'

Rose glanced at the ormolu clock by the side of her bed. It was half past nine, early for her. She was rarely up before ten. On most mornings, her day did not start much before eleven. This dislike of an early start she always blamed on her time in the theatre; actually, she had never been an early riser.

'Who is he?'

'Sir Bernard Warner.'

'The Chief Constable?'

'I saw him at the ball, ma'am.'

The girl had clearly no idea who he was. Rose frowned in annoyance, partly at the maid's ignorance, partly because she hated to receive unexpected visitors so early, and partly for another reason she could not quite understand. Somehow, this seemed more likely to be a professional call than a social one.

'Did he say what he wanted?'

'No, ma'am. Just to see you. But he did say it was an urgent matter.'

'Then I'll go down and see him right away.'

Rose waited until the girl had gone, then climbed out of bed, went into the bathroom, washed, brushed her hair quickly. She put on a silk dressing gown, walked downstairs. She had slept badly for the couple of nights her husband had been away. Not that they slept in the same bed; he had his own bedroom, his own dressing room. But the fact that he was at least near gave her a certain sense of security and solidity.

She did not like being in this big house on her own; she did not count as companions the huge staff living in attics, and her two sons and daughter in the nursery wing. The former were only paid help, the latter, children. She felt vulnerable, uneasy. What could Sir Bernard want to see her about now? Could it be something to do with Charles?

Grover had shown him into the morning room and brought him a glass of Madeira and some water biscuits on a tray. He was sipping the wine as Rose came into the room.

'I'm sorry to get you out of bed,' he said. 'But I felt I should come round right away.'

He paused.

'I've had some bad news.'

'About Charles?'

'How did you know?' he asked.

'I didn't,' she said. 'I guessed. I can't think of any other reason why the Chief Constable should call unannounced. Charles left in such a hurry that I sensed there must be an odd reason. He'd never done anything like that before. I couldn't understand it. I wondered if something was worrying him.'

'He was in Paris,' Sir Bernard said.

'Was?'

'I'm sorry to admit I have had the very gravest news, Rose. I hesitate to tell you, but I feel that at any moment of crisis, it is best to know the worst.'

'What is the worst?'

'I deeply regret to say that poor Charles has been killed by a motor van as he crossed the street in Paris.'

'Killed?' Rose gripped the back of a chair.

'Yes.'

'What was he doing in Paris?'

'I have no idea. Colleagues in the gendarmerie made enquiries and say he had been staying in a small hotel in the Place Saint Sulpice. In that area they are given over to making religious vestments, things of that order.'

'That would not influence him. Charles is – was – not a religious man.'

'Possibly not. But this was a quiet, discreet hotel.'

'Discreet? Why would he want to be discreet? He used to stay at the Crillon. We've been there often. Together.'

'I don't know why he chose this particular hotel. Perhaps he was involved in some business deal and did not wish this to be known publicly?'

'I find that difficult to believe. He liked to be thought of as a good businessman, but in fact I don't think he'd ever done a business deal in his life. He lived on the rents from his farms and other properties. On dividends. He came into a very large inheritance.'

She paused.

'Where is he – his body – now?'

'In a mortuary in Paris. I can make arrangements to bring it home, if that is your wish.'

'Yes. You are very kind. I would not want him to be buried in a foreign country. But tell me, Bernard, you were a friend of his, and I have always enjoyed the friendship of your wife. Why do you think Charles left so suddenly for Paris of all places?'

Sir Bernard shook his head.

'I've no idea,' he said. 'But one strange thing did happen there. According to the hotel manager, soon after Charles arrived he sent a telegram to his bank in London asking for five thousand pounds to be telegraphed to the local branch of the Credit Lyonnais. He was apparently actually walking to the bank to collect this money when he looked the wrong way through force of habit crossing the road, and was run over by a van.'

'What happened to the money? Is it still in the bank?'

'That is the odd thing, Rose. An Englishman, who gave his name as Brown, Jack Brown, came up just after the accident and told the gendarme he knew your husband. He said your husband had been crossing the road to meet him.'

'And?'

'The police believed this man's claim to close friendship with your husband. He told them he would bring back his passport and other papers to England. Instead of that, he went into the bank and cashed the draft. He signed your husband's name. Do you know anyone called Brown?'

'No one. This man Brown, whoever he is, forged Charles's name and withdrew the money on Charles's passport?'

'Apparently, yes.'

'Does anyone have an address for him?'

'No. He was seen walking with another man out of the bank. Then he disappeared.'

'None of this makes any sense. What on earth could Charles have wanted five thousand pounds for? It's a fortune.'

'For some business transaction, no doubt.'

She gave a sigh. 'I'd better tell the children.'

'They were close to their father, were they?'

'Our eldest son, Tobin, was. But Richard and Cecily, no, I wouldn't say very close. But of course they'll miss him dreadfully. They'll be terribly shocked.'

'I have told no one else about that money transaction involving this man Brown, Rose. I would suggest that nothing could be gained by you mentioning it to anyone. If you do, it might get to the ears of the gutter press, and all kinds of fanciful explanations could be aired. I suggest that it is sufficient to say that your husband had to leave for France on a business trip quite unexpectedly, and met with a most unfortunate accident.'

Rose nodded. She rang the bell for Grover to show Sir Bernard to the door. Then she went up to her bedroom.

Five thousand pounds. A large amount of money, but an odd sum. Not enough for a big business deal, but too much for a few weeks on the Riviera, even with a pretty woman. And she did not think her husband had been particularly interested in women, pretty or not. She was not a sensual person herself and she had imagined that her husband was also not greatly interested in sex. They had both wanted children, but that was about as far as interest in each others' bodies went.

And then, a few days before the ball, Rose had made the most disturbing discovery which quite caused her to change her mind about her husband, and, indeed, to regard him in a totally different and unexpected light.

She had run out of writing paper and, wishing to write a letter to a friend, rather than call a footman to bring her some paper from her husband's study, she had gone into the study herself. His desk had an opening lid on which

85

stood a wooden case that held envelopes and sheets of writing paper of different sizes. But on this occasion the case was empty.

She lifted the lid of the desk, hoping to find some notepaper inside, and instead found a large brown envelope. On the back was written in crude handwriting, not her husband's, the words 'Twenty prints'. For no reason she could give herself except basic feminine curiosity, she put her hand inside the envelope to pull out whatever it contained. She thought it might be a magazine – Charles subscribed to several hunting and fishing magazines. Instead, she found a wad of photographs.

She had never seen photographs like these. They were all of young boys, much the same age as her own sons, all naked, all with erect penises. She looked at them with fascination and horror – and bewilderment. Why were they in her husband's desk? She sifted through them. Some were worse than others; several of the boys had pinched, hungry faces, old before their time. They must be male prostitutes. There was no letter inside the envelope and no indication who had sent the photographs. Then she counted them. Nineteen. So one was missing.

She experienced a sense of dismay, almost of panic; not so much about the nineteen photographs, but about the twentieth. Oh, please God, she prayed, don't let it be what I fear it may be. Please not.

Rose replaced the photographs in their envelope, shut the desk and tiptoed out of the room, her original intention to find some writing paper quite forgotten. It was absurd to tiptoe, of course. But she felt somehow unclean, ashamed of what she had seen – and very worried about the photo she had not seen.

Now, walking up the stairs, she remembered this; indeed, it had never been far from her thoughts since that day. She had not mentioned it to Charles. There were many matters they did not discuss, and this must be the most delicate. To admit what she had seen would be to reveal she had been looking through his correspondence, and this could bring all manner of accusations and recriminations. This was a secret she must keep to herself. But could these photographs possibly have any bearing on her husband's disappearance? And what about the missing picture?

Curiously, she felt little grief for the loss of her husband. She would miss him, of course, but almost in an impersonal way. Perhaps grief would come later, but somehow she did not really think it would.

The most important thing now was to tell her children of their father's death. Then she must contact the family solicitor, see the terms of Charles's will and seek the lawyer's help in arranging a funeral and possibly a memorial service.

It was fashionable to hold services of thanksgiving for the life of someone who had died. But somehow the idea seemed distasteful to her. She thought again of those photographs in the drawer, went into the study to take them away and destroy them. It would never do for them to fall into anyone else's possession.

She opened the desk. The photographs were no longer there.

Richard and Tobin and Cecily were in the nursery. They had no idea why their mother had asked them to come here, but sensed it must be something important.

The chairs were part of a half-size suite, really almost toy chairs, and they sat uneasily in them. Rose checked that the door was shut so that no servant outside could hear what she had to say.

'I've called you here,' she began nervously, not quite sure of herself, 'because I have some very bad news to tell you. You are all growing up, and are old enough to understand that in life sad and unpleasant experiences happen to all of us. We have to bear them, overcome them. It's no good pretending everything's always going to be pleasant all the time. It isn't.'

She paused. She felt she was in danger of losing herself in a labyrinth of words, and yet how could she break the news without causing terrible hurt, perhaps irreparable shock? She cleared her throat and decided to be blunt with the truth, to get it over quickly.

'As you know, on the night of the ball your father was suddenly called away on important business. He had to go to France, to Paris. He promised he would be back very shortly. But I have to tell you, he is not coming back.'

'Not ever?' asked Cecily sharply.

Her mother shook her head.

'I'm sorry, not ever.'

'Why not? Where's he gone?'

'He has met with an accident. You may know that in France, traffic runs on the right of the road and not the left as here. Apparently he had momentarily forgotten this and was crossing the road, and through force of habit he looked to the right and was hit by a van. He is dead.'

'Was he killed instantly?' asked Tobin.

'Fortunately, he endured no pain. But we who are left suffer pain because he has gone. We are like a team that has lost its leader. We'll have to go on as best we can, as we imagine your father would have liked us to go on, if he were still here. Following his lead.' She paused, and again suddenly thought of those terrible photographs and felt almost physically sick. She swallowed.

'Don't cry,' said Richard, mistaking her emotion. She shook her head.

'No, I won't cry. There are some things in life that are too painful for tears, and this is one of them. But we must all look forward, not back. That's what he would have liked us to do.'

'What sort of business was it that Father was called away on?' asked Tobin.

'I really don't know. But it was terribly important. He told me so. He said it was something that affected all of us. All our futures.'

'So in a sense he was trying to help us when he was killed?'

'Yes. That's a very good way of looking at it, Richard. He was trying to help us.'

'And did he help us?' asked Tobin.

'I'm sure he did. I'm very sure he did,' Rose replied, with a confidence she did not feel.

'I think there was another reason for him going away,' said Tobin slowly.

'Really? What could that be?'

'I think Richard altering the safety valve on that engine, which caused me all these burns, affected him. I'm the eldest son. I was closest to him.'

'You were all very close to him.'

'But he's often told me the eldest son is special. He inherits everything.'

'Let's not talk about inheriting anything yet,' said his mother sharply.

As she spoke she remembered Charles admitting to her that he was worried about Tobin's face. Perhaps this story of business was a myth to cover up his own feelings about one son's scarred face, his other son's denial of what he had obviously done? She looked at Richard with a new distaste. He was a strange boy. She could not understand him at all, whereas she felt she always understood Tobin.

Richard recognised the brass-edged black smokestack of the traction engine towering above the hedgerow when he was still half a mile away. As he approached, he saw canvas roofs of tents and the varnished caravans of fairground workers and stallholders. As he came nearer, a gout of black smoke suddenly blew up out of the funnel. Birds fluttered away nervously from the lower branches of the nearest trees.

Richard paused for a moment. He wanted to see Carola. But what if she wasn't there? Then he would have to ask her father whether he had mended his toy engine, and although this was important to him, it wasn't as important as seeing Carola again. This was quite absurd, of course. He had never been drawn to anyone like this. He paused, irresolute. Should he go on or should he turn back? He wanted to tell her that his father had died. But why should she be interested? He did not even know her. After all, they had only met once. He'd look a fool; worse, he'd be a fool. He decided he'd go home. That was the best thing to do, the wisest, most adult course to take.

As he turned, he saw Carola coming towards him.

'I was following you,' she said. 'But you didn't look back.'

'I'm going home,' he explained.

'Didn't you ask where I was?'

'No.'

'But why ever not?'

'I don't know, really. I thought you might be busy. I see the traction engine's running.'

'Oh, that's my father. He always checks it's working at least an hour before he needs to connect the dynamo. Better be safe than sorry, he says. I suppose you were coming to ask about your engine.'

'Yes,' he said. 'Then I thought you mightn't be there.'

'I'm glad you've come. I wanted to tell you something. You know that mark on the back of your hand you say looks like Marco Polo's initials?'

'What about it?'

'Well, I saw you hadn't got your name, or even your initials, on the steam engine. Only the maker's inscription "The Spirit and the Speed". So I heated up a bit of solder and put the initials M.P. on the base plate. That's as good as having your own name, I thought.'

'Better,' said Richard enthusiastically. 'Thank you very much.'

'As soon as my father mends it, I'll bring it back to you.'

'I don't know if that's altogether a good idea,' he said.

'Why not? I won't come up to your room again, if that's what worries you. I'll simply ring the back doorbell, and you can come down.'

'No.' He shook his head. 'Since I saw you last something terrible has happened.'

'What's that?'

She was close to him now. He could see concern on his face, and how blue her eyes were, how she genuinely appeared interested in what he had to say.

'It's my father,' he explained haltingly. 'He's been killed in an accident in France.'

'In France? What was he doing there?'

'I don't know. Business of some sort.'

'Do you feel very sad he's dead?' she asked him.

'Yes and no,' he replied, surprised at the question – and at his answer.

It was odd, but no one else had specifically asked him whether he felt sad or sorry; not his mother, Aunt Hannah or his brother and sister. So why should this girl he barely knew care how he felt? He warmed to her for her query. Deep down he did feel a sense of loss, of course, and also uncertainty.

'I was never very close to him,' he admitted. 'My brother was.'

'The one whose face got burned?'

'Yes. He'll be rich now. Everything's left to my mother on trust, and then to him.'

'How do you mean, on trust?'

'Oh, a legal thing. So that my mother can't spend it. Say she met some adventurer who persuaded her he loved her and they got married, she wouldn't be able to leave everything to him so that none of us got anything. Nearly everything always goes to the eldest son.'

'Why?'

'Well, so it's not all split up and gradually diminished. The estate, farms, properties.'

'But what has your father's death got to do with me bringing back your toy?'

'I may not be there.'

'Why? Are you selling the house?'

'No, not that. But my mother has a sister, my Aunt Hannah. And she's suggested I go and live with her.'

'But why? There must be lots of rooms in your own house. Why have you got to move?'

'It's not a question of rooms exactly,' he said slowly.

How could he explain the situation to her? He felt he was speaking a different language, talking to someone who needed reasons for decisions which he simply accepted. But then he wasn't telling her all the truth; no one bares their heart to a stranger. For after the meeting with his mother in the nursery, there had been another meeting which cast its shadow over them all.

A middle-aged man wearing a grey suit, with a grey face and grey hair and a high starched collar had arrived to see them. He carried a black bag which he opened on the desk in his mother's writing room, while Richard, Tobin and Cecily and their mother sat watching him. He might be a conjuror about to perform a trick at a children's party, thought Richard inconsequentially. He opens his bag and a rabbit jumps out, or a white dove or the flags of the Empire. But not on this occasion; this was altogether more serious.

The man produced a number of files containing papers, some in neat copperplate, some typewritten, all tied together with red tape.

'This is Peter Once-Hogg, our solicitor,' his mother explained.

Mr Once-Hogg bowed as though she had paid him a compliment.

'If you would all be seated, please,' he said, 'I will read you the terms of the will of your late husband and father.'

This had little interest for Richard. His mind drifted, speculating what his father had been doing in Paris? Why had he suddenly left at the height of the party and then come to say goodbye to him without waking him up? Had he known then, or suspected, he was not coming back? The thought haunted him and disturbed him. The lawyer's voice droned on.

' ". . . Being of sound mind, I leave and bequeath all my worldly possessions to be held in trust for the benefit of my wife Mrs Rose Mary Rowlands and then, on the occasion of her death or, should she and the trustees so decide, to my eldest son Tobin Thomas Rowlands.

' "At the same time I leave and bequeath to my younger son Richard Peter and my daughter Cecily Anne such sums that the trustees shall decide are necessary to procure their education, to pay for my son Richard's university training should he wish to follow a profession, and to provide a dowry for my daughter should she wish to marry . . ." '

There was more about legacies and gifts of money or cottages to servants and retired retainers, a sum to the local church for a stained-glass window in his memory. And then Mr Once-Hogg paused and set down the papers, and looked at each of them in turn.

'Have you any questions, Mrs Rowlands?' he asked.

Rose shook her head.

'No. I haven't. I had no idea what my husband was leaving, or how he would dispose of his possessions. I feel rather sorry, I must say, for my two youngest children, who it would appear have been given much less than has come to me or my eldest son.'

'That was your husband's wish. It is customary in the case of handing on important estates.'

'I suppose there should be enough money in the trusts to help both my sons if they fell into difficulties, or if Richard did not wish to take a degree and decided to emigrate or join the army. A little capital then would be useful.'

'I quite agree, Mrs Rowlands. But now I have to tell you something else, which I regret is not all that pleasant.'

'What is that?'

The lawyer opened another file of papers, began to riffle through them.

'Your husband was known as a most generous host,' he began tentatively. 'His annual ball was looked forward to by hundreds of people in the county as a highlight of the social year. But this cost him a great deal of money.'

'I know that. But then he had a great deal of money.'

'He *had*, Mrs Rowlands. I fear that the past tense applies here. He did not die a rich man. Quite the reverse, in fact.'

'What on earth do you mean? We've thirty thousand acres of land here. Rows of houses, a factory in Lancashire, all kinds of securities. How can you say he wasn't wealthy?'

'I say so with the deepest regret, madam, because over several years before his most untimely demise, I find he entered into various commitments with other people without seeking my advice.'

94

'Commitments? What sort of commitments?'

'In brief, and to be blunt, for I am sure you agree that this is not the time for obfuscation, he borrowed money. A lot of money, madam. The estate, while large, as you say, does not produce an adequate return for someone of expensive and extravagant habits. On the other hand, it can provide magnificent and prestigious collateral on which the owner can borrow impressively large sums without any let or hindrance on the part of the lender. He knows that his money is well secured. In fact, he may even increase the loan. Against further security, naturally.'

'Naturally,' replied Rose drily. 'So what is the worst you have to tell me, Mr Once-Hogg?'

'The worst, Mrs Rowlands, is that, apart from this house and a hundred acres, which are, as we lawyers say, unencumbered, mortgages and other liens are held on the rest of the estate and on all the other properties you mentioned.'

'But this is incredible!'

'I fully realise the shock this must be to you, but, with the deepest respect, the rate at which Mr Rowlands lived was also incredible. In my understanding, there are roughly thirty servants inside this house alone, and perhaps as many outside. They all have to be paid each week. They are all provided with houses which could otherwise be sold, or which might, if let, bring in at least a modest rental. I am sorry to be the bearer of such grievous news, but you will, I am sure, admit that your husband lived on the scale of a millionaire. Unfortunately, he did not have the money to underpin this style of life.'

Rose looked at him, and saw in his mean eyes a glint of satisfaction. He resented them. He might work for them, but he did not work in their interests.

'So what do you advise, Mr Once-Hogg?' she asked

him, trying to keep her feelings out of her voice.

'I would advise, Mrs Rowlands, that an immediate reduction is made in the overheads of running this house.'

'I will do my best. But most of our staff have been here for many years. We cannot just be rid of them overnight. They have given us good service and total loyalty. We owe them something in return.'

'I appreciate what you say, but I have to speak as I find. These borrowings will have to be serviced or, better still, repaid.'

'Was it because of his financial situation that my husband went to Paris?' Rose asked him.

'I have no idea why he went to Paris. All I know is that he withdrew five thousand pounds when he was there, and that money disappeared from the bank, collected by someone who produced his passport, apparently, and signed his name.'

'Tobin is at boarding school. Richard is due to go next term. Will there be money to pay the fees?'

'There should be enough for the fees, yes, even if . . .' He paused.

'Even if what?'

'Even if we have to come to some accommodation with the moneylenders.'

'Who are they?'

'The North London Loan and Mortgage Company. They are known as hard bargainers. They may decline to advance any more money without additional security. And that is a move I cannot advise you to make.'

'How did my husband get into this state? Couldn't you have advised him it was folly to put himself in the hands of these people?'

'As I say, he did not seek my advice, Mrs Rowlands.'

'What interest are they charging?'

'Twenty-five per cent.'

'That is madness. Surely he could have borrowed at a few per cent from the banks?'

'He had already borrowed from the banks, Mrs Rowlands. To pay off their debt he took out other loans. Interest is very high on such transactions.'

'He never told me. I had no idea.'

'Unfortunately many wives have little or no idea of the financial circumstances of their husbands, although they depend on them. That is a tragedy of life. But there are a few stocks and shares that the lenders have not discovered. There should be enough to pay all the fees for at least one of your sons. Your daughter, what about her?'

'She is going to a day school. We would not send her to a boarding school. But if my husband hadn't been killed, what would have happened? Would he have just gone on?'

'Yes, I think that is possible. The usurers drew their interest. There was no need to foreclose – for the time being. The interest paid and owing has already overtaken the capital sum borrowed.'

'And you had no idea of this either?'

'Not when he entered into these agreements. As I say, your husband did not confide in me.'

He paused for a moment, remembering Rowlands' last visit to his office. He had come to tell him he was being blackmailed. Clearly, his widow knew nothing of this, and there was no point in telling her. It would only cause further distress. He had never liked Rowlands, but now he was dead, and as he looked at the faces of his family staring at him in disbelief, he felt a twinge of sorrow for them.

He had advised Rowlands not to pay Harper, to bluff out the threat. But although Rowlands insisted he was innocent of the charges, Once-Hogg sensed he was not telling him everything about the incident. Once-Hogg had no idea who had been blackmailing him, whether this was an isolated incident or whether the moneylenders could be behind it, turning the screw, frightening Rowlands, eager to bend or break him and then seize the estate. So now he said nothing, but busied himself with his papers, thankful for the opportunity to avoid looking into the eyes of a family facing ruin.

Standing talking to Carola now, Richard remembered that terrible scene. He disliked the lawyer. In his opinion, Mr Once-Hogg was simply another predator who had to be paid. A whole secure world had fallen in as they sat in the elegant room.

Richard could not tell Carola any of this. It was far too private, too hurtful to mention to any third party. It must remain a family secret that they were so desperately in debt. He knew now there was not enough money, even from the sale of all the shares and debentures – which were actually very few and yielded poor dividends – to pay his fees and Tobin's. Tobin would stay on at the public school, of course. He was the eldest son and that was his due, his right.

Richard felt he could not have explained this to the girl, even if he wanted to. How could he expect her to understand? Nor could he expect her to appreciate what Aunt Hannah was going to do for him.

When she had heard of her brother-in-law's death she immediately came over to see her sister Rose.

'I don't know how you're going to be left for money, Rose,' she said, broaching the subject with north country bluntness. 'I just have a feeling that, maybe, you might not be as well off as you think. I hope I am wrong. If I am, please tell me.'

'You are right,' Rose admitted. 'But what gave you that idea? I had no knowledge of it myself until the solicitor told me.'

'I don't really know,' Hannah admitted. 'Perhaps what our father taught us. Mr Micawber's theory.

Annual income twenty pounds, annual expenditure nineteen, nineteen and sixpence – result, happiness. Annual income twenty pounds, expenditure twenty pounds and sixpence – result, misery. Charles seemed to spend huge sums of money without a second thought, and I did sometimes wonder whether he wasn't living beyond his means, considerable though these were – or, at least, seemed to be. I'll give you advice you won't take, Rose. Sell up all this and pay off your debts. Then you'll be free, totally free. But as you'll obviously delay doing that for as long as possible, I'll make a practical contribution. I'd like to take over the education of young Richard.'

'Why?'

'Because I think he's got unusual abilities. And I like him. I admire him. He's a sort of one-off, you might say, not just interested in things you might expect him to be interested in with his background – fishing, shooting, hunting. He has a real flair for mechanical things.'

'Where would you educate him? If you were paying the fees, you must have some idea?'

'I'd send him to a day school.'

'As opposed to a boarding school? All his contemporaries will be there.'

'All Tobin's contemporaries, possibly. But I'd send Richard to the best school I can afford. And then in the evenings and at weekends, when he's done his homework, he can do what he really wants to do, experiment with engines. How's that steam engine I gave him, by the way?'

Rose explained what had happened to Tobin.

'I'm terribly sorry,' said Hannah. 'Was that Richard's fault?'

'He says not.'

'And you believe him?'

'Well, no one else was playing with the engine. No one

else had the chance to alter the safety valve.'

'Tobin did, from what you say.'

'Is it likely he would?'

'It's possible. Just to spite his younger brother.'

'That's ridiculous.'

'I don't think so at all. I think it's totally in line with human nature. Especially with jealous male adolescents. The elder brother resenting the younger.'

'Well, you're entitled to your opinion, Hannah. But please say no more on the subject. It's painful enough as it is. Charles told Richard he was to get rid of the engine, throw it out.'

'And did he?'

'I suppose so. But you'd better ask him.'

And Aunt Hannah did ask him. Richard looked her in the eye. 'It was given to the boot boy to throw away, but he kept it. I took it back from him.'

'So you went directly against your father's orders. Why?'

'If he'd believed I'd had nothing to do with Tobin's accident, he would never have given that order.'

'That doesn't really alter the fact that you disobeyed him.'

'I know. I'm sorry about that. But, well, that's why I did it.'

'Where is the engine now?'

'The man who worked the traction engine at the ball, he's brazing the boiler which exploded. I'm going over to get it from him.'

'Then you'd better keep it out of your mother's sight. She has enough on her mind as it is.'

She told Richard about her plans for his schooling.

'You'll have to live with me,' she said. 'It won't be like living here in the big house. But we shall survive.'

'We'll do more than that, Aunt Hannah,' Richard assured her warmly.

For the first time since Tobin's accident he felt his spirits lift. With Aunt Hannah he would feel free, really free. They understood each other. He had no need to explain to her, no need to hide anything, no need ever to lie. With her, he could be himself – and he might even find out who he really was, and who and what he wanted to be . . .

Carola's voice brought him back to the present.

'You're very quiet,' she said. 'Something else on your mind?'

'A lot,' he admitted. 'Anyhow, as I said, I'll be going away from home to live with my aunt.'

'So I may not see you again? How can I get the engine back to you?'

'You keep it,' he told Carola. 'I'm not supposed to have it anyhow.'

'I'll only keep it until we meet again,' she promised him. 'It wouldn't be right, wouldn't be fair to have it for keeps.'

'All right,' he said.

Almost without realising it, they had been walking more and more slowly, and now they stood in the lane. From over the hedge came the shouts of hustlers crying their wares. A steam organ began to play and the speed of the traction engine increased. Strings of lights hanging from stall to stall glowed more brightly.

'How can I get in touch with you?' Richard asked.

'You can't, unfortunately, for I don't know where I'll be after this. I know we have some engagements on the south coast, but we're only in each pitch for a day or two.'

'And in the winter?'

'We usually spend that with other fairground people in the yard of a public house in east London.'

'What do you do then?'

'I go round selling sprigs of lavender in the street, and

101

knocking on doors, telling people it will bring good luck if they buy one.'

'And does it?'

'To us, yes. For that's our living. We bleach it, you know, so it's like white heather. Then my father and I have to overhaul the engine and the dynamo. The brushes keep getting clogged with oil from the bearings so they won't pick up the current. We have to keep stopping it to clean them. I want to modify the design.'

'You're very clever.'

'No,' she said. 'Just doing what I like doing. When other girls played with dolls, I used to stand watching motor cars go by, wishing I could play with those. My father is good with his hands, too. He made a toy car for me, something I could push along. There are lots in the shops now, but mine was one of the first.'

'So I can't get in touch with you anywhere?'

'Not really. But I'll be in touch with you,' she promised. 'I'll write and say where I'm going.'

'You will?'

'I said so. I never go back on my word.'

Richard gave her Aunt Hannah's address, then held out his hand. They shook hands awkwardly, not quite knowing how to say goodbye, not wanting to say goodbye.

'I've never met anyone like you,' Richard said suddenly, and his voice was hoarse and husky as though he was going to cry, which was ridiculous. He didn't even know the girl. Not well, that is. The way he spoke sounded as though he knew lots of girls of Carola's age. But this wasn't true. She was the only one.

'Good luck,' Carola said very softly. 'I will think about you.'

'Me, too,' said Richard.

He watched her walk away. His eyes suddenly felt sharp and prickly. He wiped them carefully, hoping no one could see him. It was not fitting that someone of his age should be seen to cry. Then he hurried back along the lane, leaving his thoughts behind him.

Carola's father was standing, arms folded, his back against the warm boiler of the traction engine, as she came though the gateway into the field.

'Where've you been?' he asked her angrily. 'I've been looking for you everywhere.'

'You couldn't have looked far. I was just down the road,' she told him. 'Took a stroll. I wanted to get away from the continual smell of smoke and soot.'

'Lucky for some, then, isn't it?' he retorted. 'The rest of us have to work. I've mended that toy engine. At least, I got someone else to do it for me. I hadn't the time. The dynamo here's bitching herself again. Dirty contacts. Something you could well have seen to if you'd been here instead of gallivanting off. Now you are here, make yourself useful and take that toy back to the big house to the kid who owns it. And this time, don't you come back here empty-handed with some smarmy excuse.'

'Where is it?' she asked him.

He nodded towards the caravan. She climbed up the steps and went inside. The engine stood on a sheet of newspaper spread out on a small table, under the leaded lights of the window. Carola picked it up, examined the boiler critically. Whoever had brazed it had done a good job.

Her father came up the steps and stood, blocking the doorway.

'Satisfied? Good enough for you?' he asked mockingly.

'Yes.'

'Then you'd better get off with it,' he told her. 'And be sure you're back here before the fair starts.'

She put the engine back on the table. 'There's no point in going,' she said flatly.

'What the hell do you mean, no point?'

'The boy's gone away. Rather, he's going.'

'How d'you know?'

'I've just seen him. He told me.'

'So that's why you were running off down the road, eh? To meet that kid?'

'It was pure chance, Father.'

'Nothing's pure chance,' he replied, mimicking her accent. 'If you've just seen him, he'll still be at home. That's your excuse. You've brought him back his engine.'

'I can't do it,' she said. 'He'll be suspicious.'

'Why the hell should he be? He wants the bloody toy, doesn't he? And you've got it. So be off, or I'll set about you.'

His hand went down to the brass buckle on his leather belt. Carola saw the movement, and recognised it.

'All right,' she said resignedly. 'I'll go.'

'*Now*,' he told her. 'And no more fooling about.'

Carola looked around the caravan, picked up an old shirt, wrapped it round the bright metal. Then she went down the steps, out into the lane. It was empty. A few butterflies hovered over wild flowers in the banks on either side. She set off steadfastly, guessing her father would be watching her. As soon as she was out of sight of the field, her pace slowed. She looked back, saw that no one was following her, then sat down to consider what she should do.

It was really immaterial whether Richard was there or not, as far as her father was concerned. He simply wanted an excuse, any excuse, for her to get into the house and steal as much as she could carry away. But she had no intention of stealing anything, any more than she had on the night of the ball. She had run her father's errands too often, and each time they became more distasteful to her. She simply could not go on like this. And there was a further reason for disobeying her father – Richard.

She had never met a boy quite like him; he was different from others of his age, the sons of stallholders or sideshow owners, brash, rough, too ready with their hands. And he was genuinely interested in engines, not simply because he needed to know which axles to grease, which gears to oil in a roundabout or helter-skelter car, but because he genuinely liked mechanical things, as others might like dogs or cats. She felt exactly the same way, but until they met she had vaguely assumed that no one else did.

Sitting on the bank, feeling the sun warm on her face, with the steam engine by her side, Carola made up her mind: she would run away. She really had no other choice, she told herself. If she did not bring back some items of value for her father to sell, he would beat her, as he had done in the past, and each beating became harder to endure. She could see no future in a life like this. But first she would wait until she knew her father was busy with the traction engine and could not pursue her.

She climbed through a hole in the hedge, and sat on the other side of the bank. She did not wish to risk being seen by people coming along the lane to the fair. Someone might recognise her and tell her father. She heard various pony carts rattle past, with bells tinkling on the pony's harness, a few farm carts, and then people talking excitedly as they walked. In the distance she could hear the boom of the steam organ, the clang of the mechanical cymbals, and the cries of stallholders.

Now and then, she looked at her watch. It had been her mother's; she had left it behind, presumably inadvertently, when she had gone away. This was the only thing she had left, and Carola valued it. From time to time, she held the watch up to her right ear to hear the mechanism tick. This was to her an almost physical link with the mother she had lost so often, and whom she might not see again.

At half past five, she covered the toy engine with grass and flowers, came through the hedge and walked back to the fair. The traction engine was running unattended, the long belt to the dynamo slapping loosely against the boiler. Her father was obviously away drinking, or he would have seen that this urgently needed adjustment. It could easily break. For a moment, Carola thought of tightening the belt herself, for she could not bear to see anything mechanical not working at its full potential. Then she realised she had not the time to do this; she must be on her way. At any moment, her father could return.

She walked up the steps of the caravan. Inside, the air felt heavy with stale tobacco smoke from her father's clay pipe. She gathered together a few belongings, put them in a carpet bag, then sat down at the table to write a note to her father.

'I am leaving,' she wrote. 'I cannot do what you asked me to do, and I cannot stay with you if you know this. Perhaps we will meet again one day. I wish you well. Carola.' She thought of adding her love, but she did not really feel any affection for this coarse, brutish man who to strangers could seem charming and friendly, and she did not wish to write a lie.

She picked up the bag, took one last glance around the familiar caravan, with its varnished ribs on the roof and walls, the rugs on the two bunks. This had been her home for a long time. She had no idea where or how she would live now, but these were questions that time must answer. The only question to which she could give an answer now was why she was leaving. It might be a difficult decision to make, but she knew it was the right one; indeed, it seemed the only one.

She closed the door carefully behind her, went down the steps, and walked back along the lane to collect the steam engine.

Chapter Six

The first night after Carola left her father she slept rough under a hedge. She had never slept out before and had no idea that the night could be so cold in summer. A faint rustling of leaves and the crack of twigs as poachers moved through the woods woke her up at one o'clock by her mother's watch.

She sat up carefully, not wishing to be discovered. She could see three men, with lurcher dogs on long leads, walking in extended order out of a wood across the nearest field to the next thicket. Two of them carried empty sacks; the third, a metal bucket.

As they passed, the wind changed and she smelled aniseed on the breeze. She guessed they were after pheasant; not one or two for the pot, but dozens, perhaps hundreds, to sell at the back doors of hotels and public houses. The means they chose to snare the birds was to throw out from the bucket balls of flour and water paste laced with aniseed and packed with fish hooks or jagged glass splinters. Pheasants were unable to resist the allure of the aniseed; they would greedily gulp down the pellets, and then die slowly and in agony.

This cruel method had three virtues from the point of view of the poachers. First, it was completely silent, which meant far less risk of discovery than if they used a gun. No poacher found after dark in possession of a gun could expect leniency from country magistrates. Next, the bird could easily be caught and have its neck wrung. Lastly, its flesh would be completely unbruised, which would not be the case if they fired shotgun cartridges full of pellets.

Carola lay down again, thankful they had not seen her. Poachers had a rough way with witnesses, and as a girl they might easily take their pleasure with her. When she had been with her father in their caravan, such dangers seemed far away. Now, she would have to accept them.

The sun shining on her face woke her up at seven o'clock. She felt stiff in all her joints, and had a slightly sore throat. She decided she would never sleep like that again, not when there were great houses where surely she must find some kind of indoor employment and a warm bed. Then she could decide on her next step. She washed in a stream, combed her hair as best she could, trying to see her reflection in a rock pool, and then set out along the road.

A few carts passed her. Labourers walking to work nodded an early morning greeting. By nine o'clock she had reached the outskirts of a town. A news boy was running through the streets, holding a contents bill for the *Enquirer* newspaper in one hand and a sheaf of newspapers under his other arm, calling out hoarsely: 'War declared! Read all about it!'

Carola had no money, and even if she had a penny, she would have bought a bun at the baker's shop rather than a newspaper. As she reached the centre of the town, the streets were full of people, surprising at that hour of morning. Groups of women stood talking to each other outside front doors. The driver of a milk cart waved cheerily at her. Then he jumped down and went through the motions of shouldering arms with his whip.

'What's happening?' she asked him.

'Don't you know? Kaiser Bill and King George are at war. I'm taking this old cart back to the farm and I'm

110

joining up today. Can't wait to get into khaki.'

'Will there be jobs for women and girls if there's a war?' she asked him.

'Must be,' he replied confidently. 'They've been building a factory up the road for the last six weeks. I'm told they're going to use it to fill shells. My old woman says they'll be taking on people any day.'

He went off, whistling.

The prospect of such employment in the future interested Carola, but how could she survive while she waited? She needed food now, and a place to live.

She trudged on through the town. On its outskirts, half a mile up the road, she passed a set of iron gates. Stone heraldic beasts, a lion with wings and an eagle with a dragon's head, held up stone crests for the inspection of passers-by. She paused. There might be work here. She turned into the drive, went round to the back door of the house, following the sign 'Tradesmen and Servants' Entrance'.

The gravel path was well raked, the brass bell handle by the side of the back door highly polished, the step newly whitened. This was clearly an establishment where high standards prevailed. Carola knew nothing about being a servant, but then until last night she had known nothing about sleeping rough. She decided she would rather learn how to be a servant than how to survive on the road.

She pulled the brass handle. A bell pealed faintly in the dim recesses of the building. She heard footsteps on flagstones. The door opened. A woman, aged about fifty, wearing a dark grey dress with a skirt that brushed the ground, a bunch of keys hanging from her belt, stood looking at her.

'I don't buy at the door,' she announced coldly. 'No gypsies here.'

'I am not a gypsy, ma'am. I want work.'

111

'What sort of work?'

'I hear there's a factory being built in the town. They are recruiting women. I thought perhaps you might have a vacancy for a maid if any of your staff thought of going there.'

'References?' asked the woman brusquely.

'I have none.'

'Been in service before?'

'No, ma'am.'

'Where are you from?'

'I live with my father. We're travelling people.'

'You mean gypsies. As I thought.'

'No. He owns a steam traction engine. It has a big dynamo. He hires it out to light fairs, outdoor parties for the quality, and to power threshing machines. I helped him.'

'Helped? You've left him, then?'

'Yes, ma'am.'

'Odd job for a girl.'

Carola shrugged.

'You look clean enough,' the woman went on. 'But a bit untidy. Slept rough last night, did you? You have grass in your hair.'

'Yes, I slept rough.'

'Had a row with your father?'

'No. I just decided I wanted to be on my own. Making my own way.'

The woman nodded as though, despite her stern appearance, she could understand that wish. She looked more closely at Carola's neat dress and her shoes. Although her shoes were dusty, they could have been cleaned the previous day. And the girl seemed respectful – better than some of the cheeky sluts they had to employ these days.

'Come in,' she said, more kindly. 'Have a cup of tea.'

She led the way into the kitchen. Along one wall of

the huge room were two porcelain sinks with brightly polished brass taps, and a draining board of scoured wood. A coke cooking stove took up another wall. The room felt warm, homely. The woman introduced herself.

'I'm the housekeeper, Mrs Square,' she said.

'My name's Carola Marsh.'

'Sit down, Carola.'

Mrs Square crossed the room, opened a cupboard, from a high shelf took down a cup and saucer of thick white china. A kettle simmered on the hob. She made a pot of tea, put a bowl of sugar on the table with a jug of milk.

'If you've never been in service, you know nothing about it,' she said.

'I could learn,' Carola told her quickly, sipping the hot sweet tea gratefully.

'Perhaps. The mistress, Mrs Campion, is away in France with her husband. She doesn't know we've already lost two maids. One has gone this morning to marry a young fellow who is off as a soldier. The other's got above herself and is going to work in the munitions factory, whenever that opens. Couldn't wait, had to go at once. No notice, not even a day. So we are short. But references are important. The mistress always insists on them. However . . .'

She paused.

'If you've got none, Carola, I'll have to take you on trust. I've never done that before with any maid, the mistress wouldn't allow it, but times change and there's always a first time for everything.

'I'll give you a chance. One month. Ten shillings a week. We supply your outer clothes, and breakfast, dinner and tea. Hours are from seven in the morning to six o'clock at night – more if they have company. Sunday afternoons are free from when you've finished your

113

work, usually about three o'clock. What do you say to that?'

'I say I am very thankful, Mrs Square. Very thankful indeed.'

Carola was to share a room in the top of the building with another maid, Isobel. The ceiling sloped so that with one bed under each angle they could only stand upright in the centre of the room. Isobel was a short, squat girl with a bad complexion and even worse breath. She had pale blonde hair that never looked clean. She stared at Carola, appraising her.

'Not been in service before, then, have you?'

'No. This is the first time.'

'Well, there are all sorts of pickings. If you keep your eyes open.'

'Such as what?'

'When they have guests, you might get half a quid tip, but you don't know that until the visitors have gone, and then you can find they've left you nothing. So you've got to look after yourself while you can, when they're still here.

'The wife will leave a handbag open as like as not, purse inside. And even if it's closed, you can open it. It'll be packed with ten shilling notes, pounds, fivers, the lot. Take one. But not more than one. And then fold the note next to it so if she looks quickly, she'll think she's still got the same amount. It's only when they get home she'll find there's one missing. And then it's too late to complain.'

'But that's stealing.'

'So? Everyone does it. The butler's got his own bottles down there in the pantry. He pours himself port, brandy, whisky, gin, whatever he fancies. Gives us a nip now and then, just to keep us happy. They've so much money and everything, they never miss a little. Got to look after yourself in this world. No one else will.'

'But if everyone acted like that there'd be no honesty. We couldn't even leave anything in our room here, for example.'

'I never leave anything anywhere, and I advise you not to, either. Not that we've much the quality want. They don't want to steal from us. We've nothing worth stealing. So we steal from them. It's our right, isn't it? They live in the big rooms, we're pushed up here in the small ones. Doesn't matter what the law says, what the Bible says, what the preacher says, what *anyone* says. Everyone does it. You understand me?'

'Yes,' said Carola. 'But I rather wish I didn't. Don't any of the other servants ever report this going on?'

'I should think not. And don't you start sticking your nose in it, either. You'll find your eyes get scratched out, or your bed sewn up, or someone'll put a turd in your shoe.'

'So someone has spoken out against it?'

'Yes. We've had one or two people who thought it was wrong, so they said, stupid bitches. Our employers are paying us a wage, keeping us, they said, so we should be honest with them. We soon taught them where their best interests lay. They were glad to clear out – and the mistress didn't give them references. Said they were troublemakers. There's another thing. When the master comes back, you'll find he's a bit free with his hands. You can make a bit off him if you want.'

'Why is he free with his hands?'

'All men are the same. Never get enough. And the mistress, she's a bit of a cow. Cold as an iceberg, I'd say. But she's the one with the money.'

'You don't paint a very happy picture, above stairs or below.'

'Well, see for yourself. But don't go thinking you're

115

going to tell on us. They wouldn't believe you anyhow. We've all been here for years, you see. No complaints. Loyal to the core. You're the newcomer.'

Mr and Mrs Campion came back later that summer. Travel to the continent was still encouraged in the early months of the war, and indeed the traffic to the south was busier than ever. Tourists might break their journey in northern France or even in Belgium, and the chance of visiting relatives who could be serving in a rear area of the war front was an added inducement.

The Campions had no family, no one but themselves to please. They arrived by motor car late one night. All the servants got out of bed, put on their best clothes, and stood in line in the hall to greet them. Footmen carried in their leather suitcases.

Mr Campion was a small, plump man with a bald head and bulging eyes, as though they were really the eyes of a much bigger man and wanted to burst out of their sockets. He had a bristling moustache, like a ragged toothbrush. He had nicked himself while shaving that morning, and a tuft of cottonwool still stuck to the cut on his chin.

Mrs Campion was tall and slim and elegant. The skin on her face was so tightly drawn across the bones, Carola was reminded of a drumskin. She looked tense, ill at ease. She stopped when she came to Carola.

'This is the new maid, ma'am,' the housekeeper said. 'As I told you in my letter, we lost two unexpectedly. That very same day she turned up.'

'Is she good?' asked Mrs Campion without any interest. It was really no concern of hers whether the girl was good at her job or not. If she didn't suit, she would go. If she did suit, she could stay.

'Very hard-working, ma'am. But she's never been in service before. This is her first job.'

'You like it?' Mrs Campion asked Carola.

'I'm getting used to it, ma'am. I'm very grateful to have a job.'

'Well, we hope you do well here. Mrs Square is very good with new girls. She'll put you right.'

Mrs Campion moved on.

The next afternoon, when Carola was in her room changing from the morning wear of dark blouse and skirt to the smarter outfit of dark skirt, light blouse and starched apron that Mrs Square provided for her to wear each afternoon, Isobel came bustling in.

'You're in luck,' she said. 'He's taken a shine to you.'

'Who has?'

'Mr Campion.'

'How do you know?'

'I heard him talking to his wife. I listened behind the bedroom door. Said he thought you'd shape up very well. Got a good shape is what he means, more like. He enjoys a squeeze when he gets the chance.'

'*If* he gets the chance,' retorted Carola.

Isobel pouted. 'He's had his hand up my skirt a few times, I can tell you. And at half a sovereign a time, the more the better.'

Carola went to the dressing table, brushed her hair, watching herself in the faded stained mirror that hung from a nail. She noticed a faint smell in the room she could not quite place, rather like incense or scented cigarette smoke.

'Have you been smoking up here?' she asked Isobel.

'Me? No. Can't afford it. I like a drop of drink, gin and lime, port and lemon. But not smoking. Why do you ask?'

'I smell something.'

'Probably the wind's blowing the smoke down the chimney, that's all. But watch out for the old man like I told you.'

117

'I don't think there's anything to fear from him,' said Carola.

'Aah, we'll see. You'll learn.'

And Carola did learn later that same afternoon. The bell connected to the study was tinkling when she came into the servants' hall. Mrs Square glanced up at it, nodded towards a tray laid for tea for one.

'Take that into the master's study, will you?' she told Carola. 'Mrs Campion's away until dinner, playing bridge. Does that most afternoons.'

Carola picked up the tray, carried it through the sound-proofed door with green baize on one side and padded leather on the other, into the hall and up the stairs. Outside the door of the study, she knocked softly, went inside.

Mr Campion was sitting in a swivel armchair behind his desk, leaning back as he read the paper. A half-smoked cigarette lay on the rim of an ashtray on his desk. He looked up at her over his half-glasses. His bald head glistened like a sweating bladder of fat. To Carola, he appeared totally repugnant.

'Where shall I put this, sir?' she asked him.

'On the side table here, there's a good girl.'

She bent down. As she did so he put out his hand, stroked her upper arm. Carola's flesh crawled at the touch.

'I'm not going to eat you,' he said. 'Not yet, anyhow. You're a nice young girl. Now, tell me about yourself. Mrs Square says you worked in a fair.'

'Not actually, sir. My father owned a traction engine with a dynamo. He hired it out to fairs to light the sideshows.'

'Oh. Well, you must have had a bit of fun with all those big brawny fellows who put up the big top and the roundabouts and the helter-skelters, eh?' As he spoke he drew her down towards him.

'Please, sir,' she said. 'I've got to get back.'

'Not really,' he told her. 'I'm the master here. I say when you've got to get back, not Mrs Square or anybody else. Just me.'

His hands were moving over her shoulders, dropped down to her breasts. She felt them squeezed, saw his face redden. His tongue licked his dry lips.

'Come and sit on my knee,' he said.

'No, sir. It's wrong.' Whether it was right or wrong was academic. She simply couldn't bear to be pawed by this repulsive creature.

'Please yourself,' he said. 'But don't get too high and mighty. I'm the master, you know. You're the maid. Think about it. When I ring again, come in and collect the tray. Then I hope you'll have thought about it and reached the only conclusion you can reach – in your position, that is.'

He smiled up at her, reached out and stubbed out his cigarette in the ashtray. She sniffed the strange smell of tobacco she had smelled in her attic bedroom. He had been there. But why?

'They're Turkish,' he explained. 'I always smoke them. They appeal to me. Like you. Now get back to your kitchen and wait till I ring.'

Carola curtsied, went out of the room, stood for a moment on the other side of the door, leaning against the wall. Her heart was beating heavily. She couldn't stand the man, yet she needed the job. What could she do?

Mrs Square was sitting down at the table in the kitchen stirring spoonfuls of sugar into a big cup of tea.

'I've made one for you,' she said. 'Now sit down here. I want to talk to you.'

'I want to talk to *you*, Mrs Square.'

'What about?'

'About the master. He touched me, wanted to fondle

me. He will when I go back to collect the tray. He as good as said so.'

'I see. You're not the first he's done that to, and you won't be the last. But you've got to be very careful, Carola. Isobel's just come down to show me something she found under your mattress.'

'Why was she looking under my mattress? There's nothing there but springs as far as I know.'

Mrs Square ignored the question.

'She found a couple of silver spoons, wrapped in a bit of yesterday's newspaper.' Mrs Square had been holding them in her lap. Now she unwrapped them on the table.

'Well?' Carola asked.

'Is that all you've got to say? *Well?* Why did you put them there?'

'I didn't. I've never seen them before.'

'Look at me straight in the eyes,' said Mrs Square sternly. 'I know petty pilfering goes on here. It does in any big house. If you can't turn a blind eye to it when you run these places, you can't afford to live in that style. But these spoons are valuable, must be worth a pound or two. You could do time for that.'

'I haven't done anything, Mrs Square.'

'Well, they were under your bed, not Isobel's.'

'Perhaps she stole them.'

'Why should she steal them?'

'Why should *I* steal them?'

'Because you need the money,' Mrs Square said doubtfully. 'But, I don't know, you look an honest kid.'

'I am honest. But wait a minute . . .'

'Well?'

'While I was changing into my afternoon uniform, I noticed there was a smell up there, an odd sort of scented cigarette smoke. I'd never smelt that kind of cigarette before, and when I served Mr Campion his tea he was smoking one. They're Turkish, he told me.'

120

'So you think he's been up there, put his own spoons under your bed?'

'It is possible. Because then I'd be in a very weak position if I complained to his wife about his behaviour if he got any worse.'

'She'd never believe you.'

'She probably wouldn't. But then neither do you. Yet what I'm saying is absolutely true.'

'It may be true, or it may not be. But we can only go on the facts of the evidence, and they're against you.'

'I think I'd better go.'

'Where to?'

'Maybe to the munitions factory. I can't stay here. If this blows over, then there'll be something else. I can't stay here and have to submit to that horrible little man.'

'Lots of women submit to horrible little men. Their husbands.'

'Mrs Campion does, too, presumably, but that's her affair.'

'She wanted a husband,' said Mrs Square. 'She's a cold, unfriendly woman. She got passed by until she was in her thirties. And then, quite unexpectedly, an uncle died and left her a fortune. And Mr Campion appeared on the scene. He married for money. Her money. Oh, she knows what he does with the maids. She turns a blind eye to it. She's got him on a string, or a chain if you like, a hook. He's grown used to living like this, with servants, a chauffeur, two motor cars, a house in France. And she's got used to being a married woman, if only in name.'

'Is all life like this, Mrs Square? I've had a pretty sheltered life, if it is.'

'Then I think that, as you say, you've had a pretty sheltered life, Carola,' Mrs Square replied sadly.

As she spoke, the bell jangled on its spring about their heads. They looked up at it.

'The study,' said Mrs Square. 'The master.'

'I'm not going,' said Carola firmly.

'You must. You're the only maid on duty.'

'What about Isobel?'

'She's gone out on an errand.'

'I'm leaving,' said Carola. 'I told you.'

'Maybe. But the terms of your engagement are one week's notice. You have to work your time out unless the mistress agrees otherwise, which she's hardly likely to do in these circumstances. You must go.'

'All right.'

Carola went upstairs, paused outside the study, smoothed her dress, her hair, tapped on the door respectfully, went inside.

Mr Campion was standing now, his back to the window, smiling at her.

'You had a chance to consider everything?' he asked.

'I have, sir. Yes.'

'And I hope you've come to the right decision.'

'Yes,' she said. 'I think I have, though it wasn't an easy one to make. I'm leaving.'

'*Leaving?* Why?'

He walked slowly towards her as he spoke, until he was standing about a foot away. She did not move. She could see pustules on his face, blackheads around his eyes, green phlegm on hairs in his nostrils, like pollen on the legs of bees. He represented to her everything she hated, loathed, despised in a man.

'I'll take your tray, sir, if I may.'

'You may. But first I have something to say to you. I could pay you more money a week than you would ever make in any other service job as a maid, or tweenie.'

'I don't intend to be that for very long, sir.'

'What you intend and what may happen are two different things. I will give you a pound a week extra when I have my way with you.'

122

'No. Not for ten pounds a week.'

'How dare you talk to me like that, you greedy, grasping little slut from the back of nowhere!'

He suddenly put up both hands and ripped her dress. She was wearing only a chemise underneath. Her breasts, firm and young and rounded, burst out. He looked down at them. His hands moved from the sides of the cloth to finger the nipples.

Carola brought up her left knee hard into his groin. Mr Campion howled in agony and staggered to one side. She picked up the tray, went out of the door, ran down the stairs to the kitchen.

'That was quick!' said Mrs Square in surprise. 'He didn't attempt anything?'

'He did. Look at my dress. But he won't again. I'd better go now. Never mind my week's money. I'll collect my stuff and go.'

'You're sure?'

'I've no option. He came at me and I brought up my knee into what he might call his family jewels.'

Mrs Square smiled. 'It's been coming to him for a long time. But I'm sorry you've had to pay the price. Where will you go?'

'I'll try the munitions factory. Thanks for giving me a chance here. I'll not forget that. And if ever I can repay your kindness, I will.'

Then Carola was gone, racing up the stairs to her room, two steps at a time.

When Carola applied for work at the munitions factory, she was given the job of filling shell cases with spoonfuls of explosive. Next day, a red-haired girl at the far end of the line walked over to see her.

'You were up working for the Campions,' she said, making the question sound like a statement.

'Briefly,' Carola admitted. 'How do you know?'

'Isobel told me. I did a year there. And I'd still be there if this factory hadn't started. Old man Campion touch you up?'

'Tried to.'

The girl nodded. 'That's what Isobel said. Apparently you kicked him?'

'Kneed him,' corrected Carola.

'Good for you. Should have happened years ago. But it never did. For if we got sacked without a reference, who would employ us? I tell you, this factory has saved me. Maybe you, too.'

Carola shrugged. 'There seem to be no men working here,' she said, puzzled.

'Nor will there be, either. They're all in the forces and, anyhow, the owner is a woman – Lady Warren. She doesn't like men. Won't employ any. I bet she'll be interested to hear what you did to old Campion.'

'Why? Does she know him?'

'Shouldn't think she bothers with him. She's too bloody rich. But he's a man. Well, sort of. And she's always interested to hear when a woman gets the better of a man.'

'Odd, surely, for a woman to own a munitions factory?'

'That's because, like me, you don't think of it as women's work. It's for men, that sort of thing. But she thinks different. She's an odd woman, I give you that. Smokes a pipe or a cheroot, has her hair cut short, wears men's suits, swears like a sergeant-major. But I like her. She's a good sort. Looks after her employees. And she can't stand fools.'

'You know her?'

'Of course I don't *know* her. Not like I might know *you*. She's rich, you see. Got her own friends, though not many, I'd say. She speaks her mind too sharply. Causes offence even if she doesn't mean to. She comes round here once a week. If she sees a girl looking poorly or maybe expecting, she'll tell her to take a week off, and pay her.

'If she finds she already has a baby, maybe she'll give her a fiver, right there and then, out of her own purse. Not many bosses do that, I can tell you. She'll have heard what you've done all right, and she'll want to have a look at you. You never know, you could be her type of person.'

At eight o'clock the following morning, a hush descended on the early shift. The chattering that sounded like a myriad birds on as many boughs suddenly slowed and then ceased. Every woman bent earnestly over her brass shell cases, ladling into each one the weighed amount of explosive, pressing it down carefully with a circular wooden rammer that fitted closely inside the case.

Only Carola looked up to see what had caused this sudden concentration. The forewoman, a war widow in her forties, was walking down the line beside a woman of about the same age. She had an Eton crop and wore a dark tweed suit. Her very sharp eyes darted up and down the line. Carola guessed she must be Lady Warren.

'That woman third from the end has a bad cut on her hand,' Lady Warren addressed the forewoman. 'See she has it dressed. If any explosive gets into that wound, it won't do her any good. And Mrs Wright here is already several months gone. Put her on other duties where she can sit down.'

'Very good, my lady,' said the forewoman respectfully, scribbling on a pad she took from a pocket in her heavy serge skirt.

They approached Carola, walking in step, Lady Warren one pace ahead of the forewoman. They stopped opposite her.

'So you're the girl who kicked that dirty old man

125

Campion in the balls, are you?' Lady Warren asked her.

'Yes, your ladyship. Kneed him, actually.'

'And a good thing, too. Kicked any other men in the balls? Or kneed them, if you prefer that word?'

'No, your ladyship.'

'Kicked them anywhere?'

'No.'

'Wanted to?'

Carola paused for a moment, thinking of her father.

'Sometimes, your ladyship,' she admitted.

'Good. I believe that a woman's as good as any man any day. D'you know what Queen Elizabeth said when she was told a deputation of eighteen tailors wished to present a petition to her?'

'No, your ladyship.'

'She said she would see *both* men directly. As far as she was concerned, nine tailors equalled one proper man. Foreigners are even worse. So what work are you doing here?'

'Filling shells, your ladyship.'

'So I see. I've got bloody eyes, girl. What I mean is, what d'you *want* to do here?'

'I'm quite happy with this, your ladyship.'

'But not for ever. Girls who kick or knee men in the balls have bigger ambitions. Maybe they want bigger shoes.'

Several girls tittered. Carola blushed.

'You've nothing to be ashamed of, girl. I understand you worked for your father on his traction engine. Are you interested in mechanical things? Motor cars, for instance?'

'Yes, your ladyship. But I don't know much about them.'

'Then come to my house at eight o'clock tomorrow morning, and we'll see what we can do. Call at the back door and ask for me. Understood?'

'Yes, your ladyship.'

Lady Warren moved on. Carola watched her. The forewoman escorted the owner of the factory to the door and then came back to Carola.

'I want to see you,' she told her. 'Now.'

Carola followed her to the little partitioned space she had as an office.

'Sit down,' the older woman told her. 'Now don't worry about seeing her ladyship tomorrow. If she takes a liking to you, you could do very well.' She sat down beside Carola in a hardbacked chair at the scrubbed wooden table that served as a desk. 'Ever heard of Lady Warren before you came here?' she asked.

'No. Never.'

'You know nothing about her?'

'Nothing whatever.'

'You obviously don't read the newspapers. Then I'd better tell you what I know. She's a strange one, all right. No doubt of that. But her heart's in the right place. This is only one of a dozen companies she controls, all connected with the war effort, and she knows everyone, their problems, their families, in each one.

'She told me she'd heard about you and Mr Campion, that before you went into service you'd worked with your father. And that you'd left him. So she wanted to see you. To leave a father *and* an employer these days shows guts. She likes women with guts. She hates men, you see.'

'Was she ever married?'

'Oh, yes. Briefly. That's why she's Lady Warren. She's north country, born in Ashton-under-Lyne, outside Manchester. Her father was a cobbler, and a good one, too, so I've heard. He had a stall in the market. He would sell the shoes he'd made himself as well as others he'd buy from bigger makers and adapt, dyeing the leather different colours and so on. She wasn't her ladyship then, of course, just plain Antonia Nolan, and she would help him there every market day.

'Now, on the far side of the market was the biggest local cotton mill – Warren Brothers. Originally, there were three brothers. Two had died long since and old Ron Warren was the last survivor. He'd been made a knight for giving money to the Liberals, or some such thing, and he owned the whole mill outright. It was more like a gold mine than a mill, it made so much. And he was mean as they come. Tight as a drum when it came to parting with a penny.

'Sir Ron usually drove to work in his carriage and pair, smart as Burlington Bertie, top hat and all. But on sunny mornings he would sometimes walk through the market and see if he could pick up a bargain. His way lay past Nolan's stall, and one day Antonia called out to him: "Like to buy a pair of good handmade shoes, Sir Ronald? They'd go well with that fine suit you're wearing."

'She's a good-looking woman now, is Lady Warren, but when she was young she must have been remarkable. And even then, she didn't care what she said to anyone. No kowtowing to the rich or to anyone else.

'Old Warren was a widower, living with his housekeeper who I've always heard say did more for him on her back than in the kitchen. But men always like a meal of fresh meat, even when they're old as Warren. Anyhow, cheeky young Antonia caught his eye. Sometimes he bought a pair of shoes, sometimes only a pair of laces because, like I said, he was tight as a fish's arse, and that's watertight.

'Finally, he propositioned her, said he would set her up in a flat, pay her five pounds a week. A fortune. She just smiled at him, very sweetly, didn't laugh, didn't turn down the offer. Said nothing. Just smiled. And that, I tell you, Carola, is one lesson I learned from her. If you've nothing to say, don't say it. Smile. You haven't agreed and you haven't disagreed. You've kept your own counsel. So when you do make up your mind what you're going to do, you can go either way and no one can ever say you've let them down.

'Antonia was determined to keep her dearer-than-life-itself until she found the right person – willing to pay the right price. No man on a business deal goes all the way at first. No woman, either, if she's any sense. You can give away what you've got, or you can invest it, if you understand me, and that's what Antonia intended. She wanted a dividend. Finally, Warren knew he was beat. He proposed marriage.

' "I would marry you," Antonia told him very gently, "but I have no money, and everyone will say I'm just marrying you for your money."

' "I don't give a damn what people say," said the old boy, getting all horny at the thought she was about to give in.

' "I do," said Antonia. "So I would like you to give me some money first. Then they can eat their words."

' "How much money?" asked Warren cautiously.

' "Thirty thousand pounds' worth of Warren Brothers shares."

' "A bloody fortune," said Sir Ron in amazement.

' "Yes and no. You're the controlling shareholder. This amount won't alter that. It's not money, as such, Sir Ronald. Only shares – bits of paper doing nothing for you. And just look at what they will buy."

' "Outrageous! Out of the bloody question!" he told her.

'Antonia didn't argue. She just smiled, and in a couple of weeks it wasn't out of the question, it was in the bag. They married. His housekeeper went mad, of course, for now her chances of a fortune had gone right up the chimney.

'Antonia lived with the old boy for a few months, but

she soon tired him out. He couldn't cope. He had a heart attack and died. He had no relatives, so she inherited everything. Then it turned out that the mill was only one of several he owned. No one knew that locally, but she did. She'd done what she called a search in some office where all such things are listed. She knew more about old Warren's wealth than he knew himself. She told me so once, sitting where you are, in this very room.

'A very clever woman, eh? Now she's worth millions. Those mills are running twenty-four hours a day every day of the week, and there's hardly a man employed in any of them. All the workers on the looms are girls, of course, but she has women in the offices, too. Women driving the steam wagons that move the bales of cotton. Women doing all sorts of jobs. I tell you, when you go to her house tomorrow, you won't see a man in the place.'

'What about the butler, the chauffeur?'

'Women,' said the forewoman. 'I thought I'd tell you all this because it might help you. And, who knows, maybe one day you can return the favour. She's hard, but she's fair, is Lady Warren. Now, I'll put the kettle on, and we'll both have a nice cup of tea.'

At a quarter to eight on the following morning, Carola stood outside the black-painted, gold-tipped iron gates of Lady Warren's house. Beyond them, the drive stretched between parkland, with metal fences on either side. Carola was early, but the house was out of sight from the road, so it might be a good half-mile walk away, and she could not risk being late. She took a deep breath and set off along the raked gravel. The drive bent to the left behind a yew hedge, and there stood the house, Cotswold stone, mellow in the morning sunshine.

She went to the side door. Instead of a mechanical bell as in Mr Campion's house, a push-button was recessed in the wall. She pressed it. An electric bell rang loudly, and the door opened almost immediately. A middle-aged housekeeper, looking very like Mrs Square, wearing almost identical clothing, with a bunch of keys at her waist, looked at her enquiringly.

'I'm Carola Marsh,' Carola explained. 'Lady Warren asked to see me at eight o'clock.'

The woman looked her up and down, hanging price tickets on her clothes, her shoes.

'Come inside,' she said. 'Wait in the kitchen. I will tell her ladyship.'

She led the way into a kitchen, just as large as the Campions', but infinitely more modern. Here was an electric stove with hotplates, and a refrigerator; in the other kitchen, everything had been old-fashioned. Carola was excited by the newness of the equipment. This was a twentieth-century kitchen, not a left-over from the nineteenth.

As she stood, she heard a sudden baying of dogs. Another door to the kitchen burst open and two wolf-hounds rushed in, barking at her. They stood in front of her, teeth bared, watching for the first sign of fear in the face of a stranger. But Carola was used to much fiercer dogs in the fairs she had attended with her father. She snapped the fingers of her right hand in the face of the nearest dog, held out her left hand to the other. The barking stopped. They wagged their tails.

'You stupid beasts,' she said in a friendly voice. 'I know you're both wonderful guard dogs, but don't attack me. I'm not your enemy.'

'Possibly not,' said a voice behind her. 'But you're certainly brave.'

Lady Warren moved round Carola and patted the dogs. 'You're the only stranger I have had in this kitchen, woman or man, who stood up to them. I had a man here the other day, unfit for military service, who wanted a job as chauffeur. He was terrified, almost ruptured himself jumping up on the table to get away from them – not that I would have employed him, in any case. I believe women can do most of men's jobs, and the best way to show this is to give them the chance. You have passed the first test. Follow me.'

Carola, heart beating quickly, for the sudden arrival of the dogs had disturbed her more than she cared to admit, followed Lady Warren along a corridor and through a great hall hung with oil paintings of women – Queen Elizabeth, Florence Nightingale, the missionary Mary Slessor.

'They are all very dear to me,' Lady Warren explained. 'They all proved in quite different ways that women can be just as tough as men, as well as being much cleverer.'

She led the way into a study. This was almost a replica of Mr Campion's room, except that here more mirrors hung on the wall, a concession perhaps to Lady Warren's femininity. Indeed, as she passed a mirror now, she glanced into it, smoothed her hair with her hands.

'When I saw you yesterday,' she said, 'you gave me the impression you were interested in motor cars, but you didn't know much about them. Can you drive?'

'No, Lady Warren.'

'Well, that's not a very good start. What do you know about them?'

'Only what I've seen in the fairs. Some of the stallholders own motor cars to pull trailers with their gear from one ground to another.'

'And you've helped them?'

'I've watched them when they were making adjustments and so on.'

'Come out to the garage. I'll show you one of my cars. I have several, you know. The benefit of having a lot of money, Carola, is that you can have almost anything you want, if it can be bought. By that I mean people as well as things.

'I use a big car when I go a long journey, a small one to take me to the station or the factory, or any one of my factories. Then there's a brake if I have guests to stay and they need to be picked up at the station.

'Sometimes the cars won't start. If my chauffeuse is away in one and I may want to drive another, I haven't the time or the inclination to fool around with the thing. So you might just come in useful. Or, again, you might not.'

They went out of a side door into a cobbled yard. At the far end stood a four-car garage with sliding doors. The walls were decorated with Portuguese tiles. Electric lights in white china shades hung from the ceiling. Lady Warren led Carola to the nearest car.

'Lift the bonnet,' she said. 'Now, there's the engine. Assume you come in the morning to start it and it won't start. What's wrong?'

'It could be one of several things, Lady Warren. Firstly, you might not have any petrol in the tank.'

'True.'

'Then there's a tap that you turn on to let the petrol run to the carburettor. That might be turned off. The magneto could be damp so there would not be a spark at the plugs.'

'What would you do in that case, girl?'

'I'd take all the plugs out, lay them on top of the cylinders, and turn the engine over by the starting handle. If they sparked, I'd know the magneto was all right.'

'Why take them all out? Why not take one, and test that? Why make work?'

'If I were a man, I could turn the engine over on the compression of three cylinders. But I'm not and it's

133

much easier to spin the engine when all the plugs are out.'

'That makes sense. Show me if you can spin that engine when all the plugs are in.'

'You want me to start it?'

'Not necessarily. Just spin it.'

Carola walked to the front of the car. The crank handle was held to one side by a waxed leather strap. She released the strap, pushed in the handle against the spring and swung it.

'Why are you holding it like that?' asked Lady Warren sharply. 'Your thumb's not round it.'

'No, Lady Warren. If it were, and the engine kicked back, I could break my thumb.'

'So you do know something about cars,' said Lady Warren more approvingly. 'Come back into the house. I'll tell you what I have in mind for you.'

Carola followed her back into the study.

'It's not often one finds a girl with a mechanical aptitude. And of course it may just be a flash in the pan. I've been taken in by people before, you know. I'm not a fool, but when you're looking for someone or something, you often tend not to see faults or flaws. You see what you want to see.

'I've watched people digging for diamonds in South Africa bring up bits of quartz that shine in the sun. The same with gold. There's a thing called fool's gold. It's a mineral of some sort, looks just like real gold, but it's worthless. Yet at first sight it seems genuine. But we all tend to believe what we want to believe. Now, about you, I think . . .' She stopped and then continued quickly.

'I think for the moment you'd better work in the factory rather than on the cars. Then we'll see what happens when the war's over. Goodness knows, it can't last for ever, though sometimes it seems as if it may.

'I have something better in mind for you, not just cars.

134

Now I'll show you where you're going to live. Here, in the house, with me and yet not with me, if you understand. Do you?'

'I'm beginning to,' said Carola.

'Good. It says in the Bible, the fear of the Lord is the beginning of wisdom. To my employees, the fear of Lady Warren can be the beginning of something even more valuable.'

Chapter Seven

Richard Rowlands would never agree with anyone who claimed that their schooldays had been the happiest days of their lives, but as far as he was concerned he readily admitted that they had been the most worthwhile. For the first time he had access to a fully-equipped science laboratory and a science master, Mr Compton, who loved his work and could infect others with his enthusiasm.

Mr Compton, a small middle-aged man, had a calliper on his right leg. When he walked, there was a constant clink of the metal joints. His disability had kept him out of the armed forces when war was declared. He had immediately offered his services in any capacity, but had been told that the best way he could serve his country was as a schoolmaster.

Science was not a very popular subject. Most boys in their teens were anxious to put school behind them as quickly as possible and to be in uniform like their elder brothers and cousins. Every day, at assembly, the headmaster would read out a list of old boys who had been killed on land, at sea, under the sea and, increasingly, in the air. But although these numbers grew steadily, the determination of the schoolboys to join up grew in proportion. It was as though they believed that, while others might be killed or wounded or blinded, they would survive unscathed: the war would somehow simply be a more exciting extension of school life, but wearing uniform.

Richard came to Mr Compton's attention when the science master found him sketching an oscillating cylinder when he should have been making notes on the basic principles of Boyle's Law – 'The pressure of a given mass of gas is inversely proportional to its volume.'

Mr Compton asked Richard to see him after school that day.

'What do you know about Boyle?' he asked him.

'Virtually nothing, sir.'

'I thought so. But at least you're honest about your ignorance. What about oscillating cylinders? You obviously know that they work by compressed steam. What is their attraction for you?'

Mr Compton's tone was not unfriendly or critical. Richard warmed to him, and explained how he had reversed the inlet and exhaust systems on his steam engine to improve its performance, and how the boiler had blown up in his brother's face. Gradually, the whole story of his father's unexpected visit to France, his death and subsequent revelations about the family's finances came pouring out. And with it Richard's own interest in engines.

'I see you favour engineering as a science rather than chemistry,' commented Mr Compton.

'Very much so, sir,' Richard agreed.

'In my view, a wise preference. This country, most unfortunately, lags so far behind our continental competitors such as Germany and France in engineering that I despair of the future. Every morning at assembly, I hear the headmaster read out the names of boys I taught years ago, sometimes only months ago, and all now dead. And I think to myself, how many young men, on both sides, could have survived if one simple piece of engineering had been better made, better designed and assembled?'

'I don't quite follow you, sir,' said Richard.

'Let me elaborate. This war started when Archduke Franz Ferdinand, the heir to the Austrian throne, was assassinated on a state visit in Sarajevo in the southernmost part of the Austro-Hungarian Empire.

'He was not a well man, and quite unsuited to make such a visit, but his father insisted. The Archduke suffered from an infection of the lungs and coughed up blood at the slightest exertion. However, his presence in Sarajevo was considered important so, as a dutiful if weak son, he visited the miserable town.

'Things went sadly wrong. First, a disaffected student threw a bomb at his car. It missed, and the royal car continued in convoy with others. Much shaken, the Archduke made a speech, as previously arranged, on the steps of the town hall, and then the plan was for him to tour a museum. As a result of the bombing attempt, however, this was cancelled. Instead, he would visit a hospital where an officer in his entourage, injured by the bomb, was being treated.

'However, almost unbelievably, while all the officials knew of this sudden change of plan, no one told the Archduke's driver. He approached a crossroads. One way led to the museum, and the other to the hospital. Naturally, he took the road to the museum. An officer sitting beside him suddenly realised the driver had not been told of the change of plan and tried frantically to make him change direction.

"Get back!" he shouted. "Get back!"

'The driver slammed the gear lever into reverse – and here we have an example of the vital importance engineering can play in world affairs. The gear lever jammed, the cogs would not engage. The wretched man wrestled frantically with it. The car was stationary long enough for an assassin on the pavement, only feet away, to take careful aim with a pistol and kill the Archduke and his wife. That, Rowlands, was the starting pistol for the war that has engulfed all Europe. Had those gears been better machined, had the gear box been better designed, history might have been totally different.'

'I did not know that, sir.'

'Most people don't. Now, to get back to your cylinder. Steam as a force of propulsion in an engine belongs to the past, except for ships and railway locomotives. The future belongs not to steam, but to petrol. And by happy chance I think I can give you some practical lessons in this type of engine.' Mr Compton nodded towards a corner of the science laboratory.

Here, under a glass cover, stood a single-cylinder motorcycle engine. Every time Richard came into the laboratory, he would pass the case and often he would stand examining the engine through its thick protective glass.

'Has it ever worked, sir?' he asked now.

'I shouldn't think so. But it could be made to work very easily. It only wants a petrol tank with a pipe to the carburettor. The pulley for the belt to drive the back wheel is in place, as you can see. All you need do to start it is wrap a piece of thick cord round this pulley, pull it, and it should run.'

'Can I try to make it work, sir?'

'I don't see why not,' said the master. 'No one else has ever asked. So, as the Good Book says, ask and ye shall receive. But you can't start it up in this laboratory. The exhaust would smoke the place out. There's a shed near the games field where the groundsman keeps his mowers. I'll have a word with him and get one of the porters to move it there for you.'

So nearly every evening for the rest of that term, Richard spent some time working on the engine. First, he dismantled it completely because he realised that only by seeing its component parts could he hope to understand its working and discover strengths and weaknesses in the original design.

He spread sheets of newspaper on the bench, washed each part in petrol to remove oil and dirt and then laid it on the newspaper with a luggage label to help him remember where it fitted. Then he re-assembled the engine. In metalwork classes he fashioned a primitive petrol tank which he mounted on four metal legs above the engine. He fitted a screw cap on top of the tank and a tube to carry the petrol to the carburettor.

Finally, the moment came to see whether it would run. Mr Compton supplied a pint of petrol which Richard poured into the tank. He wound a length of thin rope several times round the pulley, and pulled. The engine chugged, but nothing else happened. He pulled again. A faint mist of petrol vapour blew out of the exhaust. Still the engine did not fire. Richard stood looking at it, puzzled. Where had he gone wrong?

He checked there was a spark at the points on the plug. He had just seen petrol vapour, so he knew that the valves were opening. So why didn't the vapour explode? It seemed against all the laws of physics that such a volatile mixture would not erupt when a spark was applied. Then he suddenly realised what was wrong; the word 'mixture' was his clue.

The mixture of petrol and air was not rich enough for combustion. He stuffed his handkerchief into the throat of the carburettor, and once more pulled the rope. This time the engine started and went on running with a noise from the open, unsilenced exhaust like a machine-gun firing.

He glanced in triumph at Mr Compton, who gave him the thumbs up sign. Richard turned off the petrol. The engine slowed and stopped. The two of them stood grinning at each other: Mr Compton, because his faith in a pupil's abilities had been vindicated; Richard, because he had proved he could do what before he had only hoped he could achieve.

'Now, what is the next thing you have to do?' Mr Compton asked him.

'Make it go faster, sir.'

'Exactly. Never be satisfied. Always reach out for something better. And how do you propose to do that?'

'When I had it in pieces, I saw that, as with my steam engine, the exhaust valve was bigger than the inlet, so I would like to enlarge the inlet hole and see how it runs then. That is, if you agree, sir.'

'I agree entirely. It is a pleasure to see someone so interested in a project.'

'Thank you, sir.'

Richard did not say what else he had seen and what he planned. He thought that his intentions might sound presumptuous, and it would be wise to take his modifications one step at a time. He took a week of evenings to enlarge the inlet, and when he had reassembled the engine it certainly ran more quickly, but less smoothly. So now he attempted his second modification which he had not mentioned to Mr Compton.

When the engine was in pieces, Richard saw that, as is usual in a petrol engine, the valves opened by revolving cams and were closed by the pressure of springs. For a split second on each revolution the valves would therefore be stationary before they opened or closed. If he could reduce this time by altering the angles on the cams, he could introduce an overlap between the valves which would allow them to stay open longer. More mixture could therefore be drawn into the cylinder, with a corresponding increase in speed.

For the next few weeks, to try and prove his theory, he filed away at the cams to alter their profile. This was a slow, difficult job, for the metal was very hard, but at last the work was finished. He assembled the engine, and started it on his own, not quite certain whether he had improved the performance or destroyed it. He need not have worried. The engine now ran twice as fast for the same throttle opening, so he felt he could explain what he had done to Mr Compton.

'You took a risk,' said the master, 'but first you worked out that it was an affordable risk. And if you don't take any risks in life, you achieve very little. I think myself you may have achieved something here which could have a worthwhile commercial application. Tell me, have you made any sketches of these alterations?'

'No, sir. I simply drew the outlines of the cams on a piece of cardboard, and filed them down until they fitted.'

Mr Compton nodded. 'I remember you doodling that cylinder in class. What I suggest you do in future is to draw each step you take. When you dismantled our motorcycle engine, you listed every part and tied a luggage label to it. If you also make sketches as you go along, you will find they will help you re-assemble things. Not only that, if the drawings don't look quite right, you can take it from me they won't be quite right. As you go on, you could paint them – in water colours, even oils. Then others can easily follow the steps you have taken, and maybe lead on from them. For science is really only a series of experiments – one leads on to another. And as the Chinese say – something the old voyager Marco Polo learned from them – "The longest journey starts with a single step."

'Now here's something else, two things in fact, to which you might give your attention with advantage. The first is what we call supercharging or blowing. About eight years ago, an American manufacturer of an already fast car, the Chadwick, decided to make it go even faster by blowing the petrol and air mixture into the engine rather than simply relying on outside air pressure

143

to push the mixture in. He fixed up a fan in a pipe between the carburettor and the engine and this blew the mixture in under pressure. But while the fan allows the engine to deliver more power, quite a bit of power is used up just to keep it turning. So it's a case of gaining something and losing something. That's one area that invites your scrutiny.'

'And the second, sir?'

'Altogether more revolutionary, and so more rewarding. At present, in a petrol engine, the explosion forces down the piston. In a motor car, this is connected to a fly-wheel which turns a shaft connected to the car's back axle. So you have an up and down motion, then a circular one, then you put a right-angle bend in to make the rear wheels revolve. Result – a lot of wasted energy. But if you could find a way to harness that explosion so in some manner it blows out a great jet and forces the vehicle forward, you would have a far more efficient motor.'

'But you could not use that on the roads, sir, with flames blowing out of the back of each car, could you?'

'Of course not. But what if the engines were not on the road but fitted to aircraft, in the air? Think of the speed and smoothness that would bring. No vibrating propeller, no gears, nothing but a straight jet. And as far as a car engine is concerned, perhaps the fiery jet could drive a turbine, as steam does now in our navy ships. Just ideas, possibilities. But, I think, worthy of your serious consideration – one day. So – never keep your eyes only on the ground. Look to the sky as well. I see the air force now has its own motto: "Per Ardua ad Astra – through adversity to the stars". A good motto for all of us, Rowlands, especially in times like these.'

While Carola was adapting to life in Lady Warren's house and Richard was wondering how he could translate Mr Compton's words into action, a man of whom neither he nor Carola had ever heard, but who would exercise an extraordinary influence over their lives and their country, was sitting in the corner seat of a railway carriage in Russia.

Sir James Mannering was on his way from Petrograd, formerly St Petersburg, to the Tsar's country palace at Tsarskoe-Selo, roughly an hour's journey. As was fitting for a visitor of Mannering's importance, Colonel Yovanovich, the Tsar's favourite nephew, wearing the gold-edged frock coat of the nobility, had been ordered to escort him on this journey.

Mannering was a broad-shouldered, heavily built man with thick black hair and beard, already faintly streaked with grey. Reference books never printed his age, but although quite young, he deliberately cultivated the dress and appearance of a man in his late fifties or early sixties. In his experience, people were always more willing to listen to a business proposition put forward by a man of mature years than by someone young.

He had his own reasons for reticence about his age and all details of his early life. Newspapers sometimes referred to him as a mystery man, and he saw no reason to dispel the image. Only a few suspected his background and none were willing to prove their suspicions. A man as wealthy and politically powerful as Sir James Mannering was not a person to antagonise lightly.

From time to time he glanced at the countryside through which the train was passing. Horses, heavier and shaggier than shire horses in England, pulled primitive, springless carts piled with newly gathered corn. He wished he were closer so that he could examine their crude axles and discover how the peasants greased them. He guessed it would be with pig lard, but up on the coast of the Caspian Sea, on land owned by Prince Yussoupov, whose family had served generations of Tsars and in so doing had acquired thousands of square miles of land,

Mannering had heard that peasants simply scooped up handfuls of earth to grease the axles of their carts. Mile after mile of this land was literally a soggy marsh of oil which bubbled up like tar. The owner was already so prodigiously rich – he owned more than a thousand square miles there alone – that he had never bothered to commercialise this natural phenomenon.

Oil would become vitally important in the war, and a percentage on each barrel sold could bring incalculable wealth to Mannering if he could somehow persuade the prince to change his mind.

Peasant women in black, backs bent from years of carrying heavy loads through the fields, as remote from the twentieth century as this primitive country was distant from war raging in Flanders, did not even look up as the Tsar's special train, glittering with lacquered engine and burnished brass, trundled past them. The only people who took any notice of the train were children who ran out of the shacks made of logs, branches and wattle, to wave excitedly as the engine driver blew his whistle.

'Those peasants out there,' said Mannering in Russian. 'Are they content? Well fed?'

He knew exactly how it felt to live like that, often grateful to have a cow or pig in the hovel for the warmth the beast provided, but this was not the moment to admit to such unexpected knowledge.

'Supremely happy to be citizens of His Imperial Highness,' the Tsar's nephew assured him confidently.

'There was some trouble here about ten years ago, wasn't there?' Mannering went on. 'Riots. That sort of unpleasantness.'

'There are always malcontents eager to cause disturbance. But you have had riots in England, too, Sir James, so I have read. After our war with Japan, returning soldiers deliberately provoked trouble. Our

146

newspapers had declared that our armies were well equipped and brilliantly led and so were ultimately victorious. Back home in their villages, ex-soldiers told a different story. After all, they had not won the war. They had lost it. But after some shouting and violence they soon quietened down, I'm glad to say.

'This is a big country. We have plenty of space, and agitators and their like can be moved to areas where they may purge their discontent. Just as, years ago, you in Britain sent your convicts out of the way to Australia.'

Mannering nodded, opened his cigar case, clipped the end of a Havana with a silver cutter engraved with his initials, and then offered the case to his companion.

'Thank you,' said the younger man, drawing on a cigar. 'I may say, sir, my uncle the Tsar is most appreciative of the way in which you are offering to help our forces. When victory crowns their efforts in this war against the Hun, your part in it, I know, will not go unrecognised.'

Mannering bowed his head at the compliment. He had every intention that his contribution would be recognised and, much more important, adequately rewarded.

'We do what we can to help,' he said modestly.

The train began to slow down, and stopped. A Rolls-Royce Silver Ghost, with driver and footman wearing royal livery, was waiting, engine running, outside the station at Tsarskoe-Selo – 'The Village of the Tsar'.

It was in fact rather more like a village. Twenty thousand people lived here permanently, plus hundreds more – archdukes, archduchesses, with wives, mistresses, courtiers, servants and bodyguards – who accompanied the Tsar and his German wife when they moved here to spend a few weeks or months, as the mood might take them, in their summer palace.

Mannering climbed into the car and leaned back on the pleated Bedford cord upholstery. It sped silently along the dusty road, then passed between the giant stone gateposts of the palace grounds. Numerous gardeners were raking the gravel on the drive and removing any large stones that might mar its even surface. Not one of them raised his head to watch them pass by; their task was to work, not to gawp at their betters.

The car stopped at the base of a wide flight of stone steps. Half a dozen servants stood on the bottom step and bowed as in a drill movement as they arrived. The two men got out, walked up the steps, while the servants dealt with their luggage.

Inside, the palace was everything Mannering had been told it would be. From a minstrel's gallery in the entrance hall hung the pennants and standards of Russia's most noble families. The hall was paved with white marble tiles. Flowers, brought every morning by special train from the Tsar's hothouses on the shores of the Black Sea, provided a living scented tapestry against the walls. Persian and Kuba rugs were scattered two or three deep to soak up all sounds of servants' footsteps. Carved and gilded metal braziers held wide bowls of potpourri that filled the air with their delicate aroma.

Mannering thought that the whole place looked and smelled like a gigantic funeral parlour. The flowers could be what English newspapers reporting a fashionable funeral called 'floral tributes' – to Tsarist Russia perhaps, mused Mannering. According to some of his associates in London, the Russian Empire could not long survive. If so, he had no time to lose to extract his reward before events overtook them all.

Colonel Yovanovich led Mannering into one of the drawing rooms. Chandeliers of glittering crystal hung from the ceiling like frozen waterfalls. Huge portraits of Russian nobles and their wives and children, with pet wolfhounds, lined the damask walls. A hundred painted eyes watched them. The atmosphere was of a gigantic theatrical set, rather than a home, thought Mannering. Not his style or his taste, maybe, but the prodigious power and incalculable wealth all this represented impressed him. Money was his only yardstick: what something cost or could fetch concerned him far more than whether it was old or rare or lovely, or all three.

'My uncle will be with you in one moment, sir. In the meantime, can I offer you wine? A glass of Madeira, perhaps? Or a red wine from our Crimean estates? Last year was a very good year for the red.'

'Thank you, no,' said Mannering. He wanted to keep his head clear; alcohol could cloud his brain, and his mission was too important to risk that possibility.

'But I trust His Imperial Highness does not object to my smoking?'

'Of course not.'

'I thought not. I was with his cousin, King George of England, last month in Windsor Castle. He told me he smokes five Havanas a day – and six on Sundays. I see your uncle has the same kind of portraits on his walls.'

'They are of the same people, sir.'

'Of course they are! How foolish of me to have forgotten.'

But Mannering had not forgotten; he never forgot a face or a person or even a casual remark if there was the chance of a percentage in remembering. Only the other day, in his hotel room in London, he had overheard two male servants discussing him. They did not know he was in the next room.

'Mean old bastard,' said one bitterly. 'I carried his bags all the way up here to the fifth floor and you know what he gave me? His thanks!'

'I've heard he's so tight he'd skin a turd for a farthing.'

Mannering rather liked the description; it was a compliment as far as he was concerned.

The colonel bowed and withdrew. Double gilt and

cream doors closed silently behind him. Mannering walked towards the window, stood looking out across the terrace. Nymphs and dryads and other figures from Greek and Roman myths supported cornucopia pouring water into half a dozen ornamental ponds. They were not ponds as Mannering understood the word. Each was more than a hundred feet across. Beyond the terrace lay a lake the size of an inland sea. And, as a delightful touch, the trunks of trees around it had been barked and varnished.

As Mannering pondered the scene, he heard a movement behind him, and the double doors opened. A flunkey, with a powdered wig and satin breeches, entered and bowed obsequiously.

'His Imperial Highness, Tsar of All the Russias,' he announced in Russian.

Mannering turned, stubbed out his cigar in a silver ashtray, and bowed politely to the man who came through the high doorway. He was very small, and his lack of height was accentuated by the size of the pillars, the arch above the door, the soaring ceiling. He looked a *doppelgänger* of his cousin King George V: stocky with a narrow head, pointed beard and restless eyes set close together. He wore an undress uniform of dark trousers, light blue jacket and soft leather boots.

The doors closed quietly behind him. The Tsar held out his hand. The flesh felt soft and cold, bloodless.

'You speak Russian, I understand,' said the Tsar in English.

Mannering bowed.

'I do, Majesty,' he replied.

'That is refreshing in someone from the West. The Tsarina and I often talk in English or German. Rarely Russian. But then she is German.' The Tsar looked at Mannering as though he expected a rebuke, or a sharp answer.

Mannering inclined his head to show that he was aware of the Tsarina's nationality. He also knew the unrest that this had caused in Russia since war began. She was not popular; she had even widely been called a spy, and this in a country where few cared to comment on any official matter because of the presence of the secret police. As a conciliatory gesture towards popular opinion the Tsar had changed the name of St Petersburg to Petrograd because this sounded more Russian than German, but the public dislike of the Tsarina continued unabated.

'I saw the King of England last month,' said Mannering, prudently changing the subject. 'He sends you his warm felicitations.'

The Tsar smiled his appreciation.

'And of course I send mine back,' he said. 'I greatly enjoyed my last visit to my cousin in England. Only the war has prevented me inviting him here.'

They chatted briefly about Mannering's journey. He had sailed from Hull direct to Petrograd aboard a vessel of the Wilson Line. On his arrival, the shabbiness of the city had surprised him. A general air of lethargy he put down to lack of food or purpose in the second year of the war. The Russians had enjoyed some early victories over the Germans, but within weeks the Kaiser's armies had turned this initial advance to retreat, and then the retreat to rout.

Mannering's opinion was that he had arrived in a country poised on the brink of defeat. However, this was not the moment to give the Tsar such impressions. He was here to help reverse this possibility. Instead, he spoke enthusiastically of everything he had seen, and singled out for praise the courage and fortitude of the Russian army.

'Now,' said the Tsar, 'to business. I am Commander-in-Chief of our forces, but all matters relating to the commissariat and the supply of weapons, now or in the future, I have delegated to my cousin, General Ormilov. He has my total trust and full authority to come to whatever terms seem fair and reasonable to him. I know, sir, that as a man of honour in your own country, and a confidant of the King of England, you will do your utmost to provide us with all we need. And with all the speed you can command.'

'I give you my word, Majesty,' Mannering assured him gravely.

'I ask for nothing more than the word of an English gentleman,' the Tsar replied simply.

'I thank you for your confidence, Majesty. I assure you I will do everything in my power to deserve it.'

The Tsar nodded, crossed the room, pulled a tasselled rope. The door opened again. This time a younger man entered. He had the same build as the Tsar, but broader shoulders and a fatter face. His eyes were very small, his mouth soft and petulant. Mannering gauged his character instantly: General Ormilov owed his position to his birth. He was not an officer who had fought his way up through lesser military ranks on his own ability. Indeed, Mannering doubted whether he had seen any action whatever. He had arrived at the top on the strength of his uncle's name. He was therefore unlikely to be a difficult man to deal with – or to outwit. The Tsar introduced them.

'I will now leave you gentlemen to conduct your business together. It will be my pleasure, Sir James, if you will dine with us tonight. I would like you to meet my General Staff. I feel it is most useful to know the men with whom one is dealing, rather than to rely on letters and reports.'

'I share those views entirely, Majesty.'

The Tsar nodded and left the room.

'Shall we sit down?' said Ormilov. As they did so, another officer, a captain, entered the room, carrying a briefcase. He clicked his heels, and bowed to Mannering in salutation. He opened his briefcase on a small ormolu table, and took out several folders.

'You have had a long journey, sir,' said Ormilov, 'and since you are dining with the Tsar tonight, no doubt you will welcome the opportunity of a rest before dinner. If you agree, I suggest we come to business directly, without any of the social pleasantries we might have enjoyed had we more time at our disposal.'

'You read my mind exactly, General,' said Mannering approvingly.

The aide opened the top folder, handed some papers to Ormilov who in turn passed them across the table to Mannering.

'We have set out here in English – not realising you spoke Russian so well – our basic and most urgent requirements.'

Mannering picked up the papers.

'You will see we are very short of artillery shells of all calibres,' said Ormilov. 'We are even more short of rifles for the infantry, and cartridges for them to fire. As a result of our reverses, when thousands of our rifles have been lost or, as I am ashamed to admit, deliberately thrown away by our retreating forces, five or six men may now have to share one rifle. In some cases, I can tell you in confidence, the only hope a private soldier has of securing a rifle for himself is when he takes one from a fallen comrade. Naturally, these shortages are not publicly known, but I admit them to you because we are in desperate need of your services. How long would it take for these weapons to be delivered?'

'It depends on the numbers required. I cannot buy them in England because, as I am sure you will appreciate, British forces need all that their factories can produce. I will have to find them where I can. This will take time, for the numbers you need are very large. But as soon as payment is made in gold, as already agreed, and deposited in the account I maintain for this purpose in neutral Switzerland, I will telegraph my agents. Our best source of supply, of course, will be the United States.'

'Does that not present difficulties?' asked Ormilov.

'Very considerable difficulties, since America is technically neutral. I say technically, because their armaments factories are run by practical men of business. They have no quarrel with either side in this unhappy war. It is not their war, and the money is the same, from whatever side it comes.'

'Even so, they have to maintain the façade of neutrality?'

'Of course. The rifles will therefore have to be shipped dismantled. The barrels may be described in manifests as steel tubing, the stocks as wood carvings. They will arrive in a neutral ship, flying the flag of Panama. When the weapons are offloaded, your people will have to assemble them. But to arrange this will take some time – and possibly more money. I hope you understand me.'

'Perfectly,' said Ormilov grimly. 'Now what about the shells we need?'

'Again, the explosives that go into the shell cases will have to be described as farming insecticides or fertilisers. The actual shells will be listed as scrap metal of no military value. The ship carrying them will also bring over a limited number of skilled men who can instruct your people in chosen factories as to their assembly.'

'Will these men speak Russian?'

'They will all be émigrés. I will select them for this purpose. And they will be well paid.'

'You maintain a very complex organisation, sir,' said Ormilov admiringly.

'Nothing of any worth in this world is ever achieved without effort,' replied Mannering sonorously. 'I pride myself that all the efforts I make are in direct proportion

154

to the worth of the enterprise.'

'I commend you, sir, for your patriotism and your help. There is a risk, of course, that ships may be sunk, even if they sail under a neutral flag. I understand that Royal Navy patrols are in the habit of stopping neutral cargo vessels at random and boarding parties search them. The same is true, though to a lesser extend, of the German navy.'

'Agreed, General. But that is a risk we must run, and the prices I quote will take account of insurance. Now, let me peruse these documents for a moment.'

Mannering's small sharp eyes skimmed each closely typed page. He multiplied totals, added in one percentage for his profit, another for risks involved, a third in case either of the first two were queried. He had no need to make a note, no need for anyone to check the figures. His mind checked them automatically. He had never been known to make a mistake where profit was concerned. He memorised page after page of armament requirements, adding, subtracting, dividing costs. Finally, he put down the papers. 'I can give you the total price now, if you wish,' he said, 'and follow it up with an itemised costing tomorrow morning.'

General Ormilov looked at him in surprise. He had never met anyone who could absorb so many figures in this way, and so quickly. 'I am indebted to you, Sir James,' he said. 'I did not expect such a swift response. But before you give us your final figure, there is another matter to which we would be grateful if you would direct your attention. Aircraft. Have you any experience of flying machines as used in war?'

'I have an interest in aviation, naturally, because it is the last element we need to conquer. Land we have defeated. Ships can sail on any of the seven seas, and submarines can travel swiftly and silently beneath them –

largely, I may say, through my influence. Only the air remains ours to command.

'I may tell you in confidence that just before this unfortunate war broke out, the British Admiralty sought my opinion on acquiring a dirigible airship or, if that was unavailable, a powered balloon to be stationed above the English Channel or the North Sea to watch shipping movements.

'I at once advised them to contact the Parseval company in Bitterfeld, Germany. This they were unwilling to do direct, so I acted as intermediary and bought for them a dirigible with a very useful speed of forty-six miles an hour. This airship, sir, has proved its worth time and again.'

'We are thinking specifically of aeroplanes, not airships. And although we can buy these from Britain and probably, through your good offices and influence, from America, they all possess the same flaw.'

'Which is, General?'

'Their means of discharging bullets at an enemy in the sky. They have to draw alongside to fire, like a ship coming into a harbour quay, because it is impossible to fire straight ahead without shooting their own propellers. It has been suggested that guns should be mounted on either side of the fuselage, in the wings. But experiments have not been successful. The wings are not strong enough to bear the weight of these weapons or to stand the force of their recoil as they fire.

'Coming alongside, as they have to do, means that they present a much larger and easier target to the enemy – as we know from Allied casualties on the Western Front. If you have any thoughts on this matter, Sir James, we would be lastingly grateful to you.'

Mannering nodded, musingly.

'I will come back to you on this,' he promised. 'Now, to the matter in hand. Here is my total, including amounts to cover every contingency.'

He gave him a figure.

Ormilov bit his lower lip. The sum was much larger than he had anticipated. But then his country's need for weapons and other stores of war was far more desperate than he had admitted. The entire Russian front was in disarray. Their army was virtually unarmed, without shells or other ammunition. Agitators were already calling on troops to desert. Huge numbers had already done so, straggling back to their villages. How soon before they heeded other calls to violence, murder, total revolution? Once this started, like a raging forest fire it would be almost impossible to stop. The nation's best safeguard, indeed the only one he could think of, was to provide these ragged battalions with arms and trust in God and the Tsar to produce a victory of some kind.

Ormilov knew he had no option but to agree, but he did so with a saddened heart. He was paying out millions more in sterling than he had anticipated. And in addition, there was something about this Englishman who spoke Russian so well, who had the ability to calculate pages of figures without making a single note, that caused him unease. He had never met anyone like him. The fellow's mind was more like a machine than a human brain. Ormilov hoped he did not need to meet him again. He would be relieved when Mannering's visit was over.

'I will have my clerks draw up an agreement immediately,' he said with a briskness he did not feel. 'Perhaps you would sign it, and then join me in a glass of Russian champagne?'

'It will be my pleasure,' said Mannering. 'I will await you here.'

Ormilov stood up, bowed, clicked his heels and left the room. The captain followed him. Mannering lit another cigar. As always, after completing a successful deal, he felt a great sense of ease, of infinite relaxation.

He imagined a woman might experience this feeling after giving birth to a child, but of course he did not know. His relationships with women were now never more than formal.

He strolled across the room again to the wide windows and looked out across the empty park. A tall, heavily built man wearing the uniform of a sailor in the Russian navy was coming up the steps towards the palace, carrying something on his back. His body was bent forward under its weight. Mannering watched them curiously, wondering what the heavy burden could be.

As the sailor reached the top of the steps and turned, Mannering saw he was carrying a boy, about eleven or twelve, dressed incongruously in a small copy of the sailor's uniform. He lay listlessly on the big man's back, head to one side, face waxy, eyes dull. He seemed more like a mannikin than a human being, almost a marionette, dressed for some pantomime or charade.

Mannering turned away from the sight. It displeased him. He knew he had been looking at the face and feeble body of the Tsar's only son, the Tsarevich, heir to All the Russias, a land so vast that as the sun rose on its eastern extremities it was already setting over the western borders.

The boy was haemophiliac. If he bruised himself, he would bleed internally for days, perhaps for weeks. A tiny cut could kill him. The bearded sailor who carried him never went to sea. His sole duties were to carry this princeling and to guard him against any accident. Sometimes he would push him about the estate in the carrier of a bicycle of the type used by delivery boys in England.

Mannering pondered on the strange ironies of life. Who could ever imagine that the Tsar, unquestionably one of the world's richest and most influential leaders, could have such a fearful secret which must gnaw at all his triumphs and cast its sombre shadow over the most glittering party?

Time and again, when the Tsar wished his son to accompany him on some state occasion, to take part as heir to the throne, the boy would be absent, delirious with a high temperature or enduring agonising pain. His absence would always be diplomatically explained: he had influenza, a severe cold, or some other childish ailment. The secret of his disability was closely guarded by the Tsar and his staff. Spies and ambassadors knew of it, of course, but it was not in the interest of either group to spread the news. What a terrible secret to be forced to guard!

Mannering drew on his cigar and smiled reflectively. Of course, his own secret was equally bizarre. What would the Tsar or General Ormilov or Colonel Yovanovich or the smart young captain say if they knew they were discussing a deal worth tens of millions of pounds sterling not with a British citizen and friend of the English King but with the son of a Russian shoemaker?

Despite his name, his impeccable accent, his title, despite entries in reference books that explained he had been born in Grosvenor Square, London, educated at Eton and Christ Church, Oxford, and was an Honorary Colonel of Dragoons, not one of these claims was correct.

He had been knighted for what *The Times* had discreetly described as 'political and public services', but the nearest he had ever been to Eton College was when he had driven through the town on the road to Windsor. Similarly, his only acquaintance with Oxford was when he saw it on his way to Blenheim. He had never served in any army. But reference books accepted each person's own description of their life and career; such items were never checked. After all, surely no one worthy of inclusion would be so craven as to stoop to lie about their past?

159

Mannering compared the opulence of this palace with the shack in Wilkomir, Lithuania, where he had lived as a boy with his parents. To his continual but concealed contempt, his father was content to carry on his craft to the utmost of his ability, even though his earnings were pitifully small. The fact that everyone in the small town agreed he made the best and most comfortable shoes available at any price seemed sufficient reward to him. His son could not understand this. Why did the old man not want to become rich? *He* did, and began to drink heavily to conceal his irritation at living in such humble surroundings, apprenticed to his father, spending his days cutting up leather hides, sewing soles to uppers. His father never understood where he found the money for so much drinking. Neighbours complained – but never to the old man directly – that his son Haim stole things in one village and resold them in the next.

All young men were liable for military service in the Tsar's army unless they were only sons, and Haim – Mannering's first name then – had three younger brothers. He had no intention of being called up and so left home precipitately. He attached himself to a widowed and childless aunt in another town and claimed to be her only son, and so was exempt from service. Then his aunt remarried, this time a Greek. When they moved to the Greek quarter of Constantinople, Haim moved with them, but he soon left his aunt's house and took a room in a wooden house near the church of St Demetre, in Tatavla, the poorest, seediest quarter.

In this city of eight hundred Muslim mosques, he prudently kept quiet about his background. And, as always throughout his life, he attempted to be in sympathy with everyone he met. It was safer, and possibly more profitable, to make a friend than an enemy.

He ate scraps lifted from stinking dustbins in the back

yards of hotels. Sometimes, when housewives queued against the counter of a baker's shop, he would dart in and seize a roll and then run as fast as he could. Once he was caught by the baker who beat him about the head with a rolling pin until he was dizzy and weak and retched with pain and exhaustion. Thereafter, Haim was always more careful.

Haim did not live like a stray animal for long. He gravitated to the fire service, a violent group of gypsies and down-and-outs known as the *tulumbadschi*. They were volunteers because no one who could find other, safer work wanted the job of fighting fires in streets of wooden buildings. The firemen's main source of income did not come from fighting fires, however, but from causing them and then systematically looting the blazing buildings. Even this meant risk of a kind, so some preferred to accept protection money from the landlords. If the owners refused to pay, their premises burned down.

Sometimes the owners or managers fought back, and after one such incident, which for years he could scarcely bear to recall, Haim sought a new livelihood, on the docks. A sailor off an Italian ship mistook him for a brothel tout and asked the way to the nearest whore-house. Haim took him there. He went into the house first and informed the madam he had half a dozen sailors outside. What commission would she pay if he brought them in? She named a sum. He pocketed the money, showed in the sailor – and ran away.

Thereafter, he worked for several brothels, pitting one against another, threatening to take clients to rival establishments if the one with which he was dealing at that moment did not pay him sufficient commission. He was not interested in sex, either with women, men, or boys. What interested him was the thrill of the deal. This was like a drug. He did not mind how he made a profit, or even how little that profit might be. The excitement lay in making it.

The first mate of a British cargo ship sought his services and, all unknowing, set Haim on the road to fortune. The man explained he was lonely because, as a middle-aged bachelor, he had no relations left alive. Also, he believed he had contracted syphilis and, as a homosexual, he was too scared to mention this to the ship's doctor.

Haim recognised his opportunity as they sat in the mate's cabin sharing several bottles of retsina. He suggested that the man should come with him to a new brothel, just opened, where all the boys were young-limbed and fresh-faced. The mate nodded; after so many drinks, this seemed a very good idea.

He left the cabin to make water before their trip. Haim, briefly on his own, pulled open all the drawers under the man's bunk. Nothing but clothes. Quickly, he searched the cupboard, feeling in the pockets of each jacket. A fountain pen, a pocket knife, a small .38 revolver. Then, beneath the man's pillow, soiled and sweaty with hair oil, he found a British passport in the name of James Mannering. He put this under his shirt with the mate's revolver.

He led the first mate to the brothel, then asked him to wait outside for a moment while he went in to make certain arrangements. The owner here was not female but male.

'I've brought you a man who's been infecting half the boys in the city,' Haim told him bluntly. 'He's rotten with pox. And he wants to come here. I thought I'd warn you first.'

'Thank you,' said the man gratefully. He handed Haim a banknote. 'Let the bastard in, then you go out the back way.'

Haim did so. He never saw the first mate again. But

next day the body of an English sailor, fearfully mutilated about the face, his genitals crudely cut off, was
found floating in the harbour. Haim kept away from the
docks for a few days until the mate's ship sailed. So Haim
became James and had taken his first impatient step up
the long ladder to wealth, social acceptance, a knighthood. To have a man killed was not quite the same as
killing him yourself, so he assured himself. The odd
thing was, he remembered that death above all others.
This was the first man he had arranged to be killed, the
symbolic loss of his virginity. He remembered it most
clearly, just as he had heard how women, after many
lovers, would still remember the first time, when they
had totally forgotten so many others.

Once Mannering possessed a British passport, he
began to branch out into different and risky enterprises,
because now he could escape to England if he ever
needed to do so. He sold the revolver for what he thought
was a large price. This persuaded him to organise a gang
of unemployed youths to break into a gunsmith's shop.
He then sold the weapons to former members of the fire
brigade who had decided to seek easier and less dangerous ways of making money than starting fires.

When they were armed, Mannering sold other weapons to businessmen – so that they could defend themselves. Through his contacts in the brothels he met
American and European salesmen; some represented
armaments companies. For a hidden commission they
sold him rifles, revolvers, grenades. Mannering quickly
disposed of them, first to individuals, then to the Greek
military authorities. Within a few years he was rich, but
still, in his view, only operating in a local sense. He
lusted after the vast profits to be made by working on an
international scale.

Probably the most valuable lesson he had learned
was that countries, like companies, were controlled by

individuals, and all had their price. It might be in cash or kind – a pretty girl, an amenable boy, a house in another country, an honour. The bribes could change, but the bribable did not. Mannering simply had to find the price and then pay it or, to be more accurate, ensure that, all unknowingly, the country's taxpayers or the company's shareholders paid it for him.

Although acquiring his knighthood was the most important single step in Mannering's career, because it gave him a status he knew was essential if he was to become a serious player on the international stage, in retrospect it was also one of the easiest.

He had arrived in London unknown and without a single friend or acquaintance. This proved no hardship because he had brought with him names and addresses of several Levantines who operated discreet suites of chambers in Jermyn Street and the Haymarket. From time to time they had sent requests to colleagues in Constantinople to supply a girl or a boy, or some special equipment – steel-tipped thongs, leather masks, body costumes – calculated to arouse the jaded lusts of rich and elderly customers.

They had thus done considerable business with Mannering, who felt no reason to doubt that the weaknesses of men and women in Constantinople were very much different from those of clients in London. The only difference was one of social and financial degree. In the capital of the British Empire, the customers would be infinitely richer and of incalculable political power. Mannering wanted a title; that achieved, he could be accepted socially. All doors would then open to him in every country.

Mannering presented himself at the business premises of a Mr Jones whose name was as false as his own. Mrs Jones, the madam, he did not meet; Mannering dealt only with principals. He was fond of saying that any number of names could be on the billboard of a theatre or at the head of a letter; the only name that ever concerned him was the name on the cheques.

After the usual pleasantries, cups of black Turkish coffee, an exchange of Havanas and mutual compliments, Mannering broached the reason for his visit.

'I would be greatly obliged if you could give me the name of one of your most distinguished clients – royal, if possible. Someone who owes you a lot of money. In return for this introduction, I will take over his debt.'

'That is a remarkably generous thing to do,' said Jones in surprise. Such an offer hinted at Mannering's wealth, about which he had already heard rumours. He was clearly a man to humour.

Mannering shrugged and drew on his cigar. He felt no need to give an explanation.

'Since you ask for someone royal, I can tell you there is a prince of the blood who owes me personally about five thousand pounds. Now and then he pays off a little, but always he says he has introduced so many of his friends to this house that I should pay *him* a commission! It is his idea of a jest. But that may be far beyond what you wish to pay.'

'What kind of man is he?'

'The worst. What the Cockneys in this city, in their strange rhyming slang, call a Bengal Lancer – a chancer. He is a sadist, a swine, and a liar, a man without any redeeming qualities, except of course that he is closely related to royalty. Such a bond of blood carries very long credit in this country. Make no mistake of that, my friend. He could be of immense use as a friend, if he so wished, and a most vicious enemy. His influence is enormous not only in royal circles but, because he is who he is, in politics as well.'

'You make him sound just the sort of man I have in mind. How can I meet him?'

'Very easily. Tonight, in fact. He is at present in Room Seventeen engaged in despoiling some child. I suggest I invite him to share a magnum of champagne in my private suite at midnight. He will accept, if only because the drink is not on his bill. Then I will leave you two alone.'

'An excellent idea,' said Mannering approvingly. 'Now, have you a copy of Debrett so that I can find out more about this creature?'

'Of course,' replied Jones. 'But there's very little that it can tell you. He was commissioned into one of the best regiments, naturally, and served totally without distinction. Indeed, he was asked to resign after some scandal, which was hushed up. He owns immense estates in England and Scotland, a house in Grosvenor Square. He is married to a stupid, plain woman of the type aristocrats choose in this country. Face like a horse and a voice like a foghorn. Unsurprisingly, they have an idiot child of seven or eight – a boy, I think.'

'What's wrong with the boy?'

'Mainly having the prince as his father, I would guess. I have heard it said, however, that despite the prince's prodigious wealth, he is too mean to pay for some new treatment that might help his son.'

So Mannering met the prince; a person of slight stature, narrow shoulders, with protruding eyes, a weak face, a wet mouth. He drank Mr Jones's champagne greedily.

Jones introduced Mannering as a man of foreign extraction who had been of very great assistance to the British government in some highly delicate Near East political negotiations. He did not elaborate what these were, and the prince did not ask him. After a few moments, Jones left them alone.

The two men chatted briefly while Mannering poured glass after glass of champagne for the prince. He would have liked to delay broaching the matter closest to his heart until a further meeting, but he guessed that the prince's concentration was slight, and there might never be another meeting. He would like to strike now or miss his opportunity.

'I have followed your career in the army, sir, with great admiration,' he said ponderously.

'I am much obliged,' the prince replied shortly, holding out his empty glass.

'Indeed, your whole attitude has been inspiring to many people in Greece and Turkey who look on you – as, of course, on the whole royal house in this country – as examples of rectitude and upholders of the highest moral standards.'

The prince looked at him, surprised, then poured himself another glass.

'But words,' Mannering continued sonorously, 'cost nothing. I hear privately and in total confidence that, most regrettably, the owner of this establishment, who is not a man I know well or admire, claims that you owe him money. I also hear that because of your other generous charitable benefactions, it is said you feel you simply cannot afford to pay for medical treatment on your son.'

'You hear a lot,' said the prince irritably. Who exactly was this smooth-tongued fellow? What did he want?

'I hear, sir, what I hear – sometimes, as in this instance, what I do not wish to hear. I raise these matters only because I wish to pay your debts here, whether they are real or largely imagined by our host Mr Jones, and also to pay a further two thousand pounds towards any treatment your doctors may advise for your heir. I am a man of some fortune, although obviously nothing approaching Your Highness's wealth. I make these offers as a gesture of thanks and appreciation for Your Highness's fairness of mind regarding political problems affecting the two nations I have mentioned.'

'That is an exceedingly generous gesture,' said the prince, astonished at this proposal. 'And you don't even know me.'

'I hope I will have that pleasure and honour, sir.'

'How can I possibly repay this kindness?'

'By being good enough to give me the benefit of your advice,' said Mannering, being forced unwillingly to the point. He hated being rushed in any negotiations, but time was not on his side. The prince had already drunk seven or eight glasses of champagne. His speech was slurred. At any moment he might fall asleep and the opportunity Mannering sought so desperately could vanish for ever.

'I would like a commendation from you that could earn me a knighthood,' he said bluntly. 'I hasten to assure you that I do not seek this honour for myself, but simply so that I can more effectively render certain essential political services overseas to your country. I have already achieved some understandings that will in due time bring incalculable blessings in the shape of trade and treaties of friendship between Britain and other countries. Such services, as Your Highness will appreciate, cannot by their very nature be made public, so only a few in the highest counsels of the land know of them. And they, like me, are bound by a solemn oath of silence. I do not seek any pecuniary reimbursement whatever for my efforts, although I can tell you I have lavished much of my private fortune on these matters.

'What would help me immeasurably in my efforts on behalf of the British government is the honour I have mentioned. It does not carry a pension for the recipient. It is given freely to such people as the mayors of towns in England. But I can assure Your Highness that this accolade would be more valuable to Britain than a huge sum of money paid out by the government's exchequer.

'I do not ask it for myself, but for my work. Rulers and others in high authority with whom I am involved would know then that they dealt with an envoy honoured by the King of England. That knowledge would help Britain immeasurably during future negotiations, of which there will be many.'

Mannering paused, almost overcome by his own eloquence. He could see he had also impressed the prince.

'So this is the reason for your generosity, eh? I appreciate all you say, but I have to tell you that such an honour is unfortunately not in my gift. This is a matter for the Prime Minister or the sovereign.'

'You know the former well, sir. You are related to the latter. And to demonstrate my total faith in your willingness and your ability to help me, I will give you my cheque immediately. Whether you can help Britain in this way, or whether, as you most modestly claim, you cannot, makes no difference. I admire you, sir, and so I place my money where I place my opinion.'

Mannering took from his jacket pocket a chequebook, bound in crocodile skin, wrote a cheque for seven thousand pounds, handed it to the prince.

'I have made it out to Bearer,' he explained. 'That will save any embarrassment to either of us.'

The prince examined it closely.

'But you have signed it "Sir James Mannering",' he said in surprise.

'Of course. It will be honoured the moment the title is bestowed.'

And of course it was.

Mannering smiled at the recollection, and then swiftly brought his mind back into focus. Let the past deal with the past. The present was what concerned him. This business of the aircraft, for example. He could see a profit of millions in it for himself; millions. And he had still to tackle the problem of acquiring rights to those immense oil deposits on the Caspian coast. His thoughts now on the future, he watched the big Russian sailor trudge across the terrace and disappear down another set of steps beyond the giant statues, carrying on his back the puny and sickly heir to a doomed empire.

Chapter Eight

Tobin Rowlands first saw Mr da Souza's name in a small advertisement in the back of a left-wing weekly magazine, the sort of magazine he did not usually read. In fact, Tobin did not read many magazines, and would boast that he never opened a book and barely skimmed the newspapers. But these magazines of small circulation could sometimes prove useful. So now, with the advertisement in his hand, he stood outside the terraced house off Upper Street in Islington, meaning to test the truth of Mr de Souza's claim that he could advise discreetly on medical problems.

This was a low-class area, drab, dirty. Dustbins stood outside front doors. Front steps were not whitened or scrubbed, front doors went unwashed and brasswork unpolished. Indeed, this seemed an odd place to find a medical specialist, quite unlike Harley Street or Wimpole Street.

Tobin walked along the street, counting the numbers, 27, 29, 31, 33, until he found the address. He paused for a moment, irresolute. He was never one to make up his mind if indecision was an option. But now he felt this was no longer a choice; it was a luxury he could not afford. He had successfully managed to keep out of the armed services on the excuse that it was essential he remained at home to run the farms on the estate (food production was very important). In fact, he knew nothing about farming or the farms he owned. He never visited them. He did not even know just how heavily they were mortgaged, or to whom.

When tribunals clearly doubted his claim for exemption on the grounds of food production, he borrowed money against future expectations, should his mother die, and so financed a tiny engineering works. This was so small it was easily accommodated in a large wooden shed. The workforce consisted of five old men with a couple of lathes. They produced small brackets, parts of hinges and axles. As the managing director, Tobin now successfully claimed exemption from the services. But finally his number came up. He believed that the only way he could still defer it would be on medical grounds. He hoped that Mr da Souza could help him here.

He knocked on the door. A dog barked in the deep recesses of the house. He heard a bolt being pulled, a key squeak as it turned in the rusty lock. A young woman, down-at-heel, wearing a dirty blouse, a stained skirt and fluffy slippers, stood staring at him.

'Mr da Souza?' he asked her hopefully.

'You have an appointment?'

'No. I saw this advertisement.'

He handed her the piece of paper.

She nodded.

'Come in. First door on the right.'

The corridor smelled of cabbage water and stale air. He heard the dog snuffling and truffling behind a door. The walls were greasy. He went into a small room. It contained three hardbacked seats, a table with some out-of-date magazines.

'He'll be with you in a moment,' she said.

He waited. A door across the room opened.

'Come in,' said a voice.

He went into a room slightly larger, with a desk, a chair on each side of it, a cabinet painted white with frosted glass. A man sat behind the desk. He was short, fat, bald, not English; Portuguese perhaps, with that name. Did it matter?

'You wished to see me?' he asked.

'Yes,' said Tobin.

'Sit down. How can I help you?'

'I saw your advertisement offering medical advice. I am the sole support of my widowed mother. I have a younger brother and a sister. We have some farms. I am the managing director of a small engineering works doing war work.'

'And?' said Mr da Souza.

'I wish to defer being called up and I hope you can help me. You are a doctor?'

'I was,' agreed Mr da Souza. He shrugged slightly, smiled. 'I am now, shall I say, a go-between. I introduce patients – clients is perhaps a better description – to specialist physicians or surgeons who I feel are most able to help them. Sometimes they have problems or concerns they do not wish to discuss with their own general practitioners for one reason or another.'

Mr da Souza's eyes instinctively went towards the glass-fronted cabinet. He saw no reason to explain to this rather unattractive young man, with his terribly scarred face, that because of his use of instruments contained in that cabinet he had been struck off the medical register. The charge had been that he had conducted illegal operations. He could not deny they were operations, but his argument that abortions should not be illegal was a defence that had proved neither convincing nor successful.

'Now,' he said smartly. 'Do you suffer from any disease? Ever had pox?'

'No. Never.'

'Your health has always been reasonably good?'

'Yes.'

'So on what grounds can I possibly say that it is bad?'

Tobin shrugged. This was not what he had come to hear. 'If you cannot help me,' he said, 'I will go elsewhere. But I will certainly have a word with the advertisement people at that magazine. They may not wish to take your advertisement again if you cannot help a reader.'

'I will do what I can to help,' said Mr da Souza quickly. In his wretched financial situation, he could not afford to antagonise anyone, even a person of this calibre. 'Take off your jacket and shirt.'

From the drawer of his desk Mr da Souza took a stethoscope, listened to Tobin's heart, felt his pulse.

'A bit quick, but possibly you're nervous coming to see me. I could perhaps persuade someone to give you a medical certificate and exemption on the grounds that you have had rheumatic fever which has affected your heart. If you were called up, military service would almost certainly aggravate the condition. As a result you could claim a disability pension and so you would become an encumbrance on the state. I think that might make them think again.'

'How much will such a certificate cost?'

'A great deal of money,' said Mr da Souza frankly. 'The doctor to whom I will refer you might find himself in an awkward position if your case was thoroughly examined by the medical board, or if anyone challenged the diagnosis. It will cost you one thousand pounds, paid cash.'

Tobin grimaced; he had not expected such a huge fee. 'That is not a sum I carry with me,' he said.

'I don't imagine it is. But perhaps you can obtain it and bring it back, say, within the hour? Meanwhile, I will at once get on to the distinguished specialist I have in mind. Otherwise, Mr Rowlands, I fear I cannot help you.'

'I'll come back,' said Tobin.

Mr da Souza nodded, showed him to the front door. As soon as he had left, da Souza took out a folder from his desk. It contained obituaries of distinguished physicians and surgeons, cut from various newspapers and medical journals. He selected a heart specialist who had died three months earlier, checked his last address in the medical register, then went out of the house. Four doors along the street a jobbing printer ran a one-man business in his front room.

'A letterhead,' da Souza told him. 'Very quickly.'

'I've a lot on,' said the printer pointedly.

'I have five pounds to say this can take priority,' said da Souza. He showed him what he wanted – the doctor's name, his qualifications at the top of the paper, and his address, all in heavy embossed type.

'How many copies?'

'Half a dozen will do.'

'I'll do that while you wait.'

He was as good as his word. Half an hour later da Souza walked up the street waving the paper to dry the ink, then sat down in his room and wrote a note confirming that Mr Tobin Rowlands suffered from severe palpitations of the heart and was quite unfit for any kind of manual work or physical exertion. He signed the name of the dead physician and dated the letter five months earlier.

Then he sat back and waited for Tobin to arrive with his thousand pounds. Tobin was back within the hour, as he had promised. Da Souza counted out the money and handed over the letter. Tobin read it, put it in his pocket.

'I see it is backdated,' he said.

'I thought this advisable, assuming your call-up is due shortly. A time lapse on these occasions is always safest.'

'I see. I'm surprised that you got it so quickly.'

'Life, Mr Rowlands, as I have discovered, having lived

longer than you, can be full of surprises. Unfortunately, not all of them are pleasant.'

Many boys of more martial spirit than Tobin left school early, eager to join up. To wear uniform had become a kind of tribal initiation, the mark of the warrior. Some even hoped the war would not end before they could take part in it.

Aunt Hannah had a long talk with Richard about this.

'I know you want to leave school and join up,' she said, 'and I certainly won't stand in your way. But you must pass your matriculation first because, without that, after this war you will be unable to get into any good university, and I am increasingly of the opinion that the future belongs to trained people.'

'All sorts of people with no training at all, Aunt Hannah, have made great things of their lives.'

'Agreed. But possibly even if Henry Ford applied for a job at his factory door now, he would be told he wasn't qualified for a job – any job. The standards of everything, everywhere are continually rising. Louis Pasteur might be hard put to pass medical examinations to qualify him for general practice today. Progress is not simply marching on, Richard, it's running on, and you mustn't be left behind. But you've still a year before you're eighteen – quite young enough to fight for King and country. How are you going to spend this year when you leave school and before you join the army? Have you any plans for that?'

'Mr Compton suggested I might go as an apprentice to an engineering works, Beechwood Gears. One of his old pupils, a Mr Cartwright, is a director. It's quite a small factory in north London. They make gears for aircraft engines and torpedo boats. It should be interesting and also useful to me.'

'If that's what you really want, I'll do my best to help

you. You won't get much money there, only a few shillings a week probably. So I'll pay for your digs and your food.'

Richard had no idea what an engineering works would look like. He had a vague and idealised vision of all manner of earnest, dedicated scientists or mechanics, immaculate in white overalls, working at lathes, or with other complex pieces of machinery which he had seen illustrated in the magazines that had sprung up during the war to show how munitions were made, aircraft constructed, tanks built.

Reality proved to be rather different. On the outskirts of a north London suburb, surrounded by scrubby grassland sprouting weeds and thistles, with here and there an abandoned mattress or perambulator, stood three long brick sheds with saw-tooth slate roofs. Outside, in racks, were lines of bicycles and a few motorcycles, some with wickerwork sidecars.

Richard went to the main front door, pushed it open. A man sitting at a desk looked up at him. In his left lapel he wore the round badge of a discharged serviceman. Richard saw that his right sleeve was pinned to his jacket. He had lost an arm.

'What do you want, son?' he asked Richard.

'I was told to come and report to Mr Cartwright. I'm joining the company.'

'This entrance is for visitors, buyers and directors only. Employees go round to the back door, son.'

So he went round to the back door. Mr Cartwright wasn't in. The foreman seemed to have no idea who Richard was, but allotted him a nail on a wall on which he could hang his jacket.

'And don't leave anything in the pockets. It'll go otherwise. Everything bloody walks here,' said the foreman grumpily. 'Overalls over here. They may not fit you, but turn up the sleeves and trousers if they don't.

Ever worked in a factory before?'

'No, sir.'

'Now's your chance to learn.'

He gave him a lump of metal and a file.

'I want a groove filed right through that.'

'With this file?'

'With that file. What else do you want?'

'A hacksaw would be quicker.'

'So you know it all already, do you? You get filing, boy, and I'll keep coming back, to see how you're doing.'

By half past four in the afternoon Richard had filed a deep groove. His hands were raw and bleeding, his nails broken. The foreman, who had not seen him all day, now arrived to examine his progress.

'You're doing well for a starter,' he said grudgingly. 'But you can stop now. Mr Cartwright wants to see you in the office.'

Mr Cartwright was a tall, thin man with a bad cough. He was smoking a cigarette. As he smoked, he would suddenly appear to choke on the fumes. Then he would put down the cigarette and beat his chest with his left hand, coughing all the while. His face was sallow and sweaty. Richard did not need a doctor's qualifications to see why Mr Cartwright was medically unfit for the services.

'Mr Compton spoke to me about you,' Cartwright told him. 'We've got you for a year, then, have we?'

'Yes, sir.'

'What do you want to do in that time?'

'Anything except file a lump of metal all day.'

Cartwright grinned, then coughed again as though the effort was too much for him.

'The foreman always sets them off like that. Wonder he didn't tell you to go to the stores and get a left-handed hammer. He's done that before now. Mr Compton tells me you did some work with cams on a motorcycle engine. Made it go faster.'

'Yes, sir.'

'Gears we make here, not engines. They have all sorts of applications. We produce reduction gears for propellers of aircraft. Sometimes the engine crankshaft revolves too fast for the propeller, so we have to reduce its speed, otherwise the plane would never get off the ground. Same for boats. The propeller in a boat just turns round slowly, lazily, and the boat surges along. If it revolved any faster the blades would simply create a hollow tunnel in the water and the boat wouldn't move at all. So the gears can be almost as important as the engine.

'I'll put you on gears tomorrow. Meantime, you go home and wash those hands with some carbolic soap, make sure you've got no iron filings in them. They can go poisonous.'

For the next few weeks Richard filed gear teeth, polished gear wheels, learned the first steps of using a lathe. At one end of the works was the drawing office, simply a large wooden cabin about twelve feet off the ground, approached by a ladder. The walls had windows so that draughtsmen up there could see the manual workers beneath them. This prevented them from deluding themselves they were in any way divorced from activities on the shop floor.

For the previous three months the designers had all been attempting to find a solution to a problem proposed by Sir James Mannering, who Mr Cartwright always respectfully referred to as 'the principal shareholder'. And the men on the shop floor, just under their feet, had to translate their drawings into working models.

Mannering had only visited this little factory once; it was so small, so far down in his scale of important commercial enterprises that as long as it produced a reasonable profit on his original outlay he was content to leave it alone. He had bought the place in a job lot consisting of a motor car factory, a coach-builders, a producer of truck engines. He had never found the need to spend time in these unattractive and chilly sheds. These people had their jobs to do, as he had his. Their task was to make money for him; his, to make them make as much as possible. So far, profits had been small, but oak trees grew from acorns, and while understanding nothing about mechanical matters, Mannering accepted that Cartwright and his designers were probably as good as any in their field.

He had instructed Cartwright to construct the prototype of what he vaguely called a 'mechanism' to enable an aircraft gun to be fired straight ahead instead of over the side to left or right, as at present. Cartwright proposed fitting a machine-gun on a metal tripod in front of the pilot's cockpit, high enough to fire above the propeller. But this upset the balance of the aircraft, making it difficult to manoeuvre and top-heavy to land. Beechwood's designers had worked unsuccessfully on other solutions. Now Mannering's male secretary, Frederick Batting, arrived to assess their progress.

'I know the problems involved,' Batting admitted, 'and so does Sir James. But he feels that it is within your capabilities to produce what is required. I need hardly stress its importance, and not only for the war effort.'

'What do you mean?'

'Well, Sir James is not impressed with the profit margin Beechwood Gears shows. It is not exciting. And he likes exciting enterprises.'

'Then why did he buy this business in the first place?'

'I don't think he realised he had bought it. It came with other companies of greater profitability, as you may know.'

There had been rumours that the original owner, who had built up these companies himself, had hoped to

180

create a wholly self-sufficient engineering group, making engines and gear boxes and coachwork, all for cars and trucks. But somewhere, somehow, something had gone wrong. Cartwright had heard he had then been forced to sell, not by the banks, but by the principal shareholder, who had threatened him in some way – Cartwright did not know how. But the man was ruined and had taken his own life.

This was an ugly story, but it gave Mr Cartwright strong reason to agree to whatever Mannering decreed.

'Will you stay for a cup of tea or coffee?' Cartwright now asked the secretary.

'Thank you, but no. I have a car waiting, and Sir James is leaving for France as soon as I return to his house in London. I bid you good day.'

Cartwright watched Batting go and then sat down again in his office. He could see no solution to the problem, except possibly using a hollow axle for the propeller so that the gun fired through it as through a tunnel. But that would be extremely difficult, and presented problems which he believed would be insoluble for a company of their resources. And his three designers, all middle-aged men, either too old or unfit for active service, had run out of ideas.

After some months on the shop floor, Richard graduated to the drawing office. He was fascinated by the drawing boards with huge squares of paper pinned to them, by slide rules, and electric lights on long swivelling arms that lit up even the roughest sketches.

At first, his work was limited to sharpening pencils, seeing eraser rubbers were clean, and that there was always a stock of drawing paper on the shelves. But he soon saw what the older men were working on, and sometimes stood looking over their shoulders at their sketches and plans.

'Got any ideas for this new project?' Cartwright asked him flippantly.

'I have the basics of an idea, sir, yes.'

'You reckon you can succeed where these trained designers fail?'

'I don't say that, sir. But if I could have a book of logarithms, and a corner where I could work on my own, I will put my ideas on paper.'

Cartwright looked at him sharply. 'Are you serious?' How the devil could this young fellow come up with something when these designers were still struggling without apparently any hope of a solution?

'I am serious, sir.'

'Right. Have all the paper you want and the pencils. There's an empty table in the corner with a chair. Get to work, boy. And if you succeed, you'll earn a bonus of fifty pounds.'

'Fifty *pounds*, sir? That's a fortune.'

'You have to succeed first, though. And that will not be easy.'

As Richard sat down he remembered Mr Compton's opinion that science is simply a series of experiments, one leads on to another, and the Chinese proverb about even the longest journey starting with a single step.

Richard had barely made one step in science; he knew that. But the lessons of the steam engine and the motorcycle engine stuck in his mind. For several days he sat sketching cams and cog wheels, and all the while his mind worked round the problem, as a sheepdog walks round a flock of sheep and finally herds them all into the direction the shepherd requires. At last, one evening, he sensed he had an answer. Next morning he asked to see Mr Cartwright.

'I think I've found the solution, sir,' he said.

'Well, let's hear it.'

'When I worked on the motorcycle engine, I started

from the basis that when the piston reaches the top of its stroke, it must stop before it goes down again.'

'That's pretty obvious,' said Cartwright, coughing. 'But what's your answer to our problem?'

'Working from that original premise, sir, I knew the cams must also stop turning for a fraction of a second. The interruption is so brief it probably can't be recorded. The engine keeps on running without any sign of these pauses.'

'I see all that. But how does that help us?'

'Since the propeller of the aircraft is rotated by a petrol engine which has pistons that stop, there must also be a moment when the propeller blades are stationary as well. What we do, sir, is to devise a system of gearing so that when the pilot presses the trigger of his machine-gun, an overriding gear mechanism refuses to allow the gun to fire when the blades are passing in front of the barrel. It will only fire between the blades. Since the propeller has two blades, this means that twice in each revolution there is an angle of one hundred and eighty degrees in which it will be safe to fire.'

Cartwright was roughing out the head of a horse on his blotting paper. He added big eyes and eyelashes. Then he looked up.

'You're right,' he said slowly, coughing again. Worry always made his breathing problems worse. 'Have you thought about the gearing?'

'I've done more than that. I've worked it all out here.' He handed over several sheets of paper.

Cartwright glanced at them, nodded. 'I'll get the design team working on this at once,' he said.

Mannering sat well back on the rear seat of his Silver Ghost. On a tip-up seat facing him to one side, because he would never allow any subordinate to sit close to him, rode his male secretary. Batting kept his gaze on the brocaded seat next to his master. He did not like to meet Mannering's eyes. Almost no one did. There was something cruel and magnetic in them. Batting felt he could be looking into the recesses of a terrible and tortured mind.

That morning he had received a telephone call from Cartwright who reported a 'preliminary breakthrough' in the design of the firing mechanism.

So now they were driving north up the Edgware Road to the factory, past music halls and rows of shabby houses, past trams and huge advertisements for Oxo and Bovril, and patriotic exhortations, 'Your King and Country Need You'. It was an indication of the importance Mannering attached to the mechanism that he should personally take the trouble to inspect the design.

Batting had been on many journeys with his master, and he found none of them to his liking. He wondered how long it would be before he could go home to his semi-detached house off Streatham High Street. His wife had not been well recently. Her mother was staying with them because their maid and the daily nurse who looked after their two small children had both left to become bus conductresses.

The car swept in over the rough ground, stopped outside the front doors of the Beechwood factory. The one-armed commissionaire came down the steps, saluting smartly with his good hand. A muscular footman, in fact Mannering's personal bodyguard who travelled up front with the chauffeur, held open the car door. Mannering stepped out. Batting followed him. Cartwright greeted them on the top step. He was chewing a menthol sweet to try and control his coughing.

'I'm very glad indeed you could come, sir,' he said obsequiously. 'I think we have something that will interest you.'

'I understand you have found a solution to the problem.'

'I believe so, sir.'

'You did that quickly, after my last memorandum.'

'I put the full design staff to work on it.'

'You have a model made up?'

'Not yet, sir.'

'So. What have you got to show me?'

'Drawings.'

'Let me see them.'

They went into Cartwright's office. The three designers stood nervously against the wall. They had heard much about their principal shareholder, had read about him in newspapers. Now they were standing only feet away from the legendary figure, so close they could admire the cut of his expensive suit, the high polish on his handmade lizard-skin shoes, the peculiar way in which his goatee beard was trimmed and, above all, they could see his piercing, uneasy eyes. They shifted nervously in their ready-made clothes; face to face with ruthless power they felt robbed of speech.

'Which of you solved the problem?' asked Mannering, eyeing them.

'He's not here, sir,' Cartwright replied.

'Get him here. He is the man I want to meet.'

One of the designers went out, returned with Richard.

'This is Richard Rowlands, sir, our newest recruit,' said Cartwright.

'Tell me your solution,' Mannering commanded Richard. He did not shake Richard's hand or offer him a greeting. Richard picked up the nearest drawing.

'This toothed wheel, sir,' he began, 'represents the fly-wheel of the engine. This smaller wheel engages with it constantly. Taking advantage of the fact that with a two-bladed propeller you have two half circles when it is safe for a bullet to be fired, these gears on this other page calculate when those moments are.'

'How do you know it will work?'

'It must do. It is a law of physics. The engine causes the propeller to revolve, and since for each stroke of the pistons in the engine there is an infinitesimal amount of time when they are static, the propeller must pause proportionately, although apparently rotating at a constant speed. In these pauses, a gun can fire safely.'

'I see,' said Mannering. He turned to Cartwright. 'Give this young man the bonus. You have my authority to spend whatever is needed to get these drawings into the shape of metal. But speed is of the essence. This invention could revolutionise war in the air.'

He turned again to Richard.

'Rowlands,' he said, and paused. His mind scanned the files of memory.

'Ah, yes,' he said at last. 'Are you any relation of the Mr Rowlands who was killed in a road accident in Paris just before the war?'

'He was my father, sir. Did you know him?'

'No. I did not have that pleasure. But I remember reading about the accident in the papers.' Mannering paused, looking at the young man. 'You have a brother and a sister, I believe,' he went on.

'Yes, sir,' said Richard, surprised and rather puzzled by Mannering's knowledge of his family. 'My sister is in the Voluntary Aid Detachment. My brother, unfortunately, has been declared unfit for the services.'

'I'm sorry to hear that. I know how every young man today wishes to bear arms against the enemy. And your mother?'

'She has not been too well, sir. After my father's death, we had financial problems. I think they affected her health.'

Mannering nodded sympathetically. He turned back

to Cartwright, glancing briefly at his gold watch.

'I have an appointment with the Prime Minister within the hour,' he said. 'He will be pleased to hear of your success. You must treat this design with total and absolute secrecy, and patent it immediately.'

'Then everyone in the patent office will know, sir.'

'Only if you patent it as a means of firing a gun,' said Mannering testily. 'Patent it as something else. All you need to describe are the ratios of the gears, the number of teeth on the wheels and so on. You don't mention a gun. This could be a mechanical means of ringing church bells in a peal, anything. Use your imagination. The young fellow did who invented it. Now, I must be away.'

Mannering walked down the steps to his car. The idea of these gears was very simple and ingenious. But then all good ideas were. Years ago, the idea of a submarine had been very simple, too. And he had made more money out of submarines than out of almost anything else. He smiled at the recollection.

As a young man on the docks at Constantinople, he had often seen how young pickpockets and petty thieves escaped their pursuers. They would simply dive into the harbour and, once submerged, use a metal tube to breathe while they swam off underwater. Mannering sensed that some application of this technique could prove profitable to him. In what little free time he allowed himself, he found out more about navigation beneath the surface of the sea.

He discovered that in the sixteenth century attempts had been made to construct a boat to be rowed under water. In the American Civil War, a more sophisticated submarine had been built, but sank on her first outing. Then a British company produced a vessel shaped like a torpedo, with bow and stern flattened like the tail of a fish. They called her an underwater warship. She could submerge by opening a valve to let in water, and then two vertical screws, set into the base of the vessel, would revolve and draw her down to the desired depth, when a third propeller could push her forwards or backwards.

The British Admiralty admitted that tests were successful but declined to proceed further for the extraordinary reason that if another country heard of this project, then the supremacy and safety of the British fleet could be jeopardised.

Mannering had his own ideas for selling the submarine elsewhere if the British were not interested. He approached the company, who gave him authority to negotiate any sales he could in the Near East, an arrangement that cost the company nothing. Mannering had a model submarine made and took this to Athens. Through his contacts in the brothels, he met a senior officer of the Greek Admiralty, and described the submarine to him.

'What use is that to us?' the officer asked him.

'My dear sir,' replied Mannering gravely. 'Just one of these undersea vessels would give Greece total supremacy over the entire Turkish navy, which at present is a constant threat to the freedom of Greece.'

After tests of Mannering's model, the Greek navy purchased one submarine for cash – on condition the deal was kept secret.

Mannering then travelled to Constantinople and explained to the Turkish Admiralty how he had learned that the Greeks were buying a revolutionary submarine warship to use against the Turks. He proposed that the Turkish Admiralty should buy at least two, to counter this gross and unwarranted threat to their national sovereignty.

From then on, he sold submarines all round the world, at a steadily increasing commission.

He would make more out of this new invention, though, much more. He already had three clients in mind: Britain, Russia, and Germany. He had never found it necessary to change his early policy of selling to both sides. He travelled on several passports, and each country naively believed he was really working exclusively in their interests.

'What did you make of the young fellow?' he asked his secretary as he sat back in his seat.

'A very keen youngster, sir.'

'Of course he's very keen. But odd about him being Rowlands' son.'

'Odd, sir?'

'Unusual, shall I say. The son of a wealthy man killed in a ridiculous accident in Paris.'

'Oh yes, sir, that is odd.' What was the man on about? wondered Batting. It wasn't like his master to ramble.

'Tell me,' Mannering went on, looking out of the plate-glass window as the car gathered speed. 'Have you ever been in love?'

'In love, sir? I'm married.'

'Ah, yes. Of course.'

Just for a moment, Mannering's hard, lined face relaxed. Batting, watching him carefully under prudently lowered lids, could imagine he had been handsome once as a young man, and attractive to women. But was there any one woman who had ever attracted him more than the others? And was he capable of giving any affection in return if there had been?

The three designers followed Richard out of Cartwright's office. Back in their little drawing office, the senior of the three found he was perspiring. He had a wife and three young children to support, and the prospect of meeting the principal shareholder had filled him with awe and concern.

'Wouldn't want to deal with that customer,' he remarked with feeling.

'No,' Richard agreed. 'There's something sinister, almost evil, about him.'

'You should talk, he's giving you fifty quid.'

'I'm not keeping it,' Richard replied. 'That design was a team effort. I intend to split it four ways with you.'

'I'll believe that when I see it,' said the oldest designer dismissively.

When Richard received the money, in sovereigns, he shared it out at once. Two designers were surprised he had kept his word; surprised but grateful. The third followed him out to the factory door as though he had something to say he did not wish the others to hear. On the steps he turned and faced Richard.

'D'you know a Mr Grover?' he asked him bluntly.

'Mr Grover?'

Richard shook his head – and then nodded as he remembered.

'A Mr Grover worked for my parents,' he said. He did not want to add that he had been the butler; he sensed that this might embarrass the designer. No one else in the factory was likely to have employed a butler.

'I thought so. He's my cousin. Now he's retired. Not the same, he says. Do you know what he liked most about working for your father? The interesting people who came to call or to stay. He's a dab hand with a pencil, is George, and he'd draw them all, the rich, the famous, the not so famous. With more schooling he could have been a much better draughtsman than me, but his mother was widowed and he had to take whatever job he could. I was luckier. I went to night school and then came here.

'I told him about your promise to split the money and he asked your name. That's when he told me he'd worked for the family. Know what he said? You're a gent, he said. So I knew you'd keep your word, whatever my colleagues thought. My cousin is never wrong about people. Never.'

Chapter Nine

Carola had an attic room in Lady Warren's house, with a bed and small table, a washbasin, a cupboard and a coal fire which a maid lit at six o'clock each morning. After living in a caravan with her father and then sharing a cramped room with Isobel in the Campions' house, this was luxury. Richard's toy steam engine stood on the table; it was the only ornament in the room.

She had never realised before how pleasant it was to go to bed by the warmth of a fire, and then to lie in bed seeing pictures in its red embers – castles, caverns, whole cities of flame, which slowly vanished as the fire went out. One day she would visit real cities, stranger than anything she could imagine; and she would fly to them in her own aircraft.

Lady Warren gave her the use of a bicycle to travel to the munitions factory every morning, a big, old-fashioned machine stamped 'Special Ladies' Model'. Whether this was intended for special ladies or was a special model for ladies was not clear. The rear mud-guard had a number of holes punched in it on either side. Through these were threaded black and red cords down to the hub to form a fan-shaped guard to prevent long skirts being trapped in the spokes or the chain.

One Friday, Carola saw Richard for the first time since they said goodbye in the lane outside the fairground, nearly four years previously.

The munitions factory maintained a Ford Model-T van to transport some of their lighter products. The Ford was a high, thin vehicle with spidery wheels and an engine that beat so strongly, even when only ticking over, that the whole vehicle trembled as though it might shake itself to pieces. A woman named Betty was employed as driver and she usually took a companion in the cab to help her unload boxes of ammunition and small arms cartridges.

Betty deliberately selected the prettiest girl she could find to ride with her on these journeys; the men in the factories or on the firing ranges to which they had to deliver their products were always willing to help a pretty girl offload the deliveries.

On this particular morning, however, Betty's usual helper was away; her only brother had been reported missing, feared killed. Going along the line of workers at the benches to select someone in her place, Betty caught sight of Carola.

'You there,' she said brusquely. 'I want you to come and help unload a special job we've got to take to a factory in north London. The forewoman said I can have anyone, and you look as though you've got your wits about you.'

Carola followed her out of the factory. It was a sunny day, and a pleasure to escape from routine work. In the distance, they could hear the boom of guns and a rattle of rifle fire from army practice ranges. It seemed extraordinary to think that while these troops were firing at wooden targets, across the Channel other young men of their age were attempting to kill each other across acres of mud, decomposing bodies and barbed wire.

The van had been loaded the previous evening. Betty marched to the radiator and gripped the starting handle.

'When I swing, you turn on that switch on the dash,' she said. 'The one near the steering column.'

Carola did as she was told. The engine fired obediently. Betty climbed up alongside her. The Ford did not have a windscreen and the drive was therefore much colder than Carola had expected. The fastest she had ever driven before was on the traction engine, about four miles an hour. The Ford could do forty, so Betty assured her proudly.

They drove past fields, where the harvest was being collected. Horses stood patiently in the shafts as the harvesters stacked the carts with corn and grain. They came into larger villages, north of London, then joined the Edgware Road, busy with buses, a few private cars, and horses and carts. Betty turned off the road and stopped outside a building set in several acres of waste land.

'I'll just go and check,' she said. 'You wait here.'

Carola climbed out of the truck with her and stood, eyes closed, feeling the sun on her face. It seemed unusually warm and pleasant and somehow unreal to be standing there while her colleagues were working in a stuffy factory. And now even more bizarre to imagine those young men killing each other across the Channel.

She heard someone call her name, a voice she recognised.

She opened her eyes, blinking in the glare of sunshine. Then she saw Richard running towards her.

'What on earth are you doing here?' he asked in surprise.

'Delivering some stuff to this factory. Why are *you* here?'

'I work here. I'm in the drawing office.'

'The drawing office?'

'Yes. Helping to design things.'

Carola was interested and impressed.

'What sort of things?' she asked him.

'Oh, gears. That sort of thing.'

'That's quick promotion, isn't it?'

'Maybe I was lucky,' he said modestly. 'And there isn't much competition with so many men in the services. And you?'

'Oh, I worked as a maid for a bit. Didn't like it, so I left and got a job in a munitions factory.'

'What are you delivering here?' he asked.

'Belts of machine-gun bullets.'

'Ah, we're going to test something I've had a hand in,' Richard said with satisfaction. 'Like to watch?'

'Can I?'

'Don't see why not. You're delivering the cartridges. Without you, there wouldn't be any test.'

'But why didn't you write?'

'I did.'

'I never had any letters.'

'Perhaps someone else took them, or never forwarded them on.'

Richard was going to say more, when Betty appeared with two middle-aged men wearing dungarees.

'All the stuff is in the back,' she told them. 'If you could take it out for me, I'd be much obliged.'

'We want it round behind the building, on the range,' added Richard.

The two men nodded. They each picked up a belt of ammunition, which was wrapped in a loose sack, and carried it behind the factory. Richard carried a third, and Betty and Carola the fourth between them. They were far heavier than she had imagined. She was glad to put it down on the trodden earth.

Here, under a corrugated iron roof, a crude shelter without walls, stood the fuselage of an aircraft. It lacked wings and had chocks in front of and behind its wheels. The engine and a two-bladed propeller were still in position. Several ropes stretched tightly over the body and were tied to stakes hammered into the ground.

'That's to stop the slipstream from the propeller moving the fuselage,' Richard explained.

Carola nodded, wondering what she was about to see. Facing the aircraft, ten yards away, was a concrete wall two feet thick and curved slightly inwards at each end.

'We will fire into that,' Richard explained. 'So keep well out of the way in case there's a ricochet.'

Mr Cartwright came out of the factory with two draughtsmen and a visitor wearing a dark suit, smarter than all the others – Mannering's secretary.

A little behind them stood a younger, taller man. He wore a khaki uniform with the pilot's badge of wings over the left breast pocket above the blue and white ribbon of the Military Cross. He was smoking a cigarette.

In the manner of fighter pilots, he had removed the wire rim from inside his peaked cap so that the edges flopped down casually on either side. He had a buccaneering air about him; very blue eyes, blond hair, a blond moustache. Uncharacteristically for an officer – he wore the three stars of a captain on his sleeve – his shirt collar was slightly loosened and his tie knot hung down half an inch. He looked as though he had just come from a fun party somewhere and was keen to return as soon as possible. He was clearly not awed by his companions, or particularly interested in them.

'Hullo, sports,' he greeted Carola and Richard in a twanging, nasal, unfamiliar accent.

'This is Captain Tom Gardener,' Cartwright explained importantly. 'He's Australian, over here in the Air Force. He's going to test the gun. I may tell you he's already shot down in combat five enemy aircraft using the very indifferent weapons with which our fighter planes are at present fitted. If these tests are successful, I reckon he can double that score, maybe treble it.'

'No problem,' agreed Gardener laconically. 'Well, when do we start?'

Richard and one of the designers began to feed the canvas belts of shiny polished cartridges into one side of a machine-gun that was mounted on four short metal legs just ahead of the windscreen of the cockpit.

'Ready when you are,' said Gardener. Clearly, he was not a man who cared to be kept waiting.

'We're ready now,' Cartwright replied, and coughed nervously.

Gardener winked at the two girls.

Someone brought out a wooden box. Gardener stood on it, put one foot into a slot cut in the side of the plane and heaved himself up into the cockpit with the ease of long practice. He sat, familiarising himself with the controls.

'Don't reckon we're going to fly very far without wings,' he said. 'Kiwi. The wingless bird.'

'Stand back everyone,' said Cartwright. 'There may be a blowback from these bullets, and we don't want anyone hit. This is for causing casualties to the enemy, not to us.'

Richard stood in front of the aircraft, both hands on the propeller blade which was horizontal to the ground.

'Contact,' called Gardener, and threw the ignition switch. Richard put all his weight on the propeller. It came down spongily, reluctantly, against compression. He released his hands. The blade swung back immediately into its first position.

'Put some beef in it, boy,' called Gardener. 'You wouldn't make out in The Outback with a pull like that. Wouldn't go down well with the girls back home, I can tell you.'

'You keep your mind on your job,' retorted Richard. The propeller was more difficult to turn than he had anticipated.

He swung it now with more force. The engine fluttered, fired, began to run.

198

'Warm the engine first,' shouted Cartwright against the roar and smoke of the unsilenced exhaust pipes.

Gardener raised his right hand in a half salute to show he had heard and understood.

The wingless plane began to strain against the holding ropes as though, even without wings, it would be up and away. Wind from the spinning propeller flattened the grass around the building. Gardener turned enquiringly to Cartwright. He nodded, raised one hand and then dropped it smartly.

Gardener stared ahead for a moment through the whirling blades. Only feet away he could see the rough texture of the concrete wall, but he imagined he was up in the blue sky, where an enemy waited just out of the sun.

He had found them so often like this, and sometimes they had found him. But always he had either shot them down or escaped; either way, he had been victorious. He had survived where others had not, and survival was itself victory of a kind.

The roar of any aircraft engine, the smell of hot oil and high-octane petrol always gave him a curious feeling of fear. One day, he could be caught up there. One day, someone he had not seen could come right out of the sun at him. He might be blinded by the glare and, too late, he would feel the splintering hail of bullets on thin metal, the crack of glass, and then the unbearable agony of violent death at high altitude.

He had seen cockpits in crashed planes literally drenched in blood, their screens spattered black with oil from a stalled engine. It was the luck of the game, so you told yourself. Like Russian roulette, your luck depended on so many things; the other man's engine faltering, his gun jamming – or yours.

At least with this new mechanism he should have more chance of survival. He wet his lips, opened the throttle to its maximum. He'd give these bastards the hardest test he could. It was no good just having a soft test, with the engine ticking over. Give it the gun.

When the noise of the engine and the scream of the spinning propeller, amplified by the wall, became almost unbearable, he squeezed the trigger. The whole aircraft trembled with the recoil of a fusillade.

The belt of cartridges whipped through the breech. Bullets produced a hot spray of concrete dust from the wall. He released pressure on the trigger and saw that the bullets had gouged a wide, deep scar in the wall. A second burst blew a hole through it. Again, he removed his finger from the trigger. At this rate of fire he might kill anyone who happened to be on the other side of the wall.

He saw Cartwright waving to him, grinning excitedly. He looked around; the others were clapping. He cut the engine. The propeller slowed, stopped, jerked backwards. A wisp of smoke blew out from the exhausts. The air hung heavy with the smell of cordite and carbon monoxide fumes.

'All right for you, sport?' he asked Cartwright.

'More than all right. Perfect,' Cartwright told him. 'It has been totally successful. You're the first man to fire through the blades of a turning propeller in an aircraft and not shoot them to bits.'

'This calls for some sort of celebration, then,' said Gardener. 'Aren't you going to introduce me to these pretty girls?'

'I'm afraid I don't know their names,' Cartwright explained. 'They just brought the cartridge belts from the munitions factory.'

'I'll introduce myself then, since you Poms don't have any manners. Tom Gardener from Perth, Western Australia. And looking forward to getting back there.'

'Carola Marsh,' said Carola.

'And you, ma'am?'

'Betty Morris,' said the driver.

'Good on you both. You brought these belts over here yourselves, driving that van? Wonder they let pretty girls out on their own to do that over here. Wouldn't do at all in Australia, you know. That's a man's country, where men are men, and the women are darn glad of it.'

'We've no alcohol on the premises,' said Cartwright, 'but if you'd care to come in and have some tea or coffee, you'd be welcome, Captain Gardener.'

'Why not? I'd rather have something a bit stronger, I admit, but never refuse a good offer is as good a motto as any I've heard.'

'If you will excuse me, Mr Cartwright,' said Batting with the air of someone who did not care whether Cartwright excused him or not, 'I have to get back to London. I will give the principal shareholder a full report of this demonstration.'

'Please tell him that now we have the ability to fire one machine-gun through the propeller, we'll work on modifications that will allow us to mount two machine-guns, side by side, and so double the fire power.'

Batting inclined his head but did not reply.

The others went through the factory into the office, and stood there awkwardly; Cartwright was not a natural host. Someone bustled off to make tea. They drank it out of mugs without saucers. Richard stood close to Carola.

'What time do you get off tonight?' he asked her.

'About seven.'

'Where are you living now?'

'Near Elstree village.'

'I've got digs near there,' he told her. 'Hendon. Let's meet. I've got a bike.'

'So have I. Where shall we meet?'

'There's an inn just outside Elstree, the Battleaxes.

I'll be there around half past seven, if you can make that.'

'I'm not going into a public house on my own,' said Carola firmly. She had heard from other girls in the factory what happened if soldiers were already drinking at the bar. They assumed that any girl on her own was a tart. They either made a quick, crude pass at her, or told her sharply, and often unpleasantly, to get out. A bar was a man's place, not for women on their own. She could imagine Captain Gardener taking that view, from what he said. But somehow, coming from him, the prospect did not seem so offensive; indeed, it could almost be a reasonable response.

'I'll see you outside the Battleaxes then,' Richard told her.

As Mannering grew richer, he developed an increasing and eventually insatiable curiosity about the lives of other rich men. He subscribed to an agency that supplied articles from newspapers and magazines around the world detailing the steps that had brought such men from obscurity to international wealth.

In most cases he found, unsurprisingly, that the subjects had inherited money. As one admitted, with rare candour, 'It is easier to make a million pounds when you inherit nine hundred thousand than to make a million if you start out in a doss house.'

Mannering had not even started his journey from a doss house; he had begun on the streets.

In the case of those who had not inherited their wealth, he noted that their accounts contained one common denominator: a gap in the chronology of their climb to riches. Usually this was covered by some such phrase as, 'After I had made my first hundred thousand dollars, I decided to diversify.' This, too, was perhaps unsurprising. Certainly, if he ever wrote the story of his life, the chronology would be incomplete. One incident in particular still haunted him.

As a member of the *tulumbadshi* in Constantinople, he had helped to burn down a bank building because the bank's directors had unwisely not paid their protection money. Unexpectedly, the bank manager had still been in his office, working late after the bank was closed.

Mannering and half a dozen others heard his shouts for help and went in, ostensibly to rescue him, actually to kill him in case he had seen the cans of petrol that they had secreted in various parts of the building. The manager was a tough old Greek, and recognised them all.

'You bastards!' he shouted furiously. 'You bastards!'

They came at him then with sticks and clubs. He seized a wooden stool to defend himself. Just beyond him, Mannering could see the safe, keys in the lock. There would be a fortune in notes inside – but first they had to be rid of this one witness.

Mannering struck the manager viciously in the face. The man staggered, dazed and bleeding, but suddenly, using one long leg of the stool as a lance, he ran at Mannering.

The leg gouged him in the groin. Mannering went down, screaming in pain. The manager overbalanced, and Mannering's companions instantly clubbed him to death. Mannering crawled away on hands and knees, like a wounded beast, his whole body in agony, his trousers red with blood. But even in the extremity of his anguish he remembered the money.

'The safe!' he cried weakly. 'Open it up!'

Others had already done so and were removing canvas bags of coin, metal boxes of notes. Then Mannering lost consciousness. When he awoke, he was lying on the pavement outside the building. The flames had subsided. He looked round at his colleagues.

'We'll get you to a doctor,' one promised him.

They broke off a side door and, using this as a stretcher, ran with him through the streets. The doctor, who usually confined his duties to examining prostitutes, and sometimes their clients, for pox, cut away Mannering's trousers, his shirt and looked closely at the terrible wound.

'Another inch and you'd have lost your balls,' he said bluntly.

'But am I all right?' Mannering asked him weakly.

'You'll live. I'll give you some ointment and bind you up. Keep out of circulation for a couple of weeks.'

Mannering holed up in his lodgings. One of his colleagues brought him a bag of coins, a tin box of notes. This was only a fraction of what he felt was his. But a fraction was better than nothing.

The pain took weeks to subside, and never completely left him. Every time he moved his body, spasms like hot and sharpened knives darted cruelly up his spine, down his legs, to his testicles. When he could walk, he found all lust had left him. He would stroke his phallus, trying to provoke it into some kind of erection, to make it stand up for itself, the lance of manhood, but without any result. The doctor shrugged his shoulders when he limped back to his surgery to tell him.

'You're lucky to be left with what you've got,' he said sourly. Mannering had not paid him, and by his guess was unlikely to do so. His concern was for those who did.

Mannering guessed his thoughts, took out a large denomination bank note, pushed this across the doctor's desk.

'For your trouble,' he said. 'Now can you help me?'

'No,' the doctor told him. 'No one can. You've got all your organs, but they're not connected. Nerves have been severed, and goodness knows what else. I can't look inside your body and tell you. There's this new X-ray apparatus that can see inside, but we haven't got one here. When you've made more money, go to Paris or Berlin. Maybe doctors there can help you.'

In time, Mannering went to Paris, to Berlin, to London to visit doctors in hospitals, clinics, private consulting rooms. All demanded huge fees for their opinions, which were always the same: they could do nothing.

'You will never be able to procreate,' one of them said. 'Nor will you ever be able to sustain even a modest erection. That is the bad news. But there is another more positive side to this condition. You will not know the pangs of desire, of lust. And many people I see would be pleased to be free of such distractions.'

'I am not many people,' Mannering replied shortly. 'You mean that I shall be permanently impotent? A eunuch?'

'Outwardly, no. But inwardly, yes. You will, however, be spared the agony of many eunuchs who want but can never possess and are unable to relieve the mounting tensions in their bodies. You will have no such feelings.'

Always a solitary person, the knowledge of his impotence increased Mannering's dislike of meeting people, especially women. He tended to avoid social gatherings and began to live life at second hand, one remove from reality, through written reports and photographs. And in this way he discovered a photograph of a woman who he felt embodied all the feminine virtues. This discovery was his secret to be guarded with the closeness of a lover.

His London house in Grosvenor Square possessed a huge hall, two drawing rooms, a library, a study, a billiard room. In the basement was a swimming pool, decorated with mosaics and Greek pillars. And high up, hidden among bedrooms, bathrooms and dressing rooms on the third floor, was the most secret room in the house, to which Mannering alone held the keys, and which no one else entered.

He had three keys to fit three locks on its door, which was lined with steel plate. He accepted that a servant could easily appropriate one key, an accomplice perhaps a second, but day or night, even in his bath, the third never left a metal bracelet on his wrist.

The room had one very small window, set high up, designed for ventilation rather than light, and it contained a minimum of furniture: a table at one end, and a chair. On the table stood a German slide projector.

Mannering would sit in the chair, drawing on his cigar, holding a switch attached by a cable to the projector. The far wall, painted white, served as a screen.

Mannering would stare at the larger-than-life images projected onto the wall, feasting his eyes on the woman's face, body, imagining it naked beneath her white formal blouse, her dark skirt. He would press the button a second time and another picture flashed on the screen. The woman again. A third, a fourth, a fifth picture of her followed; all taken from magazines, or bought from society photographers.

The cooling fan of the projector hummed, and gradually the air in the little room would grow unpleasantly warm from the heat of the giant bulb. Mannering never paid any attention to this. In his thoughts he was miles away, with her, dancing, in a yacht, lying naked with her, on her, beneath her, in her. And yet he was nowhere. He was a lonely man alone in a darkened room, in love with an illusion, a one-dimensional slide of a woman he had never met.

This was his secret. More, this was his secret hell. As always when he saw her photographs, he remembered the steps by which he had grown rich and the price he had paid.

He sat now in this room, alone with his dreams and his bitterness. Eventually, the warmth made him sleepy. He shook himself awake, switched off the projector, went out into the corridor, carefully turning the keys in the three locks behind him. Downstairs in his study the butler was waiting for him.

'Your secretary has returned, sir,' he said.

'Where is he?'

'In his work room.'

'Send him in.'

Mannering glanced pointedly at his gold pocket watch as Batting came in.

'You've been a long time,' he said accusingly, although in fact he had not expected him back so soon. But he knew nothing surpassed a touch of firmness to sharpen up subordinates and keep them keen and anxious to please.

'I was as quick as I could be, Sir James,' Batting replied apologetically. 'When I got out to the factory, the truck with the ammunition still hadn't arrived, so we had to wait for that. Then the gun had to be loaded, the aircraft engine started and warmed up before this Australian pilot could fire it.'

'How was the test?' Mannering asked impatiently.

'Totally successful. The pilot fired two bursts, a hundred rounds in each, and the propeller was untouched. There was not a scratch on its blades, not even a mark on the varnish to show that so many bullets had passed between them. Quite amazing. The pilot raced the engine, so it wasn't just ticking over. He gave it full throttle, to make the test as difficult as possible. An astonishing demonstration. It impressed him greatly, as it did all of us. And now Mr Cartwright is working on plans to fit two machine-guns instead of just one.'

'Good. And what happened then?

'They had a cup of tea to celebrate.'

'You didn't stay with them?'

'No, sir. I came back here as quick as I could. I knew you'd be wanting my report.'

'You are absolutely certain there was no chicanery, no faking? They weren't blanks the pilot was firing?'

'Of course they weren't blanks, sir. There were spent cartridges all over the place afterwards and the concrete wall he fired at had a hole driven through it.'

'Good. Let me have a written report as soon as possible.' He nodded a dismissal, pressed a button. A manservant entered the room.

'Tell the chauffeur I want the small car at the front of the house in five minutes.'

For journeys on which he wished to remain as anonymous as possible, Mannering maintained two small and inconspicuous cars, a Star and an Austin. He walked down the front steps and climbed into the back seat of the Austin. In his tweed suit and light raincoat, a soft hat on his head, he did not appear different from any other man of his age being driven to some business appointment. No one would guess he was a man of power and wealth. Once inside the car, he put on a pair of spectacles with heavy tortoiseshell frames, although he enjoyed perfect eyesight.

'My barber,' he told the driver.

'Very good, sir.'

They drove west along the Bayswater Road. Several riders were gently exercising their horses in the park. Cars moved along the inner road, and uniformed nursemaids in twos and threes pushed prams, chatting busily to each other. Mannering's car turned off the Bayswater Road into a side street, slowed as it passed a barber's shop, and stopped round the next corner.

The barber's shop had a faded blue and red striped pole above the window, ancient symbol of a barber surgeon. When blood had to be let, the patient would grip the pole to make his veins stand out and so ease the barber surgeon's task. Mannering sometimes thought the sign was rather apt in his case. How much blood had flowed – in the trenches, at Gallipoli, in Mesopotamia and Russia – as a direct result of his meetings in an upper room above this shop with a man whose real name he did not know?

He climbed out of the Austin, walked back to the shop. Three swivel chairs were set in front of washbasins with big mirrors; two men were having their hair cut. They looked curiously defenceless under the white sheets that covered them, their heads bent forward beneath the snip of the barber's scissors. The third chair was empty. The barber standing behind it looked at Mannering enquiringly and then recognised him.

'Mr Barnaby is upstairs, sir,' he said very respectfully.

Mannering walked past him, through a curtained doorway. He pulled the curtain closely behind him, climbed a flight of narrow stairs. He owned this shop. He also owned the whole street and the one next to it, but not under his own name, of course. He owned nothing himself, not even the clothes he wore. Everything was held by nominees.

The barber had no idea of this. He ran a profitable sideline in pornographic photographs, much in demand by richer, older men. He had no idea of Mannering's identity – he did not know the names of most of his clients. It was safer that way, for them as for him. They were simply men with a certain need which he was fortunately in a position to satisfy – at a price.

Mr Barnaby was a small man with a black pointed beard and a waxed moustache. He stood up as Mannering entered the room at the top of the stairs. It was furnished with a table and two chairs. The curtains were drawn, and the light was dim and filtered. A faint smell of brilliantine and scented soap sweetened the air. Along one wall bars of soap were stacked on bookshelves, with carboys of hair lotion and shampoo on the floor.

Mannering sat down. The other man pulled his chair

up to the table and looked at him enquiringly, obsequiously, like a dog facing a harsh master. He took a brown envelope from an inner pocket, laid it on the table between them.

'The tests have been totally successful,' Mannering told him, putting the envelope unopened in his pocket. 'You can tell your people that. Two hundred rounds were successfully fired through the blades of a propeller spinning at speed. This invention will totally revolutionise aerial warfare. There is no need for further modifications in my view, or in the view of the makers. There is a price, of course.'

Mr Barnaby said nothing. He sat watching his visitor, raised his eyebrows slightly.

'Half a million pounds,' Mannering told him.

'It has been patented?'

'Yes. But in war it is difficult to uphold patents if they are pirated by an enemy country. After the war, it will be different. But then there may be no need of such devices then.'

Barnaby shook his head. 'There will always be a need of them,' he said. 'For every weapon that has ever been invented there is a counter-weapon. Every poison has its antidote.'

'There is no antidote to this particular item,' Mannering replied shortly. 'A pilot simply aims at his target as he flies towards it and fires. Moreover, he will soon be able to have two machine-guns, side by side, instead of one. He will be unbeatable.'

'Only as long as he hits his target and his adversary does not also possess this weapon,' Barnaby corrected him. 'Eventually, we will have aircraft fighting each other, and both armed with it. So that is stalemate. However, that is not our concern. I will apply to my superiors at once. I expect their answer by the end of the week.'

'I will wait until Friday. But, remember, no bargaining. It is my sum or nothing. You will get the drawings when I receive the money.'

'My people are in Lisbon,' the man explained. 'It may take time to contact them. All letters are being opened by the censors here. Every telegram in and out of this country is checked by the security people. I may have to send a messenger.'

'That is your business, not mine,' said Mannering shortly; such details were of no concern to him. Both men stood up. Barnaby made as though to hold out his hand to him. Mannering pretended not to see the gesture. He walked downstairs, out of the shop, along the street back to his car.

'Home,' he told the driver brusquely.

He sat in the corner of the rear seat, looking out at the busy streets, but he barely saw anyone or anything. His mind was elsewhere, dealing with more weighty matters than housewives shopping or companies of soldiers marching behind their band. Such sights, such people were beneath his concern, like the Russian peasants viewed from the Tsar's train. They were all expendable pawns in a game involving nations; and he was master of that game.

He had played both sides in this war successfully for a long time. This was a risky business, possibly the riskiest, but the profits were enormous. Even so, it might be wise to retire now, while he was still unsuspected. He had always shrunk from personal involvement in violence. From his earliest years in Constantinople, he had preferred to strike at one or more remove. He must not forget this basic principle of survival. He recalled a Turkish proverb that had long impressed him: 'He who says nothing, sees nothing, hears nothing, lives for a hundred years in peace.'

How many people in that barber's shop would know

211

who he was? He had so many aliases, so many disguises, he sometimes wondered who he really was himself, and almost believed the stories about his background: his education in this country, the fact that his parents died some years before the war on holiday abroad – which conveniently explained why there were no records in this country, and no graves bearing their names.

He put his hand in his pocket, reaching for his cigar case, and his fingers touched the envelope Mr Barnaby had given him. He took it out, opened it, examined the crude photographs it contained. They showed boys, men, women in a grotesque variety of sexual poses. One feature was common to them all: an air of sadness, almost of non-involvement, on their faces. They posed against studio backcloths of painted trees, a balustrade, a fluted pillar. He must have looked like that once, he thought, hungry, lonely, despairing, ready to snatch at anything for the price of a meal.

None of the faces meant anything to him. He searched through the pictures quickly, looking for another photograph of the woman he worshipped from afar and loved at one remove, but there was nothing. He had not really expected he would find anything, but Mr Barnaby knew all manner of people and provided collectors with photographs of many kinds. There was always the chance that one day he would find another photograph that Mannering could put in his slide projector and gaze at in his darkened room, loving the likeness of someone he had never met, who, in his mutilated condition, he felt too ashamed to meet.

Richard was sitting on a bench in the yard of the Battleaxes inn when Carola arrived. He had been waiting there for twenty minutes. She had left her cycle in the hedge fifty yards down the lane and first walked up to make sure he really was there before she arrived.

He stood up to greet her. 'What will you have to drink?'

'I used to drink cider at the fair, but I think I'll have something a bit stronger tonight. A shandy.'

'That's not very strong,' said Richard.

'It'll do to start with.'

He went into the bar, came back with a pint of bitter, half a pint of shandy. He raised his glass to her.

'To our next meeting. You still have my little steam engine?'

'Of course,' she told him. 'The Spirit and the Speed. An inspiring phrase. I keep it in my bedroom. I must give it back to you, like I promised.'

'Some time,' he replied, 'but not just yet. I'm hoping to go in the army when I finish my year in the gear factory. I won't have room for it in the army, so you'd better hang on to it.'

'You look too young to be a soldier.'

'I'll be eighteen and a half when I finish at Beechwood,' he told her stiffly. 'That's not too young.'

Carola realised she was thinking of Tom Gardener, who looked much more mature than Richard. But then he was mature. He was not waiting to join up; he must have been in uniform for years, and he was the holder of the Military Cross. He had shot down five German aircraft, so Mr Cartwright said. He must be at least twenty-four, perhaps even twenty-five. She would find out. But how? She realised she wanted to see him again, to talk to him. She'd never met anyone so easygoing, and casual. She had liked him on barely half an hour's meeting.

'I suggest we take a cycle ride,' Richard was saying, 'then perhaps come back here and have some sandwiches.'

'What is there to see round here?' she said.

'Well, there's Elstree airfield, not more than a mile away.'

'Have they planes there?'

'Of course. The air force uses it for training. Ever seen a plane close up?'

'Only that one in your works.'

'That was, as the pilot said, a kiwi, a wingless bird. Come on. Finish your drink. We can cycle there.'

'Will we be allowed in?'

'Don't see why not. I've a permit from Beechwood to visit any War Department property in the course of business. And you're with me.'

'You make it sound easy.'

'Most things are easy when you tackle them head on,' Richard told her confidently. 'Now, tell me what's been happening to you?'

As they cycled through leafy lanes towards the airfield, Carola told him about the Campions, Lady Warren and her all-women ménage. They turned into the gates. An army sentry, with a rifle slung over his shoulder, halted them. Richard produced his pass.

'Looks all right,' said the sentry grudgingly. 'Who do you want to see here?'

They didn't want to say they were just looking round, then Carola remembered the Australian.

'Captain Tom Gardener,' she said. There must be a chance he was stationed here, because this was the nearest air force base to Richard's factory.

'Behind that first hangar is the officers' mess. You can't go in, of course, being as you're not officers, but an orderly will tell the captain you want to see him.'

'You remembered his name,' said Richard in surprise as they cycled on.

'It's the only name I know of anyone in the air force,' Carola explained quickly. This was true, but not the whole truth.

214

For a moment, Richard looked at her oddly. They cycled on in silence.

Three biplanes were drawn up in line outside the nearest hangar, with wedge-shaped wooden chocks against the wheels. Mechanics were filling their tanks with petrol from churns. The next building was the officers' mess. Some small fir trees were newly planted near the windows.

'They get so much noise from the engines,' Richard explained, 'they plant these trees to try and keep it out. Do you really want to see if this captain is in?'

He hoped Carola would say no. He hoped again that he wouldn't be in if she did say yes. But she said yes, and he was in. An orderly brought him out.

'Why,' he said in surprise, 'my new friends! I can't invite you in the mess. They're too stuffy here. It's different back home in Australia, I tell you. Bloody right, it is. But here, it's all old English customs, the old school tie, upper-class rules and regulations, you know? You can't beat them. Unless you're a colonial, then you have to. What brings you here?'

'I thought we'd see the planes. See how our gun could fit,' said Richard, trying to think of a reasonable excuse for being on the airfield.

'Come and look at these, then.'

He led the way across the short cropped grass to the concrete area in front of the hangar where the planes were parked. He turned to Carola. 'Ever been in a plane?'

'Never,' she admitted.

'Well, try this for size.'

'Is that allowed?'

'I'm allowing it.' He brought up a set of wooden steps on wheels. 'Just hitch up your skirt and up you go, girl. No hanging back.'

Carola climbed up the steps, peered into the cockpit.

It was bound in padded leather with big stitches, held by leather thongs like bootlaces. The seat, also of leather, seemed absurdly small. The dashboard was polished aluminium. Half a dozen dials were screwed on to it, all with black faces, white figures, white pointers. Everything seemed unexpectedly spartan and primitive. Somehow she had expected something more luxurious, like the inside of Lady Warren's Rolls.

'What do you think?' asked Gardener.

Carola told him.

'Well, it's got to be as light as possible. Fitness for purpose. And the only purpose of this plane is to fly fast and give the pilot every chance of outpacing the enemy. You could ponce it up as much as you like, even put in woolly rugs, anything, but then you have to take all that extra weight up into the sky. And every extra pound is a pound of useless flesh up there. You want the biggest engine in the lightest aircraft, and with the best gun, which, when we get that one I tested today, we will have. Then you have a good power-to-weight ratio. But you work these things out, don't you, in your factory?' he said to Richard.

'No. I just do the gears.'

'You worked on this shooting idea?'

'As a matter of fact, it was my idea.'

'Great. You must live on fish. What gave you the idea in the first place?'

'An old motorcycle engine.'

Gardener laughed.

'You get money out of it, a royalty?'

'Oh no, of course not. It's the firm's.'

'There you are. That's you English for you. The game is more important than winning. That's crap. Winning is all-important. The only thing that matters. Next time you invent something smart, sport, you make sure you invent it at a better profit for yourself. The factory's making a profit, so are the shareholders and the owner. But not you, who thought up the whole thing.'

'The owner came to see us some time ago,' said Richard proudly.

'I don't wonder with an idea like that. Who is he, anyhow?'

'An odd bloke. Sir James Mannering.'

'Never heard of him.'

'He's in and out of the papers. But never with his photograph, so I'm told.'

'Is that right?' Tom Gardener turned to Carola. 'Sorry I can't take you up for a trip, but maybe some time, when we've got a two-seater here, we can get together. What do you say?'

'I'd like that,' said Carola.

He winked at her. She winked back. Did she mean she would like a trip in a two-seater or she'd like to get together with him? All three of them wondered, but only two of them knew.

Chapter Ten

Like many other people during what was becoming known as the Great War, Sir Bernard Warner, the Chief Constable, found he had to accept an unexpected and unwelcome change in his life. First, he was recalled to the colours and posted into a branch of military movements. He disliked the inordinate amount of paperwork involved and what he considered petty and unmanly political intrigues for promotion between officers who he believed should be above such manoeuvrings. When one of his two sons was killed at Verdun, he did his utmost to secure an active service posting.

At heart, Warner was a regimental officer. On duty, years previously with his regiment in India, he had been in command of a display of marching and counter-marching staged before King George V on the occasion of his splendid Delhi Durbar. A courtier, who before his elevation to an earldom and his subsequent posting to the staff of Buckingham Palace had been a junior officer in the regiment, introduced Warner to the King.

They got on well. Warner, never a man of great charm or tact but of total integrity, possessed a certain bluff attractiveness which the King found agreeable. To someone almost continually surrounded by sycophants and place-seekers, it was refreshing to meet a man who spoke his mind without tailoring his words to royal ears, and in due course Warner was knighted.

His request to return to regimental soldiering in the war was not granted; after all, he was middle-aged, and everyone agreed this was a young man's war. He was therefore moved sideways or, as he thought privately, backwards, into Intelligence.

Sir Bernard had always believed, with Napoleon, that a spy, even if useful, was not a gentleman. Napoleon accepted that a well-placed spy could prove as valuable as a division of fighting troops, but he was still someone to keep at arm's length. By the basic nature of his calling, he could not be considered a man of honour.

But Sir Bernard was not himself a spy. His brief was to catch spies; to stop their activities, possibly to use them to lead him on to other spies, or turn them against their German masters.

For this task he soon found he had little natural aptitude. He looked a military officer; he would always look a military officer. Disguises, which some of his colleagues affected, were not to his taste. The prospect of putting on a false beard or darkening his moustache or wearing a wig or heavily framed glasses like an actor on a stage were anathema to him, although he admitted that sometimes such stratagems could produce valuable results.

In his new role, he needed a marker to follow, just as when his regiment would go on parade they needed a marker against whom they would dress off to the right to form a perfect line. He chose as his personal marker a man for whom he had a great admiration, who indeed could be said to be the founder of the British counter-intelligence service, Colonel Vernon Kell.

Colonel Kell had served as a soldier during the Boxer Rebellion in China, and after being decorated by the Americans as well as the British for his services, he retired from the army. But while Sir Bernard had been soldiering in India, sticking pigs, riding horses in gymkhanas and generally behaving as an extrovert regimental officer with private means should behave, Kell's career had followed a different course.

For several years before the outbreak of the war there had been widespread concern in Britain about the activities of Germans in the country. German brass bands toured cities and large towns. German acrobatic displays drew full houses in theatres. German tourists appeared in unusual numbers in coastal resorts – and many brought easels and painted pictures of harbours and docks, paying particular attention to naval ships and shore establishments.

Were all these activities harmless, as the German authorities declared? Or were they a deliberate attempt to gather information about Britain's defences? Vernon Kell decided to find out. He petitioned Members of Parliament to ask questions in the House about the advisability of monitoring the activities of potentially dangerous foreigners – meaning, of course, Germans.

Finally, largely to keep him quiet, Kell was provided with a room in an office in Whitehall and a male clerk and told to produce proof of his theories within a certain time.

Kell had no clear idea where to start his enquiries. He was working independently of the police, and in any case, their intelligence system was by no means sophisticated, even if he had been able to avail himself of it.

For some months, he and his clerk could find no evidence whatever of German espionage. Then a state visit by Kaiser Wilhelm to London was announced. The Kaiser stayed at Buckingham Palace, but many of his entourage were put up in Claridges. Kell and his colleague decided to follow two of these officers each morning to see where they went when they left the hotel. Kell took the first one; his clerk took the second. Diligently, they trailed them to art galleries, to restaurants, and to private houses. Nothing contrary to the behaviour of visiting foreign aristocrats came to light. And then, one day, Kell discovered something he considered unusual.

He followed his man in a taxi to King's Cross station. The taxi drove past the station and into the Caledonian Road, and, to Kell's surprise, stopped outside a barber's shop.

The German went inside. Kell kept a watch from the other side of the road. The officer was in the barber's shop for only a few minutes, clearly not long enough to have a haircut. However, he might have had a scalp massage, a brief manicure, or he could simply have bought one of the bottles of the setting or dressing lotions that stood in rows in the fly-blown window. But this seemed an odd place for such a senior officer, a man of great personal wealth, the holder of an ancient Bavarian title, to make such purchases. There were distinguished hairdressers holding the royal warrant near his hotel. So why come to this seedy shop – unless he had another reason?

Next day, Kell again kept watch on the shop and to his surprise, another officer, whom he recognised from previous surveillance, also visited the barber. A number of other foreigners called later and left shortly afterwards. Kell knew they were foreign because he approached one and asked him if he could kindly direct him to St Pancras station. The man replied in a guttural accent that he could not, as he was a stranger to the district.

Kell lacked the resources to follow up his discovery, so he passed the whole matter over to the police who accepted it with some reserve. The police kept their own watch on the shop and discovered that it was a clearing house for snippets of intelligence. Which regiment was due to be posted where? Who held the keys for the electric power stations? Where were the main submarine stations on the east coast? What was the weekly tonnage of ships docking at Chatham, and what cargoes did they carry?

In isolation, these bits of information were probably unimportant, but taken all together they could provide a valuable mosaic of facts that might help a potential enemy.

Vernon Kell was vindicated. He was given proper offices, a staff, and control of the fifth department of Military Intelligence. This soon became known by its initials as MI5. By the time war broke out, his staff numbered several thousand men and women.

Sir Bernard thought that what had once produced such positive results might well do so again, in the same way that if you fished a certain stretch of river and caught a number of salmon, it was obviously worth fishing that stretch a second time. Salmon were creatures of habit; so, he believed, were spies.

He controlled a dozen plainclothes men, mostly, like him, ex-officers of varying ranks, but none above the rank of major, and allocated areas to them, with instructions to watch barbers' shops.

If he could have thought of any other places where men would visit regularly, and where their appearance would cause no interest or surprise, he might have had them watched too, but he could not. Bars were too obvious meeting places. Public lavatories might be where homosexuals gathered, but they were ill-suited to buying or selling information. Also, plainclothes policemen frequented them in the hope of making easy arrests, and they might frustrate the class of person Sir Bernard wished to catch.

Gentlemen's clubs in St James's were not in the category. Several restaurants in Covent Garden and Leicester Square had private rooms, but it would be too expensive to keep these under surveillance. Barbers' shops, he felt certain, were safe and inconspicuous places where men could meet, and they had the additional merit of being inexpensive targets to watch.

For weeks his team produced nothing whatever, and then he received reports that a number of foreign-looking men were visiting a barber's salon in Pimlico, and another off the Bayswater Road.

There was nothing sinister in the first. Nor was there in the second until one agent, a retired major, came to see him.

'I've been watching Luigi's for the past fortnight,' he explained. 'Nothing to report except that twice in this time a large car has parked round the corner. A middle-aged man with a beard, his hat pulled down over his face, gets out and walks back to the shop. He wears glasses. I could not see his face clearly.'

'You've taken the number of the car?'

'Of course. I've checked this with the police. It belongs to a company, an import and export firm with a registered office in Finsbury Circus.'

'Who are the directors?' asked Sir Bernard, beginning to be interested.

'One is a solicitor working in Gray's Inn. There's a chartered accountant who also sits on the board of several small companies. But the chairman is someone altogether different – Sir James Mannering.'

'You mean the man the government relies on for providing so many of our weapons?'

'Exactly.'

'Is the man with the glasses Sir James?'

'I think so. But he keeps his picture out of the papers as much as possible, as you know. I've checked the number of times he's been photographed. Only twice. Once at a wedding and once at a funeral. But in both cases he saw the photographer. At the wedding he held up a hand in front of his face, and on the other occasion he blew his nose so that his face was virtually concealed by his handkerchief. He is therefore almost unknown to the public.'

'So such a simple disguise as glasses and a big hat could be effective?'

'Totally.'

'Let's bring in Mr Luigi and tell him where his best interests lie.'

'There is actually no Mr Luigi, sir. The shop is run by an Irishman, Terence O'Brien.'

'Bring in Mr O'Brien then, and we will have a chat.'

Sir Bernard had at his disposal several flats in south and west London. His section used each address for a week or ten days and then moved on to the next one. This made it difficult for anyone they interviewed to discover exactly where they were – or who was asking the questions.

In one such house, off the Cromwell Road, Terence O'Brien was brought to face Sir Bernard. They sat opposite each other in a basement room. The walls were whitewashed, and the room was bare except for two chairs and a table. In the centre of the ceiling, an unshaded bulb, protected by a wire mesh grille, shone brightly in O'Brien's face.

'Don't be alarmed,' said Sir Bernard smoothly. 'We aren't going to hurt you or harm you in any way. This is a branch of the security service, and we think you can help us.'

'If I can, sir, I'll do anything to help.'

'I am sure you will. We're interested in a gentleman who comes to see you from time to time. He wears spectacles and has a beard.'

'I know him, sir, yes, but not who he is, if you understand me.'

'He comes to you for a haircut or a shave?'

'Oh no, sir. He just comes to have a chat with Mr Barnaby.'

'And who is Mr Barnaby?'

O'Brien paused. He was sweating. The light was very bright, and he did not like the look of this man who was questioning him. He had the smack of authority. What did he know about the room above his shop? If he admitted its existence, could he be accused of any crime? Surely not. Couldn't a man rent out a room in his own premises?

'I think perhaps you are remembering something, Mr O'Brien,' said Sir Bernard quietly, watching his face.

'I'm thinking about something, yes,' O'Brien admitted.

'Tell me.'

'I don't know if it's of any interest, but I rent the upstairs room to Mr Barnaby who comes in once or twice a month.'

'And what does he do in your upstairs room?'

'He meets people. Friends, I suppose. The man with glasses is one of them.'

'Why does Mr Barnaby meet these gentlemen in this room?'

'I don't know why he meets them, sir. I don't rightly know who he is. I use the room for storing lotions and soap, that type of thing. And he came in one day and said he'd like to rent it for meeting people.'

'An odd place to choose, surely?'

O'Brien shrugged; whether it was odd or not was not his concern. All he cared about was the weekly rent.

'Do you have an address for him?'

'No, sir. He pays a pound a week, whether he uses the room or not.'

'Is he up there for a long time?'

'Not usually, sir. People come and visit him. Gentlemen, of course. Not ladies. There's nothing like that.

226

I'm not renting the room for that sort of thing.'

'I never thought you were, Mr O'Brien. You say gentlemen. Do you mean gentlemen, or just men?'

'I mean gentlemen, sir. They appear to have some affinity with Mr Barnaby. The wear well-cut clothes, handmade boots. One or two have motor cars. They don't come to my place for a haircut. Not gentlemen like that.'

'So Mr Barnaby either gives them something, or they give him something. Is that the situation in your opinion?'

'It's possible, sir, but I don't know what.'

'I see. Well now, Mr O'Brien, you've been very helpful. But don't tell Mr Barnaby you have seen us. It would not be in your interest to do that. You follow me, I'm sure.'

'Perfectly, sir.'

'To show that we appreciate your co-operation, here is a small sum to help cover any loss of earnings.' Sir Bernard took a new five pound note from his wallet and handed it to O'Brien.

'Thank you very much, sir. It's most generous.'

Sir Bernard smiled and showed him out into the street.

Hardly had O'Brien gone when the agent who had first watched Luigi's barber shop came into the house.

'I've made a thorough search of the premises,' he reported to Sir Bernard. 'There's nothing downstairs except sacks of old hair which apparently barbers of this class sell as stuffing for pillows and cushions. Upstairs, though, it's a different matter.'

'What's different about it?'

'There's only one room. In this the owner stores bars of soap, shampoos, bottles of hair oil, tins of brilliantine. In a cupboard I found a false shelf, one above the other. It had a piece of oilcloth hanging over the front to conceal the join. I lifted it off and found these.' He took from his briefcase a large brown envelope, shook out the contents onto Sir Bernard's desk.

'Pornography,' said Sir Bernard dully, not bothering to hide his disappointment. He fingered the photographs with distaste. Faded yellowish faces of male and female Levantines, Cypriots, Egyptians, photographed goodness knows where or when, and in grotesque poses, looked up at him with sad eyes. 'I suppose there must be a market for this, but Sir James Mannering? That amazes me. Still, we all have our vices, our little peccadilloes.'

As he pondered Mannering's sexual taste, his fingers stirred the photographs. Suddenly, his eyes narrowed. He picked up one photograph, showed it to his colleagues. A young woman was standing naked by the side of an Afghan hound. Apart from her nakedness, the picture was quite unerotic. Her face showed defiance, as though she hated what she was doing and yet had to do it.

'Ever seen her before?' he asked.

The man shook his head. 'Not dressed or undressed, so far as I know, sir,' he said.

'Well, I have,' Sir Bernard replied. 'What an extraordinary thing.'

'You know the lady?'

'I do. Yes.'

Sir Bernard did not mention her name. It did not seem either fitting or necessary for him to admit to a subordinate that he was looking at a nude photograph of Mrs Rose Rowlands.

Snow was falling, softly, thickly, silently, as Mannering looked out of the hotel window in Petrograd. The glass was opaque with frost and his breath hung like steam in the freezing room.

Mannering was attempting to telephone the British Embassy. Only a few months earlier, this would have been totally unnecessary. The Embassy would have sent a First or Second Secretary to meet him at the quayside and escort him to his hotel. But now, revolution was in the air. General Ormilov was not in his office. Indeed, when Mannering went to his office, the entire War Ministry building appeared deserted.

Worse, looters had stripped each room of anything portable and smashed items too heavy to carry away such as desks and leather armchairs and bookcases. The obligatory portraits of the Tsar had been gashed with knives and axes. Someone had drawn a giant hammer and sickle in human excrement beneath the Tsar's picture that hung in the general's office. Mannering walked from room to room; every one had been pillaged. He had never seen such damage, and felt fingers of fear clutch his heart as he realised what this meant: the end of law and order, the start of an age of terror.

Before Mannering left London he had been told that to make a trip to Petrograd was unwise and probably very dangerous, and he was wasting his time going there.

'They are our allies,' he had told the Foreign Secretary. 'I feel it is my duty to go.'

'It is your duty to preserve your abilities to help *us*,' was the blunt reply. 'The Russian army is packing in all along the front. It's everyone for himself there. I don't know what's happened to the Tsar or indeed any of the royal family. Apparently, they're still alive, and our information is that they are prisoners somewhere. But where is anyone's guess. I wouldn't give much for their chances, poor devils. According to our Embassy, a lot of the people we've dealt with for years are either dead or in hiding.'

But Mannering had never been one to take a negative for an answer. He had goods to sell; goods to buy; deals to make. He would not give up so easily. But, now in the cold hotel room – the heating was not working because there was no more coal or wood to feed the furnaces – he wondered whether he had been foolish. Greed had brought him here; greed and the love of money.

He wanted to sell the Russians the plans for the Beechwood machine-guns. This, he felt, was only reasonable, since they had suggested the need for a forward-firing device to him in the first place. He had delayed his return to Petrograd because he had hoped to sell it to the Germans as well. But Barnaby had returned with bad news: his contact in Lisbon had been unsuccessful.

'My sources tell me they are short of money,' he explained. 'They simply cannot raise enough to make the purchase. Not at your price or, indeed, at anything approximating it.'

'But your clients must have vast gold reserves,' Mannering replied testily. Neither man ever mentioned the nationality of any of their clients; it was safer not to do so.

'Possibly,' agreed Barnaby. 'But I hear they are financing revolution in Russia. If the Tsar can be overthrown, they hope to come to some accommodation with the Bolsheviks, perhaps persuade them to fight on the side of the Central Powers. Lenin and his crowd will owe a great deal to my client – millions and millions of marks, in fact. Indeed, without my client's backing they have little chance of success. They have helped these people in other ways, too. Some of the revolutionary leaders have been living in exile in my client's country. They were provided with a secure train and armed guards, and given safe passage through every Customs post all the way to Russia.'

'Delivering the germs of revolt,' said Mannering bitterly. 'What a short-sighted act.'

'Possibly. But so many politicians have astigmatism. They cannot see beyond the immediate gains. Anyhow, there is no further purpose in our meeting to discuss this matter. Regrettably, we must both consider it closed.'

'I suppose so,' agreed Mannering sadly.

He had, of course, received a large sum from the British government for the mechanism, and a contract specifying royalties on every piece of equipment sold, but if he could sell something twice over, so much the better. He had always done this whenever he could, right from his earliest deals with the gangs in Constantinople. Why be content with a single profit if you could have two, or even three?

So Mannering decided to go to Russia himself and describe the enormous merits of the invention to General Ormilov. He believed that when it came to selling anything, he had no rivals. One day, he feared (but resolutely tried to banish the thought from his mind), his duplicity could be discovered. He had heard of several British traitors who had ended up in front of a firing squad in the small-arms range behind the Tower of London. He was in no doubt as to the punishment for treachery discovered. From the Germans he had less to fear because he rarely met them face to face. If anything went wrong, a go-between would take the blame.

Mannering had had no real conception of conditions in Russia, despite what the Foreign Secretary had told him. He rarely accepted anyone else's assessment of any situation if it did not fit in closely with his own. Now, he wished he had.

The hotel elevator was not working. Electricity had been cut off. The main power station, he had heard, had been sabotaged. He walked down the red-carpeted marble stairs to the front hall. The reception desk was empty. He pressed the bell to summon a clerk and ask him to engage a troika, a three-horse sledge, used as a taxi when the snow was thick. There was no answer. The hotel servants had fled; they had no wish to face people's tribunals on charges of being lackeys of the capitalists. He would have to walk.

The streets were full of people, surging forward in one direction and then, like lemmings, turning and running in another. There was something fearful in their haste to go nowhere. A mindless mob was always dangerous. Mannering reached the Embassy gates. They were locked and chained. He pulled the bell handle, but no one came. He shouted through the bars of the gate, but still no one answered. And all the time, snow kept falling. He was surprised how thick and heavy it felt on the brim of his hat, on his beard, on his shoulders.

He walked back to the hotel. He would go home aboard the first available ship. It was far too dangerous to stay here. He was gaining nothing and had no hope of making a sale to these people.

As he came through the double doors of the hotel entrance, two men who had been sitting in the hall beside a potted palm stood up.

'You are Mister Sir James Mannering?' asked one in stilted English.

'Who are you?'

'The Revolutionary Council has sent us to escort you, dear sir.'

'Where to?'

'You will be told, dear sir.'

They moved towards him, positioned themselves one on either side. They wore thick overcoats and fur hats. Their eyes were cold, their faces pinched and hungry. They still had snow on their shoulders, so they could not have been long in the hotel.

'I have no appointment to see anyone in the Revolutionary Council,' Mannering told them in Russian. 'I wish to see the British Ambassador.'

They did not reply. Instead, they each took hold of one of Mannering's arms and escorted him out of the hotel door and round the side to a street where a khaki staff car with canvas hood and mica side curtains waited, engine running. The cold was such that drivers were reluctant to switch off their engines. If they did so, they might not start again.

The driver opened a rear door for the three men. They drove in silence through wide streets. Here and there, great houses were ablaze. Huge orange tongues of flame roared through smashed windows. Mannering was amazed to see firemen, trying desperately to put out the flames, being beaten back by soldiers with rifles and bayonets, and by screaming civilians wielding clubs or heavy walking sticks.

'They were once the homes of the rich, the aristocratic people,' the English-speaking man explained. 'Now they belong to us, the ordinary people.'

'So why are you letting them burn?'

'Why not?'

'But they're probably full of priceless antiques, paintings. Can't you understand that? Their contents will be worth fortunes.'

'We have no need of fortunes. The pursuit of such wealth is against the real interests of the workers. Paintings, valuables of such a kind, are the dross of civilisation.'

'They're the whole point of being civilised,' retorted Mannering angrily.

'That is a capitalist view, Mister Sir James. We have suffered for years because of such capitalist opinions. Look where it has led us.'

Mannering said nothing. How could he explain to this dolt that once he had been far poorer than almost any of these so-called workers to whom he referred, and by his own exertions had dragged himself up to his present position? The man simply wouldn't understand.

The car stopped outside a house on a square thronged

with people. The ground-floor windows were broken and wire netting had been hammered across the frames, either to keep out thieves or to stop anyone from throwing a bomb through the gaps. Mannering followed the two men up a marble staircase. Soldiers lounged on the landings, uniforms unbuttoned, leaning on rifles, smoking cheap cigarettes. Someone had lit a fire from a gilded door, torn from its hinges and chopped up with an axe. It burned smokily; the paint and varnish gave off a bitter smell. A corporal fed in new planks as they passed by, up to the second floor.

As they approached a closed door a soldier came out of a side room, holding a rifle with bayonet fixed. The man said something in a whisper; the soldier nodded. The man led Mannering through the door into the room. It was bare except for a desk, two chairs in a corner, a side table and an oil lamp. The carpet was dark green and scuffed by many dirty boots.

He had never met the man on the other side of the desk, small and bald-headed, with a pointed beard rather like his own, and dark unfriendly eyes, but he had seen enough newspaper photographs to recognise Vladimir Ilyich Lenin. The architect of the revolution, so the Foreign Office had called him. He certainly looked an unimpressive little man, his head too large for his body, so that he appeared almost a cartoon figure, a grotesque. But whatever his outward appearance, his lack of looks, Mannering accepted that his brain must be remarkable. He was one of the leaders who had arrived in Petrograd from Germany in the sealed train.

'I understand you had an appointment to see General Ormilov,' he said in English.

He did not stand up, nor did he offer to shake hands. He simply sat still, looking up at Mannering.

'That is so, sir,' Mannering replied. 'I cannot find him at his office.'

'You will never find him in any office ever again. He is dead. He was shot two days ago by a military firing squad after sentence by a people's court.'

'On what charge, sir?'

'On several charges, each of which carries the death penalty. One, he was a lickspittle of the Tsar. Two, he caused the deaths of hundreds of thousands of loyal Russian peasants impressed into the army. Three, he was found guilty of making away with funds on a great scale, and refusing to modernise the army. Those were only some of the serious charges for which his defence was judged totally inadequate.'

'I deeply regret that he has been killed. I know from my dealings with him that he was a patriot, a totally loyal officer.'

'He was loyal to himself and, I would say, to the Tsar, which amounted to the same thing. They were related, so the Tsar looked after him. Ormilov owed everything to him. However, I did not invite you here to discuss these matters. What did you wish to see Ormilov about?'

'It was a private matter, sir.'

'In this country, Sir James, nothing is private any more. Nothing is hidden, and indeed there are no hiding places. We are all equals now. We have no secrets from one another. So that we may not waste time in useless and fruitless discussion but reach the basic facts, I may tell you that your luggage has been searched. Detailed drawings of a complex mechanism were found. I am told they appear to deal with the firing of a gun in an aircraft between the blades of the propeller. Am I right?'

There was no point in denying it. Mannering nodded.

'We have taken possession of the drawings. Were you hoping to sell the plans to the Tsar? To the Tsar's army?'

'At General Ormilov's request, I put my designers to work on a mechanism that would enable a gun to fire forwards in the direction of aircraft flight. You appear to have appropriated it.'

'It is of no use to us at the moment, Sir James. Russia's interest in this imperialistic war is over. But I am having it copied by our best aeronautical draughtsmen. We will then sell it to Germany as our property. They will pay a large sum for it, in foreign currency. And this we need desperately because other countries are unwilling to trade with us. They doubt we can pay for what we buy, and they fear that the tide of communism may spread to them and so sweep away their corrupt capitalist systems.'

Mannering was hardly listening. He had been out-flanked, and the knowledge caused him almost physical pain. These communists could have no conception of the price to ask for the machine-gun gears. Without doubt, they would sell far too cheaply, a prospect which hurt Mannering almost as much as being outmanoeuvred.

He made an appeal to Lenin's patriotism.

'To sell that design is against the interests of your country, sir.'

'You mean against the interests of yours, Sir James. There is no place for war in Russia now, although your leaders would disagree. We intend to build a great communist nation and so reverse the decline of centuries, when all profits went to a favoured and ruling few. We intend to stop the blood-sucking activities of capitalists. For ever.'

'Did you call me here simply to tell me this, Mr Lenin?'

'Indeed, no. I brought you here to try to do what you would call a deal. With you. Not your government. Your past is not unknown to us. Nor is your character. I understand from my sources that you do not care with whom you do business as long as you personally make a profit. You might rather trade with a friend, of course, but friendship would not play any part in your negotiations. You would deal just as harshly with him as with anyone else.' He paused. 'When you were here last, you met Prince Yussoupov?'

Mannering nodded.

'He has left the country, too, like many wise men of great wealth and high social standing. The Tsarina got rid of him because of his part in the murder of the lunatic monk Rasputin. As you may know, her son is sickly. There is no cure for the complaint from which he suffers so acutely, only death, but Rasputin was apparently able to ease his pain.

'I think he simply hypnotised the boy so that his attitude of mind temporarily overcame his symptoms, but his mother believed that Rasputin was a holy man and the only person in all the empire who could help her son, and maybe, one day, save him.

'She came totally under Rasputin's influence, taking his ridiculous advice on political and military matters. His ideas were simply the views of a drunken, crafty peasant, which he was. Because of the disasters that resulted, a handful of the Tsar's friends and relatives decided to kill him – and succeeded. The Tsarina, of course, could not forgive them. She had them exiled.

'Prince Yussoupov had to abandon his castles, his chateaux, his art collections, and of course the estates he owns, including one hundred and twenty-five miles of coastline, with possibly the world's richest oil deposits.

'In Russia we will eventually build a country where every worker can own his own motor car if he so wishes, as only the rich do now. But in a thousand years we could still not consume more than a fraction of that oil. I want to use it to bring foreign currency to Russia. Now. And I am inviting you to organise its exploitation.'

'How, exactly?'

'We will provide tankers to carry crude oil to any port in Europe or Britain. You will pay us for it in pounds sterling or American dollars well below the market price for crude oil. You can then make what profit you like.'

'That is an interesting proposal, Mr Lenin, but as you admit, the countries of the West are not at all anxious to trade with your communist regime. I believe several European governments have already decided not to finance you directly or indirectly.'

'But you are not a European government, Sir James. You are not even a European. You are a Russian. A Jew. I wish you to give some thought to your ancestry, and to the country of your birth. You have no more right to the name of Mannering than I can lay claim to the name of Smith. The real James Mannering, I am told, is dead long since. And at your hand, if indirectly. You are alive, but you are a cheat and a murderer.

'It is possible, too, that if we in Russia have to endure hardships because of the short-sighted attitude of other nations, those of your faith may be blamed. The workers could even feel, however wrongly, that Jews have played a disproportionate part in driving down their living standards so that they could personally make large fortunes. You would not wish that to happen, I am sure?'

'Most certainly not.'

'The vehemence with which you answer my question gives me confidence that you are willing to co-operate. In addition, I wish to make a similar proposal with regard to some of Russia's art treasures. I am ordering the private art collections of the aristocracy to be brought to a central place. The pictures will be removed from their frames, and sold – to you, again for sterling or US dollars. You may dispose of them as you wish and keep the profit.'

Lenin paused, watching Mannering carefully.

'What you say interests me, Mr Lenin. On the way here, however, I saw great houses being deliberately burned down. I remarked to the man who brought me here that it seemed extraordinary for soldiers and civilians to be physically attacking firemen who were bravely attempting to put out fires which would destroy paintings and furnishings worth a fortune. That seems to me to be an odd way to safeguard art treasures and earn foreign currency.'

'On the contrary, Sir James, it is a very sound way. We have encouraged foreign newspaper correspondents to witness these fires. We operate strict censorship, naturally, so we know what they have cabled to their newspapers. If their readers believe that art treasures are being deliberately destroyed, that must increase the value of those remaining.'

'What if I don't agree to your propositions?'

'You go back to England. I hear, however, from sources in London that not all in high office there approve of your methods of doing business. And it might be in the interests of my country to demonstrate our wish to remain on good terms with Britain by throwing some light on the darker aspects of your business career, when love of money has taken precedence over love of country – any country. Indeed, all countries with which you have ever been associated.'

'I would sue anyone who made such gross allegations against me.'

'You would fail, Sir James. We would arrange for these questions to be asked in the House of Commons. Perhaps your knowledge of your adopted country's parliamentary procedure has not kept pace with your business advancement? Any Member of Parliament can raise any question, and make any statement, even about someone as rich and influential as you, secure in the knowledge that they are protected by parliamentary privilege from actions such as you threaten. Similarly, any newspaper can report parliamentary proceedings under the same protection. And I need hardly tell you that we have many political sympathisers in and out of Parliament.

'Now, we have talked enough. Those are my proposals. If you are interested, I will direct you to the people you must meet. I will also give you written authority to do business with anyone in the country. What do you say?'

'You leave me no option,' Mannering replied.

Lenin smiled and stroked his beard. 'So, the arch capitalist and the arch communist do business together. An irony worthy of Gorky or your Charles Dickens, don't you think?'

While Mannering was agreeing that this irony was indeed worthy of either of these writers, Mr Barnaby had just left the barber's shop off the Bayswater Road. He regularly met a number of people there by prior arrangement, but this morning the man he had agreed to meet had not arrived.

This was unusual, but since Mr Barnaby never gave his address to any of his contacts, it would have been impossible for the man to let him know he would not be there in the upper room.

Mr Barnaby waited for a quarter of an hour beyond the agreed time to meet, and then left the building. He walked to the Bayswater Road and took a taxi to Tottenham Court Road. He did not hail the first taxi, or the second or third, but the fourth. Then he walked down to Leicester Square and travelled by Underground to Belsize Park.

Outside this station, he bought an evening paper from a newspaper seller and stood, apparently reading it, but in fact carefully watching all the other passengers who had come up in the lift with him.

Mr Barnaby was a cautious man, and always took a roundabout route when he left the barber's shop, in case he was being followed. But now it was clear he was on his own. In the description he had learned years previously at the German army's spy school in Hamburg, he was clean.

He crossed the main road, walked along Howitt Road until he came to the terraced house where, throughout the war, he had rented three upstairs rooms.

The landlady thought he worked for a newspaper in Fleet Street, a job which explained his erratic hours. He had told her that because of tuberculosis he was unfit for any of the services. He was a very patriotic man, however, and she approved of the way he hung a small Union Jack on the sill of his front sash window to mark any Allied advance or victory.

Mr Barnaby opened the front door with his key, walked slowly up the shabby staircase. Outside his room, he took another key on a chain from his waistcoat pocket, put the key in the lock.

As he turned the key, hands seized him from behind and pinned his arms to his sides. Two wardrobes stood in the corridor, on either side of the door. The landlady explained they were really too big to fit into any room, but she liked them because they had been in her family for a long time. The two men who now gripped his arms must have been hiding behind them.

'Let go of me,' Mr Barnaby said hoarsely.

'Go into your room,' said the taller of the two men.

They went in, all three still locked together. The tall man kicked the door shut behind them, pressed the button on the lock. He released his grip as his companion frisked Mr Barnaby for a gun, a knife, or any other weapon. Mr Barnaby was unarmed; he was not a man of violence.

'Who are you?' he asked them. His voice contained a measure of returning authority.

'That doesn't really concern you,' said the tall man. 'It

is who you are that concerns us.'

'I am a British subject. I work for the *Daily Enquirer*. I am unfit for military service. I have a medical card from the doctor about that. It is in my wallet. Who *are* you? Is this a hold-up? If so, as you can see, I have nothing worth stealing.'

'We will ask the questions. You will answer them. The first is about Mr O'Brien and his barber shop, the second about Sir James Mannering.'

'I have had my hair cut several times by Mr O'Brien. He gives me a good price if I go on Saturday morning when he does not have many customers.'

'And what does Sir James give you?'

'I have never heard of the man. I don't know what you are talking about.'

The second man, who so far had not spoken at all, now produced an envelope from his pocket, shook out a blurred photograph. It showed Barnaby and Mannering walking away from the shop.

'Think again,' he said conversationally. 'And this time think clearly and answer honestly. A lot depends on it.'

'What do you mean, "a lot"?'

'I mean everything, Mr Barnaby. Your life.'

Chapter Eleven

Carola met Richard or Tom at least twice a week, but never of course together.

Neither knew nor even imagined she was seeing the other man, and Carola saw no need to enlighten them. She liked them both, but, as she kept assuring herself, in quite different ways. Richard she felt had the deeper character; he liked to ponder things, turn them over in his mind before reaching a decision. Tom was hasty, headstrong. Carola believed he needed someone to restrain him from making hasty and unthought-out decisions. But was she the person to do that? Did she even want to? The answer was, yes, she did.

One evening, out for a cycle ride with Richard, an imperative hooting sounded behind them and a two-seater car passed and then stopped a few yards ahead of them. Tom was driving, wearing his air force uniform. By his side sat a blonde girl, her hair wrapped in a silk scarf. She regarded Carola coolly.

'Hello there!' said Tom cheerfully. 'Where are you cycling off to? Gretna Green? Runaway marriage?'

'Nothing like that,' said Richard, suddenly wishing there was something like that. 'Nothing at all, really. Just taking the air, exercising the muscles. And you?'

'Borrowed this little bus from a friend. We're going out to have a drink, or four or five, then we'll see whatever the night offers. Well, mustn't keep you.'

He let in the clutch and accelerated away. The car's noisy exhaust covered them in blue smoke. They stood by their cycles, coughing.

'*Well*,' said Richard.

'*Well*,' agreed Carola and smiled.

'You see much of him?' asked Richard, suddenly sensing that this might not be the first time they had met since Tom showed them the biplane.

Carola shrugged as though this was very unimportant.

'From time to time,' she admitted casually.

'I didn't know,' said Richard.

'There's no reason why you should. You probably see people I know nothing about.'

'He's a good flyer,' said Richard, changing the subject. The people he met were all connected with his work; designers or engineering trainees unfit for military service; no one in whom he thought Carola would have the remotest interest. But Tom . . . Tom was a different type of person, very different.

'I believe he's pretty well off in Australia,' he went on as casually as he could. 'Thousands of acres, apparently. A property as big as Wales, so one of his friends told me.'

'How did you meet this friend?'

'The air force wanted some modifications to the machine-gun gears. Nothing very much. The friend came over to explain exactly what was needed. He told me.'

'So you asked about Tom?'

'Well, yes, in a way, I did.'

They mounted their bicycles and cycled on in silence. But whereas only moments earlier the silence between them had seemed friendly, almost drawing them closer together because neither felt any need to speak, now it became a chasm, dividing them.

Men are funny, Carola thought as she pedalled with her eyes firmly on the road ahead. What do I feel for

Tom? I'm not sure. He takes me out in any car he can borrow, including the one that just pulled up. Didn't think much of that girl, though. Peroxide blonde. Bit blowsy, almost a tart, really. But that type seems to appeal to some men. Yet is Tom like some men? Surely not. He's different. Isn't he? Again, the little niggling doubt entered her mind.

She thought back on their outings together. He would not meet her at the Battleaxes because, she thought, he somehow regarded that as Richard's area. He would suggest some other inn with a garden. They'd sit and have a drink, and talk. He'd kissed her, of course. Often. Not like Richard, almost hesitantly, as if this were a privilege. With Tom, it was not a privilege but a male right, his due. He would have gone much further, too, and so would she, but she was afraid. Several girls in the factory had become pregnant. Some had undergone agonising experiences with backstreet abortionists; a few girls had actually given birth. Their babies had been adopted and they missed them. Neither of these unhappy alternatives held any attraction for Carola.

Tom had taken her back several times to the mess on ladies' nights. These she found very impressive – candle-light, silver on the table, bowls of flowers, and uni-formed waiters with white gloves carrying in each course. It was difficult to remember there was still a war on with food rationing. Once, they ate steaks; another time, chicken or salmon.

'Oh, we get it where we can,' Tom had explained as vaguely and casually as he explained everything. 'Lot of us old colonials here, you know. We don't stand on ceremony. Canadians, New Zealanders, South Africans and, of course, us Australians. We all come from big countries. Here, everything's small. A land of little people, I call it. Tiny lanes, cars the size of toys. You go five miles to a party here and you're exhausted. It makes a talking point, the distance you've covered. In The Outback it may be thirty miles, or a hundred, to the nearest house. That's the scale of things. It affects how you think, how you act, how you live. You should come out to Australia after the war and see for yourself.'

'To do what, while I'm seeing for myself?'

'You could find a job for a month or two. Then just look around. I guess lots of English girls are going to do that, you know. You won't be the only one. There won't be much future here.'

'You don't think so?'

'I don't. You follow politics?'

'No. Not at all.'

'Then you should. Britain's very heavily in debt. Indeed, almost everything's hocked to the United States. They only came in the war because they had to. They were making far too much money to come in before, selling on both sides of the street. Neutrals. Even-handed to the Allies and the Central Powers.

'There are also a lot of sinister people moving money – and people – around. Bankers with middle-European backgrounds. Fellow came down here to give us some kind of talk the other week. Name of Mannering. Sir James Mannering. Richard mentioned him, said he had a controlling interest in the gear factory. Great financier, he's supposed to be. Patriot. All that. I thought he was a real crook and a bum. I'd have told him so, but the CO warned us all in advance there must be no questions or remarks of a provocative nature.'

'Would you have provoked him?'

'Too right I would. I'd have asked him who his father was, where he was born.'

'Does that matter?'

'To me it does. It says in the reference books he was born in London. I looked him up. Educated at your Eton College and Oxford. I think differently. I'd say he was maybe born on the Continent, but more likely in the Middle East, possibly even in Russia. You must never take people at their face value, Carola.'

'I'm taking you at yours.'

'You don't know my face's value.'

'You did mention you've got great estates.'

'Oh, sure, my old man has a station in Australia. But that's nothing very special to own, not out there. Just wish I were there now, though. It's a wonderful country. As I've told you, you should come and see for yourself.'

'Maybe I will. If I'm asked.'

'Maybe you will be,' said Tom, looking at her closely.

At that moment a waiter arrived. The mood was broken, just as Tom's arrival in the car had fractured the rapport between her and Richard.

Carola had sensed then that Tom was about to ask her to go to Australia – or could it even be he was going to ask her to marry him? That seemed absurd, a girlish fantasy, more suited to a novel than to reality. She didn't really know him. But then girls were marrying soldiers, sailors, airmen they hardly knew on forty-eight hours' leave. After four years of war, everyone had a sense of impermanence. She felt that herself. Somehow, to be married, to be one of a team of two instead of on your own, seemed comforting; you could face whatever ills might be in the future far more confidently. Or so it was said. Privately, Carola was not convinced. She remembered how her father's attitude changed whenever her mother left home. He'd become morose, bad-tempered, given to shouting at her, hitting her. But Tom hadn't asked her to marry him.

The morning after her bicycle ride with Richard, the forewoman called Carola into her office.

'Lady Warren wants to see you urgently,' she told her. 'You'd better go now, I think.'

'Any idea what it's about?'

The forewoman paused as though about to say more, then thought better of it.

'I think it would be best if she told you herself.'

Carola cycled back to the house, wondering what this urgent summons could mean. She had barely spoken to Lady Warren after their first meeting. Although Carola lived in her house, she ate meals in the servants' hall and used one of the back entrances. She had physically seen Lady Warren being driven away from the front door or arriving in her car a number of times, but that was about all. So what could she want to see her about now that was so urgent?

Lady Warren was in her study, smoking a cheroot. The stubs of several other half-smoked cheroots lay squashed in the silver ashtray on her desk. She was standing, back to the fire, the rear of her skirt raised to warm her legs.

'You look unusually surprised I should wish to see you urgently,' she said accusingly as Carola came into the room.

'I am, Lady Warren. We've not spoken much since you invited me to live here.'

'I've been too busy. Got other more important things to do than to speak to a rather silly girl.'

'Oh.'

'Don't say "oh" in that ridiculous way, as though you can't think what else I might have to do. You're surprised, are you, that I say you're silly? I'll tell you exactly why you're silly, bloody silly. It's obvious, or it should be obvious to anyone of the meanest intelligence, that when I offered you a place, as my guest, in my house, I did so because I felt you had the makings of someone more than just a dreary little girl, filling shell cases. I hope I'm not mistaken?'

'Have you reason to think you might be, Lady Warren?'

'Strong evidence suggests I could be. I understand you've been seeing something of two young men. Too much of them, in my opinion. One is an Australian flyer, the sort I'd call a ne'er-do-well, a rich man's son for whom the war is only a bit of fun, a *divertissement*, just as to him pretty girls like you are a bit of fun.

'The other man is a bit different. I've made some enquiries into his background, too. His father was killed in an accident in France just before the war. The boy was brought up as though he was rich. But in fact the family home is heavily mortgaged, and he is actually living at the expense of a generous aunt, who sees something in him. What have you to say about that?'

'They are my friends, Lady Warren. I see them fairly regularly.'

'Friends – or lovers?'

'Friends. I like them both.'

'They've made advances to you, I suppose.'

'That surely is my private affair, Lady Warren.'

'While you're working for *me*, living in *my* house, at *my* expense, you have no private affairs, however you may choose to define the meaning of those words. My forewoman reports you're a hard worker, but sometimes a day-dreamer. She also told me that other girls have seen you out in the company of these young men. Now I am not going to waste my time or my money on you if you're going to be like all the other little girls who just want a man and marriage and a little house and a little family. So, you've got to decide what you're going to do with your life. Now. Before we go any further.'

'I don't wish to sound ungrateful, Lady Warren, but what I do with my life is surely my own business. I'm very grateful to you for giving me a job, and putting me up here in your house. It was very kind of you and patriotic, and I will always appreciate it. But the war, so I read in the papers, is in its last stages. There's even talk

249

of an armistice. I don't know what'll happen to me then.'

'In other words, you hope one of these men may offer you marriage?'

'I think it is unlikely. But they might.'

'And if they did?'

'I might take their offer.'

'Whose offer?'

'I like them both, that's the truth – and the trouble.'

'You little fool! You think this is love?'

'I don't know what it is, but I enjoy their company – as I say, both of them. Richard is a thinker. He's got a good brain. He's already invented something that allows a machine-gun in an aeroplane to fire through the propeller blades. He'll do great things. And Tom makes me laugh. Also, I'd like to see Australia. I'm never likely to be able to go out there on what I can earn myself. So if Tom asks me, well, I'll think about it. You see, Lady Warren, you have a lot of money. I heard your husband left you a fortune. So no matter what you say about marriage now, you married yourself. Once.'

'And once was enough. I cannot recommend that situation at all. If your only aim in marriage is to secure the wherewithal to stay alive, in crude terms, to use a man as a meal ticket, earning more on your back than you can earn with your hands or your brain, then so be it.'

'I've not had much opportunity to earn much so far in any way.'

Lady Warren let her skirt drop, walked away from the fire, stubbed out her cheroot in the ashtray with the others.

'I married purely to get out of a rut that I could see myself being stuck in for the rest of my life,' she said. 'I had to get moving, and marriage was the only escape route I could see. No one offered me another way out, like I'm offering you. If I hadn't married, I could still be

250

working in a stall, selling shoes my father made. But I saw my chance, my only chance, and I took it. I'm offering *you* a chance. Now. A much better one. But whether you have the sense to take it is another matter.'

'What chance are you offering me, Lady Warren?'

'A chance that most people, men or women, never have in all their lives. So much of their time must of sheer necessity be spent earning just enough money to buy just enough food so that they can go out next day and earn just enough money to buy more food in order to keep alive *ad infinitum*. Note my choice of words. They only *earn* money. They don't, and can't, ever *make* it. I did and so I can pass on some of my good fortune to you. I'm offering you the opportunity to be someone special. Yourself.'

'That's very generous of you, Lady Warren. But how? I don't quite follow you.'

'Then you're a damned fool. More bloody silly than I took you for. Listen. I'll explain it in words a child could understand.

'Our country is in decline. It may be terminal. It may not. Oh, I know you can look around and say we've got an Empire, the biggest in the world, the largest navy. But it's past noon for us, well past noon. First, consider our casualties, largely on the Western Front. Fifty, seventy thousand men lost in a single battle, to achieve what? Gain – or lose – a few yards of mud. Ten times as many wounded, maimed or blinded for ever, driven out of their minds by their experiences.'

'But the enemy's casualties were just as large, surely?'

'Agreed, but they were conscript soldiers, forced to serve and fight. In the beginning, ours were not. Each man we lost in the first few years was someone very special, a volunteer from Britain or the Empire, not a pressed man.

'Cities and towns all over the country formed their

251

own battalions of the best young volunteers, and often lost them all in a single afternoon. That destruction of an entire generation of the bravest and best means that, in blunt terms, our future generations will largely be bred from second-raters, war dodgers, the degenerate and the effete. That is a primary cause of any concern for the future. We have not only lost the best, we have in addition lost the sons and daughters they never had.

'Next, this country's ability to keep itself in any other war without overseas help is very doubtful. To fight this war we had to place orders of immense size with the United States. We had the potential capacity to produce shells and guns and tanks and trucks and aircraft, but not in the numbers and speed required.

'All our businesses are small, usually run by families on old-fashioned lines. Maybe grandfather was a blacksmith. He prospered, brought his son in, so they could run two blacksmith shops. When cycling became popular they started mending cycles. Then instead of just mending cycles, they decided to make them.

'Lots of small companies in the Midlands produced frames and wheels and saddles, and touted them round for local firms to put together and call their own. Then came motorcycles, and cars, all built up from bits and pieces bought in, assembled in sheds or huts.

'Soon the grandsons of the founders were rich and lost interest in this sort of work. After all, they didn't need to run things themselves. So they handed over to managers and became country gentlemen. They bought estates, went shooting, hunting, fishing. The factories could run themselves. They didn't understand them or what they produced. They were above that sort of thing.

'That is why, when we needed masses of war material, in a damn great hurry, we went to the Americans. We had to or be beaten. The Americans drove very hard bargains. The Du Pont company, for example, making explosives for shells, insisted that first we had to build new factories for them to make explosives for us. These would be the property of the Du Pont company, of course. That was essential, they said, in case demand fell off after the war. And after all, who knew which side would win?

'We had to build other factories in the States to make aircraft and tanks. The Americans own them and will work on Mr Henry Ford's principle of mass production. Men stand on either side of a rolling belt, like a moving staircase, on which, say, the basic chassis of a car is put. Each man adds to it, wheels, mudguards, whatever. Then someone else drives it off at the end.

'I've introduced this system in my munitions factory and production is three times as high as with the old-fashioned way, as we make cars, bit by bit, using what I call knife and fork methods. One man has the job of fitting a headlight, say, then finds he hasn't enough nuts and bolts. So he has to cross the factory floor and look through boxes of odd nuts and bolts and washers until he finds ones that fit. Ridiculous.

'We couldn't beat Germany in terms of production. They have taken the title which used to be ours – workshop of the world. After the war we're going to be in trouble unless some people decide otherwise. And I think you can be one to carry the flag for this country.'

'How?'

'By showing that although we've lost the cream of a generation of young men, women can take their place. To do this, a woman must achieve something that catches the admiration of the world. You could just be that woman.'

'Me? How?' Carola's astonishment showed in her voice.

'By flying. I know you want to fly. And I know you've been up in a plane with this Australian. One day, people will think no more of getting into an aeroplane and flying all round the world than they do catching an omnibus today. But to bring this about we have to show that flying can be commonplace. People are used to hearing what pilots have done in the war, but they are all men. Once a woman flies, and beats the men, then they will say, "If a woman can do it, anyone can." I want you to be that woman, Carola.'

'But why me?'

'Because I believe in you, and I am not usually wrong in my assessment of people – and problems. I'm lucky, in that I have a great deal of money, more money than some of the banks. I'm unlucky in that I've never been attracted to men – nor to women, either. I've no one to follow on after me, no one to carry my name. When I heard what you'd done to that swine Campion, I thought you were the sort of daughter I would have liked to have had. The sort of girl who could benefit from what I can give you. A scientific education. And then . . .' Lady Warren paused.

'And then?' echoed Carola.

'I will finance you. For whatever it takes. I will pay the bills.'

'To do what?' asked Carola in a whisper, mesmerised by the intensity of the older woman's feelings.

'To show them what a woman can do, before men even attempt it. You will fly. But not only that. You will be the first woman to fly immense distances, to show how safe it is. There may be others who fly from Croydon to Rome, maybe to India, even to Australia. But they will be like the early acts on a music hall bill. They prepare the audiences for the real star, the top of the bill. And that's going to be you.

'You're going to make the biggest, most publicised flight in the world. The first woman, the first *person*, to fly from here to China, then over the Pacific to Los

Angeles, across the United States to New York, and back over the Atlantic.

'You'll be famous, you'll be in the history books. And you'll have shown that not only can we do it in Britain, but a British *woman* can do it. And that's important to me. There are as many women as men in this country, but in achievement we don't count for that much. You will make us count. With my money. Now do you understand me?'

'I understand you,' said Carola. 'But I don't know if I can do it.'

'I don't care what *you* know. I'm telling you what *I* know. You're *going* to do it – if you will trust me.

'When I was a young girl there used to be a fad for men to cross Niagara Falls on a tightrope. Blondin did it. Then came others. One man crossed pushing a wheelbarrow, then a wheelbarrow with another fellow inside. None of those men thought what would happen if they failed. They *knew* what would happen. They'd be crushed on the rocks, drowned by the torrent. They told themselves, we're going to get to the other side and make history. And that, my girl, with my backing, is what you're going to do in a far more worthwhile way.

'So forget these young men, the Englishman, the Australian. They'll do nothing for you except get you pregnant, and then it'll be goodbye to records, goodbye to everything. When you're married or, worse, unmarried, with a child, you're like a ship that could cross any ocean but is for ever locked in harbour, with anchors fore and aft. I don't want you to be like that. I don't want to *see* you doing that. I want you to *live*. And then I'll live through you. By proxy.' She stopped, almost breathless. 'Well? What do you say?'

'I don't know quite what to say, Lady Warren, except that I'm amazed and honoured you have such faith in me.'

'I don't want that mushy talk. What do you say to the offer, child?'

'I say "yes",' said Carola at once.

So Carola enrolled as a student of aeronautical engineering at the Regent Street Polytechnic. Not unexpectedly, she was the only girl on the course. Men students nudged each other and winked and raised their eyebrows and looked at her. She did not care. She would show them all, just as Lady Warren had said. She would put this learning, this theory, these bench tests into practice.

Like the alchemists of old who believed that one day they would find a stone which could turn base metal into gold, she would turn all she learned into a far more worthwhile achievement, not only for Britain, but for women everywhere.

The telephone rang in Sir Bernard's office. He picked it up, automatically pressed the scrambler button. The Home Secretary was on the line.

'Our legal people have been looking at this case of that Irish barber and the go-between Barnaby, which seemed to involve Sir James Mannering,' he said, without any preamble. 'The general feeling is that since they both have been dealt with, we should leave the matter there. While we probably would have a strong case against Mannering, it would at best be a messy business. He is, I am sure you appreciate, a very slippery customer with many powerful friends.

'I needn't elaborate to you all the ins and outs of the arms trade. Over the past few years, very large sums have been paid to all kinds of people to persuade them to do this or not do that. Such matters are obviously not in the public interest to reveal. But Mannering might ignore that interest if he felt he could save himself from some very unpleasant publicity, and maybe much more unpleasant retribution. You follow me?'

'Perfectly, Minister.'

'Well, since the war is behind us, thank God, and since we are facing all manner of peace conferences, and since frankly we may need Sir James's help again in the Middle East, the Cabinet decision is that we do not proceed against him.'

'Some people think we should have dealt with him at the time, Minister. We had a very good case against him. The man Barnaby told us a great deal.'

'Yes, yes, I know all that. But the matter isn't as simple as you make it sound. Anyhow, we are not proceeding with it.'

'This is a political decision, then?'

'It's a political decision, yes. But one based, I may say, on simple common sense. And we might even get a few free favours out of the gallant knight by hinting, in the phrase, that we know where the body is buried. You follow me?'

'Yes, sir.'

'Good. I thought you would. So just forget all about it. Goodbye to you.'

Sir Bernard replaced the receiver, sat back in his chair, stretched out his feet. How many times had he and others in his team uncovered some instance of gross treachery, even, as here, of trading with the enemy, only to be told there would be no prosecution because the guilty men might incriminate men of influence or men the public felt were honourable? Well, he had done what he believed was his duty. He had better follow the Home Secretary's advice and forget the whole matter.

Sir Bernard opened a drawer in his desk, took out the silver hip flask of whisky he kept there, unscrewed the top, put the flask to his mouth and drank deeply. He felt old and tired and dispirited. How different the honourable task of commanding a battalion had been, away from the mainstream of politics and corruption!

But that was long ago when he and the world seemed young. He couldn't just sit here drinking and brooding on life's unfairness. He'd lunch at his club, and hope some congenial companions would cheer him up. The fact was, he'd lost the heart for this business, and indeed, even for life.

What had hurt him more than he had realised at the time had been the death of his second son Arnold, just twenty-five. At first, Arnold had been reported missing, flying over the Western Front only days before the war ended. His eldest son had died at Verdun, and he and his wife had prayed that Arnold would survive.

They had clung to the shrinking hope that he had landed his plane on some flat field and been taken prisoner, unharmed. There had been several instances of this, but then a friend in Arnold's squadron told them he had seen the plane go down in flames. At last they had to accept that he was dead; he and how many million others?

To have served all through the war, first in the infantry, then in the Royal Flying Corps, latterly in the Royal Air Force, always without injury, and then to be shot down like a pheasant in the last days of the conflict seemed cruelly ironic. Moreover, Arnold had told him only days before that his squadron was going to be fitted out with machine-guns which through some new and ingenious mechanism could fire through the propeller blades. This meant they could attack enemy aircraft head on. But it turned out that the Germans already possessed this advantage. As several British aircraft, including Arnold's, still lacking this innovation, flew across a line of enemy aircraft in the traditional fashion, they were suddenly raked with devastating fire.

Sir Bernard sighed, pulled open the drawer again to put away the whisky flask. As he did so, he noticed, pushed towards the back under some other papers, the brown envelope of photographs taken from O'Brien's premises. He had all but forgotten about them; they must have been lying there for months and months. How embarrassing if someone had found them.

On an impulse, Sir Bernard took them out on his blotting pad, put on his reading glasses to examine them more closely before he threw them away. He found nothing erotic in any of them. They were all old poses, and yet several seemed to be printed on rather thicker paper than was usual for a photograph. Idly, he ran his thumbnail round the edge of one.

The photograph was stuck on a second sheet of paper. He looked at this more closely, picked up a letter-opener, carefully inserted the blade and peeled away the photograph. Underneath, on what had been a backing card, was part of a larger drawing. It showed gears meshing, arrows pointing, captions explaining ratios and figures he did not understand.

He put the card to one side and began systematically to peel the backs away from the other thicker photographs. Soon he was looking at a mosaic of some kind of mechanism. He fitted the pieces together – he was quite good at jigsaws when he had the time.

In fifteen minutes, Sir Bernard was looking at an engineer's drawing, cut into sections, each the size of a photograph. They showed a cluster of gears that would allow the pilot of a fighter aircraft to fire a gun through the blades of his propeller.

This, surely, would make the Home Secretary change his mind about Mannering. He knew that O'Brien had been running a clearing house of espionage in his barber's shop, and this unequivocally involved that bastard Mannering. He had been playing both sides of the street, as doubtless he had done all his life. Political decision or not, war or peace, this must be followed up. Sir Bernard picked up the telephone.

'The Home Secretary's private number,' he told the operator, and sat, holding the earpiece, staring at the drawings, thinking about his son spiralling down the winter sky to his death.

'Hello?' The petulant voice of the Home Secretary sounded in his ear.

'Forgive me troubling you, sir. Bernard Warner speaking.'

'Yes?'

'I have just discovered something I think you should know. Those pornographic photographs found in the barber's shop we were discussing just now. Each one is pasted on a piece of card. I found one loose, so I peeled the backs off all the photographs. Underneath are sections of an engineer's drawing of that gadget that allowed pilots to fire through the blades of aircraft propellers. The plans must have been sold to the Germans by Mannering.'

'If so, why is it still on your desk?'

'It must be a copy. Probably several copies exist in case one was lost or confiscated. But this is hard evidence that Mannering was, maybe still is, a traitor of the most serious kind.'

'That's your opinion, Bernard, and of course you're entitled to it. But, as I explained earlier, the war is over. We are now concerned about the peace. Mannering has a role to play in that. The Cabinet decision stands. Do I make myself clear?'

'Perfectly,' said Sir Bernard, and put down the telephone without even saying goodbye.

As Sir Bernard was leaving his office, Tom Gardener was driving Carola through Hertfordshire lanes, out towards St Albans.

She had never been in a car as powerful as his (borrowed) Sizaire-Berwick. Just inches from her feet the engine seemed to tremble in its wish to race at unprecedented speed along the dusty road.

It was an exhilarating feeling, almost as good as flying; not quite, but a fair contender. She glanced sideways at her companion. He was still wearing uniform. Most of his colleagues had thrown their uniforms away when the war ended and changed into civilian clothes. They might still technically be in the services, but because they had come from distant parts of the Empire to help the Old Country, they felt no need to wear uniform any longer.

Tom sensed she was looking at him, turned and smiled at her. But his face was grave. He looked more set and stern than she had ever seen him. He drove into a wide parking space at the side of a roadside hotel.

'Let's have lunch here,' he suggested. 'It's early, I know, but we could go on somewhere afterwards, look round St Albans. It's a quaint old place.'

'As you say.'

Carola climbed out of the car, followed him into the inn. One room had been set aside as a small restaurant with five tables. They were all laid: starched white cloths, imitation silver cutlery, polished glasses. A fire was burning in the grate. Above the mantelpiece hung a framed photograph of a young private soldier in uniform. His plain, unsophisticated face stared out at them. Carola crossed the room to read the inscription beneath: 'Private J. Leonard, Beds and Herts Regiment. Died of wounds, April 21, 1917.'

The landlord came into the room. He was in his fifties, prematurely grey.

'Your son?' she asked him, not meaning to, but somehow unable to restrain the question.

He nodded.

'Our only son,' he replied. 'He used to help me a lot. I hoped he'd take over when I retire. This is a free house, you know. Not tied to any brewery. But there you are.

That's life. But I must say, all the victory celebrations sounded a bit hollow to the wife and me.'

'I can imagine,' said Tom. 'I can well imagine.'

'However,' said the landlord, 'that's in the past. The Bible says let the dead bury the dead, but you can't bury the memories. They live on. Now, what'll be your pleasure?'

Tom said, 'We'll have a sherry each before lunch. And then perhaps we can order.'

There were two easy chairs by the fire. The landlord brought the sherries, put them down on a side table and withdrew, closing the door. Tom handed one glass to Carola, raised his own.

'To you,' he said. 'To our future.'

She heard the almost imperceptible emphasis on the word 'our' and for some reason she could not understand, she felt suddenly nervous. She had never seen Tom serious before. She didn't like him serious. He was a fun person, cheerful, laughing, but not serious; at least, not until now. He drained the glass at one swallow, sat forward in his chair, his hands on his knees, manifestly awkward.

'I wanted to see you to tell you something,' he said. 'Two things in fact.'

He paused. She waited.

'The first is, I'm going home next week.'

Of course, the war was long since over. But even so she had somehow vaguely imagined he and his friends would be here indefinitely. She could not think of life without their cheerfulness, their totally different, outgoing attitude.

'Why?' she asked. Silly question, she knew, but she couldn't think what else to say.

'Well, we've done what we came over for, that's why. I've been here four years. Bit more, really, which is long enough. And there's work to do back home.'

'You'll go back working for your father?' she asked him.

'With, I hope, not for,' he corrected her. 'We've got a big station. My young brother's there. He'll be about eighteen. He's helping my old man. We've got a number of Abos – Aborigines – who work on the station. But my old man is getting a bit past it and there's a hell of a lot to do. I feel I've been wasting time – marking time is perhaps a better phrase – for these years I've been away.'

'But you've been fighting, flying. You won the Military Cross.'

'So did lots of others. And what's going to happen to them now? I'm lucky, for I've something to go back to. Many of the fellows on the airfield haven't anything. Some have already been back to the firms that employed them and found other men in their jobs, and they don't want to leave. Some were shirkers, conchies, or were genuinely unfit. Others were too old to join up. And women are doing men's jobs now. As one man said to me, we joined up when we were wanted, and now we're not wanted.'

'But I read in the newspaper that the Prime Minister was saying there'd be homes for heroes.'

'Sure. But not enough homes, and too many heroes. And the bloke who's a hero now will be a liability in a couple of years, if he isn't already. He won't settle down easily, not after what he's seen, where he's been. People have very short memories.'

'It's not like you to be so cynical.'

'I'm not being cynical, just realistic. I asked you out here, somewhere we've never been to before, sort of breaking new ground, if you like, to tell you that.'

'I'm so sorry,' she said. 'I just can't believe you're going. I've loved knowing you and flying, and talking to you about Australia. It sounds wonderful out there. All that space and heat. Nothing crowded. None of the rules and restrictions we have here.'

He looked at her now very closely. His eyes had never seemed bluer. She suddenly imagined him focusing them along a gun sight, firing through the spinning blades of a propeller. Then from thinking of Richard's invention, her mind turned to him and she suddenly wondered where he was, what he was doing. Could he be entertaining a girl she knew nothing about? Tom's voice brought her thoughts back to him.

'I'm glad you think like that,' he was saying. 'I hoped you would. Because that brings me to the second reason I asked you here, Carola. I love you.'

Love was a word Carola had often read in novels, in newspaper articles. But no one had ever told her they loved her. Maybe her mother had done when she was a small girl, but Carola could not remember the occasion.

'I love you,' Tom repeated.

'I didn't know that,' she said weakly. 'I've always enjoyed being with you. I like the way you kiss.' Another silly remark, but it was the first thought that came to mind. 'I like everything about you. But, love . . . Are you sure?'

'I know,' he said convincingly. 'I knew the first time I saw you. Outside that factory. You'd driven up there with all those belts of ammunition with some other woman and you were standing there. And there was that other bloke, Richard. Do you still see much of him, by the way?'

Tom asked the question with deceptive, calculated casualness.

'Sometimes,' she replied with equal care. 'He's very nice.'

'Yes. And I'm very nice, too.'

He smiled in an attempt to be his old carefree self. 'Anyhow, I've never said this to any other girl. I've never really wanted to. But I'll be quite honest with you. I don't want to come to you under false colours. I've had my fun with girls, back home and here. But I've never felt for any of them what I feel for you. I just want to go on looking at you for the rest of my life.'

'You'd soon get very tired of that,' Carola told him, but feeling very flattered nonetheless. Did she want to look at him all the rest of her life? He was handsome, he was charming. But . . . But what? Before she could sort out in her mind reasons against this prospect, Tom was talking again, and she was listening.

'I don't want to beat about the bush,' he said. 'I want to come right to the point. That's the way I was brought up to do with everything. Never run away from a problem, never dodge it. Go right in.'

'Is this a problem?' she asked him, smiling.

'Hell of a problem, Carola. The biggest I've ever come up against. Like I say, I love you. I want to see you every day of my life, every hour of my life. I want you to marry me. I'm proposing marriage to you.' He looked at her.

'You want an answer now?' she asked him.

'Of course. Why waste time?'

'I'm sorry, but I can't give you an answer now.'

'Why can't you? This other bloke, Richard?'

'No-o. Though I like him. But the reason is something different altogether. I don't know if you'll understand.'

'I'll try. What is it?'

'This woman, Lady Warren.'

'Making a pass at you, is she? She's one of those?'

'No, no. Not at all. She was married once. She wants different things.'

'Like what? She's teaching you to want different things?'

'In a sense, yes.'

'What things?'

'It's very difficult to explain, but I'll do my best. Hear me out.'

265

'I'll hear you. Get talking.'

'She has a lot of money. And she wants to put that money to a cause she thinks is worthwhile. She points out that while half the population of this country – the world, in fact – are women, we don't have very much say in matters, and we don't make use of what you might call our potential in the professions or jobs. Oh, they use us in offices typing letters. Typewriters, they call us. That sort of thing, and as housekeepers, mothers.'

'But women are cut out for that. That's their natural role.'

'Sure. And you're probably cut out to be fathers, too, some of you. But you also have other careers. She knows my interest in mechanical things, which I suppose is unusual for a girl. She wants me to get a degree in engineering.'

'You can still do that if you're married. No problem.'

'Not at first, maybe. But when women have children, they get bound up with them. The moment for doing something on your own passes. There's a time, often a very short time, for everything. You have to seize what is going past at that moment, or lose it for ever. Life is like musical chairs. When the music stops, you need to grab a chair. I'm doing an engineering course now at the Regent Street Poly, and then she plans to get me some sort of job with an aircraft manufacturer so that I can learn the practical side as well.'

'And then? You want to be a mechanic in an aircraft factory all your life?' Tom looked at her in surprise.

'Not for all my life. Only for as long as it takes me to learn what I have to know to fly. I've always wanted to fly – as a pilot, not a passenger. And Lady Warren wants me to break records, to be the first woman to fly – who knows where? Perhaps even round the world.'

'That's a hell of a long flight, the longest there is. You've only been up for short times so far, and it's fun

266

then. But when you're flying for hours on end, it gets cold and lonely. You lose the ability to measure time and distance. I know. So many people have told me that if man – or woman – was ever meant to fly, then God would have given us all wings.'

'That's rubbish,' she said. 'You might as well say that if we were meant to swim, we'd have been given fins and scales. We *can* fly, and I mean to, properly, breaking records, before I get married – if I ever do marry.

'I've got to be honest about that. I like you very much. You're unlike any other person I've ever met. You're fun, all the time. I like the aura about you of a great country on the other side of the world. Vast distances. A land where there are no reasons for not doing things, just plenty for doing them.'

'So come out and join me,' he said. 'You can fly just as well in Australia; better, in fact. I was figuring I'll buy a small plane when I go back anyway, to fly about the station. It's quite simple to make a landing field, put up a wind-sock and a hut for the plane, keep it out of the sun. It's a damn sight quicker than driving by car or riding on horseback, I can tell you. You could help me.'

'I'd love to,' she said. 'I really would. But that's only a substitute for what I feel I can do.'

'So your answer is no?' He drew back from her.

'My answer is not no, but not yet. Give me time to try this, please. If I fail . . .'

'If you fail, then you'll take up my offer?' he said sharply. 'I can see that, even understand it. You want a soft landing, a silk parachute landing. But life isn't like that, Carola. There are no soft landings, and no free meals – except this one. You pay for everything, in one way or another.

'I may go back to Australia and meet someone else. Okay, maybe I won't feel for them like I feel for you, but they'll be there and you'll be here, six weeks' voyage away. I'm asking you for the last time to marry me, to say yes now.'

Carola shook her head miserably. She felt tears run down her cheeks. She did not even bother to dab them away.

'I can't,' she said. 'Not yet. You must understand. Please.'

Tom sat back, banged his empty glass angrily on the table. The door opened. The landlord looked at them enquiringly.

'A large treble whisky and soda for me,' Tom told him. He turned to Carola. 'What do you want?'

'I don't know,' she admitted wretchedly. 'I don't know.'

It was nearly midnight when Tom drove back to his billet. The lunch had not been a success. They ate in silence, and then both would begin to speak at the same time and stop and wave the other to continue. Afterwards, as Tom had suggested, they walked round St Albans, but the day was cold and cheerless, and at teatime rain began to fall. That somehow seemed to mark the end of their outing.

Tom drove Carola back to Lady Warren's house, stopping, at her request, about a hundred yards from the main gate in case someone saw them together and told Lady Warren.

He drove on alone, and then saw some fellow Australians going into a public house. He stopped the car and joined them. It was their last night in England. They were leaving in the morning by special train for Tilbury and then would go aboard a troopship. Next stop, home.

Tom wasn't quite sure what home would be like now; he had been away for a long time. He'd been only a boy when he left, he kept telling himself. Now he was a man. Did he really want to go back home? And where was home? He had grown used to messes, hutted camps, tents; home to him now was where he hung his hat.

He had a couple of whiskies, then drove on to his billet. He kicked off his shoes, unbuttoned his uniform, threw it on the floor, lay down on his bed. There was no need to keep his uniform smart any longer. He should have got rid of it like so many of his contemporaries. But he knew the reason he had not; it represented a kind of stability he had never known in Australia and somehow had grown to appreciate. Three meals a day guaranteed, a roof over his head, a regular income.

Tom lay back, already half asleep. Then he remembered a letter that had arrived just before he went to pick up Carola. He had not bothered to read it then. Now, he decided to do so.

He climbed off his bed, picked up his uniform jacket, took the letter out of a pocket, opened it. It was from his younger brother in Perth, and had been written and posted several weeks earlier.

Dear Tom,

I expect you're getting ready to come back. So I thought I would write and tell you, no bullshit, there isn't too much here to come back to.

Dad was taken for a sucker by someone who sold him shares in a gold mine. He took a mortgage on the station, certain he was going to make his fortune. He lost everything. Ma went mad. She knew nothing about this. Only when the letters started arriving.

Now the bloody bank's foreclosing. You can't blame them because we're not the only ones going through a hard time. A number of banks have shut up shop themselves, too. People have been beating on their doors trying to get their money out, their whole life savings. But there isn't any money there.

It's all gone. And the station's going, too, unless a miracle happens.

Don't get me wrong, Tom. We'd be glad to see you always and, as Mum and Dad say, this is your home. But there's not much of it left, I tell you. A few acres, a house and that's about it. So what I'm saying is this. If you can get a job in England meanwhile, at least until things get better – because believe me they can't get much bloody worse – then that would tide you over for a bit and all could be OK.

Hope this finds you as it leaves me, in good health.

Robert

Tom read the letter again, rolled it into a ball, flicked it towards the wastepaper basket. He missed. He was losing his touch. He'd never missed up there in the sky, in four years,not a damn thing. Well, he was missing now.

Odd, how he had just been thinking he might not be so keen on going back, and now that he was being told bluntly he shouldn't go back, he rather wanted to go. What the hell could he do here if he stayed on in this cold little island? It was one thing to be here in uniform. Girls were taken by your accent and your stories of Down Under, which was so different from England. A different world, of course. He'd had his way with a lot of them.

He'd not been fair, looking back, but who was it had said all was fair in love and war? It didn't matter what you told the girls to get them on their backs or up against a wall. That's what counted: to score in the sky – or on the ground.

He'd not been fair to this kid Carola, either. But she was a beaut looker and he knew he hadn't a lot of time so he'd given her the old spiel. *I love you. I want to marry you. I can't live without you.*

That had always worked before, sometimes worked too damn well. Couple of girls had told him they were expecting because of him. To one of them he'd written back a letter with a note he persuaded a friend to write, signing himself the squadron doctor, to say that he was impotent. It was therefore medically impossible for Captain Tom Gardener to father a child, and so no credence whatever could be placed on her claim that he was the father, etc., etc. It was a rough letter, sure. But Tom guessed if he could screw her, then so could someone else. And not only one; maybe lots of other blokes. So why should he carry the can?

To deal with the other girl he'd persuaded the same fellow to sign himself as squadron commander in a letter that told how Captain Gardener had most unfortunately been lost in aerial combat over enemy lines, attempting to save the life of another pilot. A bit over the top, that explanation, he thought now, but what the hell; it made a better story, and again it worked. He'd never heard another thing from the girl. He hadn't expected to; after all, it was unlikely she would waste time writing a letter to a dead man.

Lying on his bed now, he thought about those two, and about some others, but about those two especially. He hadn't done them a favour. And it couldn't be easy to have an illegitimate child on your own in this cold, Calvinistic country.

Funny thing, when the sun was warm, people were warmer, too; they took a more relaxed view of these things. But when it was cold they became tight-lipped, tight-arsed. But then, he told himself, those girls had also been screwed by other men. But even as he assured himself there must have been others, he didn't really believe it, not deep down. They had been nice quiet kids.

271

Good lookers, too. Fine pair of tits, both of them had. No doubt about it, he was the father, and he was a shit. So what? It was every man for himself in this world.

Now this girl, Carola. He'd thought he could lay her, felt certain he could, in fact. He'd kissed her often enough, got a hand under her blouse once or twice. But she wasn't easy, not like the rest. She had something about her the others lacked. He couldn't quite put a name to it. Maybe it was guts or enterprise, something like that, for her background, like his, was nothing special. Not like that bloke Richard Rowlands whose old man had owned properties and farms and a damn great house the size of Perth museum.

Yet he could tell by the way Carola looked at him that she liked him. Or was she just impressed, intrigued, like the others? Of course, he was a good-looking fellow, no question. He'd got a way with him, and a way with women. Everyone said so. Carola probably thought so, too. He'd hang around, not give up so soon. Sometimes it was difficult to pull a peach off a tree. So wait until the peach ripens and you don't have to pull; it falls.

But if he stayed on in England for a while he had to find a way to make some money, real money. He lit a cigarette, blew a smoke ring up towards the ceiling. Money. He thought of something a Pom said once, a rich Pom apparently, son of a lord or something; if you couldn't make money, then you married it. Bloody true, that. Good advice, too. Trouble was, he didn't know any woman who was rich. If he did, he'd marry them willingly. Get a settlement first, of course. Then he'd be wealthy, even if he left them – as he would if they became boring, as all women tended to.

The woman Carola kept mentioning, Lady Warren, who was paying her fees at technical college, wanted to train her to fly and all that. If he married *her* he'd be rich, but he guessed he hadn't a chance. He'd never met her, but he'd heard enough about her from other girls he'd taken out from the munitions works. She had been married once and that was enough. Of course, she had married for money herself, but would this make her more or less susceptible to a man with the same idea in mind? He was not sure, but either way his chances of success must be remote.

Maybe Carola could get some money from her. Maybe he should try harder with Carola and suggest the idea. It was really against his instincts to marry at all, because once married, you were caught, like a fish in a small-mesh net. He had seen so many friends land in that net. He had no wish to join them, for so long as he was single he was free, and while he was free other, better opportunities might present themselves.

The obverse of this freedom was that he was also free to starve. In the meantime, the only thing he knew well was flying. Could he make a living at that? Very doubtful. He hadn't got an aircraft for one thing, and he couldn't afford to buy one. It all came back to money in the end. Everything did.

What if he and maybe one or two others who also might not want to return to Australia for reasons of their own got together and started some sort of air circus? They could go round the country giving displays or, even better, offering flights. Five shillings a hop, ten shillings a longer hop. There was something in it. But could he get it off the ground?

Within a week, Tom had his answer. The whole squadron was finally being disbanded. Most had already gone, the rest would leave within days. Over a drink in the mess, the commander remarked how, because of contracts, aircraft firms were still making planes that no one wanted to buy.

'It's an extraordinary situation,' he said. 'Raw material goes in one end of the factory and planes come out at the other. And as soon as one comes out, it's just broken up for scrap. Right there and then.'

'But that's crazy,' said Tom.

'Sure it's crazy. The world's crazy. But it's all a matter of contracts. The government has agreed to buy so many planes, say a hundred. They've got to stand by that. There's no clause in the agreement that allows them to cancel, so a hundred planes it is.

'Of course, they try to reach a compromise, but the plane makers don't want a compromise. They want the profit on a hundred sales. So they work the contract out of their system. You could probably buy one of those cheaply if you wanted, you and a few others.'

Tom's pay was paid into the local branch of the bank on the first of every month. He had a couple of hundred pounds in a current account. Better see the manager, find out whether he could borrow more. An aircraft wouldn't be very expensive, but it would still be more than he could afford on his own.

The manager was a small, plump man, with a tidy mind and a tidy office. On his desk he had a blotting pad, a telephone, a pen and an inkwell. Tom noticed he had no paper to write on. But maybe life was quiet in a provincial branch?

'I'm leaving the service,' Tom explained. 'And there are two things I came to see you about. One, to thank you for looking after my account while I've been over here. And the second, to see if I could borrow some money.'

'You're staying on in this country?'

'Yes. For the time being, at least.'

'Things are bad in Australia, I hear. And you've been away a long time.'

'I had a letter from my younger brother who says things are a bit rough. He thought I should stay here for a while, get a job, see how everything worked out.'

'And what job have you in mind? Are you Captain Gardener now, or Flight Lieutenant – these new RAF ranks, they're difficult to get used to.'

'I'm plain Mister again. And I want to buy an aircraft. One for a start, maybe more later. And either on my own or with one or two others I want to see if I can run a business giving flights, aerobatic shows at country fairs, that sort of thing. I've a couple of hundred quid in my account, but I don't think that will pay for an aircraft. Or if it does, I'll still need more for running expenses. I'd have to fly the plane from place to place. You can't take it on the roads, because the wings don't fold.'

'Have you had any experience of business, Mr Gardener?'

'Not this business. But I hope I'm going to have some very soon.'

'I see. And what sort of advance do you have in mind?'

'Five thousand pounds,' said Tom, reckoning it was always best to aim high and come down if necessary.

The manager pursed his lips; this was far more than he had expected or had the authority to lend. 'On what security?' he asked.

'Me. Myself. My skills. My life. The fact that I've been over four years in the air force. The fact that I know more about flying than I know about anything else. I'm going to take a risk with this plane. I'm going to buy it, and, as I say, take other people in with me if I can.'

'That means, of course, you will have to pay them.'

'Well, maybe, to start with, a little bit. But then we can split what comes in.'

'But to do all this, Mr Gardener, you need money. And you propose doing this on the bank's money?'

'Well, that was my intention. That's how banks make money, surely? Lending. Usury. The old Shylock touch, eh?'

The bank manager frowned. This was not the sort of

275

conversation he cared to prolong.

'Have you any other securities, apart from your own skills?'

'You know I've none. Except for that two hundred in the bank.'

'That is not sufficient security on which to borrow five thousand.'

'All right. I've made my pitch. Now, what would you offer?'

'I'm sorry to say this, Mr Gardener, but without some security, tangible security, which in the event of any mishap or unfortunate occurrence . . .'

'You mean like me falling out of the sky and dying?'

'Well, yes. Or over-trading, getting into debt. In the circumstances you describe to me, I could not recommend to my superiors that they advance any money at all.'

'Shit to that. You mean I get *nothing*? I've been here fighting, risking my life, for years.'

'That is not the issue here, Mr Gardener. We all appreciate what you've done, none more than me. If it had not been for a gammy leg, I would have been in the forefront of the volunteers. But someone had to man the businesses at home. As Ivor Novello's excellent song says, "Keep the Home Fires Burning".'

'You can keep the home fires burning or you can let them go out, far as I'm concerned,' said Tom shortly. 'So your answer is no, thumbs down, nix?'

'I'm sorry to say that it has to be unless you can find a partner or colleague who has collateral.'

'I can't,' said Tom. 'But stuff you.'

'That is not an attitude which is going to promote your business affairs.'

'Maybe not. But it's lucky you have a gammy leg or I'd kick your arse. Goodbye.'

Tom stormed out of the office. He walked down the

road, trembling with rage, muttering curses at this ridiculous man and the unnamed, unknown superiors to whom he could not put his proposition.

But as he walked, he calmed down slowly. He'd blown a fuse too soon, been a bloody idiot, antagonised that stupid toad in there, and now he'd never lend him money. And maybe if he went to another bank, took out his wretched two hundred pounds, deposited it with them, they'd check with this bank and then he'd be right back where he started from, labelled as a difficult, touchy Aussie bastard.

He stood on the street corner, watching the cars go by. People needed money to buy a car; they needed money to pay for the petrol, the road tax, insurance. You couldn't live without money, but unless you could make it, that only left the option of marrying it.

As he stood there in the sunlight, he suddenly had an idea. He smiled to himself. It would take some handling, but he was equal to that, and if he was careful and bided his time, it could set him up for life.

Chapter Twelve

The Australians were having a farewell sing-song in the upper room of a pub in Elstree. They had reached the middle of one of those raucous choruses that men sometimes sing to conceal an inner sadness when their group is disbanding, breaking up. Afraid to let their real feelings show, they belt out rude rhymes with a savage, drunken intensity to conceal regrets and concerns which they fear companions might call unmanly.

The air was pale blue with cigarette smoke by the time Tom arrived; all the windows were closed. He went round the room until he found the man he wanted.

'A moment of your valuable time, Sandy,' he told him.

'What are you offering me for it?' asked Sandy, a cadaverous, lanky man with fair hair, already thin on top. He had been drinking heavily and he slurred his words.

'Whatever your pleasure is.'

'That's easily answered. A treble whisky. Neat!'

'You're on.'

'So where do you want to spend this moment of my valuable time, then?'

'In the corridor. Outside.'

'You want to watch him!' shouted someone drunkenly, waving a tankard at them. 'Keep your back to the wall, Sandy!'

Sandy grinned, followed Tom out into the corridor,

closed the door. Behind them, the singing started again.

'What have I got to do for the drink?' Sandy asked.

'What you've done before,' Tom told him. 'Remember that note to the girl who said I'd got her up the spout?'

'There are plenty of girls you've probably got up the spout. And I remember writing two letters, not one.'

'Right. Now I want you to write me another.'

'Goddammit, I've said you're dead once, and forged my name as the squadron commander. Before that I was the squadron MO and said you'd had an operation and couldn't do *anything*. So what's it to be now? You've come back from the grave with three balls like a pawn-broker?'

'Not quite. I'll tell you what to write. But first, can you get a sheet of paper with the squadron crest, and that rubber stamp with the MO's qualifications again?'

'Shouldn't be too difficult. All sorts of rubber stamps are in the billet. They're going to be thrown away.'

'When are you going back there?'

'Soon as this sing-song is finished.'

'Finish it now. I want you to get one of those stamps before it's too late. Then I'll buy you another treble. Be a pal.'

'What's the hurry, sport?'

'I'll tell you. On the way to the billet.'

Lady Warren's housekeeper came into the study. She held a salver on which lay a white visiting card. Lady Warren was writing at her desk, blowing smoke from her cheroot over the ink to dry it. She gave no indication that she had seen the housekeeper.

'What do you want?' she asked at last, not looking up.

'There's a man to see you.'

'I don't like seeing men. You know that. Who's this coming here without an appointment? Some bloody salesman?'

'No, your ladyship. He's an Australian pilot, just going back to Australia. He asked to see you especially. Said it was important.'

'When people say that they usually mean it's important to them. What's his name?'

The housekeeper examined Gardener's card.

'Tom Gardener, MC,' she read.

'So what does he want to see me about? Did he say?'

'Only that it's important. A personal matter, your ladyship.'

'The hell it is. I don't want to get personal with this man. Or with any man.'

'Very good, your ladyship.' The housekeeper turned back towards the door. Lady Warren took the cheroot out of her mouth.

'I didn't tell you to go,' she barked. 'Show him in. He's come a long way to fight for the Old Country. The least I can do is to hear what he has to say – and then kick him out.'

'As you say, your ladyship.'

Tom came into the room, bowed.

'Thank you for seeing me, Lady Warren. I've heard a lot about you.'

'And I've heard you've been sniffing around the skirt of Carola Marsh.'

'I wouldn't describe it like that, Lady Warren. But I do think she's a very nice person. And I know she owes a great deal to you.'

'Who told you that?'

'She did.'

'So you've been talking about me behind my back?'

'No, your ladyship. She is immensely grateful to you. I've asked her several times if she'd come out with me, but she always says she has to study instead, and not let you down.'

'Really? Look, Mr Gardener, I may be a widow

281

woman, but I'm not a damn silly widow woman. She has been out with you, quite often, so I understand.'

'Well, sure, now and then. But there's nothing more to it than that. Except for one thing.'

'Which is?'

'I would like to say, as a pilot myself, that I believe she has all the talent you think she has for flying. And possibly more. I feel she could really do great things, fly to places where probably no one has flown before, certainly no woman. She has guts, if you'll pardon the expression.'

'I'll pardon any bloody expression,' replied Lady Warren. 'Go on. Don't mealy-mouth me.'

'She has the guts of any two men I've ever met. If she'd been a man, she'd have made a great fighter pilot.'

'So you've come here to tell me that, have you?'

'I've come to tell you that, yes. And something else.'

'Which is?'

'I would like to teach her to fly. Not just what she could learn in a flying school – though that would be pretty good – but all the tricks of the air I learned the hardest way of all, with my life at stake. The sort of things flying schools don't teach because the instructors just don't know. How to conserve your fuel in an emergency. How you can use air currents to your advantage when you've bad engine trouble or are low on fuel. How you can cut your engine if you have to, and glide if you're out of petrol. How to survive if you must make an emergency landing – as we were taught to survive if we came down over enemy territory.

'I learned these things the hard way, Lady Warren, by doing them. I'd like to pass them on to her, because they're an extra skill which, if she goes into record-breaking flights seriously, she'll need.'

'What did you do before you joined up?'

'I worked on my father's station in Australia.'

'Are you going back there?'

'Eventually. I'd better tell you why I'm staying here for a while.'

'Because of this girl?'

'No. Because things are very bad economically in Australia. I have just had a letter from my younger brother. He says I should take a job here for a bit, if I can find one, till things improve at home. I thought I might buy one or two unwanted aircraft, and make a living stunt flying at fairs, giving five-shilling hops to country yokels, that kind of thing. But the bank wouldn't lend me any money. I'd no security except myself and my experience in the war as a pilot, and that just wasn't enough.'

'I should think not,' said Lady Warren. 'Money's a hard thing to come by. And you'll never get much help from banks. They'll shower you with money when you don't need it. But when you do and you ask to borrow ten pounds, too often it's goodbye. Unless you have twenty pounds' security. So, having failed with the bank, you thought you'd come to me and offer yourself as a flying instructor to Carola, with me paying the bill. Am I right?'

'I'd pay it myself if I could. But I can't.'

'I see. Sit down. Don't just stand there. You smoke?'

'No.'

'I smoke twenty of these cheroots a day and I feel all the better for it – so I tell myself. Now don't give me what you'd call bullshit. What you really want is to hang around Carola, get her on her back, in crude terms, don't you? Then maybe you want to do what you might call the decent thing, and marry her.'

'I don't want that at all. I want to help her dedicate herself totally to a career I am certain she has, a great career. If you're going to be a concert pianist, you have to practise every day of your life. If you miss practising one day, *you* know you've missed it. If you miss two days, the audience knows. There's no let-up, no time to relax or for distractions. If you seriously wish to succeed you have to go at it wholeheartedly.

'Carola has a natural interest in mechanical things, which in my experience is very rare in a girl. She's also keen on flying, and that is another rare thing for a girl. Add the two together and you're looking at someone who has a lot to offer aviation and, more important, to this country. Most important of all, she can show the world that what a man can do, a woman can do just as well.'

'Nice speech, Mr Gardener, but I still think you'd like to have your way with Carola.'

'Lady Warren,' said Tom gravely. 'I wish that could be true. But unfortunately it cannot be so.'

'What the hell do you mean? You're young, you're fit. What's the matter? You a pansy? One of those?'

'No, Lady Warren. Since, in a sense, I'm being interviewed for a job, I think it would save us both embarrassment if you would kindly read this letter.' He took out an envelope from his jacket, handed it across the desk.

Lady Warren shook out a letter, put on a pair of pince-nez, read it aloud. So much for saving embarrassment, thought Tom.

To whom it may concern. Tom Gardener MC.
As senior medical officer of the air section of the
Imperial Australian Expeditionary Force, I have
examined this officer over a period of several
months. I have to report that, owing to severe back
and abdominal injuries to the body and the central
nervous system, sustained as a result of being shot
down over enemy territory, captured, maltreated
for months, and then escaping via a neutral country

to British lines, he has suffered irreparable damage to his reproductive system. He will never be able to become a father.

More than that, any kind of sexual gratification is denied him. He has been examined by leading medical and surgical specialists, and all agree with my opinion. We consider this a grave tragedy for one so young and of such promise, and especially since his skills and bravery have contributed so much to victory in the air.

The damage to this officer's personal life and welfare is impossible to compute. He may be considered fortunate in that he is a single man, not engaged to be married. I have to put on record that in fifteen years of specialist practice in this field, I have never come across a case of a man whose injuries have resulted in such total and irrevocable impotence at such a young age.

'Who the hell is this intended for?' Lady Warren asked.

'See the bottom of the page,' said Tom.

She read again: 'To the Chief Medical Officer, London Medical Pensions Board, Roehampton, SW. So,' she said briskly, 'in simple terms, what all that pious rigmarole boils down to is that you're a eunuch. Yes?'

'I suppose that is the harsh description of my medical condition, yes.'

'You can't get a child?'

'That is so.'

'You can't even get it up?'

'That is the situation, as you rather bluntly put it.'

'And you're carrying this letter about with you as a sort of insurance policy?'

'Not at all. I'm due at the Pensions Board later this afternoon. I came to see you two hours before I see them.

In view of your remarks, I thought it best to show you the letter.'

'You think you'll get a pension for what you've lost?'

'Maybe. Maybe not. Pensions are for old men with no hope, no future, only a past. They paid in for them. I suppose you could say I paid my premiums in the skies above France. But what I want now is the chance of a job where I can pass on my skills in flying to someone else. I want to teach Carola Marsh to fly as I'd like to fly if I were learning all over again. I am tired of flying myself. I've had enough of it. Now I want to pass on my knowledge, all my experience, to someone who's starting.'

Lady Warren handed the letter back to him. He put it in his pocket. For a moment neither spoke. Then Tom stood up.

'I have said what I had to say, Lady Warren, and obviously I haven't persuaded you I am the man to teach Carola to fly. I'm sorry about that. But before I go I would like to wish you and her every possible success in the future.' He turned to the door.

'Wait a minute, you stupid, headstrong Aussie,' said Lady Warren roughly. 'Who said you haven't persuaded me? I'll take you on. I'll give you a lump sum to teach Carola. How much do you want?'

'I'm not a businessman, as the bank manager reminded me.'

'All right, I'll name a sum. To teach that girl to fly well, how long will it take?'

'How long is a piece of string?' he replied. 'It's generally reckoned that anyone who needs more than sixteen hours' dual flying is not necessarily going to make it. There's a lot of technique to learn, but a total of, say, twenty-five hours' dual and solo should see her on her way. But flying is not a finite art. There's always something new to learn. Where is she now, by the way?'

'I'm paying her fees to take a course in all aspects of aeronautical engineering. This will be very valuable to her when she starts on long-distance flights. And then she'll do a special apprenticeship with Vickers at their factory in Surrey. They're preparing a plane to attempt to fly the Atlantic, so I hear. Working at Vickers with that going on should give her an idea of the dedication required.'

'I agree. How many are going to make the attempt?'

'Two. Pilot and navigator.'

'Why not let her fly the Atlantic?'

'When?'

'When she's ready. Obviously not a day, not an hour before. I could navigate for her. She'd get all the credit for flying, for that's where the credit should be, keeping the plane in the air. The navigator just works out with maps and compass and sextant where they are and where they should be heading. The pilot has to fly.'

'That's in the future, a long way off,' replied Lady Warren. 'She has to finish her course first. I never believe in leaving any job half done. If you do, it's twice as difficult to go back to it.'

'I agree with you entirely,' said Tom.

'You talk a lot of sense sometimes, for a man.'

'Coming from you, Lady Warren, that is a compliment. Are you, by any chance, free for supper tonight? If you are, it would give me great pleasure if you would dine with me at Kettners in London. I should be back from the Pensions Board by seven.'

'No. You dine with me. Here. Now ring the Pensions Board. Put 'em off. You know their number?'

'I could find it,' said Tom.

Lady Warren pressed a button. The housekeeper appeared.

'Look up a telephone directory for the Putney area,' Lady Warren instructed her. 'Get the London Medical

Pensions Board on the phone. Then bring the telephone receiver in here. Mr Gardener needs to make a call.'

She turned to Tom as the housekeeper left the room. 'For a man who has lost so much, you still have a certain crude charm,' she said, and smiled.

Tom smiled, too, not from pleasure at her remark but to conceal his unease. He had no appointment with the Pensions Board; they had never even heard of him. But with any luck, so many people would be making or cancelling appointments that he could conceal this from Lady Warren.

She lit another cheroot as the housekeeper came in, carrying the telephone receiver on a long cord.

'I have asked the operator for the number, your ladyship,' she explained. As she spoke, the telephone began to ring.

When Richard finished his year at Beechwood Gears, he at once volunteered for the army. The local recruiting sergeant told him that no more recruits were being accepted. The war was over.

Aunt Hannah knew a professor at Oxford, and on her suggestion Richard wrote to him and applied for a place at the university. The reply was that ex-service students would have first priority.

In the event, however, fewer ex-servicemen applied to become undergraduates than had been expected. The casualty rate among young men qualified for university places had been disproportionately high. And of those who survived and were eligible, many had spent several years in the services and were reluctant now to spend three more years studying for a degree. So Richard went up to Oxford in Hilary term, 1919, to read for an engineering degree, specialising in the internal combustion engine.

Most rooms in Oxford colleges were arranged off small

landings on staircases. The treads of these wooden stairs had been worn smooth by the feet of generations of undergraduates over the previous two or three hundred years. The room under Richard's was occupied by a gregarious American, Jonas B. Brackley. In place of poster-size reproductions of Toulouse Lautrec's paintings favoured by many undergraduates, Brackley's walls were covered with advertisements for straw boater hats, soft drinks and American cars. He was a genial fellow, but not accepted by all on his staircase because of his habit of boasting.

To Jonas Brackley, size was all-important. Everything American, because it was generally bigger than anything British or even European, must therefore be better. He did not make friends by constantly reiterating this theory, but no one really knew him well enough to question whether he actually believed what he said.

Richard assessed him as a genuine enough fellow, if not the sort of person to whom he could ever be close. Their backgrounds were so different, but Brackley gave regular drinks parties, and he had a love for machinery which Richard could quite understand.

One evening, in Richard's second year, they met in the doorway of the college; Richard was going out, Brackley coming in.

'A bit of news for you,' said Brackley excitedly. 'I've got a real car coming, a real automobile that'll take the pants off anything you've got over here.'

'What's that?'

'A Jordan.'

'Never heard of the make,' said Richard.

'You will,' said Brackley confidently. 'It'll be a sensation.'

'When is it due?'

'Any day now. I've heard it's already been offloaded at Southampton docks. Your Customs guys have got to go

through it, of course, with all the usual British thorough-
ness and attention to useless detail, and then it will be
here.'

'I look forward to seeing it.'

He saw it that Saturday morning. Richard was still a
couple of hundred yards away from the gates of the
college when he noticed a crowd standing around the
entrance doors. In the centre stood an enormous car,
bright red with yellow wire wheels, white walls to its
tyres. At the wheel, a cigar in his mouth, straw boater
pushed to the back of his head, one arm resting
nonchalantly on the back of the seat, sat Jonas B.
Brackley, basking in the pride of ownership. He saw
Richard approaching and waved his cigar at him in
greeting.

'Come and look at this,' he called excitedly.

The crowd parted to let Richard through. Brackley
jumped out of the seat, opened the bonnet.

'Look at this motor. It goes so goddam fast, the tyres
leave streaks of rubber on the road.'

The long five-litre, six-cylinder Continental engine
filled the space impressively.

'Never seen anything like it,' Richard admitted. 'This
is the Jordan you were telling me about?'

'As ever is. The mighty Jordan. One more river to
cross, and that's the river of Jordan. It's a great car.
Made in Cleveland, Ohio.'

'A bit big for our roads, surely?'

'Other cars will just have to get out of the way, then,
won't they?'

'One way of looking at it, I suppose. So long as they
do.'

Richard walked round the car. The finish was impeccable: leather seats, an engine-turned dashboard, white
coach lining round the edges of the mudguards and along
the sides of the doors.

'I'll ask the question everyone else must ask about it. What'll she do?'

'I'm not quite sure, but what I am sure of is that it'll beat anything you've got over here,' said Brackley simply. '*Anything*.'

'That's quite a statement,' said Richard doubtfully. Some of the richer undergraduates owned remarkably fast cars. One ran a Hispano Suiza; another a Rolls; a third, one of the new Bentleys. Undergraduates were not supposed to own cars of any kind, but they garaged them beyond university limits, so when they hared up to London to see a show or visit a night club, the university authorities did not know they were driving themselves in their own cars.

'Want to bet?' Brackley asked him.

'I've no car to bet against you,' replied Richard. 'I'll just have to take your word for it.'

'I'll put my money where my mouth is if anyone else wants to take me up. I'll give a magnum of champagne to anyone who can beat me, Sunday morning from here to the Bear at Woodstock. We'll have a first-class breakfast, loser to pay. Who'll take me on?'

The undergraduates looked at each other. Some shrugged their shoulders and moved away. This could be interesting to see, but not to become involved with. Then someone spoke up from the rear of the crowd.

'I've got a Beechwood,' he said. 'A three-litre. Not new, by any means. But I think it'll still give you a run for your money. You'll have two litres' engine capacity to your advantage.'

'You're on,' said Brackley quickly. 'Sunday. Start at Magdalen Bridge eight o'clock. We'll be in Woodstock long before half past. Just in time for a champagne breakfast. *And* a champagne lunch. You still game?'

'Totally.'

Richard knew the other undergraduate by name, Peter

Drummond, but he had never spoken to him. He was a thin, tall, quiet person who wore glasses. There was nothing particularly special about the Beechwood car he drove except for its solid construction and its very good road holding. Since the Beechwood Car Company was in the same group as Beechwood Gears, Richard felt a certain loyalty to the make. But Brackley's Jordan had an engine nearly twice as large, and it was new, while the Beechwood was not. However, it was nothing to do with him. He had no money on the outcome.

Brackley looked round at the crowd. His eyes fastened on Richard.

'Ride with me, will you?' he asked him. 'All racing cars need a riding mechanic, and I know you're no slouch in that area.'

'If you wish, I will,' Richard agreed without enthusiasm.

'See you here, then, Sunday, quarter to eight, to warm up the oil.'

At a quarter to eight on Sunday morning, the two contestants drove their cars from the college gates, along the High Street to Magdalen Bridge. Then they turned them round so that they were facing back up the High towards the centre of Oxford.

News of the contest, originally intended simply to be a private challenge, had spread widely, which was not what Brackley had intended. He had no wish to alert the proctors – in charge of university discipline – to the race; it could result in both drivers being rusticated for a term as a punishment for infringing regulations about owning motor cars, or even being sent down permanently for taking part in such a competition on public roads. But despite the early hour, a crowd of undergraduates, some on foot, others with cycles or motorcycles, thronged the bridge. Many had spent years in uniform, and this unexpected challenge seemed a return to an earlier age when outlandish wagers had been made and met.

An older undergraduate, a wartime major in the Army Service Corps, appointed himself as starter and general marshal. He addressed both drivers and anyone else near enough to hear him.

'The rules are simple,' he said. 'No reckless driving on the wrong side of the road. Obey all traffic signs and laws. No undue racing of engines. Remember, this is the Sabbath morning. We don't want to annoy too many people. The first car to reach the Bear at Woodstock is the winner. If neither reach it, for whatever reason, the race is null and void. Are you both absolutely clear on these points?'

'Totally,' said the American.

Drummond, the Beechwood driver, nodded.

'And you will abide by them?'

'Of course.'

'Each car,' the marshal went on, 'will carry one passenger, designated as riding mechanic. I'll stand on the pavement here and give you a count of five. When I drop my arm, may the best man and the best car win.'

An undergraduate Richard did not know climbed into the front seat of the Beechwood. Drummond vaulted over the side; that particular model did not have a driver's door. He started the engine, blipped the throttle. The burble of a straight-through exhaust echoed back from the stone walls of the bridge.

Richard climbed in beside the American. He was surprised to see how nervous Brackley appeared. He had never driven with him, and now felt slightly uneasy. Was the man safe at speed?

'You'll be all right,' Richard assured Brackley, hoping to calm him. 'You should win hands down with this car.'

'I hope so,' Brackley replied. 'But I'm not sure I should be doing this. Trouble is, I'd had a couple of pink gins just before I suggested the wager, and having shot my mouth off, I couldn't back down.'

'Not had any gins this morning, I hope?'

'Hell, no. Only a large black coffee.'

He started the engine. In comparison with the Beech-wood, the Jordan's note was subdued, almost muted.

'I am beginning to count,' called the marshal. 'Five . . . Four . . . Three . . .'

He raised his right hand, holding a striped silk hand-kerchief that fluttered slightly in the early morning breeze.

'Two. *One!*'

He dropped his hand.

The Jordan accelerated with a jolt that flung Richard back against the leather seat. On his left he could see the Beechwood driver already changing gear, gloved hand gripping the outside gear lever. For a moment the two cars ran hub to hub. Then the Jordan steadily drew away. Brackley changed up into second gear, then top.

There were only two stretches of road where it would be relatively safe for a fast car to overtake a slower one: here in the very wide High Street, and beyond the centre of the city, in St Giles, where the road was also unusually broad. Whoever led in either section had the best chance of winning.

The two cars roared up past University College on the left, Queen's on the right. St Mary's Church went by in a blur of stone, then a row of shops on either side.

The Beechwood was the more manoeuvrable of the two cars, but it lacked the Jordan's power. Brackley kept ahead easily and was leading as they approached the crossroads at St Aldates and Cornmarket Street, but he was clearly the less skilled driver.

He did not change down for the sharp righthand bend but swept round in top gear, relying on his engine's power to give him a good getaway. The car slewed to the left as he fought the heavy steering. For a moment,

Richard thought they would hit the lefthand kerb and overturn. He had a sudden pin-sharp view of shop fronts, saw fear and horror etch the faces of a young couple walking arm in arm along the pavement. They leapt to one side, and then the Jordan was past them, accelerating ahead.

But this lapse gave Drummond the chance he needed. He dropped down a gear and surged past the Jordan, totally ignoring the narrowness of the road.

Past the Randolph Hotel on the left, the Martyrs' Memorial to the right, they raced, and then reached St Giles, the second and last wide section before the road divided into two. The righthand fork led to Banbury, the left to Woodstock.

Brackley had barely four hundred yards in which to overtake the Beechwood or lose the wager, for the Woodstock Road was little wider than a lane, and already other traffic was coming towards them – a two-seater car, a horse-drawn milk float, three cyclists in line. This made overtaking dangerous, if not impossible.

Brackley trod the throttle to the floorboards. The big car bucked under full power but still he could not pass. The Beechwood was just in front, holding its position – and now perhaps only a hundred yards remained in which Brackley could pass.

'Drop down a gear!' shouted Richard. 'You'll never do it in top!'

Brackley nodded, surprised. He was not a sporting driver. He had not realised the significance of using a lower gear to boost acceleration. Like most people accustomed to driving large, powerful cars, he changed down from top as little as possible. Now he double-declutched down to second.

Instantly, the big car took wing. They came up alongside the Beechwood, their front wheels running parallel with its rear wheels. Then they drew ahead, and finally the Beechwood fell away, as though being pulled backwards by an invisible cord.

Brackley swung left along the Woodstock Road, and changed back to top. He turned to Richard, gave the thumbs-up sign. The race had still several miles left to run, but for practical purposes it was already over. They coasted into Woodstock, stopped outside the Bear. Seconds later, the Beechwood pulled up alongside them. Drummond switched off his engine. He jumped out from behind the wheel, crossed to the Jordan, shook hands with Brackley.

'Congratulations,' he said warmly. 'It was a good race.'

'Agreed, but maybe I was lucky. I say, let's make it only the first of three. Best of three should prove who's best conclusively.'

'Not with me,' replied Drummond. 'I can't afford to risk being beaten three times and have to pay for three champagne breakfasts for the four of us. You've got the faster car, as you said. I'll let it rest at that.'

As he spoke, other cars were arriving. Undergraduates jumped out, cheering. Motorcyclists with pillion riders pulled up to offer congratulations and commiserations.

'And I thought you were a sportsman,' said Brackley.

'I am,' protested Drummond. 'That's why I'm footing the bill now.'

'Come on, best of three. Be a man!' Brackley took a coin out of his pocket. 'Toss for it, if you like. Heads you race, tails you don't.'

Drummond shook his head. 'No,' he said. 'Once is enough.'

He did not add that on the previous day he had received a letter from home. His father had invested heavily in platinum shares, for which a great future had been forecast. Platinum was used in the ignition system of every car, and the motor industry was booming, so how could platinum shares yield anything less than a brilliant return? In the event, his father's shares yielded very much less; the mine ceased production. Overnight, his shares became virtually worthless.

The Beechwood would have to go, and it would be impossible to sustain any further extravagant expenses, such as champagne breakfasts. Worst of all, he might even have to leave Oxford. To pay his fees and even the most modest living expenses needed a relatively large amount of money. Drummond could not expect this American show-off to understand this, and he had no intention of explaining to him the nakedness of his financial situation.

Brackley's face clouded with discontent, and Richard was suddenly reminded of his brother Tobin.

'One moment,' he said quickly. 'If Drummond changed his mind and he won, what then?'

'What d'you mean, what then?' asked Brackley petulantly. 'I pay for the breakfast. That's what then.'

'At present, with an engine so much less powerful than yours,' said Richard, 'he can't possibly win. But what if I had a look at his engine and advised one or two changes? Would you have any objection? He might at least have a better chance then.'

'You can advise what you like,' retorted Brackley. 'But I'm so sure I can beat him whatever you do, I'll increase the stakes. Champagne breakfast *and* a hundred guineas to the winner.'

'Drummond and I will discuss it,' Richard told him.

'There's nothing to discuss,' said Drummond shortly.

'There may be,' replied Richard. 'There just may be. Now, let's go to breakfast. You're paying for it, so the least you can do is to eat it.'

After breakfast, Richard drove back to college in Drummond's car. They did not exchange a word until they reached the front gates.

'Let's have a look at your engine,' said Richard.

Drummond raised the bonnet. 'Well? What can you do to improve things?'

'Probably not a lot,' admitted Richard. 'But I could suggest some modifications that might be worthwhile.'

'Could they make my car go fast enough to trounce that American loudmouth?'

'I think so. Your car holds the road much better than his, so all you need is to extract more power from the engine.'

'How?'

'I would alter the valve timing. Make the valve openings overlap. I did that with a motorcycle engine once. It went like the clappers.'

'That would mean having the cams filed down.'

'Yes, but that shouldn't present a problem. I worked for a firm in the Beechwood group making gears before I came up to Oxford. I can ask my old employers to let me have a spare camshaft.'

'Even so, it would be expensive,' said Drummond. 'And now that we're on our own, I can be quite frank with you. I simply can't afford it. My old man has lost all his money. I'm broke. But I don't want Brackley to know.'

'I could get it at cost. And I'll do my work on it for free, of course.'

'It's very kind of you,' said Drummond, closing the bonnet. 'And I appreciate the offer. But I must repeat, I haven't got any more money. So that's that.'

'I'll pay for it myself,' Richard persisted.

Drummond looked at him in surprise. 'But why should you? What's your interest in me winning?'

'I don't particularly like our American colleague's manner either. And also I'd like to prove to myself, if to no one else, that I can do what I think I can do.'

'You might ruin my engine and then I couldn't even

298

sell the car, which, as things are, I'll have to do pretty damn quick.'

'There's no possibility of that. If my plan doesn't work, I'll simply put back the old camshaft. Then everything will be just exactly as it was. But I am pretty certain I won't need to. And you could be richer by a hundred guineas.'

They walked into the college together, paused outside Richard's staircase; Drummond's rooms were in another quadrangle.

'All right,' said Drummond reluctantly. 'On the absolute understanding I don't have to pay a penny, go ahead.'

'Agreed,' said Richard. They shook hands.

For the next few evenings he worked in the stables of the house on the outskirts of Oxford where Drummond garaged his car. He drew the sharper profiles he needed on the camshaft and sent the drawings and the camshaft to Mr Cartwright at the gear factory. The new one arrived at the end of the week. He fitted it and, as he had expected and calculated, the engine produced roughly a third more power, probably enough to pass the Jordan early in the race. The race would still be in the large car's favour, but at least the Beechwood now had a chance.

That evening, on his way through the college gates, Richard went into the porter's lodge. The porter, who had lost an arm in the retreat from Mons, was sitting at a desk, behind a hole in the glass screen, reading a newspaper. He looked up, nodded to Richard.

'Evening, sir,' he said.

Richard took a ten shilling note from his back pocket, folded it to the size of a postage stamp, pushed it through the hole. The porter's hand closed round the note with practised skill.

'I want your help,' Richard explained. 'Where can I find an honest bookie in this city?'

'That's a bit like finding a hen with teeth,' replied the porter. 'But you might find Douglas MacNab in the Bear. He usually sits in the corner, drinking beer and whisky. I've placed bets for many young gentlemen with him. He's always honoured his bond, no matter how high the odds or how strange the wager.'

When Richard walked into the Bear, he saw Douglas MacNab sitting on a high stool, elbow on the bar. Next to his hand stood a pint tankard of best bitter and a large glass of MacAllan the Malt.

The bar was almost empty; it was early in the evening. Richard crossed the floor, ordered a beer for himself, nodded towards the drinks.

'The same again, Mr MacNab?'

'Aye. But how d'you know my name?'

'Mutual friend. College porter.' He gave his name.

'Oh, aye. I ken him well. He's an old friend, right enough. We were in the army together.'

They raised their glasses to each other.

'He gives you a very good reference, Mr MacNab.'

'Glad to hear it. And what can I do for you? I assume you're not buying me a drink simply because we both know your college porter?'

'I want to ask you something. Did you hear about the race between two cars to Woodstock on Sunday?'

'I did indeed. Pity I didn't know about it before, though. I'd have made a bob or two. It seemed a pretty foregone conclusion – big 'uns usually beat little 'uns. But there's always someone who will take the other view.'

'You're talking to someone like that now,' said Richard. 'Remember David and Goliath.'

'Aye. But then David used his brain.'

'There's going to be another race this Sunday. Same cars, same drivers.'

'Are you riding in one?'

'I'm riding with the American in the big car, as I did last time. Simply because he asked me. But I've done a bit of work on the engine of the other car. I think that now it has a better chance. The American knows I've done this, there's nothing underhand about it. He's still totally confident he'll win again.'

'I can believe that. I thought there might be a rerun, so I had a word with a man I know in the garage where he keeps it out on the Iffley Road. He tells me that the Jordan's engine is nearly twice as big as the Beechwood's. Short of a miracle, or running out of road, it must win.'

'So what odds would you offer against the Beechwood winning?'

'Very large indeed,' said MacNab, watching Richard closely.

'Even though I've told you I've worked on the engine?'

'You can't work a miracle. I was brought up a Presbyterian. I remember that the Bible said a man can't add a cubit to his stature by taking thought. And I say you can't add enough power to that engine to make it beat one nearly twice as big – not over a short distance, anyway.'

'You're probably right, Mr MacNab. But I repeat, what odds will you offer for the Beechwood to win?'

'It's a shame to take money off a young man like you.'

'Don't let your better nature deter you, Mr MacNab.'

'I was quoting a hundred to one against the smaller car. I've taken a bit of money on the race already. But since you seem to know something I don't, I'll cut them. I'll give you eighty to one.'

'I'm not a betting man,' said Richard. 'So you must excuse my ignorance. If I put on a pound and win, I get back eighty pounds? Is that correct?'

'Yes. Plus your one pound back.'

'Right. I'll put on a hundred pounds.'

MacNab sipped his whisky slowly, considering the

proposition. 'You're either very rich, or very foolish,' he said at last.

'Certainly not the former. So I must be the latter.'

'On the other hand, you may be a genius with engines.'

'I've been called other things.'

'Aye. So have we all. It's not in my nature to refuse money. That is not how the great fortunes were made. So let's have a sight of it, and you're on.'

Richard took out his chequebook, wrote out a cheque to Bearer, handed it to MacNab.

'Cash it tomorrow,' he told him. 'If I win, where do I come to collect? Here?'

'Aye. And if you lose, still come. I'll buy you a drink. At a hundred pounds it'll be the most expensive drink you're ever likely to have.'

Twice as many people gathered on Magdalen Bridge to see the start of the second race as had watched the first one. Richard saw Mr MacNab looking at the cars pensively. The undergraduate who had acted as marshal stood on the pavement again with his silk handkerchief.

'Same partners as before,' he said. 'Same rules. Are you ready?'

The drivers nodded.

'Start your engines,' the marshal ordered.

Richard climbed into the Jordan.

'I hear you've been spending quite a bit of time on that little Beechwood engine,' said Brackley. 'It's all a waste of time, though. I'll beat him now as easily as I did before. Maybe even more thoroughly, for I'm going to use your tip about dropping down a gear when I accelerate.'

The marshal began to count.

'Five . . . Four . . . Three . . .'

The sound of the next two numbers was lost as both

drivers accelerated, slipping their clutches, watching his handkerchief. As it dropped, both cars surged forward. Brackley led by eight feet. Then, as both men changed gear, the Beechwood drew level and moved ahead. The distance between them grew steadily. By the time Drummond was passing St Mary's Church, Brackley's car was still only opposite University College, a couple of hundred yards behind.

There was no doubt in anyone's mind now that Drummond's Beechwood had as good as won, and barely a quarter of a mile from the start. He kept ahead all the way, along the Cornmarket, into St Giles. And then Richard saw a faint puff of blue smoke from the Beechwood's exhaust. The smoke quickly changed colour, light blue to black. More black smoke blew out of the ventilating louvres on the sides of the car's bonnet. Drummond coasted to a halt at the roadside. As Brackley raced past, sounding his hooter in triumph, Richard saw oil the colour of treacle dribbling out from under the other car's engine.

Brackley lifted his foot off the accelerator. His car slowed, stopped. He and Richard climbed out, walked back to the Beechwood. Other cars and motorcyclists who had been following them also stopped and gathered round the winner and the loser.

'What went wrong?' asked Brackley.

'You'd better ask him,' said Drummond angrily, pointing to Richard.

Richard crossed to the car, raised the bonnet. The smell of very hot paint and boiling oil rose up like incense. In the righthand side of the crankcase he could see a big hole, as though it had been punched by a hammer. In a sense, it had.

He bent down and moved the end of a connecting rod. It had snapped and gone right through the side of the case with the force of a sledgehammer blow.

What a fool he'd been. The Beechwood used aluminium connecting rods, strong enough to take the power of an ordinary engine. But when he had tuned it to develop one-third more power, they simply could not stand the strain for more than a few minutes. He should have thought of this, and asked Mr Cartwright to make steel connecting rods. If only . . .

He lowered the bonnet. 'My mistake,' he said contritely. 'I told you nothing could happen to your engine, and it has. Never mind. I'll pay the bill for a new one.'

'That's going to cost you,' said Drummond.

'I'll put it down to experience. A fee to the university of life, engineering division.'

One of the following cars came up in front, stopped.

'Want a tow?' the driver called.

'Badly,' Drummond replied.

'We were going pretty well, you know,' Drummond told Richard grudgingly. 'I thought we had it in the bag. I even borrowed money for a bet. Oh, well, put not your trust in princes nor in any son of man.'

Brackley turned to Richard. 'I'll give you a lift back,' he said. 'You certainly know your stuff, whatever you did. But it didn't last.'

'There's nothing for nothing in this world, and probably not in the next,' said Richard. 'I forgot that basic truth. I'll remember it next time.'

That evening he went into the Bear. MacNab was sitting in the same corner with the same drinks on the bar. When he saw Richard he waved.

'Sit down,' he said. 'What'll you have? Something stronger than beer?'

'No. Beer will do me.'

The barman drew him a pint. He raised the tankard towards MacNab, began to drink.

'You look a bit depressed,' said MacNab.

'I have much to be depressed about. But you should

look cheerful,' Richard told him. 'You don't have to pay out eight thousand pounds to me. And I thought I was going to be rich.'

'Aye. We all think that from time to time. I thought I'd make some money on this myself,' said MacNab.

'Well, didn't you?'

'No. The wager stated the winner would be the first car to the Bear at Woodstock. The marshal made that clear at the first race. Neither car got there. So it was no race. All bets to be handed back.'

'So I haven't lost?'

'Not really. And maybe you've learned something. Maybe when you do again whatever you did to that Beechwood car, you'll do it so that as well as going faster, it also lasts longer.'

'Damn right I will,' said Richard. 'I think that calls for another drink. You've been pretty fair with me.'

'Aye. But the college porter was good enough to recommend me to you. I don't like to disappoint a friend.' MacNab winked. 'There's been a young lady in here asking for you,' he went on. 'A pretty young lady.'

'Did she give her name?'

'No.'

'How did she know I would be coming in here?'

'I think your college porter said you might be. I suggest you ask back at the college. If you don't hang about, she might still be there. There's an old Scots motto – never run after a pretty girl, but equally don't push your luck too hard. And if they've run after you, never keep them waiting. At least, that used to be my motto – before I became an old Scot!'

The only girl Richard could think of was Carola. Hoping she would still be waiting for him, he walked back to his college, climbed the stairs to his room. He opened the door.

Sitting in an armchair, smoking an Egyptian cigarette in a long tortoiseshell holder, sat the prettiest girl he had ever seen. Then he corrected himself. He had seen her before, several times, once riding with Brackley in his car, again in the first row of the stalls at the Playhouse, and in photographs in *The Isis*, *The Tatler*, *The Sketch*. He had seen her but he had never met her. Like most of his contemporaries, he had simply admired her from afar.

'Hello,' he said now. 'What do you want?'

'To talk to you. I'm Eleanor, Eleanor Blake.'

'I know,' said Richard.

'Why haven't we met before, then?'

Richard shrugged. She moved in a set for which he had not the money, if even the will, to join. They went to parties at the Trout at Godstow, the George at Dorchester. They booked boxes or stalls in London theatres, and then went on to expensive night clubs. In a word, they had so much money that any whim, any mood of the moment could instantly be gratified.

'I want to talk to you,' she said. Her voice was as he had imagined it must be; soft, melodious, soothing.

'But how did you know who I was?' he asked.

As soon as he spoke, he realised the absurdity of his question. You could find out who anyone was, where anyone lived, through the university directory. It was too simple. But he was nervous, and conscious that his heart was beating unusually fast.

'I saw something in *The Isis* and then in London papers to the effect that the "bright young things", as the reporter called them, had organised a car race in Oxford, quite against all the university rules, and there was bound to be trouble. But there had been years of war, and this was something of an antidote. "The other side of the medal," they called it. Your name was mentioned and your college.'

'I had no idea,' Richard said. 'Would you like a drink?'

'I'd love one. What have you got?'

He paused. He had two bottles of sherry – one medium, one dry – a gin, some tonic water, and an odd collection of glasses. Really, he must get himself organised. He was living like a monk in this place: talking about engines, working with engines, thinking about them. And there was a whole different life out there, a life of fun and laughter, of wine and roses, and he had no part in it. But did he really want that life, when he found his engines, his drawing, so satisfying?

'A sherry?' he suggested.

'Thank you. Dry, if you have it.'

'I do.' He poured two glasses, handed her one.

'Bad luck about the race,' she said. 'I was in St Giles because I thought that was where your car, if it had any steam at all, would pass Jonas.'

'It passed long before, in the High.'

'So I heard. Then it expired right in front of me. A lot of oil and horrible black smoke.'

'You know how it ended, then. Why come to see me?'

'To tell you I was very sorry.'

'Morally, Peter Drummond should have won. I made a big mistake.'

'So Jonas told me. The connecting rods or something should have been steel and they weren't.'

'You know about these things?'

'Some of them. You've also got quite a bill to pay for Peter Drummond's car.'

'That's right. I persuaded him to race when he didn't want to do so, and I assured him his engine wouldn't be damaged, and it was. It's a matter of honour to put it right.'

'You seem great on honour and morals.'

'I wouldn't say so. But, anyhow, what can I do for you?'

'First, I'll tell you what I'd like to do for you,' she said.

'Oh?'

'Yes. I'll pay all the repairs for Peter's car. You did your best. As my old man says, anyone who does his best deserves a second try.'

'But why should you pay for it? It will cost a lot of money, perhaps a hundred pounds.'

'My dear Richard, I *have* a lot of money. You don't know who I am, do you?'

'Yes. You've told me. I know who you are. Eleanor Blake. I've seen your picture often. And I've seen you in Jonas's car.'

'My mother is American. She inherited the Zimbro Car Company in Detroit. They had enormous contracts from the British government to build staff cars, trucks, tank engines, during the war. Then the Americans came in. Now they're turning out about a hundred cars a day. They're only beaten by Henry Ford's lot at Dearborn.

'My mother doesn't take a great interest in the firm; only in the results, the dividends, the profits. Though we're selling lots of cars now, as you are over here in England, too, she believes there'll be a slump one day. She thinks that the boom with people coming out of the services and spending gratuities will suddenly end. There'll be unemployment, and to keep in business at the rate we're doing we need our cars to be a word in the language – like a Ford, a Buick, a Rolls. A Zimbro. It was started with Portuguese money. Do you know what the word means?'

'I've no idea.'

'It's Portuguese for a juniper tree. They make gin from juniper berries. My grandfather should know, he died from drinking the stuff. But that's not why I'm here, to tell you about my family. If you can make Peter's car go so fast, you could do the same for some of ours. Not all, obviously. But, say, the top models. I'm interested in taking over some of the work in the factory.'

'Not on the bench, surely?'

'No. On the advertising side. I think if we can win races at your Brooklands track, our Indianapolis, reliability rallies, that sort of thing, and sell a car that is faster than anything else at the price, *and* has a cachet, we could ride out any slump. So I thought I'd come and ask you, would you be interested?'

'In doing what, exactly?' Richard asked cautiously.

'In coming on the payroll. Working for Zimbro. We'd give you a better salary than you'd get elsewhere, for a start. We'd also give you a laboratory and testing facilities, anything you ask for, so long as you produce results.'

'And if I don't?'

'Well, then we'd have to look closely at the reasons why you don't deliver. But I think you will. I wouldn't make this offer otherwise.'

'When would you want me to start?'

'What year are you in here?'

'My second.'

'So you've one more year to go. Say, as soon as you get your degree. Are you interested?'

'Very.'

'You'll have time and maybe some facilities to pursue other interests, though not in direct competition with Zimbro, of course.'

'It seems a very generous offer.'

'It is. But then I'm a very generous girl – with company money. So, what do you say?'

'I say yes.'

'Good. If you're going to invite me out to dinner, I'd say yes, too.'

'I'd love to,' said Richard, pouring out more sherry.

'This is the second break I've had today. I was one down with the Beechwood blowing up, because I bet the car would win. I lost my bet. But the bookie decently returned me my money as the race was declared invalid since neither car finished. That was my first break. Now you're offering me a job. That's my second. Dinner could make it third time lucky.'

Eleanor raised her glass in a mock toast. 'Who for?' she asked him. 'You or me?'

'Both, I hope.'

The provost of Richard's college had spent all his academic life, upwards of thirty years, studying Anglo-Saxon. He therefore found it difficult to bring himself back to the present. He felt much happier in a world of mead halls and horn-handled knives and battles with shields and swords. The present day seemed somehow alien to him; Beowulf and the Battle of Maldon were more real than anything in the twentieth century.

And especially alien and repugnant of all his duties were interviews he sometimes had to conduct with an undergraduate who, in his opinion or the opinion of the proctors who safeguarded the discipline of undergraduates, had offended against the university's largely unwritten code of rules.

The provost was a small man, not given to using one word if six would do. He sat in a huge chair with a footstool, otherwise his feet would not have reached the floor. Across from his desk stood Richard, wearing a gown and the stiff white collar and white bow tie of one called either to sit examinations or to explain himself to the head of his college.

He waited uneasily, wondering at the nature of the summons.

That morning his scout had told him that the provost wished to see him in his study at eleven o'clock. He had checked with the provost's secretary, and received a cold affirmative. What had he done wrong? He could not think of anything either particularly wrong or right. Now he stood in front of a man who preferred the tenth century to the twentieth.

'I called you here, Rowlands,' the provost began, 'because I want to give you a full opportunity of answering serious allegations that have been made against you. I do not refer to you being a passenger in an open motor car of the sporting or racing type, being driven at what I am told were breakneck speeds through Oxford on two separate occasions. The driver of this car, an undergraduate of this college, has been rusticated for the rest of this term and is very fortunate he has not been sent down. You, as passenger, while being present in the vehicle, were not in control, so I pass by what at best was a most unwise participation. What I wished to see you about concerns a matter of much greater gravity.'

He paused, opened a folder on his desk. Richard saw that it contained five or six bills. Upside down he could read the letterheads of a tailor off the High, a bootmaker nearby, wine merchants in St James's, shirt-makers in Jermyn Street.

'These bills,' said the provost, 'total the not insignificant sum of twelve hundred pounds. In each case the tradesman concerned tells me they gave you credit as being a member of this college. When they applied for payment, you refused it to them, not in person, but on the telephone. You said, according to the tailor, "You can whistle for it." What have you to say to these charges?'

'Could I see the bills, sir?'

'Of course. I am sure you are already acquainted with them.'

Richard skimmed through them, handed them back. 'I

311

have never been into any of these shops in my life,' he said.

'Really? Then how do you account for these?'

'I cannot.'

'Unfortunately, we have recently had a number of cases of undergraduates living above their means, running motor cars illegally and against the statutes of the university, and also getting credit which apparently they have no intention of paying. Before the war, tradesmen could afford to be patient, believing that when their student customers went home and their allowances came through or they took up their careers, they would pay. But things are rather different now. They want their money.'

'But these are not my bills. How were they ordered, sir?'

'According to the tradesmen, you called in person.'

'I would like to take one of these bills back to, say, the tailor and ask him about it.'

'You may do so. But this is a very serious offence, Rowlands. If they hand the matter over to the civil authorities, you may appear in court. This will not do you or the college any good. I think, therefore, that if you have no satisfactory explanation, it would be best for you and for the reputation of the college if you cease to be a member.'

'You mean you're expelling me?'

'Sending you down, is the phrase.'

'Can I have time to see at least one of these people, sir?'

'Today is Monday,' said the provost. 'You have until the same time, eleven o'clock, on Wednesday. Good day.'

Richard put on his mortar board, took it off and bowed three times in the established ritual for saying farewell to the provost. Back in his room, he changed into more comfortable clothes, walked to the tailor's shop. An assistant was talking to the manager behind the counter.

'Good morning,' said Richard. 'My name is Rowlands.'

'Rowlands,' said the manager coldly. 'I'm glad you called in. To settle your account, I hope, sir.'

'No. Because it isn't my account. Can you tell me how it came to be placed in my name?'

'A young man came in – I thought you, sir – ordered six shirts, paid cash for a couple of silk ties and then, saying he was out of funds, asked that the goods should be sent to him at the college and he would settle up.'

'And were they delivered?'

'They were about to be, by messenger, as is our custom, when he called on the telephone and said he would collect them, which he did. On four separate occasions we sent him the bills. He telephoned once and when my colleague here asked for a cheque to settle the bill, he was abused.'

'This is a very serious matter. Did you see this person?'

'Of course I saw him. He came into the shop here, standing where you are now. The light was as good as it is today – except he had a scarf that muffled his face and a rowing cap with a big peak. I couldn't see his face very clearly.'

'Would you recognise him again?'

'I think I would. In those clothes, at least.'

'Was there anything wrong with his face?'

The manager looked enquiringly at the assistant.

'I was also here in the shop, sir. I saw him as he came in the door. His face was disfigured, badly scarred. I think that is why he wore a scarf. It was not a particularly cold day, and he had his cap pulled right down.'

'Was he about my height?'

'Yes. And your colouring. But looking at you now, sir, I would say he was at least a couple of years older.'

'I see. I have a good suspicion who this person is. But I am being blamed for this and for bills he has run up in my name with other tradesmen, here and in London.'

'There's quite a bit of that about these days, sir. People got used to living above their means during the war, as captains, majors, and now it's back to reality.'

'My provost says I have until Wednesday to settle up with you or prove I do not owe these bills. Could I ask you to help me in this matter?'

'Certainly. What can we do?'

'I want a small piece of cloth of the same type of each of the shirts that were ordered.'

'There are a number of them, sir.'

'Then let me have the same number of samples.'

Richard walked from the station to his mother's house. He took a short cut across the fields in case anyone saw him coming up the drive. He was surprised and depressed to see how uncared-for the grounds looked. He had not been home for some time. Docks, thistles and cow parsley waved in the wind above uncut grass. The house also looked unloved. Window frames needed painting, a length of guttering had come away from the roof. Rainwater had left long green streaks on the stonework.

He let himself in through the back door, climbed up the well-remembered service stairs. He walked along the corridor, past his old bedroom, came to Tobin's room, knocked on the door.

'Come in,' Tobin called.

Richard was surprised. He had not expected his brother to be home. He opened the door, closed it behind him, stood against it.

'Hello, stranger,' said Tobin. 'What do you want back

here? We don't see you often.'

'I understand you told Mama that I shouldn't come here.'

'It distresses her to see you,' Tobin explained, flushing slightly at the obvious lie.

'I'm sorry to hear that. But I've got some news that may distress you.'

'Really? And what is that? Not that you're coming back to live here? Now that would distress me.'

'Not yet,' said Richard. He took a bill from his pocket, gave it to Tobin.

He glanced at it briefly, handed it back. 'This is yours, isn't it?' he said.

'No.'

'But it's in your name. It's marked here, delivery to the college. Can't be clearer.'

'The instructions can't be clearer, I agree. But I never gave them. You did.'

'Me?'

'Yes, you. For some reason, you hate me. Not just because of the steam engine, it goes back further than that. You want to discredit me. So you've run up bills in my name, refused to pay them. You hope I'll be sent down from Oxford, disgraced.'

'You're mad. Why should I bother with such a thing? I don't care a damn what you do.'

Richard crossed the room, pulled open the top drawer of the chest.

'What the devil are you doing in my private things?' Tobin asked him angrily.

The drawer contained underpants, silk vests, a mass of handkerchiefs. He closed the drawer, pulled open the one underneath it. It was full of striped shirts. He took out the drawer, tipped the contents on the bed.

'Do you mind!' his brother shouted.

Richard took the samples of cloth from his pocket,

held them against three shirts. They matched.

'These are the shirts you ordered in my name. I'm sure the same is true of the suits and everything else.'

'You're bloody mad.'

'No. Just bloody angry. Now listen, Tobin. I haven't got time to mess about with you. I want the money to pay these bills. Now.'

'You'll get nothing from me.'

'These are your shirts. You bought them in Oxford. They even have the name of the shop on the collar backs. Do you have a receipt for them?'

'No. I paid cash for them.'

'Not for these, you didn't. The manager of the shop is downstairs. I wanted to spare you this humiliation, but if he comes up and identifies you, as he will very easily, I will have no alternative but to call the police. I cannot have someone impersonating me, running up bills in my name.'

'You wouldn't dare.'

'I'll give you three, or I bring him up.'

Richard looked at the flickering second hand on his wristwatch.

'One.'

'Don't be a damn fool.'

'Two.'

Tobin said nothing.

'Three.'

Richard walked to the door, turned the handle.

'Wait,' said Tobin. 'I don't know anything about this. There may have been some mistake, a clerk or someone mixed up the bills. I wouldn't like to cause you trouble.'

'I don't want excuses. I want the money.'

'How much money, exactly?'

'For all the bills, twelve hundred pounds.'

'I'll give you a cheque.'

'No way. Come down to the bank with me and we'll get a banker's draft.'

For a moment, Tobin hesitated. Then he nodded sullenly, followed Richard down the stairs, out into the grounds.

'Where is this bloody tradesman?' he asked.

'You wouldn't want to see him, I'm sure. Otherwise when he does identify you, he may wish to place charges himself. And that would be out of my control.'

Tobin grunted.

It was just as well Tobin had not insisted on seeing the manager, Richard thought. He was actually miles away, in his shop.

Chapter Thirteen

Lady Warren picked up the ivory and silver speaking tube in the back of her Rolls.

'Stop the car,' she told the chauffeuse.

The huge car pulled in to the side of a lane overlooking miles of rolling Surrey woods and fields. Beneath them, in the grounds of a great private estate, lay a circular concrete track a hundred feet wide, two and three-quarter miles round. In the centre stood several buildings, a clubhouse with a clock, and behind them a row of hangars with two names painted in huge white letters across the front: Vickers, Brooklands.

Lady Warren lit a cheroot and turned to Carola.

'I want to explain the background before you arrive,' she said, gesticulating out of the open window. 'This is Brooklands motor racing course. It was built as an act of patriotism by a friend of mine, Hugh Locke King. A great and generous man who, like me, believes in this country. In 1907 he built this track with his own money. He engaged two thousand workmen who lived in huts with roofs of fir branches. They worked day and night, literally, using flares. Their only times off were Saturday and Sunday evenings. They cut down thirty acres of woodland, shifted the River Wey in two places. They built bridges, laid a railway line to bring in thousands of tons of gravel and cement. The total cost was one hundred and fifty thousand pounds, all out of his own pocket, remember. And within three months the motor racing track was finished. An amazing achievement.

'He built it because there was nowhere in this entire country then where British cars could run at a speed above ten miles an hour. Of course, not long before that motors were required to have a man walking in front of them with a red flag to show how dangerous they were. Imagine trying to drive from London to Manchester with someone walking in front of you all the way!

'But here, as in every branch of engineering, the Continentals were way ahead of us. French, Italian, German cars beat us hands down in speed and reliability. Locke King built this track to give our manufacturers a chance. And because cars are like aircraft – they both have petrol engines, they both travel fast – right in the centre there's Vickers aircraft factory. They've made some of the greatest planes of the last war, and they're going to build some of the best planes for the future. And that's where I'm putting you, to work with the men who actually design and build the aircraft. Then, when your time comes – as come it will, my girl – and you are the first woman to fly alone round the world, you'll know exactly how every part of your plane works. Then, if anything is out of tune, you'll know instantly. Your record, and your life, could depend on what you learn here.

'Under various nominees, I have a huge shareholding in the company. They know that, though they don't know exactly how much. Never let anyone know too much about your business. They only get above themselves if they do. Here you'll learn about flying and aircraft the hard way, which is the only way. Now, no questions. No comments.'

She picked up the speaking tube.

'Drive on,' she told the chauffeuse.

The works manager interviewed Carola personally.

'It is unusual for a girl to wish to work in an aircraft factory,' he said cautiously. 'You've had some experience in mechanical work, I understand.'

'Very little,' Carola admitted. 'I don't want to start here under false colours. I'm at the Poly studying aeronautical engineering, and before that, some time ago, I did a bit of work on steam traction engines.'

'Good,' he said. 'Well you've certainly come with a very good recommendation – from one of our most important shareholders, so I understand. You've also come at a most interesting time. I expect you've read about the offer by the *Daily Mail* to pay ten thousand pounds to the pilot who makes the first Atlantic flight. The offer was first made before the war and then, of course, it had to be abandoned. Now Lord Northcliffe has proposed it again. A number of aircraft companies are interested besides us, because we're all convinced air travel is the thing of the future. But it's only about ten years ago that the Frenchman Blériot flew the Channel – a hop of twenty miles. The flight across the Atlantic would be a hundred and twenty times longer. One day, people will fly right round the world and think nothing of it. But that day is some way off. To bring it nearer we have to fly the Atlantic first.'

'From East to West?'

'No,' the works manager replied. 'West to East, to catch the prevailing wind. This will mean they don't have to carry so much fuel. We've got a great plane to make the attempt, the Vimy bomber, which acquitted itself very well in the war.

'I'll put you, first of all, on the bench, where everyone works to begin with, filing things, measuring them, generally getting the feel of the place.'

'Thank you,' said Carola. 'I'll do my best.'

'I know you will. You've the look of a fighter about

you. Odd for a girl to want to work in an engineering factory, but you'll be all right.'

Carola was the only woman apprentice in the works. At first, the other apprentices did not know quite what to make of her, and treated her with some aloofness. Then gradually, as she proved she could work as well as any of them, that she neither asked nor expected any favours because of her sex, they began to accept her. Several invited her out for evening rides on the pillions of their motorcycles, to have tea out in the country on Saturday or Sunday, or to watch the motor races at Brooklands track.

Carola regretfully declined all these invitations. She did not know whether Lady Warren had someone in the works to report on her progress, but she thought it possible. Lady Warren always seemed to be unusually well-informed about any person or project which interested her. Any one of these young fellows could be telling her how her protégée was getting on, how she was spending her spare time. Had she any boy friends? Was she working hard enough? Did she ever criticise Lady Warren?

Apprentices, fliers, motor racing enthusiasts and their mechanics would meet in their spare time in the Bluebird Café at Brooklands track. Here, after some initial reserve on the part of other habitués – young men wearing casual clothes, overalls, breeches, leather jackets – Carola was also accepted. There was a Bohemian air about the place which she found exciting. She met pioneers of flying, like Tom Sopwith – the Sopwith Camel had been one of the great aircraft of the war – and A.V. Roe, who founded the Avro firm.

Generally, the talk was technical. She did not understand it all at first. But she soon learned what inherent stability meant, and an angle of incidence, what a gyropter was. Arguments and discussions would continue from one day to the next, seemingly without ever being completely resolved. How many engines did an aircraft need for optimum performance? Some held that the propeller should face the rear of the plane, and be a pusher rather than a tractor, the name given to aircraft with propellers in front. But many took the opposite view, and just as vehemently.

One morning, sitting at one of the tables with a cup of coffee and a doughnut, discussing the merits of various engines, Carola heard a familiar voice and turned. At the far end of the café she saw Richard. She called to him. He came over.

'What are you doing here?' she asked him in surprise.

'I was going to ask you that,' he replied.

She explained and introduced her friends.

'You're not flying, too?' she asked him.

'Not me,' he said. 'Engines are my thing. I've got a job with the Zimbro Car Company.'

'Pretty dull cars, those,' said someone. 'If I may say so.'

'But they're reliable and if I have anything to do with their development they won't be dull for too much longer.'

'You have something up your sleeve, then – apart from your arm?'

'More than up my sleeve. On the drawing board,' he replied. 'In fact, one of our cars is outside now with some of my modifications. Come out and have a look at it. We're down here to try it over a few laps.'

It was the custom for manufacturers to arrange for prototype models to be brought to Brooklands and driven round the track by a works driver. Sometimes they lasted for one lap, sometimes for twenty. The rough concrete, with crude joins that cracked in winter frosts, quickly showed up any faults in steering and suspension and braking. Engines which, on paper or during a bench test, seemed far in advance of anything else, would boil unexpectedly, even blow up, when faced with mile after mile in top gear at full speed.

Carola followed Richard out to the track. It was a hot day and the air was heavy with a smell which she now associated with flying and cars and speed, the smell of dope. This was not a drug, but the cellulose with which the fabric skin of aircraft bodies was painted to harden it and provide a flat, waterproof finish. In the heat of the sun, dope gave off a peculiar odour, rather like nail varnish remover. Added to this were other evocative smells: hot oil, blistering paint and rubber torn from the treads of spinning tyres.

The Zimbro was a two-seater with a pointed tail, two little humps on the dashboard in front of passenger and driver to carry the wind over their heads. There was no windscreen.

'You're not going to sell that as it is?' she asked Richard.

'I hope so. With a few creature comforts, of course. This is the prototype of the sports version.'

He lifted the bonnet. In front of the engine she saw a rough, round aluminium casting, ribbed like a huge grenade.

'What's that?' she asked.

'The blower, the supercharger. I don't want to try and teach you to suck eggs, but inside a standard carburettor is a very fine jet. The pistons go down and draw air into the cylinders over this jet, which releases a spray of petrol, thin as a mist. The blower has vanes which revolve at high speed and so it blows in the petrol and air mixture, and thus increases the engine's speed.'

'Your idea?'

'No. It's not original,' he admitted. 'Been around since the early years of the century. But the particular way I'm working on it is. In the factory they've given me a nickname – Blower.'

'I rather like that,' she said. 'It seems to epitomise speed, being blown along. I wish you luck, Blower.'

'Thank you.'

'How did you get the job?'

He told her about the race through Oxford and Eleanor Blake.

'Is she pretty?' she asked, almost without meaning to.

'Very,' he said, grinning. 'And rich.'

'I should feel jealous?'

'Not really. She's my employer. I was advised in the gear factory, never dip your pen in the company ink-well.'

'Don't be crude,' Carola said disapprovingly.

'And how did you get here?' he asked her.

'Courtesy of Lady Warren. She's a shareholder, sheltering behind nominees so no one knows just how big.'

'A strange woman,' he said. 'I can't understand her. All that money, so patriotic, and the consuming determination to force forward the cause of women, yet she's so lonely herself.'

'How do you know?'

'I've read any number of articles about her in the papers, but she's never with any friends, men or women. She's always alone, always crusading. A loner.'

'Maybe that's what I am, too. And you?'

'Could be. You know what they're doing here at Vickers, don't you?'

'Well, making planes.'

'They're preparing for a record flight,' he said. 'Across the Atlantic. Lots of other companies are in it, too, nearly a dozen here and in the States. It could be the biggest earner they'll ever have, so they're all keen.'

'Oh yes, I know about that,' Carola said. 'It's the main topic of conversation here. In fact two pilots are down

325

here today discussing it with the chiefs. One is John Alcock from Manchester. He's a great fellow, a real flier. The other one is Arthur Whitten Brown. His parents were both American, but he was born in Glasgow. His particular interest is navigation, so I gather.'

'Well, you're certainly at the centre of things here,' said Richard admiringly. 'I shall be down here testing Zimbro cars quite often, so we should meet, have a meal. You could come out with me in one of these cars.'

'I'd love to,' said Carola. 'But . . .'

'But what? The Australian? He's gone back Down Under, hasn't he?'

'I think so. I haven't seen him for ages.'

'Well? Is absence making the heart grow fonder?'

'It's not that,' she said. 'It's Lady Warren.'

'What about her?'

'She feels that any involvement with young men will draw me away from the main object of her investment of time and money in me.'

'Which is what?'

'It sounds ridiculous when I've never flown anything, and here I am surrounded by veteran war pilots, and she wants me to have a go at long-distance record breaking. To show what a woman can do.'

'Good for you. And good for her. But I don't see how an evening out can possibly interfere with that. Rather the reverse. The old saying is that all work and no play makes Jack a dull boy. Since we've got sex equality in what you're attempting, that must also make Jill a dull girl. But if that's how you want it, Carola, I'll say goodbye. Or rather, I won't. I'll be back.' He smiled, winked. She watched him walk away down the track.

Three weeks later, Carola was moved from the general engineering division to a special part of the hangar. Here the Vickers Vimy was being prepared for the

326

Transatlantic flight. Its original two separate cockpits had been combined to make one large one so that Alcock, the pilot, could sit side by side with Brown, the navigator.

At the front of the plane, the nose skid, fitted like a ski, in case the aircraft came down to land at too great an angle, had been removed. Space taken up by bombs and bombing gear during the war was now filled with extra petrol tanks for the flight. One of these tanks doubled as a buoyancy craft, with rope handles fixed to it in case the aircraft came down in the sea. A sealed can of iron rations was fitted into the rear of the aircraft as in a lifeboat. When the aircraft's two Rolls-Royce Eagle twelve-cylinder engines had been designed by Henry Royce in the early days of the war, they produced 200 brake horsepower. Now, with modifications, they produced 360.

Carola had never stood so close to such a large plane. It was over fifteen feet high, forty-two and a half feet long, with a wing span of sixty-eight feet. The fuselage had to carry 865 gallons of petrol, and fifty gallons of oil. The cruising speed was only ninety miles an hour, the landing speed half that, the maximum barely ten miles more. It seemed impossible that such a huge structure could ever lift itself off the ground, let alone fly the Atlantic Ocean.

'Well, there she is,' said a man behind her. She turned.

'I'm Jack Alcock,' he explained. 'And I've got to fly this bus. And you?'

Carola introduced herself.

'Unusual to see a girl interested in these matters, isn't it?'

'She's an unusual girl,' said the works manager proudly. 'She's very keen, and knowledgeable. So don't go sending her off for a left-handed spanner or something of that kind. She's been through all that before.'

A taller man joined them, introduced himself.

'Whitten Brown.'

They shook hands.

'He's got the tough job,' Alcock explained modestly. 'I've no doubt whatever about that. I believe I can pilot the aircraft across the Atlantic, but it'll be a jolly sight easier with a good navigator on board.'

He walked over towards one of the engines, began examining the four-bladed propeller.

'I'm very concerned about these,' he commented. 'They're wooden, as you see. In the war, I was ordered to bomb the marshalling yards on the Bosphorus, and we ran through a lot of Turkish anti-aircraft fire. We had just come out of that unscathed, or so it seemed, when suddenly the wooden port propeller just broke up and flew off in pieces. I had to bring the plane down in the sea. The navigator and I swam ashore.'

'It'll be a longer swim if you have to do that this time,' said Brown drily.

'I don't intend to,' replied Alcock. 'I'm not taking a swimming costume.'

What they were taking was the most up-to-date navigational equipment. They also had a radio transmitter and a receiver. Because of the drain these would impose on the batteries, a small generator with a tiny propeller was fixed on one of the wings to keep the batteries charged. They had borrowed a special compass from the Air Ministry. Their fleece-lined flying overalls were fitted with thin electric wires along the legs, and the backs and arms.

'They'll keep us warm when we switch them on,' Brown explained. 'It's a new idea, electrically heated flying suits. Gets damn cold up there.'

This sounded very professional on the face of it, but Carola could not help thinking that some of the equipment seemed rather primitive.

'You think you can carry enough fuel for the journey?' she asked.

'We should do. We've worked it out time and again. The plane has a range of nearly two and a half thousand miles and we'll have the wind behind us. There may be storms, of course, and they could slow us down. But once we're over halfway, we can't turn round and go back. The shortest way home is straight on. And in this sort of flight, over the sea, if we can't go on, we'll have to come down. We're going to go on.'

Afterwards, over coffee in the Bluebird, Carola asked them what they thought was the most important factor in any record-breaking flight. Both men considered the point, stirring their coffee reflectively. Alcock was the first to reply.

'The main thing, in my opinion,' he said, 'is total dedication. You must give every record attempt your whole life – or maybe you'll lose your life. First, you must follow the engines from assembly to testing. Check every control, every lever, every pipe, every joint. It's no good assuming things are working correctly, that it will be all right on the night, because if it isn't, what do you do when you're ten thousand feet up in the air at midnight and that one little union you didn't check plays up? Maybe it was in an awkward place and to get a good look at it you'd have to dismantle something else, so you let it go. Now it's gone – and maybe you're going, too.'

'I agree with all that,' said Brown. 'And I've only this to add – determination. You are going to win. *Nothing* will stop you, not engine failure, weather conditions – or you yourself. You must have the will to go on against all odds, all setbacks. There are always so many reasons why people don't want to go on. They'd rather give up, it's easier. They've had a good try and there's no disgrace in failing. It's too difficult, too dangerous, to continue. Or they're just plain tired.

'You want none of that. You're up there to win. So much depends on it, and so many people. Hundreds, thousands of people are directly or indirectly involved in this attempt. Their careers, their jobs, their future. Then there's the prestige of the country. We lost a lot of good men in the war. I think we have to show the world we still have bright brains left who can build planes that can fly the Atlantic, the longest flight that's ever been made.'

'Do you think a woman will ever do it?' asked Carola.

'Women will do everything one day, probably even go to the moon. Why, are you planning it?'

'Oh, it was just a question,' she said, embarrassed.

'If you are,' said Alcock, 'get a good navigator to go with you. Then at least you'll know where you are going – not just where you've been.'

'Thanks. If ever the time comes, I'll take your advice.'

They smiled at Carola, amused by the enthusiasm, not thinking she was serious. Although they were not very much older in years, they were separated from her by long experience of war and death, by aerial dogfights, bombing raids, wounds and capture.

She realised that this flight was something they had to do, not just for the reasons Brown had given her. They were also flying for all those other young men they had known, who would have been just as keen as they were but who hadn't survived to make the attempt. They were doing it for them; for the honour of the dead as well as the living.

Sir Bernard Warner slit open the envelope of the only letter that had arrived by the afternoon post. The handwriting was very poor, and he frowned as he tried to decipher it.

Dear Sir Bernard,
    You don't know me, but we saw each other

330

several times, years ago. I was the butler to Mr
Rowlands. You came to his last ball before the war,
remember? I am retired now and in poor health, a
widower, living with my unmarried daughter. I
would like to see you, if you could spare the time,
and tell you something about Mr Rowlands' trip to
France. It was a bit of a mystery why he went. I
can't write more, but I feel I must tell someone,
and I believe I can trust you.

Yours respectfully,

Joshua Grover

The address was an unfashionable suburb in south-east
London; the notepaper was pale blue, of the cheapest
quality, with the imprint of a flower in one corner.

Sir Bernard could not recollect meeting Grover, but
then there was no reason why he should. He regarded
butlers and footmen as ciphers, merely mannikins in
livery. Unless you personally employed them, you did
not need to know their names. But what a strange letter
to receive so many years after Charles's death.

For a long time he had felt guilty about Rose Rowlands. He had seen her on two or three occasions at other
people's dinner parties in the years between then and
now. He had no idea how she was, or whether she was
even still alive.

The fact was that if you were friendly with a husband
and he died suddenly and unexpectedly, you felt embarrassed at attempting to carry on the friendship with his
widow. Also, after the loss of their two sons in the war,
the Warners did not lead a very active social life. Both
found it painful to meet the sons of friends who had
either survived the war or who, like Tobin Rowlands,
had somehow managed to avoid any active involvement.
They could not help thinking of their own sons, and
what they might be doing now if they had survived. They

disliked being faced with such hurtful and poignant reminders.

Sir Bernard glanced at his watch. Four o'clock; too late to visit Grover that afternoon. But he was doing nothing much on the following morning. He had been retired for some time now, and he welcomed the chance of something to do, even if it was only to look up the former servant of a dead friend. He would drive over to see the fellow after breakfast. Grover might have fallen on hard times, and this could simply be a rather circuitous attempt to extract a tip. Well, he could afford a fiver. But there was also just the faint chance that Grover did have something of interest to say, even if he had waited years to say it.

As Sir Bernard put down the letter, he glanced at the photographs of his two sons on a side table. Boyish, cheerful faces smiled out from the silver frames. Every day he remembered them, and every day he grieved that so many of the young and brave had died, while so many others he considered unworthy had lived to prosper.

From the *Enquirer*
SIR JAMES MANNERING'S GREAT PLANS FOR MOTORISTS
Famous Financier To Open
Countrywide Garage Chain
To Sell Cheap Petrol
By our Motoring Correspondent

Sir James Mannering, the immensely wealthy but publicity-shy financier, announced last night that he has bought 100 petrol filling stations in England, Scotland and Wales. They will sell his own brand of petrol exclusively under the name of PPP – People's Petroleum Products.

For several years this company, which he controls, has been importing large quantities of petrol from Russian oil-fields. Owing to Sir James's advantageous purchasing, this will now sell at 6d a gallon less than other brands from sources in the United States and the Middle East.

To control so many roadside garages marks a great step forward for his company. This ambitious new enterprise will also benefit British motorists – already burdened by increasing licence costs and rising insurance premiums – and may start a fierce war of price cuts as other oil companies are forced to respond.

Sir James, a great patriot, put his international contacts and unparalleled expertise in financial matters freely at the disposal of the British Government during the late war. It is understood that he founded PPP at the suggestion of the Russian Government during a visit to that country before the Bolshevik Revolution.

Grover lived in a bow-fronted Victorian house in a long terrace. Halfway down the street a barrel organ was playing 'Keep the Home Fires Burning'. A tired monkey sat unhappily on the lid, rattling its chain and sucking an orange skin.

Sir Bernard knocked at the front door. A middle-aged woman answered it with a promptness that suggested she had watched his arrival from the front window.

'You must be Sir Bernard Warner,' she said at once, taking in his well-cut suit, his highly polished Tricker brogues. 'My father thought you would come.'

Sir Bernard followed her along a narrow corridor into a back room. He recognised Grover as soon as he saw him, but his face was fat and flaccid; it was like looking at a photograph that had somehow been over-exposed. He was now a bloated caricature of the

urbane butler who had taken his coat at the Rowlands'
ball so many years before.

Grover was sitting in a high-backed chair. He struggled to get up as Sir Bernard went in, but the effort was
too much and he sank back wearily. He was clearly in
poor health.

'Don't disturb yourself,' said Sir Bernard. 'Of course I
remember you. And that night, too. A wonderful party.'

'The last, sir,' said Grover.

'I suppose it was.'

'Oh, yes, sir. After that, with Mr Rowlands going, and
the war and everything, it all changed. Wasn't the same
at all.'

'I agree,' said Sir Bernard with feeling.

'Would you like a cup of tea?' Miss Grover asked him.
Sir Bernard shook his head.

'Thank you, no.'

'I will leave you, then,' she said.

Sir Bernard sat down in the only other chair the room
contained. The air felt hot, stale. Flies buzzed wearily
against musty windowpanes. The clock had stopped at
half past seven, but whether in the morning or the
evening, he had no idea. There seemed a timelessness
about the room, as he had often noticed where old people
were concerned. Their future was now so short that their
thoughts almost constantly focused on the past. The
present seemed unimportant; it was merely a staging
post, possibly a final one, on a journey now nearly at an
end.

'Admiring the drawings are you, then, sir?' asked
Grover.

'The drawings?' What did the man mean? Sir Bernard
looked around the room, and was surprised to see a
likeness of himself above a calendar. He had not noticed
sketches on the wall. Next to this hung a good likeness of
Charles Rowlands and Rose and their son Richard.

'Who did them?' he asked politely.

'I did,' Grover replied proudly.

'You've certainly got them to a T.'

'My hobby,' Grover explained. 'If I'd had the chance I would have liked to have been an artist, full time. My cousin went to night school to learn. He's a draughtsman in a factory in north London where Mr Rowlands' younger son was working.

'Young Rowlands was offered fifty quid for some idea he put up, and like the gent he is he insisted on sharing it with the others, my cousin included. Made a great impression on him, that did. Isn't too much generosity about these days, sir. So I thought, one good turn deserves another. That's why I wrote to you, sir.'

'I see,' said Sir Bernard, not quite following this reasoning. 'And what have you to tell me that does anyone a good turn?'

'When I was in service I used to draw the quality. Everyone who came to the house. My wife said I should try to sell them copies, but I never liked to. It's different when you're below stairs.'

'Quite so,' Sir Bernard agreed patiently.

The old man put a hand down one side of his chair, picked up a large brown envelope, shook several sheets of sketching paper out onto a small table.

'You know about that Mr Harper, I suppose,' he said. 'He told him to go to France.'

'Go on,' said Sir Bernard, puzzled.

'Well, this Mr Harper came to see Mr Rowlands. He wanted five thousand pounds. Blackmail, I thought. He said Mr Rowlands had invaded the privacy of a young boy who needed the money to emigrate and build a new life in one of the colonies.'

'How do you know?'

'I listened. I always did. So did all the rest when they had the chance. The quality forget servants are

335

human. They'll discuss all kinds of things in front of us. You'd be amazed at the intimate things they say. They think we're just creatures who can't hear anything, or if we do, we don't understand it. So if they don't care what they talk about when we're in the room, why shouldn't we listen when there's a door between us? How do you think these writers in the newspapers pick up all their news about what's going on in society? From servants, of course. They get paid for what they pass on. Trouble is, the papers are afraid to print the really juicy bits.'

'Go on,' Sir Bernard repeated, more sharply this time.

'Then your two policemen arrived, Sergeant Gonville and the other man – I didn't get his name – and took Mr Rowlands away.'

'You're certain of this?'

'Oh yes, sir. Positive. I was there.'

'Of course. Tell me, did Mr Rowlands ask to see their warrant?'

'Sergeant Gonville offered to show it to him, but Mr Rowlands said it wasn't necessary. The sergeant explained that you were tipping the wink to an old friend, sir. If Mr Rowlands got out of the country then and there, he'd be all right. But if he stayed, the police would have to act. So he hadn't much choice and no time. He packed while they waited for him and then they took him in their motor to the station.'

'Do you believe Mr Rowlands would have anything to do with a boy in the way you suggest?'

Grover shrugged. 'Impossible to say, sir. Since you ask me direct, I'd say no. But he was always very concerned about his position, what people thought of him, what people might say about him. In confidence, sir, I'd say he felt he was doing nothing with his life. He'd never had a proper job. He was just frittering away his time, living on money others had left him. Little things that you and I wouldn't even think about became very important to him. I always say that if you want to kill time, the best and quickest way is to work it to death. That's the trouble with so many of the quality, sir. They've no work to do and no need to do any, so they fill their heads and lives with rubbish. But he always treated me fairly, that I will say. But that Mr Harper, he left an envelope with Mr Rowlands. Afterwards I had a look in it, of course.'

'Of course,' agreed Sir Bernard, trying to keep irony out of his voice.

'I was surprised what it contained.'

Grover dug down at the other side of the chair and pulled out a square of brown paper. He undid it, shook out some photographs onto the table. Sir Bernard picked them up. He had seen them already; they were duplicates of the pictures in the room above the barber's shop. He examined the edges. They had nothing concealed behind them.

'There's one more in this set,' he said. 'Have you got that?'

'Then you know about it?' asked Grover. 'You're right, sir. There was one more, but I didn't want to mention it.'

'Because it's of Mrs Rowlands?'

Grover nodded. 'It didn't seem right to keep it when I was working for her and she was always kind to me, and to my lady wife. I threw it into the back of the fire.'

'Can I borrow these?' Sir Bernard asked, indicating the sketches.

'By all means.'

'Who are they of, exactly?'

'This one's Mr Harper. And I expect you recognise Sergeant Gonville and the other policeman.' Grover looked anxiously at Sir Bernard.

'Of course,' he said at once. 'You certainly have a gift for drawing. Now, is that all, Mr Grover?'

Just for a moment, Grover hesitated. Then he dug into his chair once more and pulled out another envelope. Sir Bernard saw that it was addressed to Rose Rowlands and had been steamed open and resealed inexpertly.

'What's in it?' he asked sharply. There was no need to ask whether Grover had read it.

'I'd rather not say, sir. But perhaps you could give it to her. It's of a private nature.'

'Where did you find it?'

'With the photographs, sir.'

'So you took the lot?'

'Yes, sir.'

Sir Bernard removed a ten pound note from his wallet. 'Perhaps you would allow me to buy the sketches. Would this be in order?'

'Most generous, sir,' Grover replied with alacrity.

'Tell me, why did you take these pictures out of the drawer?' Warner asked him. 'Why not leave them there?'

'I thought they would be discovered. Wouldn't do anyone any good leaving them lying around.'

'I wonder why Mr Rowlands left them there.'

'I've no idea, sir. But he had to keep them some-where.'

'I suppose so – if he wanted to keep them at all.' Sir Bernard paused. 'Was the letter to Mrs Rowlands in the brown envelope, or did you find that later?'

'Later, sir. After Mr Rowlands left, I had a look-see in the drawer and found it then.'

'I see. Now, anything else?'

'No, nothing, sir. That's the lot.'

Sir Bernard let himself out of the house. In the street he paused for a moment, thankfully breathing fresh air after the foetid atmosphere of Grover's room. Half a hundred yards away, the barrel organ began to play 'Roses of Picardy'.

From the *Enquirer*
INTERNATIONAL FINANCIER'S NEW VEN-TURE
Sir James Mannering Opens
London's Latest Art Gallery
By our Arts Correspondent

Considerable interest has been aroused in artistic circles by the announcement late last night that Sir James Mannering, the world-renowned financial expert, is opening an art gallery in Bruton Street, London, W.

This will be known as the Mannering Gallery and its first exhibition, largely of portraits, will be formally opened by Prince Edmund next month. The first exhibition will, I understand, be unique in that all the sitters were members of the Russian aristocracy. Most of them perished tragically at the hands of the Bolsheviks during the revolution of 1917.

Sir James, I am told, has been fortunate in being able to secure more pictures than can be displayed in a single exhibition. He has plans to open another gallery in New York later in the year, and in due course hopes to have exhibitions of paintings by British artists.

Chapter Fourteen

Lady Warren's car sighed north, slicing through traffic in the Edgware Road, past rows of shabby terraces, corner shops, music halls, public houses, out to Stanmore where the houses were larger, with trees and gardens. It travelled over Brockley Hill, along the old Roman Road, Watling Street, to Elstree, then towards the airfield. Lady Warren lit another cheroot and turned towards Carola.

'You know this airfield well, I believe,' she remarked.

'Not well, Lady Warren. But I used to visit it from time to time, yes.'

'Eight times, if my information is correct, and it usually is. You had your first flight here with that Australian fellow.'

'That's right, yes. I did.'

'And what about that other young man? You've been seeing him again, I believe.'

'Richard Rowlands? We've met a few times. I bumped into him at Brooklands. He has a job in a car factory. They were testing a new model.'

'So I heard. It blew up, I'm told. No wonder his nickname is Blower. However, nothing worthwhile in life is ever easy and straightforward. As he is no doubt discovering. And so will you.

'Now, to the matter in hand. I've arranged for a very good instructor to teach you to fly. You will start in a simple aircraft, and then progress to faster ones. He's also going to teach you many things that could save your life when you start your long-distance flights. How to survive if you crash-land in the sea, in the desert, anywhere. You will learn a lot that other fliers know nothing about.'

The car turned off the main road, went past a long fenced wood with notices 'Trespassers Will Be Prosecuted'. At the Battleaxes inn, Carola half expected to see Richard waiting with his bicycle. They drove on through the airfield gates. The Rolls stopped outside the nearest hangar.

'Follow me,' said Lady Warren.

She led Carola into the administrative building. A clerk looked up, then rose to his feet smartly when he saw them. Although he had no idea who Lady Warren was, her presence was commanding. Also, he had seen her car arrive. This visitor was clearly someone of wealth and influence.

'I have brought this young lady for her first lesson,' Lady Warren told him. 'We have booked an instructor. I am Lady Warren.'

'Oh yes, your ladyship. He is waiting for you.'

'In fact,' said a voice from the door. 'I'm not just waiting, I'm ready to begin!'

They both turned. Tom Gardener stood smiling at Carola.

'*You!*' she cried in amazement and delight. 'I thought you were back in Australia.'

'Well, I'm not. I've been helping run a flying school. Didn't you wonder why I hadn't written? I told you I would.'

'I thought that was all talk.'

'Now you can see it's not talk. I'm here.'

'But Lady Warren, surely *this* isn't my instructor?'

'He is. And, I believe, the best.'

'I didn't know you even knew him.'

'There are many things you don't know, girl. And many things you have to learn in life. All is not ever as it seems. Nor are people. I do not often make mistakes, but when I do I admit them, frankly and freely. A characteristic that you and everyone else would be wise to follow. And I made a grave mistake about this brave young man. Now, I am pleased to say, he is going to teach you to fly. I will leave you in his good hands. A car will be sent for you in three hours' time. I bid you both good day, and good luck.'

Carola watched her walk out of the building. Then she turned to Tom.

'Is what she's saying true?'

'Perfectly. I went to see her. There was a misunderstanding. She thought I was an old roué.'

'Whereas you're just a young roué.'

'Just young,' he said, smiling. 'And raring to go. Now, let's begin your first lesson.'

Carola had no real idea what to expect. Her previous flights had all been with Tom as pilot, and she had always felt confident of his abilities and experience. She had looked down over the side of the cockpit, past struts and wires and wings, as the fields, rivers and roads of southern England unfolded far beneath them, like a colourful patchwork quilt.

But now, wearing goggles, a leather helmet with earphones and a borrowed set of flying overalls, several sizes too large, she sat in the rear cockpit while Tom explained what was going to happen.

'At your feet are the rudder pedals. They are connected with the pedals in my cockpit, so don't put too much weight on them. Just let your feet go with them easily as I steer, and then gauge how hard you will need to press.

'You will find you only need to touch them lightly, but

fairly often, to keep the plane on a straight course. We will set off in a straight line easily enough, but winds and hot-air currents and so on can deflect us.

'The lever in the centre, known as the joystick, controls the ailerons and the elevators.

'I have a speaking tube in my cockpit which is connected to your earphones and if I give you orders – not instructions – do exactly what I say and at once. No argument, no hesitation. Up in the air we have to act fast, with instant thought and reaction. We can't have any discussions and explanations. Just do what I say. Quickly.'

'You won't have any discussion or argument from me,' Carola answered him.

'Right. Well then, let's go.'

The cockpit was edged with padded leather; her seat was also black leather, creased and polished by use. Everything seemed very small and spartan. Wires controlling the rudder and the elevators ran on either side of her feet. There was no attempt to conceal them or protect them. A mechanic swung the propeller. The engine fired.

As they began to taxi along the grass runaway, Tom kept talking.

'Almost any fool can take off,' he said, his voice sounding hollow and metallic through the speaking tube. 'And once you're up in the air, it's still not very difficult to fly. Landing is what sorts out the men from the boys – or the women from the girls, in your case. So watch how I do it, and remember when your turn comes.'

They flew up and turned above the airfield in a wide circle.

'I'm coming in now to show you just what I mean,' he went on. 'I aim to make a three-point landing so that our two wheels and the tail skid – all three points – touch the ground at exactly the same time. This means that the pilot has to work out speed, height, how long the runway is, what the wind's like, and so on before he – or she – can come down.

'And remember, each time you land, the equation will be different. Some people can never land cleanly. You will see them come in and then sail off again without touching down. They've funked it, so they have to try a second time, or a third. But we all have to come down eventually, so it's best to make it the first time. Now, watch this.'

He came down, landed neatly, taxied to the end of the airfield, turned and took off again.

'See what I mean? Now we'll do it again, and again, to get you used to the feeling.'

Week after week they were up in the air whenever the weather allowed. After several sessions, Tom let Carola control the plane in the air, then told her to land. The first time, she muffed the landing. He simply opened the throttle and the plane took off.

'Now try again,' he told her. 'And this time do it properly.'

She looked over the side, trying to work out how high she was from the ground. All she knew for certain was that she was above the treetops.

'Keep your nose straight. Keep your nose *straight*!' warned Tom. 'Aim at the far end of the airfield, and hold it there. Now, come on down. Gently does it.'

Carola began to ease back the joystick with nervous, jerky movements. Between each one, she felt her heart beat slowly and heavily, like a muffled drum. She knew that she was bringing the plane in too low and too fast. And then, before she could correct it, bang, bump, bump. The wheels hit the ground before the tail skid.

'Too fast, too fast,' said Tom wearily and opened the throttle. Up and away they went. At the fourth attempt she made a three-point landing. How and why, she was not quite sure, but she had done it. And that meant she could do it again and again. Didn't it?

Tom's attitude towards her was always strictly formal. He was the instructor, she was the pupil. Sex did not enter into it. No one would ever suspect he had once asked her to marry him. She did not know that Tom also felt concerned in case Lady Warren had a spy among the mechanics. He had too much to lose to risk anything at this point.

After each flight Carola was driven back to Lady Warren's house, sitting in the back of the car behind the chauffeuse. Every time, Lady Warren asked her how she'd done, how she was progressing. Could she land yet? Could she take off? Had she flown solo?

Five weeks later, Carola could answer that she had. She flew the plane alone for the first time from the rear cockpit. Taking off was easy enough, as Tom had told her. After all, she was starting from the ground. She went through the drill slowly, repeating each check aloud in case she'd forgotten anything. Once airborne she gained height and flew south above the outskirts of London. She wheeled north, then east, and so back until she could check her position from the straight line of the Edgware Road. Soon she was above the airfield again, easy to recognise because it had a wide expanse of water to one side, a reservoir or a lake.

Suddenly, she realised why she was flying aimlessly. She was too afraid to attempt to land. She felt terrified, almost petrified with fear at the prospect.

She was up on her own, alone in the sky, like some human bird with mechanical wings. Soon she had to fly down to the nest, and for a moment she could not think how. Her mind seemed totally blank, devoid of every memory, every recollection, everything Tom had taught her. Panic gripped her with sharpened iron claws. Perspiration dampened her forehead, her back, her hands.

She leaned over the side of the cockpit and felt cold wind on her face, and wondered whether she would be physically sick.

Carola knew she had to beat this feeling of total helplessness. She must get down there somehow, or quite simply she would die. If she did not land, she would eventually just fall out of the sky, like a bird with broken wings, and die as she hit the ground.

She calculated she had probably two hours of petrol left in the tank, and every moment she delayed, she would find it more difficult to reach a decision. She had to go down. *Now*, before all correlation between brain and memory and muscle vanished.

She came down to five hundred feet, then hastily climbed again. Not just yet. Wait a minute. I'll feel better in a moment. And when I feel better I'll do it then. So round and round she went. She did not have a wireless in the plane, and no means of talking to Tom on the ground or anyone else in the airfield control tower who might help her to break this deadlock and talk her down. The only way she could communicate was by shouting, futile against the roar of the engine and the shriek of the wind, and in any case what could she say? Tom had told her often enough what to do. Now she had to tell herself.

Finally, she made up her mind to attempt a landing. She *had* to do it this time. No more muffed attempts. It must be now or never. She came down too fast, at the wrong angle of approach, overshot the runway, went up again. But she had nearly made it. Nearly. She was probably only within feet of making it. Next time she'd do it.

She came down more slowly now, easing the stick gently. Down, down, ease the throttle, check you're heading towards the end of the runway, not at an angle but dead straight. Now, the stick, then back with the throttle lever, and bump, bump. She was trundling along the grass, throttling back to slow the plane.

She turned, taxied to the clubhouse and stopped. Tom came out and waved to her. Carola expected warm congratulations, tributes to her skill. Instead, he waved her back into the cockpit as she started to climb out.

'Back!' he called. 'Do it again. Twice more.'

'I've proved I can do it,' she replied sulkily.

'So prove you can do it three times in a row. *Now!*'

He was right, of course. She had nearly lost her nerve and she felt, deep down, if she didn't go up now, she might never fly again. She had to go because she hated it, because she was afraid to go. And no one could ever fly with such fear as their co-pilot.

The second time was no better than the first. She overshot again, but landed at the next attempt. The third time, she made the landing in one.

Thankfully, Carola climbed out of the aircraft. Mechanics put chocks against the wheels as she walked towards the clubhouse. She felt quite shaky, almost as if she might faint. She had not realised how hot it had been in the cockpit. Usually, she was cold in the air, but that was when Tom was in charge, not when she was up on her own. This was not a matter of temperature, of flying on a hot day; this was the sweat of fear.

She pulled off her helmet.

'You look about all in,' he said sympathetically. 'Come into the clubhouse and have a drink.'

'It's not good to drink and fly. You've told me that often enough.'

'You're not flying any more today. Have a brandy. To celebrate.'

Carola accepted thankfully. She had felt more afraid in the air than she would ever admit to anyone.

'We're going up again,' Tom announced suddenly.

'I'm not,' she replied, surprising herself by her own

vehemence. 'Three landings. That's enough. You said so yourself.'

'This time, you'll be the passenger. I'll pilot you. Take off those flying overalls and we'll go.'

'Where to?'

'A surprise. Like those holiday coaches on the coast that take old folk on a mystery tour. We're going on our own air mystery tour.'

For most of the flight, Carola kept her eyes closed and leaned against the hard back rest, thankful she was not at the controls. She had no idea how long they flew, but it was probably only for about twenty minutes. Then they came spiralling down, landed on a wide field near a river. Its banks were thick with willows and osiers. The sun felt very hot. She glanced at her watch. Twelve o'clock. Why, it wasn't even lunchtime. This must be the longest day she had ever known.

'The end of the run,' he told her. 'We get out here. Leave your helmet in the plane. It's too hot to wear flying gear.'

'Where are we, exactly?'

'On the edge of the Thames.'

'Whose field is this?'

'Oh, a farmer's. He said it would be all right,' Tom assured her easily. 'That's where we're heading.'

He pointed towards an inn near a wooden bridge and a weir. They walked to it through long grass. The air smelled sweet with the scent of hay and herbs. Tom put out one hand to help her up a slight slope, and when they reached the top and came down on the other side he did not let go. The sun felt very warm through her thin blouse. She was conscious of being relaxed, at ease. It must be a combination of brandy and being out of the plane – and Tom holding her hand.

She feared flying; that was the root of it all. Out of a

349

plane she felt safe, released, relieved. In the cockpit, at the controls, she felt trapped. She held the only key to her freedom and she was afraid to use it. She'd had no idea what flying alone would be like until she had done it. She had been infatuated with a dream, an imagined ideal, not reality. Perhaps in thinking she was so attached to flight she had really, deep down, been trying to fly away from her problems, her drab life with a rough-handed father, an uncertain future.

Compared to the life she had glimpsed, if only at second hand, with Lady Warren, she had been existing, not living. Flying still remained her best escape route; possibly the only one. But she was terrified of taking it. Yet, if she wished for Lady Warren's help, she had no other choice. And if she didn't, she had no choice at all.

They reached the inn. The landlord was laying a table under the trees. She suddenly remembered that other inn outside St Albans, when Tom had told her he was going back to Australia. But he hadn't gone. He was still here, by her side. Had he ever intended returning, or was that simply a story, a ploy to gain her sympathy, make her show regret so that he could discover whether she really cared for him?

Cutlery and glasses reflected the sun like tiny, welcoming, reassuring heliographs. They symbolised a world she yearned for: elegance, grace, no skimping, no meanness. Swans glided past on the river, heads and beaks sheltered under their wings. The peaceful atmosphere reassured her. She was overwrought, still tense after her solo flights. She needed to relax, to unwind.

'You must have known we were coming, sport,' Tom told the landlord cheerfully.

The landlord looked up at him in surprise. He had not seen them cross the field.

'That your aircraft, sir?' he asked. 'I saw it circling round.'

'It is. What have you got for lunch?'

'Fresh trout, caught this very morning. And some beautiful fillet steak, from a local farmer.'

'Then we'd like trout to start with, followed by two steaks, rare. You have any wine?'

'We have, sir.'

'We'll have a cold Chablis, and a claret to follow.' Tom turned to Carola. 'Is that all right with you?'

'I suppose so.' She had never had a meal ordered for her in this cavalier way before. In fact, she'd not had many meals ordered for her at all. Richard always asked her what she'd like. It was rather exciting to be told what you were going to have. Eat that, or else.

The landlord brought out a bottle of Chablis and a bucket of ice and glasses. Tom sipped the wine appreciatively.

'Great,' he said. 'Great. It's got a good nose.'

'I'm glad it's to your satisfaction, sir.' The landlord poured two glasses and left them.

'What do you mean by a good nose?' Carola asked.

'Damned if I know. But posh Poms talk like that, the ones who think they know something about wine. And it always goes down well.'

The trout was firm, the steak tender. Tom ordered black coffees and insisted she tried a Drambuie.

'For the king across the water,' he explained.

'What king?'

'All the kings, who one day will be across the water. Let's drink to that day.'

'You're against the royal family?'

'I'm against no one. I'm all for everyone getting as much as they can, and as soon as they can. I certainly want my share. The royal family's just got a lot more than the rest of us, and they've held on to it for far longer.'

'So they must have some points in their favour.'

'Maybe they're good judges of people who can keep it safe for them. Anyhow, what's it matter? Drink up.'

A brandy, plus the strain of three solo flights and now two different wines and a Drambuie made Carola sleepy. Worse than sleepy, she felt wuzzy, as though she was listening to a conversation rather than taking part in it. She was not used to drinking anything stronger than a shandy with Richard.

Tom watched her shrewdly.

'Come for a walk,' he said. 'It's a good thing you're not flying, for I think you're just a tiny little bit over the top.'

'You've drunk as much.'

'It's nothing to what I drink when I'm really trying,' he replied shortly. 'Nothing at all. I could have drunk those two bottles just for starters and then gone on to the hard stuff without feeling any strain. But, come on. It's you I'm concerned about, not me.'

They walked along the bank of the river. Carola felt a little unsteady, so Tom took her arm. She was glad of the support and leaned towards him gratefully. He seemed to be the sort of man she could rely on; strong, impossible to flurry, a head as steady as a rock. And yet a tiny doubt hung in her mind like the clouds that were already drifting across the afternoon sky.

Why had Tom said he was going home? And when he didn't, why had he not contacted her? After all, he had told her twice he loved her, had asked her to marry him. Why had he allowed Lady Warren to introduce them again? And what had made her suddenly change her low opinion of him? These questions chased answers and never caught them, like painted horses on a merry-go-round.

They walked on in silence. The day suddenly seemed oppressive, the air unusually warm. Only the gurgling water in the river gave an illusion of coolness somewhere, but not in her mind.

'You're all in,' Tom said gently. 'The first solo's always difficult. But I was right in making you take two more.'

'You were right,' Carola agreed mechanically. She deliberately spaced out the words, otherwise they would have run together, out of her control – as the aircraft had felt up in the air.

Tom was leading her towards a grove of trees, dark, friendly, welcoming. The grass beneath them was shorter than the grass in the field for it saw less sun. Under the overhanging branches, the air felt cooler.

'Here,' he said and took off his jacket. 'Sit down on that. Then the grass won't stain your clothes.'

She sat down inelegantly and then thankfully lay back. Tom sat down beside her, picked a blade of grass, held it between his thumbs with two hands pressed together, and blew a warbling sound.

'The pipe of Pan,' he explained. 'Pan, the ancient god of the countryside. Town people are afraid of Pan and what used to happen in the country in the sacred rites of fertility and birth and death. But it's in our background, in all of us. The country's still a wild place, even here in this tiny island. But you should see it in Australia.'

'Maybe I will, one day,' Carola replied, and closed her eyes. For a long time Tom sat, looking at her, saying nothing.

She must have dozed because, when she awoke, he was lying down beside her, his face against hers. As she opened her eyes, he turned her face towards him, kissed her. She could taste Drambuie on his lips, and wondered dreamily whether he could taste the same spirit on hers. Then she felt a hand at her blouse, gently undoing the buttons.

'No,' she said weakly, trying to sit up. 'No.'

'Never mind Lady Warren,' he replied firmly. 'She's not here. I am.'

Carola laughed – she did not really know why – and with the movement of her body Tom slipped his hand in the open blouse, undid her brassiere. This was a new one, of which she had felt rather proud. It had two clips at the front. According to the saleswoman in the shop, this made it man-proof. Maybe she should go back and ask for a refund.

Tom was kissing her again, and now she could feel his warm expert fingers stroking her nipples. They hardened beneath his touch. She felt as though this was a dream, or happening to someone else. His other hand strayed down, outside her skirt. Slowly, gently, inexorably, it slipped underneath the skirt, as though with a mind of its own. Then on up, to the top of her stockings. It reached the bare space of her thighs, and passed on to its secret goal.

'No,' Carola said sharply, but not sharply enough. Vague memories of warnings from her mother surged through her mind – and then out again. 'You shouldn't.'

'Give me two reasons,' he suggested.

'Well, it's wrong.' She paused.

'That's one reason. What's the second?'

She could not think of one.

'Don't tell me it's wrong,' said Tom, and his voice had changed subtly. Now it sounded thick and hoarse, and barely louder than an urgent whisper, as though he feared he could be overheard. But there was no one to hear them, no one to see them; no one knew they were there.

'People have been doing this since the world began. Otherwise there wouldn't be anyone in the world, would there?'

'But . . .'

'But nothing.'

Slowly, he undressed her.

'Someone will come,' she said warningly, but somehow the prospect of discovery only increased her feeling of excitement and anticipation.

They made love. This was the first time any man had made love to her. Before, she had known the theory but, as the workmen in Vickers would have said, this was the practical.

'I'm afraid,' she said as Tom moved on top of her, pressing her body into the soft grass. 'I don't want a baby. Please, I mustn't have a baby. You do understand?'

Memories of girls in Lady Warren's munitions factory, put, as they described it, in the family way by soldiers or sailors on leave and then left alone, miserable and frightened, forced to rely on Lady Warren's bounty, flashed warning signals in her mind. No matter what ecstasy now, the subsequent humiliation and ostracism could be incalculable. It was a totally unequal equation – a few moments of bliss, against years of bringing up an unwanted child. Odd, how even in this context she thought of the pleasure and the pain in engineering terms; an equation. But Tom was talking.

'I'm taking precautions,' he said.

She drew away slightly.

'So you thought this might happen?' she said, disappointed. He had planned it and she had foolishly imagined their feelings were spontaneous.

'I never think anything *might* happen,' he replied. 'I just like to think ahead.'

The first time it was rather painful, not quite as she had expected. The second, better. The third, best of all. Then they slept, and when they awoke, both at the same time, it was five o'clock by her mother's watch, and the sun had moved down the sky. There was an unwelcome chill in the late afternoon air. She began to dress hurriedly, brushing blades of grass from her clothes.

'I'd better button myself up, too,' Tom told her in a

matter- of-fact tone. 'We'll have to take off soon. I hope I didn't hurt you?'

'Only at the beginning. But then I liked it.'

'I thought you might. But don't tell Lady Warren. It's a long time since anyone did that to her.'

'Perhaps they never did,' said Carola, and they both laughed.

'That could be her trouble,' said Tom. 'But, you never know. She might be lucky one day.'

Carola snuggled against him, wanting his arms about her, his body against her, in her again. She yearned for the warmth, the strength that seemed to radiate from him. She told herself she had achieved two firsts on this remarkable day; a solo flight and virginity lost. She could let others know about the first, but the second was a secret only they could share. She told Tom.

'You make it sound like the end of a chapter,' he said gently. 'But this is only the beginning. To use a wartime comparison, sex for the first time is rather like ranging a big gun on a target. First shot, you may fall short. Second round, maybe you overshoot. Third time and it's a bull's eye on target. And from then on, you have the range, speaking in terms of firing a gun.'

'I like *your* gun,' she told him, and they both laughed, and liked each other more because of the laughter.

Carola kissed him lightly, a butterfly kiss on his lips, his nose, his forehead.

'I'll tell you something now,' she said. 'I was *terrified*.'

'Of this?'

'Oh no. Of being up in the air on my own. No one to help me if I did something silly. You weren't there to guide me down. There was no one but me.'

'We're all a little bit afraid in the air when we have to come down,' he explained seriously. 'But gradually the fear wears off. It's like making a high dive into a swimming pool. The first time you're up there alone on the top board you'd give anything, absolutely anything, for any excuse not to dive. But once you've done it, the second time's easier.'

'It wasn't much easier for me,' she said.

'It's like making love,' he said. 'It'll be much better each time. And easier.'

'You know?'

He nodded. 'I know. When it's with someone you like, someone special.'

'Have you ever done it with someone you didn't like? Someone not special?'

Tom laughed the question away, but Carola noticed he did not answer it.

'You ask too many questions,' he said easily. 'Come on, time to go.'

He took her hand, which went some way towards mollifying her, but not the whole way. Hand in hand, they walked back over the grass to the aircraft. The sun had left the sky now and a wind was rising, ruffling the water on the river. The swans were diving, swimming slowly in wide circles. Everything looked much the same, but Carola knew that for her, at least, nothing would ever be quite the same again. Two firsts in one day.

They reached the plane. A stockily built, red-faced man was standing by it. He wore leather leggings, breeches, a tweed jacket and he was smoking a pipe. He carried an ash walking stick. A bulldog sat at his heels. He could have been a stand-in for John Bull.

'This your plane?' he asked Tom gruffly.

'It is.'

'Then what the hell's it doing in my field?'

'I'm sorry. I thought I'd asked for permission to land.'

'You asked for nothing. And I'll tell you something, young man. You're damned lucky I didn't put my bull in the field to keep it company. I've had people picnicking here, parking their cars, walking all over the crops without so much as a by your leave. Now I've even got people coming in from the sky. Don't you land here again or you'll be in trouble, I'm telling you.'

'I'm sorry,' said Tom contritely. He motioned to Carola to climb in. 'If you'd just move further away for a moment,' he told the man, 'I'll start the engine and we'll be up and away from your field for ever.'

The man took a step grudgingly to one side. Tom walked to the front of the aircraft, put his weight against the warm wooden blade of the propeller, pulled it down hard. The blade jumped back as if on a spring. He pulled it down a second time. The engine fired. Gouts of blue smoke puffed from the exhaust. Tom swung himself up into the pilot's seat, opened the throttle. The plane bumped slowly across the rough field. As he pulled down the throttle lever in its quadrant, the engine roared. He waved to the farmer as they took off.

Back at Elstree, Lady Warren's chauffeuse was waiting for Carola with the runabout. Tom turned to Carola as they walked to the clubhouse.

'I hope you enjoyed the trip,' he said.

'I enjoyed everything,' Carola admitted happily. 'Especially you. Only one thing worries me a bit.'

'You won't get pregnant, I promise you.'

'I trust you. It's not that, so much. But you told me you'd got permission to land.'

'I thought I had. It must just somehow have slipped my mind.'

'Do many things slip your mind?' she asked him, looking into his incredibly blue eyes, wondering how she could be so attracted to this man, whether she could ever really trust him.

And in watching him, she knew the answers to both questions.

As Sir Bernard came up the long drive to Rose Rowlands' house, he felt depressed by the sad changes since his last visit. Casting his mind back, that must have been for the funeral service of Charles Rowlands. Then, the drive had been neatly raked, grass verges trimmed and cut, black iron railings on the edges of the paddocks newly painted. Now lawns were overgrown and weeds sprouted unchecked in the gravel. The railings were rusty, and where a cow in the park had butted them they had bent badly, and not been straightened.

At these obvious signs of neglect and lack of money, he felt even more guilty he had not been to see Rose before. But at least he was going now, although he wished he wasn't. He stopped outside the house, climbed out of his car and looked up at the pillared portico. In days gone by, servants would already be coming down the steps to bow and open the car door for him, and guide him up as though he did not know the way. Then Grover the butler would show him in to see whoever he had come to visit.

Sir Bernard climbed the steps on his own and tugged the bell pull. Its brass handle was tarnished, pitted by wind and weather. The suns of many summers had blistered the dark green paint of the front door. He waited for a long time before it opened, and Rose stood framed in the doorway.

'Come in,' she said. 'Tobin said you rang to say you were coming, but I hadn't expected you so soon.'

'Is it inconvenient?' he asked, offering her his hand, hoping she might say yes so that he could go away from this house of memories, this mausoleum of what once had been.

'No, no. Come in,' she said. 'I'm just doing a bit of dusting. I've only a daily char now. All the other servants have gone, long since. Just as well, really. I've no money to pay them.'

'And you've a lot of garden to keep up, as well as the grounds to look after.'

'Oh, well, the farms have been sold to pay interest on the mortgage Charles had arranged on the most terrible terms. We've a few acres left, and when they are sold I don't know what will happen. I'll have to go into an old people's home or something – if there's any money left for that. He always had such grandiose plans, Charles. And really without the money to carry them out. Huge parties every year, trips abroad. It was all so important to him, keeping up appearances of being very rich, when he was anything but.'

Rose paused as though to collect her thoughts.

'Cecily's married now. Lives in Canada. Winnipeg. I think she was glad to get away and start a new life. She never got over her father just walking out and not coming back. I thought she hadn't minded – she was very young – but I was wrong.' Her voice faded.

'And Richard? He was at Oxford last time I heard.'

'Oxford?' Rose looked at him for a moment as though she was not quite sure what he meant, then she nodded vaguely. 'Oh yes, Oxford. The university. My sister Hannah knew a professor there. The college was quite glad to get undergraduates, I think. So many potential ones had been killed in the war. Richard's working for a car firm now. Always was keen on mechanical things.'

Sir Bernard followed Rose through the hall into a side room. French windows opened on to balustrades and statues, now chipped and green with moss. Beyond lay the unkempt lawn, the overgrown flowerbeds.

He was as surprised at the change in Rose's appearance as in the condition of the property. He remembered her as a vigorous woman, an energetic hostess. Now she appeared vague, almost senile. Was this extraordinary change in character due to the loss of her husband – or money? Or was she ill?

Tobin followed them into the room. Sir Bernard smiled at him, trying to appear friendly, but unable to rid his mind of the cruel contrast between this plump, soft-fleshed young man who had somehow kept out of the war and the memory of his two dead sons, who hadn't.

'Haven't seen you for years,' he said, as brightly as he could.

'You haven't called, that's why,' Tobin answered rudely.

'You're quite right. I feel very guilty about that. But there it is.'

He would have said more, but he did not care for Tobin, his scarred face, his mean pig's eyes set so close together. Tobin regarded him with unconcealed hostility.

'Please sit down, Bernard,' said Rose nervously. She turned to her son. 'I think perhaps our guest would like a sherry.'

'No, no. Don't bother, please. This isn't really a social call. I just thought I should look in.'

'I'd describe that as a social call,' said Tobin coldly.

'Please,' said Rose beseechingly. 'Don't start.' She turned to Sir Bernard apologetically. 'He gets belligerent sometimes, Tobin,' she explained. 'He doesn't mean it. He's only trying to protect me.'

'From whom? I should think you've a lot of friends, Rose.'

'The usurer wasn't a friend,' said Tobin sourly. 'And I had my doubts about our lawyer. A very weak fellow. And as for my brother Richard . . .'

'Does Richard come here often?' Sir Bernard asked quickly.

'No.'

'Well, you asked him not to,' Rose pointed out gently. 'You told him it upset me to see him. I don't know why.'

Sir Bernard sat down uneasily on the edge of a chair. The chintz cover was soiled where dogs had curled up in it. Their hairs were everywhere. One had scratched a hole in the arm rest. He smiled weakly, wishing he were elsewhere, that he had checked Rose was on her own before he came to see her. He could not say what he had to say in front of this son.

'Well?' asked Tobin abruptly. 'What does bring you here, if it's not a social call?'

Sir Bernard looked at him. There was no point beating about the bush.

'I wanted to see your mother privately,' he said.

'You mean with me not here?'

'Privately,' Sir Bernard repeated.

'I can take a hint,' said Tobin. 'But I'll find out afterwards from her what you've been discussing. I can't stand people talking about me behind my back.'

'I can assure you we won't be talking about you.'

'Oh? What else have you to talk about that you don't want me to hear?'

Sir Bernard shrugged. He did not wish to become involved in a futile argument. Rose waved a hand feebly. Her thin fingers fluttered like the blades of a Chinese fan.

'Please go, Tobin. You were going in any case, I know. You have some shopping to do.'

'That can wait.'

'Well, if Sir Bernard wants to speak privately, he's come a long way . . . I don't know . . .'

Tobin sidled towards the door, looked balefully at Sir Bernard. 'I'll be outside,' he announced.

Sir Bernard waited until the door was shut, then turned to Rose. 'Could we walk in the garden? I remember it so well on the night of your ball.'

'Everything's changed now,' she replied. 'You'll hardly recognise it. And to think we had I don't know how many full-time gardeners, and sometimes even they didn't seem enough. Now we've one old man who comes in from the village to cut the lawns when he feels like it. I'll come out, certainly.'

Sir Bernard felt relieved she had agreed so easily. He guessed that Tobin would be listening on the other side of the door, and what he had to discuss was not for his ears.

Rose fumbled with the verdigris-covered handle on the French windows. The wood had swollen; they had not been used for years. Sir Bernard pushed them open sharply, and walked down the steps to the long grass.

'I'm sorry I haven't been to see you before,' he began. 'I should have come. But I was involved in Intelligence during the war, and I was away a lot. And somehow, quite wrongly, I felt I was your husband's friend rather than yours. I didn't want you to think I was pushing my nose into your affairs.'

'You'd never do that, Bernard,' Rose assured him. 'Charles thought very highly of you.'

'I'm proud to hear it. I held the same opinion of him. Now, the main reason I have come to see you is to deliver a letter.'

'A letter? From whom?'

'It's rather a long story. You used to have a butler, Grover?'

'That's right. Rather a shifty fellow, I always thought. I knew he stole drink, and I think some other things as well. He was for ever listening behind doors. But servants were all the same then. They felt part of the big house establishment and wanted to know everything that was going on. Then they'd compare notes with servants in other houses. It's different now, of course. Almost no one has servants. Can't afford them. But what about Grover? Is he still alive? He must be quite old. He left some time ago.'

'He's alive, but not very well. He wrote to me out of the blue, said he wanted me to see him. He remembered me from the old days, apparently. He's on rather hard times, wanted money really, I think. When I saw him, he gave me this letter.'

'But it's addressed to me!'

'Yes. He said he found it in a drawer in your husband's study.'

'You mean he stole it from the drawer?'

'You could say that. Anyhow, he's got a conscience about still having it. Maybe he thinks he's nearly at the end of his life and wants to settle things while he can. So I brought it over to you.'

'Do you know what's in it?'

'I've no idea. But I should think he does.'

'Of course.' She examined the back of the envelope. 'Even I can see it's been steamed open.'

She reached into a pocket of her shabby cardigan, took out a pair of spectacles from a metal case, put them on, opened the letter.

'It's from Charles,' she said. Her voice sounded strange, as though she could be about to cry. 'He wrote it just before he went to France that night. You can see the date. What an extraordinary thing.'

She said no more until she had finished reading the letter. Then, her face pale, she handed it to Sir Bernard. 'Here, you'd better read it for yourself. I can't bear to tell you what it contains.'

Sir Bernard put on his reading glasses, looked at handwriting he had not seen for so many years.

My dear Rose,

I find it very difficult to write this letter, but not as difficult as it would have been to tell you face to face what is happening.

I've told you I have to go to Paris on business. And so it is of a kind. A couple of weeks ago I had a visit from a man called Harper. He claimed to be

364

some kind of investigator. He said he wanted five thousand pounds, apparently to help a young fellow emigrate. He claimed I'd been involved with this young man. This is rubbish, of course, but he brought with him a number of obscene photographs. I believe some shady people in London hawk these things round to names taken from reference books, hoping they may find a buyer. Among them was a photograph of you, naked and obviously recognisable.

I don't know how Harper came by this. I don't know whether it is a fake or not. I pray it is. But we have never been able to discuss many private things between us, so I did not care to mention it to you.

I got Once-Hogg to look into the matter. Harper's address was only an accommodation address. I did nothing, hoping the whole matter would just die. But it hasn't. This evening, at the height of our ball, two policemen have arrived. They tell me that serious charges could be preferred against me, but Bernard Warner has very decently said that if I get out of the country for a time, things would blow over. This is obviously Harper's doing.

I am quite innocent, but this picture of you could be sent to one of the scurrilous newspapers. Probably they could not print it, but they might use part of it or publish some gossip item about you posing nude, which would be almost as bad because we wouldn't be able to deny it. We'd be ruined socially. Ostracised, finished. I could not face that and what it would mean for you.

Tonight, as I leave for France, I have suddenly realised that my whole life has been lived on the efforts of others, ancestors I never even met. Most of our friends live in the same way. We all keep up a façade we think is important, and this photo could shatter that for ever as far as you and I are concerned. For me that would be fatal, for this façade is really all we have. I have borrowed heavily to live in the style we do and the moneylenders would move in for the kill if our social standing suffered such a terrible blow.

When I get to Paris I'm going to think again about lots of things. First, I'm going to fight this man Harper. I can't write more now for the policemen are waiting, but I will be in touch. Remember, I'm doing this for you as well as for me, and for our family. God bless you all.

Although I may never have told you as often as I should, I love you.

Charles

Sir Bernard handed back the letter.

'Did you send two policemen as Charles says?' Rose asked him.

'No,' he replied. 'I sent no one. I had no idea of any of this. Whoever they were, they weren't policemen. Grover gave me the name of one, Gonville, or at least the name he used, and I've checked there's no one of that name in the police register. They were probably working with Harper, whoever he is.'

'But why?'

'Blackmail. The first attempt failed, so they tried again. Once they had Charles in France, on his own, probably frightened, cut off from his influential friends, he was far more vulnerable. He was run over in Paris in a genuine accident, and in any case it's unlikely blackmailers would offer him violence because they would regard him as a source of income for years ahead. But one of them cashed his cheque there for five thousand pounds.'

'The nerve of it! Is there any chance of finding out who he is and where he is after all this time?'

'I'll do my best. But there wasn't much to go on even then. There'll be much less now.'

'For years I've wondered why he went. And now I know. And he says he loved me. He never told me. Not properly. Only in this letter.'

Sir Bernard put his hand on her arm. 'Of course he loved you. We all knew that.'

'I didn't,' she said dully. 'I didn't. We had totally different backgrounds, you know. He was always rich, or seemed to be. Father, grandfather, goodness knows who else. Someone generations back had been a trader out East and made a fortune. Everyone else had lived on that money ever since.

'My family wasn't rich. I'd been on the stage. Not in London. In the provinces. Touring. I was desperate once, when I was very young, eighteen or nineteen. The manager had run off with the takings and our company was stranded in the Midlands. One of the girls knew a photographer who promised us a couple of pounds each if we'd pose nude. There was a market for such pictures, so he said. I wasn't keen, but I was hungry.

'I needed the money, Bernard, I needed it so badly I'd have done almost anything for it. You won't understand that, I know, but it's the truth. That's why I posed for that picture.'

'I understand that totally. During the war, Rose, I learned that all sorts of surprising people would do terrible things against their conscience, their training, their upbringing, their country because, like you, they needed the money. It was that or starve. But don't tell anyone in your family about this. We will deal with it privately. Together.'

'What about Tobin? Can I tell him?'

'No,' said Sir Bernard grimly. 'Certainly not Tobin. Not anyone.'

Chapter Fifteen

Carola had never been to a lunch like this.

The main banqueting room of the Savoy Hotel in London was filled to capacity by guests honouring the historic achievement of John Alcock and Arthur Whitten Brown in making the first flight across the Atlantic from St John's, Newfoundland, to the village of Clifden in Ireland. They had flown 1,890 miles nonstop in fifteen hours and fifty-seven minutes, at an average speed of 118.5 mph.

Winston Churchill, Secretary of State for War, sat with them, and everyone of consequence in the design, building and flying of British aircraft had been invited. All the tables were decorated with long streamers of specially treated canvas, the type used to cover aircraft wings, and red, white and blue flowers in the form of RAF roundels. The flags of Britain, Ireland and Newfoundland were draped across the walls. More baskets of flowers, made in the shape of aeroplanes, were suspended from the ceiling. Before each guest was a special commemorative menu carrying a picture of the Vickers Vimy and photographs of the pilot and navigator.

First course of the lunch was *oeufs poches Alcock*, followed by *suprême de sole à la Brown*. The main course was *poulet de printemps à la Vickers Vimy* with *salade Clifden*, then *surprise Britannia*, and finally *gâteau grand succès*.

369

After the meal, speech followed speech, each more eulogistic than the last. The editor of the *Daily Mail*, Thomas Marlowe, deputised for Lord Northcliffe who was ill. Northcliffe's interest in flying, and his offer of a prize of £10,000 for the first person to fly the Atlantic, had first aroused international interest in the possibility. Marlowe praised the remarkable achievement of the two fliers.

'It is a flight that will never be forgotten, and that adds the names of these two men to the brief list of classical heroes,' he declared to round after round of applause.

Then Mr Churchill rose. In trenchant style he described their experiences as they flew 'through clouds and storm and darkness to their destination.

'Think of the broad Atlantic, that terrible waste of desolate waters, tossing in tumult, in repeated and almost ceaseless storms and shrouded with an unbroken canopy of mist,' he said. And he reminded everyone how 'at every moment in this voyage they were liable to destruction from a drop of water in the carburettor, or a spot of oil on their plugs, or a tiny grain of dirt in their feed-pipe, or from any of the hundred and one indirect causes which in the present state of aeronautics might drag an aeroplane to its fate.'

At the end of his long speech, Mr Churchill announced that King George V wished to make pilot and navigator Knights Commander of the Order of the British Empire. At this, the applause and cheering, the clapping, the shouts of 'Bravo!' to the enthusiastic stamping of feet lasted for five minutes.

This was a moment Carola knew she would remember all her life. Earlier she had heard from Alcock and Brown about some of the worst moments of their flight. During a storm their plane dropped from a thousand feet to barely a hundred as they tried to fly their way through thunder and lightning, the wind and the rain.

They came down so close to the surface of the sea that spray from breaking waves lashed the underpart of the Vimy's wings. They climbed out of that storm – and flew straight into another. Now clouds engulfed them, dark and thick as a range of hills. They heard the rigging wires hum like violin strings in sympathy with the roaring wind as the plane struggled on. In the fierce hail and cold they crouched, freezing, behind the tiny windscreen in their open cockpit, the electric elements in their flying suits useless against the frenzy of the weather.

Once, Brown's goggles froze up entirely. The intense cold also affected the engines. They lost power and the aircraft began to fall slowly, steadily. Six times, Brown climbed out over the fuselage, inch by inch, to chip away pieces of ice with a pocket knife from the air intakes, while hail pummelled him like grapeshot. Gradually, the engines regained power. They flew on.

Guests at the lunch might guess at these near catastrophes, enduring hour after hour of freezing cold, always listening for the first tiny, telltale tremble and falter of an engine that could be the forerunner of fatal calamity. But Carola felt privileged, for they had told her their feelings, and she fully understood the immensity of their achievement in an open cockpit plane.

The flight was as much a tribute to the designers and builders of the aircraft as to the pilot and navigator, but now she appreciated for the first time just how large a part luck played in all record flights. As Winston Churchill had said, 'I really do not know what we should admire most in our guests – their audacity, their determination, their skill, their science, their Vickers Vimy aeroplane, their Rolls-Royce engines – or their good fortune.'

She came out of the hotel and stood in the Strand watching the crowds hurry past. Lady Warren and Tom had already left. She was to find her own way back. She walked along the Strand in a daze, passing the cut-price jewellers' shops, the clothing stores perpetually shutting down. Her mind was miles away, flying out of the sun, navigating by the stars. Alcock and Brown had done what she must do. But she would be flying alone. What would happen if her luck ran out? It did not bear thinking about; she knew the answer too well. As she walked, she began to feel terrified at the prospect Lady Warren had in store for her. But like Alcock and Brown, when they passed that point of no return more than halfway over the Atlantic, she could not go back. She had to go on.

Lady Warren's Rolls effortlessly overtook other, lesser cars. She lit a cheroot from the silver-plated lighter.

'What did you think of the lunch?' she asked Tom.

'I was very impressed. What those two men did was absolutely fantastic. You've never flown, Lady Warren, have you?'

'No. And I don't intend to, either.'

'I've flown for years. I've fought in planes, I've bombed from planes. But I take my hat off to them. The distance they covered, the conditions they endured, out of touch with everyone, absolutely on their own. Two men and two engines in the sky. And they won through. It was a wonderful, magnificent, almost unbelievable achievement.'

'Of course, but how can we use it? What about Carola?'

'You mean that she should attempt to fly the Atlantic?'

'Yes. Why shouldn't she?'

'Because she couldn't possibly undertake that journey yet.'

'With you as navigator she could. You suggested it yourself. Remember?'

'Yes, but not yet. You need long experience, so that if

you're tired, if you feel ill, if you even fall asleep, the wheel in the mind, what I call the automatic pilot in your brain, will somehow pull you through, keep the ship on course. You only acquire that gift when you've flown for many, many more hours than Carola's flown. Or when you've been in dangerous situations and been forced to draw on reserves you didn't know you had, because if you didn't, you'd die. She hasn't reached that point yet.'

'But you have. And you'd be with her as navigator.'

'Events have overtaken my proposal. Two men have just flown the Atlantic. Now if a man and a woman – a woman and a man – do the same thing, no one will really care. Whoever does it next has to do it on their own. Another dual flight wouldn't be the same. We need a solo attempt.'

'You're certain she couldn't do it on her own in a week or two – say a month or two?'

'Positive. You'd be sending her to her death. Those storms out there, waves forty feet high. Freezing conditions, everything icing up. You get disorientated. You can be tipped upside down in a storm so you don't realise where you are, what direction you should be taking, whether you're coming or going. And that's not just for a moment or two. It could be for hours. Your instruments block off, your engine cuts. In those conditions, you haven't a chance, haven't any hope whatever without years of experience – and not too much if you have that.'

'You disappoint me. I thought you had more guts than that.'

'It's not a question of guts, Lady Warren. It's a question of feasibility. If you send that girl up now, you will be guilty of murder.'

'I wouldn't do that.'

'But you're thinking about it.'

'In every achievement there has to be some pain. You have to take risks.'

'Agreed. But only when there's a reasonable chance of it succeeding. With Carola, as she is, there isn't any chance at all yet.'

'Your attitude displeases me.'

'I'll have to live with that,' said Tom shortly, and lit a cigarette from a match struck on the sole of his shoe. 'But I'll come up with something good when she's ready for it. Make no mistake about that, Lady Warren.'

'What concerns me is whether I've made a mistake about you,' Lady Warren retorted.

Sir Bernard Warner had deliberately selected his hotel room in Cannes because it overlooked the yacht basin. He stood now, well back from the window, shielded by the thick curtain. Through his powerful field glasses he could see activity on the deck of Sir James Mannering's 150-foot steam yacht.

She had sailed in early that morning from a Mediterranean cruise, and Sir Bernard had watched the hotel messenger deliver his letter to an officer on deck. Now he recognised the tall figure of the owner coming down the gangway. He wore light trousers, white yachting shoes, a dark blue blazer and a panama hat. Sir Bernard smiled sardonically at the familiar two blues of the Old Etonian tie and hatband to which he knew the wearer was not entitled.

Several paces behind Mannering walked two other men, also in yachting clothes. Sir Bernard recognised one of them from Grover's sketch. The other was a stranger. Both were of heavy build. They must be Mannering's bodyguards. Sir Bernard knew that Mannering never walked alone when abroad, and never ate on his own in any public restaurant. In England, he felt the risks of personal attack or even kidnap were small. After all, most of his important business dealings there were with members of the British government. Abroad, it was different. He was more vulnerable. Intermediaries and go-betweens lay between him and the decision-makers, and too many people knew him for what he was, and hated him for that. He had acquired too many powerful enemies over too many years to discount the possibility that someone, somewhere, would decide to repay an old debt – finally.

Walking in step, the three men came up the marble stairs onto the hotel terrace. The commissionaire, scenting the presence of immense wealth and power as a hog smells out truffles, saluted Mannering smartly.

Sir Bernard gave his field-glasses to another man who sat well out of line of the window.

'He's coming up the steps,' Sir Bernard told him. 'I'll talk to him on the terrace. We'll sit where you can get a clear view of him. Then I'll see you here afterwards. Right?'

'Right, Sir Bernard.'

He left the room, took the elevator down to the entrance hall. He walked towards Mannering and then paused, as though hesitating. It would be unwise to approach the man too directly. He might guess that he had been watched, targeted.

The two bodyguards moved closer to Mannering's side as Sir Bernard approached.

'Excuse me, sir,' he said diffidently. 'Am I right – you are Sir James Mannering? I sent you a personal letter this morning.'

'Ah yes, about my yacht,' Mannering replied. 'Then you're Sir Bernard Warner?'

'Yes, I am. Would you care to join me in a drink?'

'I never drink alcohol,' Mannering told him brusquely. 'It dulls the brain. One glass can kill millions of brain cells.'

'So I've heard. But for some of us the brain has reached a stage where nothing can dull it further. I sometimes feel like that, I must admit.'

Sir Bernard led the way to a table, offered Mannering a chair facing the hotel. The two bodyguards sat at another table close by.

Sir Bernard signalled to a waiter. 'A bottle of Krug, please, and two glasses.'

'One,' Mannering corrected him sharply. 'A Seltzer water for me. Now, to business. How did you find out I owned this yacht? She's not registered in my name.'

'I read in one of the yachting magazines that an owner was thinking of disposing of a splendid vessel. A detailed description was given, and since only two or three private yachts afloat possess such power and luxury, I made some enquiries.'

'The agent had my strict orders not to reveal my identity to anyone.'

'Ah, Sir James, we may give orders, but rich as we may be, we cannot guarantee they will always be carried out. And to be fair to your agent, he did not admit you were the owner. I deduced that fact myself.'

'I do not wish to discuss business in a public place, Sir Bernard.'

'Of course not. Neither do I. But it simply struck me that while we both, by chance, happen to be here in Cannes at the same time, we might talk over the proposition in a friendly way before we come down to hard figures. But if you wish otherwise, so be it. We can meet in London if you prefer. I will be back there next week.'

'No. Since we are here, as you say, let us talk. You know the price – one and a half million pounds sterling. No offers. The price to be paid in full on completion of the deal, which must be within seven days of my acceptance.'

'You drive a hard bargain, Sir James. But I see nothing too difficult about the price. However, I am sure you will understand that I would like to look over the vessel before I commit myself.'

'It is inconvenient for me to show potential buyers over the yacht now, or indeed at any time,' Mannering replied shortly. 'I am not a yacht broker. That is why I employ an agent. I suggest you agree a mutually agreeable time with him to inspect the vessel. She will be here in Cannes for several more days.'

'Of course. In the meantime, have you any photographs that would give me, and especially my lady wife, some idea of the stateroom furnishings and so on?'

'I have none. I do not keep photographic records of any of my possessions.' Mannering drummed his fingers on the marble table top. He was beginning to feel uneasy. He did not know why, but the antennae in his mind that had so often in the past picked up distant signals of approaching danger had always been accurate. He could not ignore them. There was something here he could not understand, and that disturbed him. He had checked Warner out in a reference book in the library aboard his yacht. The man had been a serving soldier, then a chief constable. The entry did not give any details of war service, but then possibly he was too old to have been involved. Now, in retirement, he was a director of several important companies. He was probably just a rich fool who wanted to impress his wife – or more likely some other woman, maybe someone else's wife – by buying a splendid yacht.

He could check him out more thoroughly in London, but why should he make the effort? What could conceivably be dangerous to him in such a simple deal? He would be glad to be rid of the yacht, and if he could do so here, in France, so much the better. He could then cut out the agent's commission; at ten per cent this would mean a saving of £150,000. Not a vast sum, agreed, but much better in his pocket than in the agent's.

He felt it was becoming increasingly unwise to own such a craft, with communism spreading and threats of violence increasing against even the moderately rich. He had his guards, of course, but how far could they be trusted? Everyone had their price. It was absurd for him to advertise his arrival in such style, all white paint and the crew in smart uniforms. It was more important to preserve anonymity. He must have been mad ever to buy the thing in the first place – not that he'd actually bought the yacht; he had taken her in part payment of a debt.

'No photographs?' said Sir Bernard, shaking his head in perplexity. 'I do not share your dislike for such records. In fact, I have a photo here that I think may interest you.'

He took one from an inner pocket and pushed it, face down, across the table. Mannering turned it the right way up and looked at it uncomprehendingly.

'Rather an odd picture,' Sir Bernard explained conversationally. 'It shows a wall behind the Tower of London, something tourists don't usually see. This wall screens a row of targets on the small-arms firing range. During the war it was used more than it is today.'

'What has this got to do with me or my yacht?' asked Mannering testily.

'In the front, here,' Sir Bernard continued, pointing to the picture, 'you will see several white stones. They mark the graves of German spies shot there in the war. We gave them a court martial, then they were taken out, blindfolded, and shot. This stone on the right belongs to one who had rather a good run but, sadly for him, it came to an abrupt end. The name he used in London was Barnaby. Not his real name, of course. He was an Irishman with a German mother.'

'Barnaby,' repeated Mannering. He spoke slowly because his throat had suddenly become constricted, as though a hand was clenching it, tightening round his windpipe. 'Why are you telling me this? I've never heard of the man.'

'I'm surprised to hear that since you used to meet him in the room above Luigi's barber shop, oddly enough run by another Irishman, one O'Brien.'

'I don't know what you're talking about,' said Mannering sharply and stood up. 'Whoever told you this was misinformed or a deliberate liar. I understood from your letter, sir, that you wished to discuss buying my yacht. Instead, you tell me things which are of no concern to me and in which I have no interest whatever. I will bid you good-day.'

The bodyguards also stood up and moved closer, alert and tense.

'This most certainly does concern you,' said Sir Bernard in a cold, hard voice. 'And it is very much in your interest to listen to what I have to say. But first, send away these two men. I dislike eavesdroppers.'

'They are officers from my yacht.'

'Then send them back there. Now. I will not meet you again, but others may.'

Mannering stared at him angrily. Sir Bernard stared him down. Mannering turned to the two men. 'Go back to the yacht,' he told them crisply. 'I will see you aboard.'

They bowed smartly and left, walking in step. Mannering sat down.

'I warn you, Sir Bernard,' he said, his voice tight, 'your insinuations are not only unfounded, they are defamatory. If you are trying to threaten me in any way, I will at once inform my attorney in Nice.'

Sir Bernard shrugged.

'By all means, Sir James, if that is your wish.'

Mannering looked at Sir Bernard. Was he bluffing? He thought not. He never could trust the English; they seemed so smooth and harmless and stupid, and then underneath they turned out to be hard and ruthless. 'Will you please get to the point,' he said at last.

'Certainly, Sir James. This man Barnaby was a spy, or rather a go-between. Our people picked him up in his rooming house in north London. He helped us a lot. But that did not balance out the grave damage he had already done. So there was only one punishment. The firing squad.

'Mr O'Brien was also helpful. But then he got above himself and tried to leave London for neutral Ireland without our permission. Unfortunately, on the ferry to Cork, he stood too close to the rail and fell overboard. Some have even said he was pushed. No matter. He is dead.

'We know you tried to sell weapon development secrets to the Germans, Sir James. In the event, the Russian Bolsheviks did that deal instead. The Home Secretary was unwilling to proceed with charges against you after the war, but many individuals who lost fathers, sons, brothers, possibly as a result of your involvement, do not take such a magnanimous view. I do not myself. I lost both my sons in the war, one due wholly to your sale to the enemy of a British machine-gun invention.

'The newspapers are always eager for news about the rich, especially bad news. It could be very harmful for you if any details of your double-dealing came out, let alone all of them. And I know all of them.'

'You talk a lot, Sir Bernard. Maybe too much. You might have an accident yourself, like this man O'Brien you mention.'

'Of course. And with that possibility very firmly in my mind, full details of what I know about you and your terrible record are lodged in several banks in France, England, and the United States. If any accident, of any kind whatever, whether fatal or not, should happen to me, they will be sent at once to newspapers. You may recall the words of Lord Northcliffe who founded the *Daily Mail*: "News is what somebody, somewhere, doesn't want printed. All the rest is publicity." This news, and its attendant publicity worldwide, would destroy you.

'My reason for our meeting, however, is not to threaten you but to make a deal with you, to come to an accommodation.'

'You mean you're trying to blackmail me.'

Sir Bernard raised his eyebrows, as though perplexed by the suggestion. 'Not at all,' he said. 'I wish to try to help someone who has lost a husband through the actions of one of your employees. A Mrs Rose Rowlands.'

Mannering was silent, and very still.

'But first, do you still wish to call your lawyer? If so, I will wait here for him. He will be interested in what I have to say.'

'I will not call him – yet,' said Mannering, and hardly recognised his own voice.

'A wise decision in all the circumstances. So let me explain the background. Before the war, a friend of mine, Charles Rowlands, was visited by a stranger named Harper who wanted five thousand pounds from him to keep quiet about some ludicrous charge involving a pageboy. He had in his possession some indecent photographs, including one of Rowlands' wife. Rowlands thought that this particular photograph might be made public and would ruin them both socially. You and I might feel that he was being unduly sensitive over this, but then you and I have made our own way in the world. He hadn't. He owed his position, everything, to his family's money and so anything that he felt could impugn family honour was of the utmost gravity to him. He heard nothing further for some time and so hoped the matter would die down – a foolish hope where the

Harpers of this world are involved.

'Then two other visitors arrived to see him. They said they were policemen and claimed to be acting on my orders – I was Chief Constable then. They told Rowlands that if he would go into virtual exile, the matter would be dropped. Again, you or I might not have accepted this so easily, but we do not share his trust in people.

'These two men, needless to say, were impostors. They were not policemen, and I would never have made such a ridiculous proposal to anyone. However, Rowlands did what he believed he had to do. To him it was the only honourable course to take. He left for France.

'In Paris, he cabled for five thousand pounds to be sent over to the local bank. On his way to collect the money he was run over – a genuine accident. Thereupon, Harper forged Rowlands' name and collected the cash. Harper was in Paris on your orders, Sir James.'

'You are totally mistaken. I have never heard of this man. You are out of your mind if you imagine I have.'

'Harper is one of the two men who accompanied you ashore, who you claim are officers aboard your yacht. While in your employ, he seemingly went into business on his own and pocketed five thousand pounds. A dangerous man to employ. You may want to look into that transaction, Sir James. After all, can you trust a man who would do such a thing?

'In view of all this, I believe you owe Rose Rowlands and her family something in return for what you caused to happen.'

'What happened was nothing to do with me. This man Harper acted on his own initiative.'

'Under your authority.'

'Prove it.'

'I will, if necessary. But I do not think it will be necessary. My proposition is this. Help Mrs Rowlands –

and help yourself. What do you say, Sir James?'

Mannering cleared his throat to dismiss and deny the whole affair. But then he looked again at the photograph of the plain headstone, marking the grave of a man who had moved so easily and confidently from one side to another, just as he himself had done, seemingly above all laws and regulations, travelling across Europe and Russia in a world at war.

And all the time these effete English had been watching Barnaby, as a man with a net patiently watches and waits to catch a rare butterfly flitting happily from one sweet-smelling flower to another, totally unaware of its fate. Too many people had talked too much. Barnaby, O'Brien, hoping for leniency; perhaps the Russian general Ormilov, even the Tsar's nephew, bargaining for a new passport and a new beginning in another country. The only thing that mattered to Mannering now was how he could escape the net.

Sir Bernard lit a cigar and regarded him coldly through a haze of pale blue smoke. 'Does the North London Loan and Mortgage Company mean anything to you?' he asked abruptly.

'Nothing whatever. Why should it? Do you imagine I need a loan?' Mannering allowed himself a thin smile at this grotesque idea.

'Through a number of holding companies you control this bunch of usurers who operate off the Finchley Road.'

'Nonsense.'

'I can prove it, Sir James. But I won't have to. You know it's true, I know it's true, so let us be done with this play-acting. This loan company holds a very heavy mortgage on the late Charles Rowlands' estate. Interest is twenty-five per cent every year on the original sum borrowed, payable in advance and unreducing. So, even if his successors only owed one pound at the end of the loan period, they would still be paying twenty-five per cent on thousands. I want you to redeem the mortgage. Immediately. And before you begin your futile protestations of ignorance and innocence once more, I repeat, I can substantiate all my allegations. The newspapers would have a field day. You would be ruined. Every time your name was mentioned in conversation or appeared in print, your background would be recalled, plus such apt descriptions as newspaper headline writers love – the Merchant of Death, the Salesman of War . . .'

There was a time to kill, a time to flee, a time to compromise, Mannering reflected. He decided on the third course.

'I may not be back in London for some time,' he began.

'There is an efficient telegraph system from Cannes, and an international telephone system,' Sir Bernard pointed out sharply. 'Redeem the mortgage from your yacht. The family lawyer who handles the Rowlands' affairs is one Peter Once-Hogg. Contact him.' He took out a sheet of notepaper on which he had written Once-Hogg's address.

'I will not forget this conversation,' said Mannering grimly.

'It is my earnest hope you will not,' agreed Sir Bernard. The two men sat in silence, while bubbles rose in the single glass of champagne.

'All right,' said Mannering at last, concealing the turmoil of his fear and rage behind a mask of indifference. 'I will do as you ask, not because of anything you could do to harm me, because I do not believe you could. You might bring your ridiculous charges, of course, but the jury could be bribed. And you only need one out of twelve to disagree. You might guess I would do that, and switch the case to another court.

Then I could bribe the judge. With enough money, Sir Bernard, you ride above every law, all law. You can buy anything and anyone. I shall co-operate because of my high regard for Rose Rowlands.

'You may laugh at that, but it is true, although I have never met her. I first saw her picture years ago in a society magazine announcing her engagement. She seemed to me to embody all the virtues of a beautiful young woman, far out of my reach, out of my class, if you like the English word. Later, I saw other photographs of her at parties, charity functions, that sort of thing. I looked into her past. She'd been an actress, without great success. I discovered that once, out of work and hungry, she posed nude for a fee of a pound or two.

'I bought all the photographs of her that I could find. I would telephone her home. When a woman answered, I would ask, is that Mrs Rowlands? But it was always a maid or a housekeeper. Then I would ring off without giving my name. I spoke to her once – I think. At least, I spoke to someone with the sort of voice I imagined she would have.'

'If you felt so warmly towards her, why did you cripple her husband, and cast a shadow over her life, with this mortgage? Why try to blackmail him and send him into exile? That was surely a strange way to show your regard?'

Mannering shrugged. 'Her husband was a snobbish fool. He didn't deserve her. I thought that when she discovered his weakness she would feel contempt for him.'

'And so favour you?'

Mannering did not reply.

'Why didn't you get introduced to her? It would have been very easy.'

'I did not wish to meet her. I had my reasons.'

And clearly he wasn't going to explain them, thought Sir Bernard, puzzled but content. He had achieved what he had set out to achieve.

Mannering stood up, gave him a curt nod and without a word turned and left the terrace.

Sir Bernard let himself into his room with his key, crossed to the bathroom, washed his face and hands thoroughly as though to scour away the memory of his interview with Mannering.

He heard faint taps on the bedroom door; three light ones, two heavy. He opened the door. His companion came inside, put a shorthand notebook down on the table.

'You get it all down?' Sir Bernard asked him.

'Every word, sir.'

'Good.' He had a record now that Mannering could not deny. If he went back on his word to help Rose, these shorthand notes would swiftly bring him back into line. 'Then you deserve a drink. Whisky?'

'Yes, sir.'

'Help yourself. There are bottles and glasses in that cupboard.'

The man poured himself a MacAllan, drank it neat. 'It was fortunate Sir James doesn't drink,' he said.

'Why?'

'When a subject has a few drams, his lips go slack. It's very difficult to lip-read accurately then, sir.'

'I suppose so. I never thought of that. But then we all have problems no one else might ever think of. Sir James in particular.'

'Very true, sir. Very true,' agreed the shorthand writer. 'But of course he is very rich.'

'Even the rich, sometimes especially the rich, find that money does not buy happiness.'

'So I've often been told, sir,' the shorthand writer

replied. 'All I'd like is the chance to prove it myself.'

'Wouldn't we all?' agreed Sir Bernard, and refilled the man's glass.

Chapter Sixteen

Every weekend, weather permitting, Carola flew some-where, either alone, or taking part in one of the amateur air races that had become fashionable. More and more people were finding they could afford to buy or rent an aircraft and were keen to learn to fly. Those who did not contemplate flying themselves gathered in their hun-dreds, sometimes thousands, to watch those who could. This was a new and fashionable activity. Magazines featured pictures of society figures at aerodromes as spectators or in flying gear.

Carola flew in contests to Brighton, to Birmingham and Bristol. Sometimes, she and other members of flying clubs were invited to fly to a charity fete or garden party. They would land in a field and perhaps present prizes to children for running in a sack race or an egg-and-spoon race. There was a continual demand for their services and involvement because nearly every day the newspapers printed a new story about women pilots, of whom there were now several. And all the time they were making or breaking records.

The Duchess of Bedford flew with a co-pilot from Croydon to Cape Town. Lady Bailey, wife of a South African industrialist, established a world record for flying at a high altitude. Lady Heath flew alone from South Africa to England, and took part in air races in the United States. Amy Johnson, daughter of a Hull businessman, and the

American Amelia Earhart were two more women pilots who looked set to break new records.

To the general public all pilots were romantic people; to fly was to conquer the last element. To see a woman fly, actually to talk to a woman who could climb into an aircraft and take off and loop the loop and race a hundred miles and return, and then enjoy a cup of tea as though nothing out of the ordinary had happened, was remarkable. If pilots were rare, a girl pilot was very much rarer.

Carola enjoyed this role. She had never felt special before. She knew that if she could follow Lady Warren's plans, she could make a whole new career for herself, however much the actual business of flying might terrify her. Oil and petrol and tyre companies might sponsor her to use their products. She could write about aspects of flying as well as flying herself; maybe she could teach others, run a flying school, anything. But everything depended on her, because up in the air, she was on her own. The moment the aeroplane left the runway, no one else could help her. And this knowledge caused her many sleepless nights. She would dream that suddenly the engine stopped, or the propeller broke up, as had happened to Jack Alcock during the war, and there was nothing she could do to help herself, nothing at all.

She would wake up, mouth dry, heart racing. It had only been a dream, she assured herself; it was all in the mind. But what if this happened when she was flying, if this recurring nightmare became reality?

Never once did she admit the full extent of the terror she felt when she was airborne on her own. She never felt fear when Tom Gardener was at the controls because then such potential problems were his to deal with. If the engine failed or a control wire snapped, if they flew into fog and lost their bearings somehow he would cope and find a safe way home. His experience would assure them of survival.

But on her own, Carola was always conscious that she was inexperienced. Flying alone in these tiny, often underpowered and temperamental planes, was something like Russian roulette. The more flights you undertook, the greater the chance that something would go wrong.

After a minor race in which Carola had competed against two young men flying similar aircraft and won, Lady Warren told Tom she wanted to see him urgently. He arrived to find her swinging in a hammock in her garden, smoking a cheroot as usual. A canvas chair had been placed beside the hammock. She motioned him to it.

'I think it's time you got Carola doing something more newsworthy, more important, than these little trips and flights she makes every weekend,' she said without any greeting, any preamble. 'She's not progressing. She's had a few mentions in local papers, but nothing in the nationals. She should be a household word by now, a woman synonymous with flying. If you don't move soon you'll be too late.'

'I accept there is need for speed, Lady Warren, but we must make sure she is able to do whatever she sets out to do, and on each of these flights she is gaining experience, and clocking up useful flying time.'

'Maybe. But surely she has enough experience now to try the Atlantic. There's this girl in America, Amelia Earhart, whose father has bought her a sports biplane. She's been practising spins and stalls and flying through fog blindly, making forced landings, with the obvious aim of attempting record-breaking flights. I read the other day that she climbed to an altitude of more than fourteen thousand feet – top height for a woman pilot. Now she plans to fly the Atlantic, on her own. Amy Johnson is talking of flying to India and on to Australia soon. And what is Carola doing? Nothing worth a toss.'

Tom sat for a moment, thinking of a reply. She was right, of course. The time to act was now if Carola was not to be left behind; soon almost every pioneering flight would have been made. And those remaining became infinitely more difficult and dangerous because they were so much longer.

'Well?' said Lady Warren irritably. 'Don't just sit there. What have you got in mind?'

'Have you anything in mind, Lady Warren?' Tom asked diplomatically.

'I'm not in the business of having such things in mind, young man. You have the training of this pupil. That is your province, your job. I pay all the bills, and have done for years. But I want results, and soon. What we need is something spectacular that will instantly get Carola into headlines all over the world. And we must have it very, very soon. Or else we forget the whole thing.

'The public are very fickle. Look at the actors and actresses, novelists, dramatists, singers who enjoy tremendous prestige and immense publicity – for a time. Then suddenly, almost overnight, it often seems, they drop out of the limelight. You never hear about them or read about them again until they become the subject of articles with such headlines as, "Where Are They Now?". And where the hell *are* they now? Out of fashion, out of work, out of funds.

'The newsreels need new stunts to film. We've had people squat on the tops of poles on the roofs of skyscrapers in New York. Men walking tightropes over Niagara Falls. Planes flying upside down, while a girl walks out on the wings.

'People are becoming more and more blasé all the time through seeing and reading about these things. Then one day all this record-breaking will go out of fashion. Bam, just like that. Land speed records, water speed records, air speed records – they will continue to be broken by a mile or two an hour at a cost of thousands of pounds. The return for record breaking is rapidly diminishing because people are losing interest. It's all been done before, they say. They want something new. So what have *you* in mind to bring our candidate into the public eye before we're beaten by someone else?'

Tom nodded, as though pondering the problem.

'Could I have a drink?' he asked unexpectedly.

'Bit early in the day, isn't it?'

'Depends when you start the day,' he replied.

Lady Warren pressed a bell-push on the end of a long flex that led into the house, and a maid appeared. 'Mr Gardener would like a drink,' Lady Warren told her.

The maid withdrew and reappeared carrying a tray of bottles and a single glass.

Tom poured himself a large whisky, added a little soda, drank slowly. He had an idea in his head, but he wanted to give Lady Warren the impression he was considering what she had said. She was a clever woman but, like all women he had met, clever or otherwise, pretty or plain, she was vain. He believed that if she thought he had decided on any proposition before he arrived, she was likely to demolish it. If, however, he could persuade her that she had planted the idea in his head, then she would treat it more kindly.

'Well?' she said testily. 'You've had your drink. Now let's have some ideas.'

'There is something she could do that would bring her immense publicity and should cost very little as long as we handle it right.'

'Yes?'

'The airship – R.101. It's due to take off in the autumn, September or October, for India. A handful of government personages are travelling on it – I believe the Secretary of State for Air, Lord Thomson, is going, and Sir Sefton Brancker, the Director of Civil Aviation.'

'He's a good man, Brancker,' said Lady Warren approvingly. 'Excellent fellow, in fact. I hear he's been trying to get a place for Amy Johnson aboard that airship, too. So he's got a good eye for publicity. But apparently the government won't agree.'

'I heard the same,' said Tom, who hadn't. 'I propose we smuggle Carola aboard and she makes the flight. When they reach Karachi in India, she admits who she is and what she has done. Her story will be published in every newspaper in the world. More so because in Karachi she can hire an aircraft and fly back here on her own. So she goes out in a lighter-than-air machine and comes back in a heavier-than-air machine.'

'Sounds ingenious,' admitted Lady Warren grudgingly. 'Can the R.101 fly that far?'

'It should do. The airship R.34 has flown successfully to the United States and back again. That's much more dangerous, because it's over water all the way. Flying east, you're mostly over land.'

'How will she stay undiscovered during a voyage that may take two weeks?'

'Because the airship weighs much more than the designers originally intended, they're cutting down on the number of passengers. They'll be taking only ten or twelve, in place of the hundred the vessel's intended to carry. Carola can use an empty cabin. I'll fix it with a steward that he brings her meals.'

'She's almost bound to be discovered, and then there'll be hell to pay.'

'When the R.34 flew to the United States from England just after the war she carried a stowaway, and that fact brought ten times the publicity the trip would otherwise have attracted. But even if she is discovered, so what? They can't drop her over the side in an open boat, can they? At worst she'll be discovered on the first lap of the flight from here to Egypt, in which case she'll be

394

aboard until they reach Ismailia, which is halfway. Then maybe she could go on as a legitimate passenger. If she's found out on the second leg of the journey, she stays in the airship until Karachi.'

'It's possible, I suppose,' said Lady Warren doubtfully. 'How do you propose to get her aboard in the first place?'

'The R.101 is kept in its huge hangar at Cardington or moored to a mast outside, two hundred feet high. There's a lift inside this mast to take up stores and crew, and there's also a circular staircase. Now, on the day of the flight there's bound to be strict security. Newspaper reporters and all kinds of people will want to get up there, and they'll be prevented. But if we dress Carola in uniform, as one of the people working for the catering supplier, it's different. She'll have gone up and down a number of times before. Whoever's on duty in the tower will recognise her, and let her through.'

'You think so?'

'Let's try it.'

'Right. You have my permission. Start right away. But keep my name out of it. And don't breathe a word to Carola until you have all the problems sorted out.'

After Tom had left, Lady Warren lit another cheroot – she still had five to smoke before she reached the total she allowed herself every day – and walked up and down the lawn, pondering on the discussion.

He was a clever fellow, Tom Gardener – for a man, that was. Quite attractive and pleasant, too, when he wanted to be. He didn't take too much on himself, he didn't presume to know more than she did.

Anyway, his idea was quite clever. It also had the merit of gaining an enormous amount of publicity for Carola at very little cost. But no idea was so good that it could not be improved. He had suggested Carola could hire an aircraft in Karachi and fly back. This might prove impossible. There might not be any planes for hire, or if she found one, it might only be suitable for short journeys, not a long trip from India to England against the wind. She'd improve on that right away. This was one of the benefits her money brought; she believed she could improve on anything.

Lady Warren returned to her hammock, pressed the bell-push, twice this time, thus summoning her secretary. The woman came out, notepad open, a pencil held to the page by a rubber band.

'Take a letter,' said Lady Warren brusquely. 'Send it to the Managing Directors of Vickers at Brooklands, De Havillands out at Hatfield, and half a dozen other aircraft manufacturers. You'll find their addresses in the file.

'I want their best and quickest firm quotation for their sturdiest aircraft, two-seater, with the second cockpit modified to carry an extra petrol tank for a very long flight. This aircraft should be capable of flying from India to England. They are to explain how it can be dismantled to go on board ship in a crate for the outward journey. Would mechanics need to travel with it to assemble it in Karachi? If so, please also quote for their time and passages. The whole matter to be treated with the utmost secrecy. If any word of this gets out to the newspapers or aeronautical press, the contract will be cancelled, no matter what stage it has reached. But stress the importance in publicity to the company chosen after the event. Answers within a week, to me.

'Send that by registered post, and mark each letter "For Managing Director's eyes only". That is all.'

Lady Warren puffed contentedly at her cheroot as the woman walked back to the house. Yes, Gardener was a clever man. But she was his match. No question of that. He had proposed. But, like God, she had disposed.

Richard sat by his mother's bedside, watching her pale,

waxy face. She lay, eyes closed, scarcely breathing. He put out a hand and gripped hers firmly. It felt thin, frail, almost like the hand of a child. He wished they had held hands many times before this, when he was young, when she was healthy.

The doctor had telephoned him on the previous evening.

'I'm the junior partner here, Mr Rowlands,' he explained. 'I don't think we've met. Your mother is one of my patients and you are the only relative for whom I can find a telephone number.' He paused.

'What's the matter?' Richard asked. 'Is she ill?'

'I'm sorry to say, yes. She's been in failing health for some time, as you probably know, but suddenly she's taken a turn for the worse.'

'Last time I saw her she seemed a bit vague about names and people, but I thought that was just because she's getting on a bit.'

'It may be a symptom of something more serious, Mr Rowlands.'

'Who's looking after her?' Richard asked, feeling guilty that he seemed to have grown so far apart from his mother that a third party had to tell him she was ill.

'There's an old woman in the village who used to work in your house when you had a number of staff. She comes in every day. A Mrs Jones.'

'Oh, yes,' said Richard. He vaguely remembered the name, but could not put a face to the person concerned.

'Is my brother Tobin there?'

'No. He's abroad, I believe.'

'Is there anything my mother wants?'

'I don't think so. She's unconscious a lot of the time. But when she's awake, I know she'd like to see you. She'll recognise you.'

'It's as bad as that, then?'

'I think you'd better come and judge for yourself, Mr

397

Rowlands. It might be a good idea if you could plan to stay for a while.'

So Richard packed a suitcase and drove over. He had arrived the night before and now sat in the once familiar room, looking at the shabby wallpaper, the faded paint on the woodwork. The curtains looked threadbare, seeming somehow symbolic of his mother's appearance. They had been thick curtains when he was a boy, heavily lined.

His mother had always seemed healthy, if remote. Now, as he looked at her face, he sensed she had not long to live. He was sorry for all the years that had passed when he had not visited her. And for all the years before then, when he was a boy, when it seemed that they were little better than friendly strangers, sharing a house, a name, but nothing else.

He heard shuffling footsteps on the stairs; heavy, laboured breathing. An old woman came in carrying a tray with a pot of tea and two cups, a jug of milk, a bowl of sugar. She put the tray down on a side table.

'I'm Mrs Jones and you'll be Master Richard,' she said.

'A long time since I was Master,' Richard replied, standing up.

They shook hands. He remembered her now, but her face, like his mother's, seemed faded, only just recognisable, like a photograph slightly out of focus.

Mrs Jones glanced around the room, wrinkling her nose in distaste. 'Things wouldn't have got into this state in the old days,' she declared. 'Dust, things dropping apart. It wouldn't have been allowed then.'

'Where is my brother, Tobin?' Richard asked.

'The south of France, your mother said. She hasn't an address for him. I sent your sister a telegram on your mother's instructions, but even if she left Winnipeg the moment she received it, it'll be days before she can get here. Would you like a cup of tea?'

'Very much,' he said. 'Please join me.'

She poured two cups. 'I won't wake your mother. It's best for her to sleep when she can.'

They sipped their tea, then both paused at the same moment. They had heard the crunch of tyres on the gravel outside, the click of a car door. Richard put down his cup and saucer, walked to the window. A Rolls cabriolet stood outside the front porch. A liveried chauffeur sat at the wheel; a footman had jumped down to open the car door for a tall man with a grey beard. He stood now looking up at the house.

Richard recognised him. Sir James Mannering, the principal shareholder, as Mr Cartwright at Beechwood Gears used to describe him.

'I'll go down,' said Richard.

He ran down the stairs, opened the front door.

'My name is Mannering,' Sir James began.

'I know,' said Richard. 'I met you at Beechwood Gears during the war.'

'So you did. The clever young man who solved a problem no one else could solve. What are you doing now?'

'I'm with Zimbro Cars.'

'I hear they've got financial troubles.'

'Lots of firms have, now the boom is over,' Richard replied. 'What can I do for you here?'

'I wanted to see Mrs Rowlands. Mrs Rose Rowlands.'

'My mother?'

'Yes, of course. Your mother.'

'She's not very well,' said Richard hesitantly.

'Nothing serious, I trust?' His voice sounded tense.

'She's asleep just now. I don't want to waken her. She's very weak.'

Mannering glanced back towards the car. The two liveried servants were sitting bolt upright in their seats, looking straight ahead. They might have been statues, but they still had ears.

Richard said, 'You'd better come in.' He took Mannering into the morning room. They sat down.

'It's rather a strange visit,' Mannering said, feeling some explanation for his arrival was needed. 'I've never actually met your mother, you see. But in a sense I feel I know her well. I followed her when she was on the stage. I've always read with interest of her charity activities and so on. I had no idea she was unwell.'

'Since the death of my father, she's lived very quietly. Why do you especially wish to see her now?'

Mannering paused, wondering what excuse Richard would be most likely to accept – and find acceptable.

'I had a most odd feeling that she might be in some kind of trouble,' he said at last. 'I don't know what, but something. Today I found I was driving virtually past your front gate, so on the impulse I told my man to make a short detour so that I could call and introduce myself to her. I thought that if she was in any kind of difficulty, there might be some way I could help her.'

'But you don't know her. You never even met her, you tell me.'

'People can meet in the spirit,' Mannering replied enigmatically. 'I have admired her from afar for many years.'

'Have you ever had any dealings with my mother?'

'Not directly, no. But since you are a son of the house, I can admit to an indirect dealing with her some time ago.'

'In what way?'

'Quite by chance I heard from a mutual acquaintance that she was concerned about a large mortgage that had been entered into by your father who, although a man of great charm, was not perhaps so

400

astute a man of business. I was able to arrange for that mortgage to be cancelled at once.'

'*You* did that? I understood from my mother that this was her solicitor's doing. She said he'd looked into the terms of the mortgage and had discovered that the mortgage company had miscalculated, as he put it, and not only was the mortgage paid up, there was a large sum owing to her.'

'That was my doing,' Mannering replied stiffly. 'I am not accustomed to spreading falsehoods.'

As he spoke, recollections of other lies he had told so easily and so often rose unbidden to his mind – years of betrayals, broken promises, pledges unredeemed. Men had taken their lives because he had not kept his word. Others, who had trusted him as an English gentleman, a knight of honour, had been ruined financially.

'Then perhaps you had better come up and see her,' said Richard. 'As I told you, she's sleeping, but when she wakes, no doubt she would like to meet you.'

Mannering followed Richard up the stairs, into her room.

'She has opened her eyes once,' Mrs Jones told Richard, trying not to stare at the stranger he'd brought into the room. Who on earth was he? 'She's not sleeping heavily. Just dozing.'

Mannering stood, looking down at Rose Rowlands. Richard, watching him closely, was surprised to see his hard face soften. A look of pity and tenderness came into his eyes for a moment. And then his mood suddenly changed. His faced returned to its set and saturnine appearance. But emotion had been there, if only briefly.

'Have you ever spoken to her?' Richard asked him.

'Spoken to her?' Mannering repeated the question slowly, as though he had difficulty in understanding it. 'No, I had no cause to,' he said at last.

'Why don't you speak to her now. She may hear you.'

Mannering cleared his throat, as though he was about to make a declaration, but when he spoke, his voice was hushed, barely above a whisper.

'Mrs Rowlands,' he said, 'you don't know who I am. I could have come to see you before, but somehow I never did. I preferred to admire you from afar. To me you have always personified everything I admire about English women. You always looked poised in every photograph I saw of you. When you were quoted in a newspaper, what you said always made sense, and was always in perfect taste. And you were never a seeker after the limelight. But now, late in our lives maybe, we are at last face to face.'

As he spoke, Rose opened her eyes, shook her head slightly. She looked at Richard first, smiled, and then at Mrs Jones, and finally at Mannering.

'Who are you?' she asked him weakly. 'The new doctor?'

'No. Just a friend,' he replied.

'Of my son here?'

'Yes. Of your son. And, I hope, of you.'

'But I don't know you. I've never seen you before.'

Her voice was as Mannering had always assumed it would be: soft, gentle.

'I was passing, so I thought I would call in. Mannering is my name. James Mannering. I have been a fan of yours for a long time. I saw you first of all in Jim Bangle's *Scandals* in Birmingham, then in Manchester at the old Hippodrome.'

'Goodness me,' said Rose, smiling at the recollection. 'You were there in the audience, then? That was *years* ago. Before I married. Long before.'

'Yes. I have photographs of you in both those shows.'

'So have I, somewhere,' she said. 'I thought I was going to be a star one day. But old Bangle ran off with the takings. I had a hard time for a while. Then I got married. And now I'm here. I never imagined then what my life would be like, that it would end like this.'

'It's not ended yet, Mother,' Richard declared stoutly.

She smiled, shook her head feebly. 'It's the last act,' she said. 'I know when the curtain's coming down. In the profession, we always do.'

She closed her eyes. Richard put out his hand, felt her pulse again. It was much feebler. He nodded to Mrs Jones. She followed him out of the room.

'Please call the doctor,' he told her. 'I don't think it's going to be long now.'

Mannering joined them. 'I don't wish to intrude,' he said. 'I had better go.'

'If you think so,' Richard agreed. His explanation as to why he had come in the first place seemed somehow unreal, unlikely. 'I'll show you out.'

'If there is any news, either way, please let me know. I usually carry a card but I don't seem to have any on me today.'

'Come into the study. I'll find some paper for you to write on.'

The study table was covered with Richard's drawings and sketches of engines, gears, blowers, some in black and white, others in colour wash and oils.

'Who did those?' asked Mannering, looking at them closely.

'I did.'

Mannering picked up the nearest, in oils. It showed a fly-wheel with two connecting rods and pistons for a horizontally imposed two-cylinder engine.

'Is that your design, too?'

'Yes.'

'I like these very much. I might almost be looking at the metal castings. You have a remarkable ability to bring this machinery to life. Have you had art training?'

'A bit in the vacations at Oxford. And draughtsmen

here and there have kindly given me hints and tips. That's about it.'

'Remarkable.'

Mannering took out a gold fountain pen, scribbled a telephone number on a piece of paper.

'A direct line,' he explained. 'It's unlisted. I haven't put my name to it, because I do not wish people to telephone me. Except you, of course.'

They walked to the door.

'Those paintings and sketches,' said Mannering casually. 'Do you sell them?'

'No. When I take down an engine I find it's easier if I draw it in pieces. It helps me when I come to put it back together again. I've made hundreds of drawings and paintings, just for my own use.'

'I ask because I own an art gallery in London and another in New York,' said Mannering slowly.

They were standing by his Rolls. Sunshine glittered on the car's rich maroon paint, its silver plate. Even the tyres were polished black.

'I know. I've seen articles about them. You specialise in paintings from Russia – portraits of the Tsar and his relations.'

'Yes. That is how I started, but I'm always looking for more modern paintings that express the idiom of today, that capture the spirit of our age and its endless quest for speed. The spirit and the speed. You do this magnificently. May I tell my London gallery manager to arrange a time to come and see your drawings and paintings?'

'By all means,' Richard replied.

'Perhaps we could arrange an exhibition?' Just for a moment, Mannering's voice grew hard as he pondered the topic closest to his heart. 'Mind you, if we did arrange one, the gallery would have to take its percentage of sales. It would all be on a commercial basis, of course.'

'Of course,' Richard agreed. The matter did not seem

important to him, not with his mother dying in an upper room. He watched Mannering depart, and then stood in the porch waiting for the doctor to arrive.

Mannering sat back against the buttoned Bedford cord upholstery of his car, trying to analyse his feelings.

He had seen Rose Rowlands, had actually spoken to her, after all these years of trying to guess her character, attempting to picture her likes and dislikes from old photographs. He had known she was ill – he had always made it his business to know all there was to know about her – and had finally resolved to see her – before it was too late.

He had always assumed – possibly imagined would be a more accurate word – that he was in love with her. Certainly, he had spent a large part of his waking life fantasising about her, and now that he had stepped out of his dream into reality, what did he find? Simply an old woman dying in a shabby room.

He thought he would have felt devastated at the prospect of her early death, but instead he felt nothing at all, neither sadness nor regret. Meeting her, even so briefly, had exorcised all the tortured thoughts and dreams he had harboured about her so needlessly and for so long. He felt he was in the same situation as a man who for long has suffered an aching tooth and sucked at it, drawing some perverted satisfaction from the constant, nagging pain. Then he has the tooth extracted and for the first time in years is free of the hurt.

He could have released himself from his mental bondage long since, but somehow he had not chosen to do so. Now at last he was free of all desire, all regret. For the first time, he appreciated what one of the specialists had told him years earlier, that many men were relieved to be free of the demons of lust or desire.

He had been generous to Rose, he thought; he had

lifted that mortgage and also given her a lump sum, just to cover himself should Sir Bernard Warner have second thoughts about his situation. He could afford it, and viewed strictly as a monetary loss, it could be set against profits made by another of his companies. Rose's son Tobin, whose background and character he had already closely investigated, might well be persuaded to remortgage the estate with him when he inherited it. How strange and ironic that he could so calmly contemplate this, which would involve the death of a woman he had worshipped at one remove for so long.

His mind began to consider how best to entangle Tobin, and how to make sure that Richard spent more time drawing and painting. That young man possessed a rare and prodigious talent – and seemingly no idea of its value. Sir James had, and as the car sped on, he lit a cigar and decided exactly what he would do.

Chapter Seventeen

As Richard drove his little two-seater north out of London towards the Bedfordshire airfield where he had an appointment at noon, he thought back, without any pleasure, on the unsatisfactory sequence of events that had resulted in this journey to meet people who had never heard of him.

For his first years at the Zimbro car works, Richard had spent time in different sections of the factory. He had worked with the designers in the drawing office; then on the shop floor, and in the engine foundry; then with the body builders, the spray painters and, finally, with the bookkeepers, finding out what each car cost to build. Here he learned how much the factory paid for basic components they bought in, such as chassis frames and wheels and brakes, the discounts given for cash or for a maximum of thirty days' credit.

The cars themselves he found unexciting. They were saloons with four- or six-cylinder side valve engines, smaller copies of existing American or continental designs, with a few unimportant additions to avoid charges of infringing patents. There was almost no original thinking. Models overlapped, in competition with each other. Zimbro did not have a clear-cut strategy regarding sales – or even any strategy at all. It was difficult to assess how much profit the company made on each car. On some, he was certain they made a loss,

407

relying for a token profit on selling extras, such as spotlights, or loud horns, or luggage carriers to take a trunk on the back of the car. No research was being done on improving the suspension, the steering or engines. All these were bought from suppliers who produced identical items for many car manufacturers.

If a competitor introduced something that appealed to the public – two-colour paint finishes, opening sun roofs – then Zimbro would simply copy the innovation. Sometimes the makers of a particular size of engine went out of business, and then Zimbro had to cast around to find a substitute, almost any substitute, quickly.

As Richard looked deeper into this state of affairs, he found that other car makers were conducting their business in much the same way. The war had provided a boost for their products, good or bad. For a time, almost any car would sell. Motoring was a novelty, so who needed to spend money on research when the public queued up to buy what they already had to sell? The boom conditions did not last, but every suggestion Richard made for innovations or improvements to boost sales was turned down by the Zimbro board on the grounds of cost. Then Zimbro bought a job lot of engines from a bankrupt manufacturer who had lost his money on the design, which was ahead of its time, with an overhead camshaft instead of side valves. This had many advantages – fewer working parts, lighter weight, more scientifically designed cylinder heads. The engines were kept in store; there was no need to use them while stocks of other old-fashioned types remained.

Richard calculated that if Zimbro made use of these engines in a new and modern-looking sports car, the company would make a handsome profit. Then they could go on to greater production runs. But first he had to design a supercharger that would increase the power beyond anything comparable on the market. The one he had tested at Brooklands when he met Carola in the Bluebird Café had exploded after the car had covered only two laps at high speed. The test driver had shrugged his shoulders as he climbed out.

'We just haven't got metal that will stand up to these pressures,' he declared. 'That's why supercharging has never caught on here. The blower adds power but it's unreliable and it also takes power from the engine to drive it. So you win and you lose. And the most serious loss is reliability. No one will buy an unreliable car.'

So Richard had redesigned the blower. Instead of blowing the air and petrol mixture into the engine at a pressure of ten pounds to the square inch, he reduced the pressure by half. The car now ran perfectly. He had a new prototype built, which he called the Blower Zimbro. He showed it to the directors, and attended a board meeting to answer any questions they might have.

The boardroom was panelled in rosewood and hung with portraits of past directors who looked down from huge gilded frames. As soon as Richard met the directors, all men in their fifties and sixties wearing black, high-buttoned suits and wing collars to allow their Adam's apples freedom to move up and down like captured marbles, he realised they would be totally against all change.

The chairman, a retired colonel called Blenkinson, welcomed Richard to the meeting and then asked the company secretary for his comments.

He was a thin accountant, with a face the colour of old parchment. He pursed bloodless lips and nodded grimly. 'We've costed this out very carefully, Colonel Blenkinson. Because it is supercharged, owners will have to pay an increased insurance premium on each car. This may be as much as five or even ten pounds a year according to their age and whether they live in a town or the country. And people don't want more expensive motoring. They want cheaper cars, cheaper to run.

'Then there is the extra discount we have to build into each car for the dealers. They will almost certainly have complaints from owners who are not used to the complicated mechanisms. Things will go wrong – they always do with new designs – while the cars are still under guarantee. Claims will be made. The dealers, and in turn ourselves, will have to pick up the bill for that. A few of these Blowers, as Mr Rowlands calls them, may explode, like the first one at Brooklands. And then we could lose the profit on ten or twenty other cars.'

He turned his pale eyes towards Richard.

'You appreciate that, Rowlands?'

'Entirely, sir,' Richard replied. 'But that was the first version, working at high pressure. I have modified it thoroughly and now it's working at only half that stress. There should be no claims at all under the guarantee because of the blower, but an immensely improved performance.'

'We've been in the car business a long time, Rowlands,' said Blenkinson, 'and it's our experience that *every* added complication in the end costs money – our money, our shareholders' money. There is more to go wrong, and usually it goes wrong in the warranty period – or people claim it does, which is much the same thing as far as we're concerned. We have to make a profit. I'm sorry to harp on this, but without a profit we're dead. We are now enjoying good sales, and I do not wish to prejudice our reputation for reliability. It could have the most serious repercussions on sales of our other models.'

Richard kept a tight rein on his irritation. 'I still say, sir, that we should produce a small number of these sports cars, and put some money towards subsidising good, fast, professional drivers. We might then pick up a number of first-class wins and awards in races, which would be very useful publicity. The car will get talked about in the motoring press and, more important, among enthusiastic motorists.'

'There are only a very limited number of motorists who would like, or who can afford, a two-seater car with a supercharger,' said a third director. 'Most of our buyers are family men with two or three children. They've in-laws, fathers and mothers, grandparents. They like to visit them at weekends, take them out for a spin to the coast. They can't possibly do that in a two-seater.'

'These cars, sir, are intended for young, single people with some money, a good job, or young marrieds without children. Or maybe even as a second car in a two-car household. They are not meant to displace our saloon models, but to add to them.'

'Most motorists can barely afford one car, Rowlands, and only a handful of the very rich and foolish want sports cars. Aiming at them would not keep us afloat.'

'It's not my aim that it should, sir. My aim is that it should bring the name Zimbro before a wider public.'

'Point taken. But, with the greatest respect, that is a public in whom we have really no interest.'

'It's a very vocal public, sir. If we could keep the name Zimbro in the newspapers, on the newsreels, show it winning races, people would talk about it. Look at the MG. The Midget is only basically a Morris Minor, a tiny little car with a wooden body of the type and cost I propose, and a fabric universal joint. The sort of thing you might find in a motorised pram. But it still wins race after race after race. People talk about the MG as the Magic Midget. They could talk about the Zimbro in just the same way.'

'Well, Morris makes these sports cars very well, I know, but they're only a sideline for him.'

'It would just be a sideline for us, too, gentlemen. But it would get the name known.'

'We feel the name is already known among people who

matter,' said the chairman. 'So, for the moment, gentle-men, I would suggest we put this project to one side until, perhaps, people have more money to spend. Our young friend may think they have a lot of money to pay out on a car now, but the fact is, every year cars become harder to sell.'

So the Blower Zimbro was shelved. After the meeting, one of the directors, who had not spoken, came to see Richard. He was a kindly man with a son about Rich-ard's age; he did not want to kill the young fellow's enthusiasm.

'I liked your idea of using these engines we've got lying about,' he said. 'Waste not, want not, eh? But have you seen those big eight-cylinder jobs we bought from the States when some of the board thought we should go into truck manufacture?'

'No. I've never even heard of them.'

'Not surprising. It was generally thought to be a mistake and a waste of money, and no one in business ever cares to admit being associated with a failure. Mind you, we bought them cheaply from our parent company in Detroit so it's only a book entry. We've not actually put out money on them. But I've an idea how we could use them and, as you so rightly said at the board meeting, get a lot of good publicity for Zimbro at the same time. I might add, for your ears only, that this could only do you personally a great deal of good with my fellow directors.'

'What have you in mind, sir?' asked Richard.

'I don't know if you follow the press, Rowlands, but there's a lot of talk about heavier-than-air machines and lighter-than-air machines. An aeroplane is heavier than air. It is kept aloft by its wings and its propeller drawing it through the air. An airship is kept afloat by a huge amount of lighter-than-air gas.'

'I have read about that, yes, sir.'

'I've several good friends working on the two airships

now being built in this country. Up in Howden in Yorkshire, a private enterprise firm, the Airship Guarantee Company, is building one that will be called the R.100. The R stands for rigid, as opposed to the soft inflatable gas bags used during the war.

'Meanwhile, the government is financing a rival, the R.101. This is being built in a special hangar in Cardington in Bedfordshire, with a good deal of state interference, as you can imagine in any government-sponsored project.

'I don't know what engines they're going to use on the R.101, but I think you might possibly be able to interest them in our truck engines. Their great selling point is that they are made of aluminium, not cast iron. They have steel liners in the cylinders but, apart from that, they are very much lighter than anything else on the market. And lightness is something you need a lot of in a lighter-than-air machine.

'I suggest you go up to Cardington – I'll give you an introduction to one of the designers, Paul Baxter – and you try to sell our engines there. It's a long shot, but in my view one well worth taking. My friend has told me confidentially that they are already getting worried about the weight of everything. These lighter engines could save them several tons weight at a stroke.'

So now Richard found himself in his little car, trundling north towards Cardington. He came up Brockley Hill, then into Elstree, stopped at the crossroads in the village to let a lorry pass in front of him. Standing by a bus stop he saw a familiar figure: Carola. He waved to her.

'Want a lift?'

'Depends where you're going.'

'Nearly to Bedford.'

'I'm not going that far,' she said.

'Well, I can drop you off on the way.'

She climbed into the little car.

'I've been waiting ten minutes for the bus,' she said. 'It's great to get a lift. As a matter of fact, I have the day off.'

'You mean your female dragon has actually let you free for the whole day?'

'Oh, she's not bad really. She's just a determined person. I can't help but admire her. What takes you up to Bedford?'

'Well, it's not to Bedford, actually. It's to a place near it, called Cardington, where they're building the airship, R.101.'

'Are you going to work on that or something? Or just having a look round?'

'Neither. I'm acting as a salesman. Not my forte, I must say. But my job with Zimbro isn't going too well for me at the moment.'

'Why not?'

'What your Lady Warren would call a British reason. No one wants change. Whatever has been, must be and will always be. I've been trying ever since I joined to persuade them to improve their image. Make a reasonably exciting little sports car, which could win races and get the Zimbro name known. It would cost them almost nothing, because lying in a shed they've lots of engines far better than anything they're using. But the board won't wear it. They say a sports car will only seat two people; and they want to build saloons to seat four or five. So many reasons for not doing anything.'

'There always are,' she said. 'Everyone here has their own reason for not doing something. That's why I think I'd like to go to Australia, a new country, where there must be reasons *for* doing things, for taking risks, having a go.'

'Why Australia? What happened to that Australian chap, Tom Gardener, by the way?'

'He's around,' she said casually.

'I thought he went home.'

'He decided to stay.'

'He's not the person who taught you to fly by any chance, is he?'

She nodded, blushing.

'Presumably Lady Warren knows?'

'She introduced us. Said he was a wonderful man.'

'Amazing. He must have something I lack.'

'It's what he calls bull,' said Carola drily. 'Anyhow, let me off here in St Albans. I've some shopping to do.'

'Why not come on and see the airship, then do your shopping? I can drop you off on the way back.'

'But on what basis could I see this airship?'

'Well, you are a pilot. You can be my assistant for the day.'

'You think so?'

'I'm saying so.'

'All right. I'm game.'

They drove on together, both glad he had made the offer and she had accepted.

When they were still half a mile from Cardington, they saw the huge mooring mast, nearly two hundred feet tall, designed on the lines of the Eiffel Tower. It soared up into the sky from a wide flat field. Then the hangar came into view. This was more than three hundred yards long, proudly described in newspapers as the largest building in the world and specially built to house the airship.

Richard drove past the sign 'Royal Airship Works', stopped outside the administrative end of the building. He and Carola went into an office. A cheerful man in his forties greeted them.

'You are Mr Rowlands from Zimbro? Glad to meet you. My name's Paul. Paul Baxter. My friend said you'd be coming along. And this is . . .?'

'My assistant, Carola Marsh. She is an air pilot. I

thought it would be useful to have her here.'

'Of course. We don't often see a lady pilot. Lighter than air?' he asked Carola.

'No. Heavier than air,' she corrected him.

'Well, maybe you'll fly our ships, too, one day. Pleased to have you here.' He turned to Richard. 'I'm told you're an engine man. And that Zimbro might have some engines we could use. Well, I doubt that, good as yours may be, because ours are already in place. But come and see for yourself and give me your views.

'I must tell you that we have already examined Rolls-Royce aero engines, and although their Condor is excellent, it runs on petrol – probably like yours. We've gone for diesel, because of the highly inflammable nature of hydrogen gas which fills the gas bags that keep the airship in the air.'

'How do you start your diesel engines?'

'A small petrol engine, linked to each one, starts them up. As soon as the diesels are firing, we stop the petrol engines.'

'Even so, there must be a fire risk from that?'

'Well, true. But there's a risk in crossing the road. And we can't think of any other way of starting the diesels. They're big motors, you know. Eight cylinders each one. A man couldn't possibly crank them, and I've not seen a lightweight electric motor powerful enough to start them. Anyhow, come with me and I'll show you both round.'

They walked along the side of the vast hangar and came to a door in the centre. Baxter opened it with a key.

'After you,' he said.

Carola and Richard went in – and were immediately faced with a solid silver wall that stretched as far as they could see in either direction and up to the roof.

'What the devil's that?' asked Richard in surprise. 'Where's the airship?'

416

'This *is* the airship,' replied Baxter drily. 'It completely fills the biggest building in the world, because it is the biggest airship in the world. I always like to bring strangers in face to face with it. That's the only way they can get a true impression of its size. As you can see, it has a clearance of only a few feet on each side and at the top. Now, follow me.'

He led the way between the wall of the shed and the silvered canvas of the airship. This was so high that men working even halfway up had to use firemen's ladders.

'How do you get her out of the shed?'

'With great difficulty. And never if there's so much as a gentle breeze. So, first of all, we have to choose the right day. We've only been out for trials when it's sunny and there's no wind. We then send lorries round all the military stations in the area to try to get hold of three hundred men. If we can't get them all, we take unemployed from the labour exchange and labourers off the farms, and bring them here. Each man is given the end of a rope which is fixed to some part of the airship, and they walk her out.

'Once they're outside they've got to hang on until a steel rope is dropped from the top of the mooring tower and picked up by another rope on the airship's nose. Then a man on top of the tower winches the ship in and she's moored like a liner in the sky, about two hundred feet up.'

'If a wind comes up, can that tower cope with something nearly two hundred and fifty yards long and only held by a steel rope?'

'So far, it has. Mind you, we've also got hawsers attached to concrete blocks embedded in the perimeter seven hundred and fifty feet away from the tower. They help to hold the airship firm.'

'I see. But if you're flying on a commercial basis you'll

have to take her out when it's wet and windy, and even fly in bad weather, surely?'

'We'll come to that when we come to that,' Baxter replied carefully. 'Right now, I can tell you, we've enough problems simply flying in fine weather. She's quite a handful to control, as you can imagine.'

The airship hung like a gigantic silver fish in a cave closely tailored for it, neither floating freely nor resting on the ground but secured by ropes. The air inside the hangar was sickly sweet with the smell of dope, the cellulose with which the canvas cover had been painted. The airship, Baxter told them, contained two miles of longitudinal steel girders with six miles of smaller girders and eight miles of side and base struts to hold them apart – a total of eighteen thousand struts in all. The bracing cables that pulled in the huge sides, like corsets, were eleven miles long. Another twelve miles of webs strengthened the girders. The hull contained twenty-seven miles of tubing. Nearly half a million rivets helped to hold everything together.

'So that you can appreciate the job our – or your – engines will have to do,' Baxter said, 'we use seventeen gas bags to lift the ship and keep her in the air. They are so large you couldn't get them into the entire length of Westminster Abbey. As a comparison with the Italian airship, the *Norge*, that flew over the North Pole a few years ago, just one of our bags has more lift than that entire airship.

'This is the biggest thing ever to fly, and the most complicated. Although we've built airships in the past, there's never been one of anything like this size and capacity, and so we have problems, for we're pioneers, learning as we go. But big as these problems are, we're solving them.'

'This is larger than an ocean liner,' said Carola in amazement.

'Much. Bigger even than the *Mauritania*.'

'How many passengers do you expect to be able to carry in her?'

'Well, we're hoping about a hundred.'

'What weight can she carry?' asked Richard.

'The total load should be about twenty tons, with passengers, luggage and boxes of mail and so on. But right now that seems a bit optimistic, because the intention is to fly to hot countries like Egypt and on to India. These airships – the R.100, and this one – will be the forerunners of a whole fleet of airships which will fly on what the politicians call the all-red route, the Empire route, from Britain to India, probably on to Australia and back. But in a hot climate the gas in the bags expands and we will have to release it, or the bags will burst. Obviously any loss of gas cuts the lift the airship possesses.'

'So this structure, as large as the largest ocean liner, can at best carry no more people than, say, two London omnibuses, with a load you could put on the back of a small lorry,' said Carola. 'I know nothing about these lighter-than-air machines, but this seems an extraordinary calculation, like using an elephant to carry a lady's purse.'

Baxter shrugged. 'That's politics. First, the Labour government wanted it. Then the Conservatives were elected and couldn't cancel the plans. Now the Socialists are back in power, eager to see its completion. I hear everything you say, but we've reached a point of no return. Our careers, our livelihoods and those of thousands of workers in firms that supply us with everything from screws to wicker chairs for the lounge depend on us going on. There can be no possibility of going back.

'Just to show how desperately dangerous any non-essential weight can be in an airship this large, we have calculated that a layer of dust on the top of this airship adds *one ton* to its total weight. And in heavy rain, water will lie on top of the canvas making it sag down between the girders. In a storm, that weight could be enough to pull the airship down, because it cannot possibly shake off so much water. We're trying to cut weight wherever we can, so I was interested when my friend at Zimbro suggested they might have some ideas about engines. But first I'll take you up and show you what we've got. I hope you've a head for heights, Miss Marsh.'

'I'll cope,' Carola assured him.

They climbed one of the fireman's ladders, went through a door into the bowels of the vessel. A catwalk nine inches wide led to another ladder down to the nearest nacelle that housed an engine. The nacelles were shaped like teardrops, with propellers at the back. From the centre of each propeller a hawser ran out to a mooring point fifty or sixty feet further astern in the body of the airship.

'That's to take the strain when we accelerate,' the designer explained.

'It seems a very crude idea,' said Richard.

Baxter shrugged. 'I agree it's not perfect, but it works. As I said, we've had to be pioneers here as well as constructors. And because we're running against time, we have to accept what we might not accept if there was no hurry. But we've been building this thing for six years and enough critics are constantly harping on about waste of time and money. We've either got to finish it soon or pack it in. And that is absolutely impossible. Now, here is the engine.'

He pointed to an enormous cast-iron eight-cylinder Beardmore diesel. Attached to it was a smaller petrol engine which could be cranked by one of the two mechanics who would travel in each nacelle. As soon as the petrol engine was running, the mechanic engaged a gear so that it could start up the diesel. The petrol engine then cut out.

Richard walked round the diesel. 'They look enormously heavy,' he said. 'Needlessly so. What do they weigh?'

'A little over three and a half tons each.'

'And how many have you got?'

'We only wanted four, but we've got five. The total weight is seventeen tons. Petrol engines are lighter – the Rolls-Royce Condors for example, which the R.100 is using. Their total weight would be about nine tons. And if we used the engines the German *Graf Zeppelin* employs, they only weigh a total of seven tons. Diesel fuel oil, however, costs only five pounds a ton as against twenty-three pounds for petrol, which is a bonus. And to carry the airship two thousand five hundred miles, we'd only need about seventeen tons of fuel oil as against twenty-three tons of petrol.

'There's also the great hazard of fire with petrol, which I've already mentioned. We've five and a half million cubic feet of hydrogen, the most explosive gas in the world, just above our heads here. We can't risk a backfire or a spark. Diesel engines don't need sparking plugs. As you know, they work off compression in each cylinder, so they're much safer.'

'Even so, you've still got the petrol starting engines.'

'Agreed. But as I said, we can think of no other way to start the diesels.'

'But why have five engines instead of four?'

'Again, largely because we're so short of time and money. When this airship comes in to moor on the mast, her nose must fit snugly into a cone at the masthead like an egg into an eggcup. If we come in too fast, in a strong wind, say, we smash the whole front of the airship and probably rock the mast off its foundations as well. When an ocean liner comes into harbour, the captain reverses

421

propellers so that he can control his speed of arrival.

'We wanted to use propellers with variable pitch, that could be feathered like oars, and so save fuel. Then we could reverse the pitch as we approached the mooring mast, and come in slowly and under total control.

'But we couldn't get them to work well enough. These propellers are eighteen and a half feet across. The engines, I may tell you, were not designed for them. They were originally four-cylinder engines meant for Canadian rail locomotives. We got them cheap on the understanding that the makers would join two together, making one of eight cylinders in line. Anyway, we can't use them to reverse, so we have to carry a fifth engine at the rear that does nothing at all until we need to moor the airship. Then it reverses us into position.'

'The noise of these diesels must be tremendous for engineers working on them all the time.'

'It is. And the heat's so bad they're almost roasted. We've cut slots in the nacelles to let some air in, but they let in rain as well. We issue earplugs to the mechanics, but they won't wear them.'

'Why not?'

'Because we use an engine telegraph. Fast ahead, slow ahead, starboard engines only, that sort of thing. They can't hear the bell ring if they're wearing earplugs. It's hard enough to hear without them.'

'This has been built like a ship, then?'

'Of course. Nearly all the people involved were in the Royal Naval Air Service. We will actually wear naval uniform, with R.101 on our naval caps, when we make our maiden passenger flight. These are air *ships*. They're steered by a coxswain with a ship's type wheel. Passengers and the crew have cabins and bunks. The passengers even have imitation portholes with electric lights behind them. A promenade deck runs round the airship with rails to lean on and passengers look out through mica windows. Not left and right here, either, but port and starboard. This sort of thinking is partly to blame for the weight. In a navy ship you need weight, strength, rigidity. Of course, you want the same rigidity and strength in an airship, but not the weight. This is meant to be lighter than air, but right now it's heavy as hell.'

'Could we look over the rest of the ship while we're here?'

'Certainly.'

They went up into the lounge.

'Sixty feet by thirty-two feet,' Baxter explained.

Richard tapped what appeared to be a mahogany pillar.

'They're all alloy,' said Baxter. 'With wood veneers on them.'

'But you've got plants here in pots!'

'It adds a touch of luxury. What passengers aboard a liner expect.'

'These wicker chairs, card tables and lights on top of the pillars are what you might find in the palm court lounge of a south coast hotel. Not, surely, in an airship?' said Richard in surprise.

'Well, our passengers will expect the best.'

A corridor extended for six hundred feet through the heart of the airship. From this, ladders and companionways branched off into the vast dimness.

'I feel like Jonah inside the whale,' said Carola. 'The size is absolutely staggering.'

'That's part of the attraction, of course. When we fly out to India for the first time, we're going to stop in Ismailia, outside Cairo, and invite local dignitaries aboard for dinner. We can cook a meal for a hundred people. Well, so they say. We only have three cooking stoves. But we'll fudge up something. Probably have it brought up already cooked from caterers on the ground, so we only need to keep it warm.'

'From what you say, there seems to be quite a lot of fudging up.'

'There has to be with a vessel of this size. And, as I say, always working against the clock.'

'How do you know where you're going?'

'We have a lookout right up on top. He's in a sort of cockpit. In time of war, he could have a machine-gun to defend the airship. At the front we've a bow lookout and a stern lookout in the rear. They report by speaking tubes to the control which is underneath.'

Richard did not reply. The entire conception of the design, almost moving a liner from the sea into the air, with traditional and old-fashioned ways of construction and control, seemed so bizarre that for the moment he could not find words to express his astonishment.

They climbed down to the ground, went into Paul Baxter's office. He ordered tea. They sat round his desk sipping the warm liquid. For some time, no one spoke.

'Well, I'm all ears,' said Baxter at last.

'As you may know, Zimbro's parent company in the States produces cars, trucks, tractors, all kinds of motor vehicles,' Richard replied. 'We have several of their engines which we were going to use in trucks, but then there was a change of plan, and they are simply lying in a shed.'

'But is an unwanted American truck engine any improvement on a Canadian locomotive engine?'

'In this case, yes, a big improvement. Instead of being cast iron and weighing literally tons, these are revolutionary, all aluminium. The cylinders have steel liners so you have the virtues of strength *and* lightness, which I can see is absolutely essential for you.'

'Are they petrol or diesel?'

'Petrol.'

'But I've told you, we can't have petrol. It costs too much and is too dangerous. And, anyway, what could we do with our diesels? They can't just be broken up for scrap. There's a great economy drive on, you know. There have been so many mistakes already over ordering, and changes of plan. The Air Ministry, for example, bought so many tons of ferro-silicon. Then some bright civil servant calculated they had bought too much and so sold off what he thought was surplus at four pounds a ton. Then he discovered that *he* had totally miscalculated. They hadn't bought too much, but too little, and they had to buy it back again at twenty pounds a ton.

'Then we agreed fixed-price contracts for making the girders. But so many changes in the design were required we've had to pay out thousands to the constructors as compensation.

'We spent forty thousand pounds building one tiny section of the craft to see how it would stand up to various strains and stresses. This was quite unnecessary. The money was simply wasted. And yet, when I put in for a calculating machine so that our engineers, working on the mathematical stressing of the airship, could produce results more quickly – what they take two and a half working days to do, the machine can do in under an hour – the request was refused. No money, I was told.'

'How much would that have cost?' asked Carola.

'Fifty pounds,' said the designer bitterly. 'Fifty miserable pounds. That's the sort of thinking we're up against.'

'I see your problems,' said Richard. 'But if you'll give me a few facts and figures on a piece of paper, I'm sure I could come up with something that might help you.'

'What did you make of it?' Richard asked Carola as they drove back down the Edgware Road.

'The size, as he said, is so impressive that somehow it seems to blot out all criticism,' she said.

'Yet for all its size, it's only going to carry a handful of

425

people. An ordinary Imperial Airways aircraft can carry more and probably average a hundred and twenty miles an hour.'

'But only in the hours of daylight,' Carola pointed out. 'That airship may travel barely half as fast, but it will be by day and night. Also, there is something reassuring about its sheer size.'

'There wasn't much reassuring about the size of the *Titanic*.'

'I'm always terrified when I fly myself,' Carola replied. 'I get pains in my stomach, at the back of my head. Sometimes my muscles seem to turn to jelly. I have to force them to do what I want them to do when I have to bring the aircraft down. It's so small and I'm so conscious of speed, the rushing wind, the roar of the engine. But the R.101 is like a calm whale in the sky, moving slowly, ponderously. That must have a soothing, soporific effect, a great silver ship up in the clouds.'

'Maybe. But some of these ships in the clouds seem to have been designed by men with minds in the clouds. They're so convinced that lighter-than-air vessels are going to beat ordinary aircraft that they don't listen to any other voice. Ships in the clouds can sink just as easily as ships at sea if there's a bad storm.

'I've had a quick glance at the figures Baxter has given me. These Beardmore Mark 1 Tornado engines are supposed to develop seven hundred brake horsepower at a thousand revolutions a minute. In point of fact, they don't even develop six hundred. Then they've got a bad period of vibration at idling speed, between three fifty and four hundred revolutions a minute, and again at eight hundred and twenty revs. When they should be pushing the airship along steadily at cruising speed they tremble so much the mechanics fear they could shake themselves to pieces. That means they have to run them faster when they should only be ticking over, and slower when they're cruising.'

'So anything you propose could be an improvement?'

'There's nothing I can think of that could be worse – short of having steam engines.'

Back at the Zimbro works Richard discussed the problem with two of the senior designers. He adapted one of the American engines so that it could not backfire or blow back into the carburettor and cause an explosion, and fitted a blower of his own design to increase its power. Richard managed to persuade the directors to keep the price of each engine low. The publicity that could accrue would be of the greatest value. This contract was well worth subsidising heavily and, in any case, the original cost of the engines had already been written off. The weight of each one was just over a ton. By using these lighter engines, and without any other modifications, the airship would be able to carry about twelve tons more weight of passengers or luggage.

Paul Baxter kept the engine for several days and then wrote a short note to Richard regretting that it was impossible to go ahead. The airship was scheduled to fly with the Secretary of State for Air and other important passengers to India in October of that year.

'You will see that there is simply not time for us to fit and test the engines,' he wrote, 'even if I could persuade my colleagues to use petrol engines instead of diesels. But thank you very much for your interest, which I assure you is greatly appreciated.'

There was time all right, thought Richard sadly. What was lacking was the will.

Chapter Eighteen

All that Saturday, motor coaches, cars and motorcycles had been arriving at the bleak airfield outside Bedford to watch the airship R.101 take off on her great flight. Richard joined a queue of vehicles whose tyres, spinning on the damp trodden grass, threw up sprays of mud. Rain had been falling steadily since early afternoon, but despite being soaked, the crowds waited patiently and expectantly, stamping their feet and swinging their arms against the raw October chill.

Above them, shining silver, as though carved from solid metal and yet appearing strangely ethereal in the harsh glare of the searchlights, the gigantic torpedo-shaped airship floated silently at her mast. For six years the families of the hundreds of workmen employed in her building had listened to stories of progress, of setbacks overcome. They had shared growing concern that she might not be completed on time, that the inaugural flight might have to be postponed. Now, at last, the moment of departure was at hand. At a time of universal economic depression, this huge structure, suspended unbelievably only yards above their heads, seemed a symbol of better times to come. Her tapering nose pointed not only towards India, but towards a greater and far richer goal: prosperity.

Richard drove beyond the latticed mooring tower and parked his car. That morning he had received a telephone call from Paul Baxter. 'I thought I should let you know,' he said, 'that finally, we are due to sail – odd how the terminology of sailors persists! We should be away by dusk, which is pretty early this time of year. Come over if you can and wish us well. I'm sorry we're not using your engines, but you know the reason.'

Richard climbed out of his car and stood for a moment surveying the scene. It was very cold. People were shining torches up at the airship, their breath fanning out like haloes of mist. The murmur of their conversation was broken now and then by a faint cheer as someone recognised a family friend going aboard. Richard walked towards the mooring mast. A uniformed official stopped him.

'Only passengers and crew allowed aboard, sir,' he said firmly.

'I know,' said Richard. 'I was here seeing Mr Baxter some time ago. Engines. He telephoned me this morning wanting to see me.'

'Oh, yes, I remember you now, sir. Just make sure you're down before she sets sail.'

'I will be,' Richard promised him. 'I'm not dressed for India.'

The man laughed, opened the door at the base of the tower.

Richard walked into the lift, pressed the button to ascend. Slowly, sluggishly, the lift moved up to the top platform. He climbed out, closed the trellis door behind him, then stepped across the small gangway into the airship.

Where a bleak corridor had stretched, seemingly to infinity, on his earlier visit, he was now surprised to see that a thick carpet had been laid across the floor. He started to walk along it, not quite sure where he would find the designer – in the control room, in the lounge, maybe in one of the engine nacelles? Halfway along the corridor he heard a call behind him. He turned. Baxter was standing in a doorway.

'Glad you could come,' he said.

'So am I,' said Richard. 'But what is this carpet here for?'

Baxter groaned and rolled his eyes. 'To impress our important passengers – all six of them. I told you how a layer of dust on top of this airship adds a ton weight. What the carpet adds, God only knows.'

'You'll take it up before you go, presumably?'

'No. That's the worrying thing. It travels too. Because of this we've had to cut down drastically on the amount of kit the rest of us can take – only ten pounds' weight each. A pair of shoes, a jacket and trousers, and that's it. We have the Secretary of State for Air aboard, and he's brought with him twenty separate leather suitcases, the sort that are heavy enough empty, let alone full.'

'You can't mean that,' said Richard, shocked.

'Unfortunately I do. We could use your lightweight engines now, I tell you, but unfortunately we didn't have the chance.'

'Well, I wish you the best of luck and a safe flight.'

A telegraph bell began to ring. Richard looked at the designer, puzzled.

'That means we're casting off,' Baxter said in surprise. 'Rather earlier than scheduled.'

Richard ran back to the door, but it was already closed. Through the mica window he could see the nose cone drop at the top of the mast. The whole metal structure of the airship began to tremble as the engines took the strain.

'We're leaving!' he shouted in horror. He tugged frantically at the door. It was locked and already, through the window, he could see the masthead diminish in the gloom. He was on his way to India. 'The man at the bottom of the mast said there was time to see you,' he told Baxter.

'Probably there was then. Maybe the weather is changing and they've just had word. This ship has never been out in the rain, so the sooner we fly through it, the better.'

'I can't go to India,' said Richard. 'This is ridiculous.'

'Well, you can't get off now, that's for sure,' said Baxter sympathetically. 'We have room for a hundred passengers and we're only carrying six and four servicemen, so there's bags of spare accommodation. Find yourself a bunk and stay in it until we're well over the Channel. Then join the others for dinner, if you feel inclined. If anyone asks who you are, explain you're an engineer involved with the engines, which is pretty nearly true. There's nothing anyone can do to get you off until we dock at Ismailia in Egypt.'

'But can I tell anyone in England where I am? In case they worry?'

'We have a wireless telegraph aboard. Once all the official messages are out of the way, I expect we can send one about you. In the meantime, my advice is keep your head down and say as little as possible – nothing if you don't have to. But after this watch – see what I mean about maritime terminology? – I'll look you up.'

He led Richard along the companionway, turned off into a tunnel that opened out into a larger space divided into cabins. Richard went into one, took off his overcoat, scarf and hat. He sat on the edge of a narrow bed. This had been made, and the blanket and sheet were turned over. He saw his face in a mirror on the wall, pale, worried.

He sat there for half an hour, hearing the faint, deep hum of heavy engines far beneath him, feeling the enormous length of the airship move and creak against unseen eddies of air. There was a faint sensation of rippling movement. Now and then, the airship dipped and rolled against unexpected gusts of wind, and then shook herself, like a dog coming out of the rain. He glanced at his watch. Half past seven. Where the hell was he? Over London already? Or Kent? It was impossible to say in this tiny room with its imitation porthole made of frosted glass, illuminated by a tiny bulb to give a grotesque illusion of daylight. He felt as though he was in some kind of cell, trapped beyond all measurement of time or movement.

He stood up, determined to ignore Baxter's advice and go out into the lounge. At least in a larger space he might escape this cramped feeling of being incarcerated in an aerial cell. A discreet tap on the door scattered his thoughts.

'Come in,' he called out. Better see who this was instead of arousing suspicion by pretending the cabin was empty. A steward entered and bowed smartly.

'Cocktails are now being served in the smoking room, sir.'

'Thank you.'

As the steward turned to leave, Richard called, 'Wait!'

The steward looked at him, surprised. Then they recognised each other.

'Carola!' said Richard in amazement. 'What the devil are you doing here?'

She was wearing a dark blue uniform, her hair piled up under a peaked cap with R.101 embroidered on it in gold. At first sight and without make-up she could pass for a young, slightly built steward.

'I could ask you the same question,' she replied.

'Remember Paul Baxter, the designer who showed us the engines? I had a telephone call this morning from him, asking if I could come and see him leave. I had virtually just said hello when it was time to say goodbye. They'd cast off.'

'So you're not meant to be here?'

'Of course not. I've got my car down there. No one even knows where I am. The only clothes I have are what I'm wearing. What about you?'

'Rather different,' she admitted. 'But again, by rights I shouldn't be here either. Lady Warren thought it would make good publicity if I could be a stowaway. I came aboard as one of the catering staff.'

'And then?'

'She has sent an aircraft by sea to Karachi with mechanics to assemble it and check it out on arrival. When the airship reaches Karachi, then I admit I've stowed away. She's sure that will generate immense publicity and interest in my flight home.'

'On your own?'

'Yes.'

'But you've never flown anything like that distance on your own. This is madness.'

'Not necessarily. I've tried the aircraft. It's very safe and solid. In place of the passenger seat they've fitted a huge extra fuel tank. It has all the instruments I need. And I'm not flying over the sea much of the trip. I'll be going from one Empire airfield to another, so there will be RAF mechanics in all of them to check over the plane and service it. I'll be all right.'

'I hope so. But who aboard the airship knows who you are?'

'No one.'

'But you're obviously not one of the crew.'

'No. The catering was done by an outside firm. The food has been brought aboard ready cooked and can be heated up in the ovens. We wear uniforms to look smart, I suppose. When everyone else went down in the lift, I stayed.'

'Have you a cabin here?'

'Like you, I've taken one over.'

434

'Do the crew know you're here?'

'Only one or two. They think I'm a sort of lucky mascot. Rather like a rabbit's foot or some such thing. They just assumed I'd missed my chance to leave. No one knows I'm doing it for publicity or about my plan to fly home, obviously.'

'So we're both, for different reasons, bound for the East at government expense but without government permission?'

'That about describes it. Over the Marco Polo route. Now, I must go, but I'll see you later. What's your excuse for being here, by the way, if any of the passengers ask you?'

'What Tom would call bullshit,' Richard replied simply. 'I'm here as an engine expert. They don't know me. I don't know them. That explanation should just about last the journey. Maybe in Karachi we could strip the extra petrol tank out of your plane and you could give me a lift home.'

'Maybe,' she said, and kissed him lightly on the cheek. 'In the meantime, I'm in cabin 8B. If you call on me, give three small taps on the door, then one loud one. Okay?'

'Okay.'

Lady Warren heard the noise first, a faint and sonorous droning as of some enormous swarm of bees passing slowly overhead. She glanced at the clock on the mantelpiece: ten minutes past ten. On the easy chair on the other side of the fire sat Tom Gardener, smoking a cigar.

'Don't you hear it?' she asked him sharply.

'I hear it,' he said, and checked the time on his watch.

'She must be almost directly overhead,' said Lady Warren. 'Let's go out and have a look.'

She led the way through the hall out of the front door. They stood in the drive, looking up at the dark sky. The night was cold; rain was falling. Above them, moving at

435

an angle, not straight ahead as they had imagined she would move, they could just make out an outline like a giant fish in the sky. Red and green riding lights gleamed, and they could see a faint glimmer from the saloon windows. The exhausts of the nearest engines glowed dull red in the sky. The propeller blades produced a distinctive whackering sound.

'She's flying very low,' said Tom dubiously. 'I wouldn't like to fly a plane at that height in this weather.'

'It's different with an airship,' Lady Warren assured him. 'She's lighter than air. They'll have checked it all.'

'That's just newspaper talk, so I'm told. There have been no proper tests of the thing. It's simply a socialist political stunt. They've been building it for years. Now they have to prove it flies or that's the end of airship development.'

'Do you think she'll be all right?' asked Lady Warren, meaning Carola, not the airship.

'Sure. If they don't make Cairo, then they'll put down somewhere else and give some plausible excuse – bad weather, a passenger ill. Anything. They're a pretty expert crowd flying her. If I thought anything was likely to go wrong, I would never have suggested Carola went along, would I?'

They stood in silence, watching the airship lumber slowly out of sight. Then the wind changed and blew cold specks of rain into their faces like tears.

'I hope you're right,' said Lady Warren slowly. 'I damn well hope you're right.'

Tom hoped he was right, too. But this was not the moment to display the slightest doubt. This was the moment for which he had plotted and planned, for which he had rehearsed, as an actor rehearses a pivotal speech in a difficult play. This was the moment by which he would stand or fall. He could not afford to concentrate on anything else.

He followed Lady Warren inside, shot the bolt on the front door.

'The housekeeper sees to all that,' Lady Warren told him testily.

'I like to make sure,' he replied.

They went into the study. Lady Warren threw the stub of her cheroot into the back of the fire, lit another.

'Would you like a drink, Lady Warren?' he asked her.

'Yes. I would. A brandy and soda. And you?'

'The same.'

'Ring for the butler then.'

'No, I'll pour them,' he told her.

This was what he had decided he would say. If Lady Warren reacted as he hoped, she wouldn't send for the butler.

She nodded. 'All right. Not too much for me.'

He poured out two brandies, added a dash of soda, handed a glass to her. She sat down, not in the leather armchair she had previously used, but in a settee facing the fire. She raised her glass to him. Through the spirit, the fire glowed gold.

'To the fliers,' she said. 'All of them.'

Tom raised his glass silently and sat down at the other end of the settee. It was a three-seater, so there was possibly a yard's space between them. He turned to her, swirling the drink round in the balloon glass.

'I wanted to see you for some time on your own,' he began hesitantly, as though he were a boy about to ask a favourite aunt for a favour and not quite sure of her response.

'Why?' she asked. 'I'm on my own most of the time. I live on my own. I don't call servants and such people companions.'

'Lady Warren,' he said, 'I've been with you, off and on, for quite some time now. I still call you Lady Warren.'

'So you should. I don't like familiarity.'

'Not even between friends?'

'Between friends, possibly. All right, have it your own way. My name's Antonia. Tony for short. I don't like it particularly. But at least it's better than my other name, Esmerelda.'

'I feel that I am your friend,' said Tom, speaking slowly and deliberately, as though he had been running uphill and needed to conserve his breath. He saw Lady Warren look at him sharply. She blew a smoke ring, said nothing.

'I don't quite know how to find words to say what I mean,' he went on nervously. In the light of the fire Lady Warren's face appeared grave, almost sad. Tom took a deep breath. This was the moment for the plunge, the time when, in a power dive in a plane, you pulled the stick back and prayed desperately that the plane would come out of the spin. If it didn't, you were dead.

'When I first came to see you, I wanted a strictly commercial relationship. Nothing more, but certainly nothing less. I was broke. There was nothing back home for me, and very little more here. I'd no qualifications, no training except as a pilot. You had a girl protégée you wished to be taught to fly – with all the survival hints she could pick up. So I applied for the job and got it.

'But working with you, getting to know you a little better, my feelings have changed. And as I said, I don't know quite how to phrase what I'm going to say, so I'll say it in the simplest way, the most direct way, which I hope you will appreciate. To be blunt, I've fallen in love with you.' He stopped. He had fired the gun; all ammunition was gone. Had he hit the target?

For a moment, Lady Warren said nothing, just drew on her cheroot. Then she turned and looked at him closely as though she'd never really seen him properly before, didn't quite know who he was.

'Is that a proposal?' she asked him quietly.

'I would like it to be so. I'm not expressing myself well, I know. Yes. It is a proposal of marriage.' Tom felt relaxed now. It was almost incredible how a woman as shrewd as Tony Warren could fall so easily for intelligent flattery. But he knew he had a way with words and with women. It wasn't all empty flattery, of course. He really quite liked her, as he might like a relation with whom he had little in common but who possessed a quirk of character that appealed.

Lady Warren inhaled, blew the smoke out towards the fire, stubbed out the cheroot.

'Now listen to me, young man,' she said firmly. 'You made a nice speech. You could have been a good actor. Probably the qualities needed for acting and flying are much the same – courage, the ability to be out there on your own, total faith in yourself.

'Well, I also have faith in myself, and I have to say I don't believe a bloody word of your speech. I would like to believe what you say, but I cannot.

'Since you first came to see me, I've had a few people look into your background. I've found that the letter you showed me claiming you were not as other men was forged. The doctor, whose notepaper it was written on, left for Australia the week before the date on the letter. I then discovered that a brother pilot of yours, called Sandy, had apparently written two other letters for you claiming medical problems in one and death in the other, to get you out of two paternity suits.

'You tried to con me. Indeed, you did con me – for a time. I am not often conned, although many have tried, but there's no fool like an old fool, as my father used to say when he was selling shoes off his stall. I expect you were sweet on Carola, and you thought you'd try your chances with me. See if I would fork out some money to help you. Or maybe you thought even then you could walk me up the aisle to become Mrs Gardener. Then you could get your hands on the lot. Am I right?'

Tom looked at her in horror. She was not speaking angrily but quietly, more quietly than he had ever heard her speak before. Her dignity impressed him deeply, and suddenly he felt enormous relief. There was no need now for more play-acting. And yet it hadn't all been play-acting. In fact his feelings for her at this moment came very close to love.

'You're right and you're wrong,' he said. 'I did think that if I could persuade you to marry me, all my financial troubles would be over. Right. But you impressed me when I first met you. I admired you. I still do. I always will. You're a character. You're yourself. You're not beholden to anyone. You don't trim your opinions. You're more than a ship sailing into a dangerous wind, you're the wind itself. I really think I could fall in love with you, although I'd never imagined I could. That's the truth.'

'Is it? I am twenty years older than you are, as I need hardly remind you,' Lady Warren said slowly. 'And I don't like men. I don't like many women, either, so there's nothing on that score. But somehow, after many, many lies, I think you are telling the truth.'

'I am. I'm like a fellow up in the sky in a fighter plane with only one round in his machine-gun. I've fired that round. I can now get out of the way or be shot down. I've never run away before. But there must be a first time for everything.'

'You're not running now,' she said. 'I like you, too – in a sense. I could make something of you, Tom. In your own way, you're a character too, an Australian original. You don't fit in here in this tiny, over-regulated island. We haven't many characters left. Too many died in the war. I like you for what you are, not for what you tell me.

'Several men have proposed marriage to me because

they want my money – my husband's money, to be exact. You're the first who's had the balls to admit it. I rather like you for that. And I'm going to make you an offer which may surprise you. I'm going to give you some money. In fact I'm going to give you a lot of money – one hundred thousand pounds sterling.

'I will write out a cheque for you this evening. You can cash it, spend it, buy a little girl, a big car, a house, a yacht, an aeroplane – anything or all those things. Or you can use it to get yourself out of the rut; to buy that station back home in Australia that's mortgaged. You're honest, after your fashion, and so am I, after mine. We'll still be friends. But we'll be nothing more. I do this because I want to, because it pleases me. I have no other reason. All I ask is that you finish the job you started with Carola and see her through until she joins the ranks of Britain's record breakers. Now, what do you say to that?'

'I don't know what to say. It's unbelievable.'

Lady Warren poured them two more brandies.

They sat for a moment in silence, and then she stood up, left the room. She walked to the front door, opened it, stood outside in the drive.

Rain was still falling and she turned her face up to the darkened sky. She wanted the rain to fall so that it would conceal her tears. How strange, how wonderful it would have been if Tom, or someone else she could like, had been speaking the truth and had genuinely loved her. She felt indescribably lonely, surrounded by everything money could buy her except the one thing that was beyond all price: love.

She turned, went back into the house, sat down at her desk and wrote out a cheque for £100,000, payable to bearer.

In the radio room of the airship the operator tapped out a Morse message to Cardington.

'Crossing coast in vicinity of Hastings. Strong south-westerly wind. Cloud base at fifteen hundred feet. Engines running well at cruising speed, giving 54.2 knots. Gradually increasing height to avoid high land. Ship behaving well generally and we have already begun to recover water ballast.'

In fact, the airship was not behaving well; she was rolling and pitching like a flat-bottomed boat in a storm at sea. The captain was having to pump water from one ballast tank to another to try to steady her. A scoop on top of the airship caught more rainwater and a complex control board of valves directed this through a network of pipes to whichever tank needed to be refilled. But all this rainwater added yet more weight to the already sluggish airship.

People who came out in the streets of towns and villages along the south coast thought she must be having engine trouble because she was flying so low. They were right. The mechanics had stopped one engine and only three were running. Oil pressure in this engine had fallen, and the men were now searching frantically for the cause. Rain drummed constantly on the thin cover of the nacelle as they worked in the confined space, heavy with the smell of diesel fuel.

Above their heads, the handful of passengers, who earlier had sat in the lounge, feeling lost in its wide, bleak emptiness and the disconcerting falseness of hollow pillars and palms, moved on to the smoking room. Here, apart from being smaller and therefore more agreeable than a lounge designed to seat a hundred, the room felt warmer.

They were unaware that the airship was gradually losing height. She crossed the Channel little more than five hundred feet above the waves.

Richard came out of his cabin, walked along the companionway, peered out at the engine that had stopped. Rain washed the smooth metal of its egg-shaped nacelle. The stationary propeller shone like a polished ebony carving. He glanced down below the engine – and was astonished and alarmed to see waves breaking in white clouds of spray. They were already far too low, and still dropping. As he stared, the airship gave a sudden downward lurch, then her bows came up like a ship riding a storm.

In the control room the captain took the elevator wheel from the coxswain and spun it rapidly until the airship began to climb.

'Now don't let her go below a thousand feet,' he told the coxswain.

'Aye aye, sir.'

In the smoking room, Lord Thomson and Sir Sefton Brancker sat in wicker chairs, drawing on their cigars. It was a curious sensation to be smoking here at the centre of five and a half million cubic feet of hydrogen. And yet they had no qualms. They felt perfectly safe from fire.

Richard walked back along the companionway. A trapdoor into the heart of the airship was open above his head. He peered through. Along a maze of latticed girders he could see members of the crew climbing carefully like steeplejacks to inspect the gas bags. They wore thick woollen sweaters and rope-soled canvas shoes, so there could be no risk of striking a spark on any metal.

It was high as any cathedral up there, and nearly two hundred and fifty yards long. In this echoing space, wires and chains that contained the gas bags creaked on their pulleys and then sprang tight with a clanking of links as the airship rolled.

All around him Richard heard the hiss of escaping gas through the throats of the valves. To the men up on the girders, this constant, uneasy noise sounded like elephants breathing in the dark. The gas bags moved like living things within the confines of their harnesses as air

443

pressures changed. They were not made of rubber or canvas, but by an almost mediaeval method of joining thin strips of membrane taken from the intestines of bullocks. Each piece measured exactly thirty-five by thirty inches and stuck together like a patchwork quilt to make each gas bag. Richard had heard that more than a million oxen from meat canning firms in Chicago had supplied the covering for these bags.

The largest contained more than half a million cubic feet of hydrogen, and all leaked constantly from the primitive seals. With changes in outside air pressure, as the R.101 rose and fell, the valves opened and closed automatically. There was no means of replacing gas lost, and when it reached a certain low level, the airship would sink steadily.

Each man carried a basket of patches to paste over the most serious leaks. The sight of these men swarming just above Richard's head in the dim, echoing vault depressed him. How could this flying anachronism, a strange, uneasy amalgam of ancient and modern technology, survive the flight through a storm and then the baking deserts and snow-capped mountains that lay ahead? An engineer climbed up the ladder from the stalled engine.

'What's the trouble?' Richard asked him, glad of any excuse to take his thoughts away from what he had seen.

'Thankfully, not too much,' the man replied. 'The oil-pressure gauge is faulty, that's all. We had to shut the engine down in case she seized. But we're running again now we know what was wrong.'

As he spoke, they could both see the propeller begin to turn slowly and then spin, a silver disc in the rainy sky. The floor beneath their feet dipped and rose again, like a corridor on an ocean liner in a rough sea. Joints creaked and groaned with the stress of the storm and under the increasing weight of rain accumulating on top of the airship.

Richard went into the lounge. It was empty. Wicker chairs had been pushed back from little round card tables as though a clutch of clubmen had left them unexpectedly. The air was still heavy with stale smoke from cigars and cigarettes. He sat down on one of the chairs. By his side a tray of glasses and a soda siphon stood on a table. As the ship rolled, their rims touched and rattled. He felt uneasy, sitting here on his own, at the centre of a storm he could feel and hear but not see. On the impulse, he stood up, went back towards his cabin.

On the way, he knocked on Carola's door with the prearranged signal, three small taps, one loud. She opened the door. She had taken off her hat, and her hair cascaded down over her shoulders.

'Anything the matter?' she asked him.

'I don't know,' he said frankly. 'But we seem too damn low The wind and the rain keep pushing us down. I think we may have to make a forced landing in France.'

'In this weather? In the darkness?'

'We may not have any option. Better to land under control than the other thing.'

'It's as bad as that?'

He shrugged. 'It could be. Being safe is better than being sorry. Have you brought much kit with you?'

'No. Only a small bag.'

'Well, pack your things in it.'

'Why? Are we leaving?' Carola tried to laugh.

'If anything happens, and the lights go out, you'll never find everything in the dark.'

She nodded; that made sense.

'Meanwhile, I'll have a walk round,' he told her. 'I'll be back if I hear any news.'

He went out into the corridor again, leaned over the hand rail, peering out of the window. Rain streamed back from the bows of the airship; he might have been in a submarine about to submerge. He could not remember a storm of such ferocity. All conventional aircraft would be grounded in such weather. Their flight should also have been delayed, but political expediency had prevented any postponement.

Above his head he heard a constant squeal as the gas bags rubbed each other, surging against the restraining wires as though they had a life of their own and wanted to be free, going their own way, up to the hidden stars. More gas was escaping now, belching, whistling through valves and leaking patches.

He strained his eyes as he suddenly saw a sharp point only feet away from the window, raised like a warning finger. Then he reeled back in disbelief and horror. He was looking at the top of a church steeple. The airship was down to roof level.

He ran back to Carola's room, beat frantically on the door.

'Come out!' he cried. 'At once! It's urgent.'

She came out, holding her bag. As she did so, the airship lurched suddenly and dropped. The door slammed shut behind her and she collapsed into his arms. He held her tightly, smelling perfume on her face, her hair.

'We're going to crash,' she said in an awed whisper.

'Yes. We've just passed a church steeple. I saw it out of the window. If they can't get any more height, we're for it.'

The tone of the engines changed abruptly as the captain increased to maximum revolutions. The airship's nose reached up feebly. Then the nose came down again and instead of remaining horizontal it began to dip. Richard clasped Carola tightly. They heard feet drum above their heads as crewmen raced along the catwalks in the huge envelope to escape from the gas bags in case they exploded.

The floor keeled over sharply to the right. They heard

a crash, a great splintering of wood as tables and wicker chairs tumbled across the floor of the lounge.

The airship was still moving, but only sluggishly, like a beast with a broken back, although the engines were roaring at top speed. Then the whole vessel stopped so suddenly that they were flung against the wall. All the lights went out. They were still on their feet in the dark, in each other's arms. Above and around them, girders snapped under immeasurable strain with booms like cannon firing.

'This way,' Richard told Carola. He seized her hand, began to lead her along the tilted corridor to the door.

'Put your other arm out,' he told her. 'Touch the side so we can feel our way.'

He did the same on his side. The tips of his fingers brushed lacquered metal, sheets of varnished canvas. The engines stopped. In place of the reassuring growl of their exhausts came a roar as though a forest was taking flame. One by one the gas bags exploded. Through portholes, they could see fire blaze at the stern of the airship. This gave them enough light to run.

They reached a door, held shut by half a dozen levers. Richard forced them down one by one, pushed at the door with all his strength. It opened slowly. Rain blew in, bringing with it great gouts of smoke and the smell of burning canvas, smoking rubber, and the stench of roasting human flesh.

The airship was down in a field. Flames lit up an expanse of grass and a row of trees. The tail of the R.101 was totally engulfed in fire. Girders, red-hot, sizzled in the driving rain. Beyond the blaze, on top of the tailplane, incongruously untouched, the Royal Air Force ensign, which had flown throughout the journey, still stood proudly in the storm.

The doorway was several feet off the ground. Richard

was about to jump when the exit was suddenly engulfed by flames.

'This way!' he shouted and pulled Carola back along the corridor. He heaved open the trapdoor that led down into an engine nacelle. They climbed down the ladder, shut the door behind them. Now they crouched, imprisoned in a metal egg while fire raged all around them. The diesel oil wouldn't catch, he knew that, unless the flames reached a certain temperature. If that happened they would be burned to cinders within seconds. And then he saw the tins of petrol, used for the starting engine, strapped together on the floor. If they went up, they were dead. He tested each filler cap; all were tightly closed. He tore off his jacket, draped it over them to insulate them from heat.

'Get down on the floor,' he told Carola. 'Cover your face and your head.'

She pulled her coat up over her head. He crouched opposite her. At the heart of a furnace, he felt desire move within him. He reached out, kissed her. She pushed back the coat from her head, opened her mouth to speak, but a sudden roar of flame which engulfed the engine nacelle drowned her words. He put his arms round her, drew her further down so that he was shielding her with his body.

Paint inside the nacelle began to blister, then crackle and blacken with heat. He looked fearfully at the petrol tins. The bottom part of the nacelle was out of the flames, but the top now glowed an ominous red. The temperature rose, but so long as the flames did not spread down to the base of the nacelle, they should survive. Then gradually the fury of the fire passed them. They could hear rain drumming with angry fingers on the thin metal above them. The red glow faded and died.

'Time to go,' Richard told Carola. He put on his

jacket, picked up a spanner and began to hammer at the side of the nacelle. The metal was too strong. He could not make a hole. Tied by a leather strap to a wooden rack of tools was a heavy hammer with an axe head. He picked it up, smashed it again and again into the metal until the blade punctured the shell. Then he hacked at it until he had made a jagged opening just large enough for them to climb through.

He could see mud, grass, white wood split from the trunk of a tree, all streaming with rain. He took Carola's hand, pulled her through the hole into the field.

At first, they could see no one. Then, in the dimness and the rain, he made out three figures.

'Are you all right?' he shouted. They did not hear him. They were searching the wreckage for survivors. Dazed, burned, bewildered, they did not realise that with Richard and Carola, they were the only ones.

'Come away,' he told Carola. He was afraid of the sights she might see, of grotesquely burned bodies, blackened corpses wearing charred uniforms. He pulled her through the fields towards a small house where a candle glimmered in a window. They beat on the door. A man opened it. He was in a nightshirt with a nightcap, his feet bare.

He stared at them without speaking. Their faces were blackened with oil and smoke. Wafers of charred canvas clung to their hair.

'Anglais,' Richard said inadequately, and pointed back towards the wrecked airship.

The fire had almost burned itself out, but flames still lit up the airship's huge metal framework. The man made the sign of the cross, indicated they should come inside. He left them in the front room and went into the only other room the house contained, returned with two metal mugs and a bottle of brandy. He poured three fingers in each mug, gave it to them. They drank,

449

toasting him and each other, and all the brave souls they
would never know again.

Chapter Nineteen

The muted bell of Lady Warren's bedside telephone purred discreetly. She reached out an arm from the pink silk sheets and switched on the bedside light, picked up the receiver. It was a direct line. Only a handful of people knew the number. She had no need to say who she was. She recognised the voice of the caller: a contact in the newsroom of the *Sunday Enquirer* newspaper.

'We've just had a phone call from France,' he said. 'The airship's come down. Apparently it lost height in bad weather and hit a hillside outside Beauvais in northern France.'

'What happened then?'

'The details aren't clear. It's a very brief news flash. They'll be following it up later. Apparently there was a fire.'

'Hydrogen?' she asked.

'Yes. Hydrogen.'

'Any survivors?'

'Not known. But there can't be many.'

'How far from Beauvais?'

'A couple of miles off the main Paris road.'

'Thank you.'

She replaced the receiver, thought for a moment of lighting a cheroot, then decided against it. She did not like people who smoked in bed. They could doze off and the bed catch fire. Fire. She thought of the airship burning. She could imagine the screams, the terror, the unbearable agony. Poor Carola. After all her dreams, her hopes, her work, to end like this.

She swung herself out of bed, put on a silk dressing gown, walked down the corridor. She opened a door without knocking, switched on the light.

Tom started up in bed, eyes blinking in the sudden glare. He'd been dreaming he was in a dog-fight and his engine was missing on two cylinders. His gun had jammed and he was diving and turning and swinging and sliding to no effect at all. The German came on, so close that he could see the sun reflecting on his goggles. Tom swallowed as the dream faded. He always had bad dreams when he slept in a strange bed, but Lady Warren had insisted he stay close at hand until they knew Carola had reached her destination safely.

'What's the matter?' he asked hoarsely. 'What's happened?'

'I've had a telephone call from Fleet Street. The airship's down.'

'My God. Where?'

'In northern France. Near Beauvais. Get on to Croydon Airport, engage a closed aircraft capable of seating four people at the minimum. Say we'll collect it in an hour. We also want a pilot and Customs clearance for France.'

Tom was already out of bed, searching for his clothes. Lady Warren went back to her room, picked up the house telephone. It rang in the housekeeper's room. A sleepy voice answered.

'Yes, your ladyship?'

'I want smoked salmon and chicken sandwiches, two Thermos flasks of coffee, half a dozen glasses, two bottles of Hine brandy, packed in such a way that they won't get broken, all in a wicker basket. Now. Mr

Gardener and I are flying to France.' She replaced the receiver, began to dress.

Dawn was already painting the sky with streaks of pink as the chauffeuse drove them to Croydon. They sat in the back of the Rolls with heavy motoring rugs wrapped around them. Even so, they both felt very cold.

'Do you think she's dead?' asked Tom.

'What's the point of thinking? We've got to know.'

'I'm sorry,' he said. 'It was my idea.'

'I agreed with it. You can't blame yourself. I'm just as much to blame. It seemed a good idea at the time.'

'So, presumably, did setting off in an airship that was untried and too heavy, in the middle of a storm.'

'Yes,' she agreed, and looked out of the window so that Tom would not see tears glisten in her eyes.

It was weak to cry. She sat back and closed her eyes. The car sped on into the early morning.

The aircraft was out on the concrete when they arrived. The engines had already been run up to warm the oil. Dew lay heavy on the grass around the runway. A Customs officer checked them through. The pilot shook their hands. He knew Tom.

'We're heading for Beauvais,' Lady Warren told him.

'Yes, your ladyship.' He paused. 'I understand the airship's come down near there.'

Lady Warren nodded. 'I know someone aboard her. How long will the flight take?'

'Probably two hours, with this wind.'

'Are you ready?'

'Whenever you are, your ladyship.'

'Let's go then.'

They walked out to the aircraft, climbed inside, sat down on the wicker seats. A faint smell of dope and petrol mingled with the scent of polish used for cleaning the windows. They took off, flew over the Channel, above northern France. The pilot was separated from the saloon by a small door. Tom went through.

'Everything all right?' he asked, really for something to say.

'Yes. I know the route. It's not far off the Paris run. I do that once a week.'

Tom went back to his seat. Lady Warren poured them each a coffee, added brandy. They drank gratefully, warming their hands on the cups. Mist hung over promontories. A few cars moved like toys along ribbons of roads far beneath them. The plane began to bank.

They looked out of the windows. Below them lay an enormous smoke-blackened skeleton, like the bones of some giant prehistoric fish left on the shore when the tide has receded. It was difficult to believe this was the frame of an airship that had flown from England only the previous evening and not the girders for a great new building to be constructed among the trees.

On the tip of a tail fin the Royal Air Force ensign still flew, the only piece of fabric not consumed by the flames. Everything else had gone. The fire had also burned away a great swathe in a wood of hazel and oaks. The R.101's nose was buried among the trees as though in an attempt to hide itself. The tail, high as the latticed entrance of Paddington Station, was well out in the open field. The airship's rudder moved slowly to and fro, left to right, right to left, in the morning breeze. Gas bag harnesses still remained, looking like the webs of great spiders. Tom could see metal gas valves, part of a staircase, the ballast water tanks – and then they were down.

The pilot taxied across the rough field, turned into the wind, cut his engines. He came back into the saloon, opened the door, let down the steps.

'I'll wait for you here, your ladyship,' he said.

'Do that,' she said. 'Let no one in and don't take off

without my specific instructions, no matter who orders you. Understood?'

'Understood, your ladyship.'

Lady Warren and Tom walked across the muddy field. The rain had stopped but the earth felt cold and damp through the soles of their shoes. Bodies, covered with sheets, had been laid out on the edge of the wood. Some peasants had already placed posies of flowers near them. A few others, mostly old women in black, with shawls over their heads, had brought out candles and knelt in prayer. British officials of the government's Airworthiness Inspection Department had already arrived. One knew Tom. He glanced curiously at Lady Warren, puffing on her cheroot.

'I recognise the face,' he said to Tom. 'Who is she?'

'Lady Warren. She has a friend aboard the airship.'

'Must be her only man friend, then.'

'I've heard rumours there was a girl aboard,' said Tom cautiously.

The official shrugged. 'It's impossible to tell until all the skeletons are examined.'

'Are there any survivors?'

'Three. In the local hospital.'

'Where's that?'

'A couple of miles away.'

'Who are they? Do you know?'

'I've got their names here.' He read out names that meant nothing to Tom.

'Who were they? Their jobs, I mean.'

'Engineers. All Bedford men.'

'No one else at all?'

'Not as far as I know. People have been looking for survivors for hours. It's unlikely they'll find any more.'

Tom walked over to Lady Warren, told her what the official had said.

'Do you want to visit the hospital?' he asked her.

She shook her head. 'I don't think there's any point. But if you were in this airship when it crashed, Tom, and somehow you survived, where would you go?'

'To the nearest house. To try to telephone someone. You, probably.'

Lady Warren nodded, looked around. Two or three tiny cottages were on the far side of the field. 'There are no telephone wires,' she said. 'No poles. Say you'd gone to the cottages and they couldn't help you. Where next?'

'The station. There's always a telephone there.'

'Exactly. Let's go.'

They walked across the field, reached the main road, kept on walking. On the outskirts of Beauvais a sign pointed to the station. They walked up the approach road. The station had two platforms and a single line. The booking office was open. The clerk was smoking a Gauloise, reading a special edition of the local paper with a description of the crash.

'Could you help us, monsieur?' Lady Warren asked him in French.

'If I can, madame. Where are you going?'

'Nowhere. We want information. We're looking for a young girl on her own. Might be a bit dishevelled, perhaps shaken at the news of the airship crash.'

'I've been on duty since five o'clock. No young girl has been here, madame. She's French?'

'No, English.'

'But on her own, you say?'

'Yes.'

'No. But there was an English girl with an Englishman. He didn't speak much French.'

'Where did she go?'

'They're in the waiting room. She was very distressed. She wouldn't get in the train. Her companion took her into the waiting room to sit down.'

Tom and Lady Warren ran along the platform to the

waiting room. Huddled in a corner, his arm round a sleeping Carola, was Richard.

'Thank God you've come,' he said.

'What the hell are you doing here?' Lady Warren asked him. 'Did you come out specially by train?'

'No. On the airship.'

'You mean you stowed away, too? You knew about Carola?'

'Of course I didn't know about Carola. Not until we met in the air and I had a message from one of the designers I'd met. He said he hoped I'd come and see them take off. I drove up to Cardington, went up in the lift. I'd only just got inside when the airship was launched.'

The ticket collector had followed them along the platform and now stood in the doorway, beaming.

'Ah, you have found her. It is love?'

'Possibly not,' said Lady Warren sharply. She gave him a ten franc note. 'Please get me a taxi as quickly as you can. We want to go back to the airship.'

When Lady Warren's chartered aircraft landed at Croydon, she drove Carola, Tom and Richard to her house, and then instructed the chauffeuse to take Richard on to his own home. They had agreed to say nothing about being aboard the airship. To admit they had been travelling without any authority would only result in a horde of newspaper reporters arriving at their doors, and could not help anyone involved with the catastrophe.

Richard opened the front door of his flat, kicked out of the way several letters lying on the doormat that had arrived by the Saturday delivery, went on into the kitchen. He boiled a kettle of water, made some coffee and sat down.

He felt weak with reaction. He had a bath and then, wearing his dressing gown, he opened his mail. Except

457

for two, the letters were all bills. The first letter he opened was from Eleanor. He had just begun to read it when the telephone rang. He picked it up. Eleanor was on the line.

'Have you got my letter?' she asked him immediately.

'I was just about to read it.'

'It was simply to say I wanted to see you. Can I come round?'

'You mean now?'

'Of course. Now.'

'All right.'

She sounded worried, not her usual urbane self. Richard got dressed and then punched up the cushions on the sofa, washed a few dishes in the sink, tried to make the little flat look more presentable. He heard a car stop outside the house, went downstairs to open the front door. Eleanor was wearing a sable coat, and for the first time in their association she seemed ill at ease, almost embarrassed.

'Would you like a coffee?' he asked.

'Thank you.'

He poured two cups.

'I wanted to see you before you read about it in the papers,' Eleanor said. 'My mother has sold her majority holding in the Zimbro Car Company.'

'Why?'

'She isn't really interested in cars, and sales over here are very slow. She was advised that it wasn't much of an investment. She could make more if she invested in other stocks – on which, of course, her brokers would take their usual large commission. This opinion arrived at the same time as an offer for Zimbro. Indeed, I wonder if this new buyer, or someone close to him, didn't suggest to the stockbrokers how to soften up my mother.'

'Who's bought it?'

'Your brother.'

'My brother? You mean Tobin?'

'Yes. He told me that before your mother died, he managed to get the mortgage on the estate lifted, as presumably you know. The house and grounds he inherited are worth a fair amount, and he decided to take out a loan against them to buy fifty-one per cent of Zimbro shares.'

'He told you he'd managed to get rid of the mortgage?'

'Yes.'

'Interesting. So who's lent him the money now?'

'Apparently the same people who held the mortgage. The North London Loan and Mortgage Company.'

'He must be mad. Their rates of interest will be usurious. They were over the mortgage, and I shouldn't think they've changed.'

'Well, that's up to him. Anyhow, I thought I'd tell you. He's in command now. Very much so.'

'Thank you for letting me know.'

'There was something else I wanted to see you about. To tell you before anyone else did.'

'What's that? More bad news?'

'It's about Tobin and me.'

'What about you?'

'He's asked me to marry him.'

Richard's jaw dropped. His first instinct was to say, 'You're not serious? You can't marry him, he's a psychological case. He doesn't want you, but what you represent – money, power, influence.' Then he looked at Eleanor, saw she was serious, was regarding him with wide, nervous eyes.

'Well, this is a surprise,' he managed to say instead. 'He's a very lucky man. I hope you'll both be very happy.'

'You've not been very close as brothers, have you?'

He shook his head. 'No. Not from boyhood, I'm sorry to say. I think he hates me, always has, since we were toddlers. But I don't know why.'

Eleanor put out a hand, stroked his wrist gently. 'You're a funny boy,' she said. 'When I came to your room at Oxford, all those years ago, I offered you a job. I also dropped a hint I could like you. You took me out to dinner, which you could barely afford at that time.'

'I know.'

'It was fun. I enjoyed it so much, I even stole the menu from the table, and kept it. But you never took me out again. You never kissed me. You never seemed to want to get to know me better, as I wanted to get to know you.'

'I thought you were terribly attractive,' Richard said, 'the prettiest girl I'd ever seen, let alone met. But I was so bound up with my work that everything else, and everyone else, took second place. And then you've always had money, while I've grown up in a curious sort of way, with money taken away from me, and under the shadow of that enormous mortgage, my mother driven ill by worry. At Oxford you were in with the richest set. I felt I couldn't compete. So I didn't try to. I decided to concentrate on what I thought I was good at, prove to myself I could invent something. That was the most important thing to me then. If I had my time over again, it wouldn't be. But it's no use saying that now. And after all that, I haven't been too successful, have I?'

'You were with the machine-gun in the war.'

'That's a long time ago now. I haven't achieved anything with Zimbro Cars. I hadn't the muscle to persuade the directors to innovate.'

'You never asked me to use my muscle.'

'I never thought of asking you, to be honest. I thought I could carry them on the strength of my arguments. But, in the event, I couldn't. I hadn't reckoned with the inertia of my own countrymen, their ingrained hatred of change, even for the better. I see now I should have talked to you.'

'I wish you had, Richard.'

'Well, that's all water under the bridge now.'

They sat talking for an hour, and then he saw her to her car.

'Good luck,' he said. 'In everything you do. Always.'

He watched the car drive away and went back to the room to look through the bills that he put on one side. The only other letter was from Zimbro's company secretary. There was to be an emergency directors' meeting on Tuesday at three o'clock. His presence was requested.

Richard entered the boardroom through one door, and the directors through another that led to an anteroom. Richard could see from their flushed faces and their air of unusual if forced cheerfulness that they had been drinking. They filed in, led by the chairman, and then came Tobin. He looked across at his younger brother, nodded coldly, said nothing.

They all sat down at the oval table. The company secretary read the minutes of the last board meeting, which were passed unanimously. A few points of order were raised, contracts with suppliers discussed, approved or cancelled. Then came 'Any Other Business'.

The chairman took off his pince-nez, laid them down carefully on the blotting pad in front of him.

'I have called you here, gentlemen,' he said, 'in advance of anything you may read in the press, to tell you formally that our American parent has decided to sell the Zimbro Car Company.

'I take this opportunity of saying how much we have enjoyed the association with the American company, who have given us great freedom of action. But I would be less than honest if I did not say I am glad that a new era of independence now lies before us.

461

'I would like to introduce to you our new controlling shareholder, Mr Tobin Rowlands. We all know the experimental work that his brother here, Richard Rowlands, has been doing, and although I regret we have not been able to make full use of his suggestions and proposals over the years, we have always had the highest regard for his technical ability. I am sure we will all work in equally close association with Mr Tobin Rowlands.'

The directors looked at each other, nodded sagely. Richard glanced at each one in turn. He had come to know them over the years. He liked them well enough as individuals but held little respect for their ability. They were all middle-aged, careful, cautious. None could afford to lose a directorship.

'Mr Rowlands has intimated that we will all remain as directors and I will continue, at least for the foreseeable future, as chairman. Now, that said, what else is under the title of Any Other Business?'

'This, sir,' said the sales director. 'We have a large backlog of unsold cars. This is, of course, because of the general economic slump. People cannot afford to buy new cars, even on the generous deferred payment system we can offer. Fewer cars are being registered this year than last. The indications are that next year there will be fewer still.'

'How many cars are unsold?' asked the chairman.

'At this moment, sir, we have seven hundred and forty-nine of all models assembled, currently parked in fields a few miles from the factory.'

'Why are they away from the factory?' asked Tobin.

'Many car buyers like to come to the factory personally to collect their new car at the factory gates rather than entrusting delivery to a trader who may not care how fast he drives the car so long as he delivers it quickly. It would be very bad for our reputation if customers saw hundreds of unsold cars. They might wonder whether they were making a good purchase.'

'I see,' said Tobin.

The chairman turned to him. 'Have you any suggestions to make, Mr Rowlands, as to how we could move these unsold vehicles?'

'None, I fear,' said Tobin. 'None at all. I leave that to you gentlemen. You're the experts.'

'Anyone any ideas?' The chairman looked enquiringly at each director in turn. They shook their heads. He glanced at Richard. 'What about you?' he asked.

'I think we should emulate William Morris. He had the same problem some time ago – too many unsold cars – and his factory in Cowley was pushed to the verge of bankruptcy. Accountants and solicitors told him the only thing he could do was to declare himself bankrupt. Instead, he slashed the prices of every model until he was making only about a fiver on each car.'

'The dealers wouldn't like that,' interrupted the chairman.

'Possibly not. But while a man with gangrene in one leg may not like having it amputated, that is better than dying. Morris sold every single car, and created such a demand for them that the company decided to drop the prices on new models. They still made a good profit, because by then they were selling so many. That is the solution I propose, gentlemen. Cut our prices to the bone.' Richard looked round at the directors. None met his eye. The chairman turned to Tobin.

'Well, it's a revolutionary proposal,' he said nervously, 'but your brother's proposals for engineering modifications have always been revolutionary. I was foolish to imagine that he would be anything else when it came to sales proposals. What is your opinion, sir?'

'What Morris did in the past worked in his case,' said Tobin, speaking thickly as though he had a heavy cold. 'But would it work in ours, now? I think not. The country's economic position is quite different today. I propose we step up our sales campaign, increase our advertising budget, and weather the storm. But of course I leave the decision to you gentlemen.'

The chairman looked at each of the directors. 'Do you vote to cut our prices, or shall we follow the advice and opinion of our controlling shareholder?'

They nodded in favour of the latter option. It was safer to agree.

That month, a spokesman for Zimbro Cars announced that the company had sustained such a heavy trading loss, no dividend would be paid to shareholders.

Next month, Morris Motors announced they had sold more than fifty-eight thousand cars in the previous year, and they expected this to double within the next twelve months.

At the same time, Richard received a letter from the chairman, terminating his contract with Zimbro.

Chapter Twenty

Lady Warren ordered that the aeroplane she had sent to Karachi for Carola when she landed there in the R.101 should be returned without any publicity. It was then reassembled and kept in a hangar at Croydon Airport. Lady Warren had decided that the aircraft should be further modified and then Carola would attempt a round-the-world flight. She felt she had waited long enough, had bowed to Tom's opinion too often. Amelia Earhart had already flown the Atlantic on her own from Newfoundland to Burry Point, in Wales. The time for action rather than talk had come. Carola must attempt a round-the-world flight. Out of work and with time on his hands, Richard offered his services, which Lady Warren was happy to accept.

Carola made a number of test flights. After these, Richard suggested modifications to the engine, mostly to give greater power on full throttle, in case she had to climb in a hurry in bad weather conditions. These were only partially successful, so he designed a blower to give the engine much more power throughout its range of speed.

Tom installed a second extra petrol tank. One additional tank already filled the second cockpit in anticipation of Carola's flight from Karachi. This second one, shaped like a cone, fitted in the rear part of the fuselage.

With all the tanks full, the aircraft felt much more

sluggish than Carola had anticipated or wanted. It seemed heavy, almost dead. By a system of taps which she could control, she could use the fuel in this rear tank first, to restore the balance of the plane as quickly as possible. But even so, she was not happy about the way the extra weight, totally unenvisaged by the aircraft's designers, affected its handling.

'It feels all wrong,' she told Lady Warren. 'It's like someone with a headache or a hangover trying to conduct a complicated conversation. I bank, I turn, but the plane only answers sluggishly. She doesn't respond as she should.'

'You'll be flying in a straight line when the tank is full,' Lady Warren replied shortly. 'You won't need to bank or turn. When the fuel's used up, you go over to the tank in the cockpit. Then you'll be all right. You must have faith. The plane's made by one of the best makers in the world. They know what they're about.'

'I know what I'm about, too,' retorted Carola. 'I'm nervous with all this weight. That plane's nothing but a petrol tank with wings.'

'All other record breakers face the same problem. This is a basic fact of the business. They survive. You'll be all right, believe me.'

Carola nodded reluctantly. She wanted to believe her, but she found it difficult.

She made two false starts on her round-the-world flight. Fortunately, there was no publicity whatever about her intentions. She was just another woman pilot apparently setting off on a flight to Vienna. Then, if anything went wrong, there would be no adverse comment in the newspapers, and no hint given of her real aim, which might alert a competitor.

On the first attempt, she planned to leave at dawn on a Monday morning. On the Sunday evening, she packed her small overnight bag with washing materials, under-

466

wear, a sweater, a pair of shoes, stockings, a dress – she might have to appear relatively smart at RAF officers' messes when she came down to refuel each evening. She would be flying in overalls and tennis shoes with her trousers tucked into the tops of a pair of woollen socks, but this was not how British officers stationed in Basra, Karachi, Calcutta or elsewhere might wish to entertain her. She had to appear feminine to them, like the girl friend they might have left back home in Camberley or Woking.

She had just finished packing when Tom telephoned her.

'One or two things I'd like to see you about before you go,' he said. 'A little bit of paperwork. Shall we have a meal together?'

'I don't feel much like eating,' she replied. 'But I'd like to see you.'

They agreed to meet at the flat he rented on the outskirts of Croydon. He had prepared a bachelor meal: steak and onions, a bottle of red wine, an ice-cream sundae bought from a grocer's shop.

'No wine,' she told him firmly. 'That would be madness. I'm off at five in the morning. I can't risk a hangover, or even just feeling sleepy.'

'The steak will do you good, though,' he insisted. 'I've some orange juice in the fridge, too. That'll help you.'

They sat down, one on either side of his small table.

'You're going to be all right,' he assured her, seeing how tense and nervous she appeared.

'You think so?'

'I know so. I've taught lots of people to fly. And I've seen lots of other fliers taught by other instructors. And you're the best. You're a natural flier.'

'You've never told me that before.'

'I didn't need to. But I think it's only fair to tell you now, when you're off on the greatest flight ever made by man, woman or beast. Beats Marco Polo. I see Richard has stamped a copy of his birthmark on the blower casing. The one that looks like the initials M.P. Let's hope the great journeyer's spirit goes with you. Now, I've one or two papers I think you should sign. They deal with the rights for any books you might write or want written. Newspaper serials, newsreels, maybe even a film of your flight.'

He pushed a mass of papers over the table to her. Carola read the first words.

'Whereas it is agreed by both parties of the first part . . .' There followed various other legal phrases: 'Notwithstanding anything that may be further agreed, said, written or suggested, we the undersigned . . .'

She pushed them away.

'I can't read all this rubbish now,' she said. 'I just can't. I'm not in the mood. What do these papers actually mean?'

'They give me authority to act in these matters for you. It's no good me offering to a publisher or a newspaper the rights to your own account of your flight if I haven't your okay to do so.'

'But you have. Without you I'd probably never be doing this.'

'Then sign here.'

Carola signed at the bottom of each page and saw with some surprise that he had already put another signature on the last page where it said 'Witness'.

'Who's that?' she said.

'I made it up. Lawyers like these things to be witnessed,' he replied easily. 'I didn't want anyone else reading the documents, for then they'd know exactly what you're up to. And we've all agreed to keep mum on that until you're over the halfway mark. Here, you take one copy.'

'It's only extra weight.'

'Not very much. And it could come in useful. You might be short of toilet paper or something!'

Tom fitted one set of papers into a big envelope, licked the flap, sealed it, handed it to her. 'You'll make a fortune out of this,' he assured her confidently.

'You think so?'

'I know so. I keep telling you, but still it doesn't seem to sink in. It's the first time this has *ever* been done. A pretty woman going round the world on her own.'

'I don't feel pretty.'

'You are pretty,' he told her. He leaned across the table and took her face in both his hands and kissed her.

'Oh, Tom,' she said, and began to cry. 'I'm afraid. I don't like flying. I'm not a natural flier, whatever you tell me. I do it because I have to. Because I want to get out of the rut and it's the only way I can think of. I suppose Lady Warren's determination has got through to me. Make something of my life, she's always saying. I don't even know if I want to do that. But I've got no life at all unless I have some money. I'm just a gypsy.' She smiled ironically.

'Rubbish,' he said.

He moved round the table, sat by her, put his arm round her. She felt his hand, warm and comforting, on her breast. His expert fingers stroked her. She began to relax.

'Come to bed,' he said. 'That's the best way of getting rid of all this tension.'

'You think so?' she asked the question, not really caring what he answered.

'I know so,' he said and led her into the bedroom. She noted without surprise that his big double bed was already turned down.

Next day, the weather was so bad, with an electric storm and hailstones, quite out of season, that it would have been foolish to take off.

'You learned one lesson in the R.101,' Tom told her, 'Don't start a long flight in the rain. Wait for the sun.'

Better weather was forecast for later that week, and this time Richard telephoned her.

'I felt I had to ring and wish you all success.'

'Thank you.'

'What are you doing tonight?' he asked her.

'Nothing, really. I'm packed up, ready to leave. I've asked the telephone operator to give me an early call at four for a five o'clock take-off.'

'Come round and see me,' he said. 'We'll have supper together.'

'I'm not hungry.'

'Nor am I,' he admitted. 'I feel as though I was flying with you. And I *hate* flying. But I do want to see you.'

He picked her up in his little car, drove her to the flat he rented on the top floor of an old house near Brooklands. She wondered what sort of meal he would have prepared. Not steak and onions, she hoped. It wasn't. His supper was pasta with a garlic and tomato sauce.

'This'll be terrible on my breath,' she said.

'Garlic's a wonderful herb,' he told her. 'Got medicinal properties. It soothes you, makes you sleep better.'

She knew how the evening was going to end, how it must end, as it had ended before with Tom. At half past ten they were in bed together, naked, body to body.

'I love you,' he said.

She smiled in the darkness. Why did men think it necessary to say this?

'You don't believe me, do you? But it's true.'

She remembered Tom in the pub outside St Albans, years before, saying he loved her. She doubted it then. Now, she wasn't sure. She would like to believe him, but whether it was true or not somehow seemed less important than she expected. She liked him, liked them both. Wasn't that enough?

470

'I don't know if I love you,' she admitted. 'I have to be honest.'

'Well, thank you for that,' he said without rancour. 'After all, we've not seen much of each other. Only every other year, it seems.'

'The fact is, I don't know if I can love anyone, Richard. I've never been loved much. My mother never even said she liked me, let alone loved me. My father just found me useful.'

'I like you because you're you,' he told her. 'Because you're brave. Because of your indomitable spirit, like old Marco Polo. Maybe he didn't want to make the journey, but he did it.'

'I don't want to make it, either,' she said. 'I'm terrified. While I'm up there on my own, there's no one to talk to, no one I can speak to, or who can speak to me. No one I can reach out and touch. I'm absolutely alone, out in the emptiness of space, crouched in a tiny little metal and canvas cocoon with a huge engine roaring away just feet in front of me, and hundreds of gallons of petrol all round, just waiting to explode. It's madness. What am I doing this for?'

'Because that is what you were born to do.'

'Nonsense.'

'No. It's not. Most people are born simply to live and die. A few are born to do great things. You're one of them. Like Marco Polo's travels, your journey will take its place in the history books. And once a pioneer blazes the trail, others follow. What is originally a lonely trail becomes a main road. But someone has to point the way first. That's what you're about to do.'

'Dear Richard,' she said gently. 'I wish I could believe you.'

'Try,' he told her firmly.

They made love gently, as always with him; not the hard, fierce taking which characterised Tom's advances.

'I love you,' he said again and again, and kissed her. She did not reply, but he felt her tears wet on his face.

Next morning, the take-off was again delayed. The weather was fine but a misfire developed in the engine. This was traced to a faulty plug lead. By the time it could be repaired, it was nearly noon and too late to go.

Take-off was finally agreed for the following day, but then, on the eve of Carola's departure, Richard discovered that an oil feed pipe was weeping at a joint. This could be due to many causes, such as vibration or tired metal or a lack of solder in the joint.

He discovered that the plane had travelled out to Karachi as deck cargo, not under a waterproof cover as had been specified, but simply lashed to the deck – at the tail end of the rainy season. This made it imperative to examine all electrical wires and connections for any belated evidence of corrosion and to check all fuel and oil pipes and unions. Several had to be replaced, and so finally a new departure date was agreed, some weeks ahead.

A few days before she was due to set off, Carola booked an appointment with a doctor in Harley Street under the name of Mrs Oxford. She bought a cheap gold-plated ring from a pawnbroker and wore it on the third finger of her left hand. She was determined to keep her identity secret.

She sat now in his consulting room, facing him. He was an elderly man with a high wing collar, thin hair, heavily brilliantined. He wore a black jacket and striped trousers and pressed the tips of his spatulate fingers together as he looked at her across the desk.

'We have the results of your tests, Mrs Oxford,' he said, 'and I am happy to tell you your own belief is entirely justified. You are pregnant.'

'Are you certain?' asked Carola, hardly recognising her

voice. Her throat had gone dry; her tongue seemed to fill her entire mouth. Pregnant. This could ruin everything. And pregnant by whom? By Richard or by Tom? It could be either. Could it be both? She was not sure and she did not like to ask the doctor.

'Of course I'm certain, Mrs Oxford,' he replied testily; he did not take kindly to patients who questioned his diagnoses.

'It isn't possible that my papers could somehow have been confused with someone else's?'

'Utterly impossible, my dear lady. Utterly impossible. But why are you so concerned? This surely is a moment of joy, not sadness. I've had women sitting opposite me, as you are now, weeping because they could not become pregnant, because they had to face up to the fact that they never would be pregnant.'

'It's my husband,' said Carola quickly. 'He doesn't want a baby.'

'That is not uncommon,' said the doctor smoothly. 'In fact, lots of husbands say that until the baby arrives. Then they're very proud to be a father.'

'Not my husband,' said Carola firmly.

'Well, I'm sorry to hear that. If you care to bring him along here one day, we could have a chat about it. I could perhaps persuade him to think otherwise.' He paused expectantly, hoping that Carola would agree, perhaps even make an appointment.

She said nothing.

The doctor shrugged his shoulders. 'Well, since you said you were going abroad, I have taken the liberty of making out my bill.'

He pushed an envelope across the desk. She opened it, wrote out a cheque hurriedly, handed it back to him. He blew on the form to dry the signature, looked at it in surprise.

Damn! Without thinking, she had signed the cheque

473

in her own name. Why hadn't she thought to bring enough cash? What a bloody fool!

'But Mrs Oxford,' he said, 'you've signed it Carola Marsh. You're not the aviator, are you?'

'I wanted to keep that secret,' Carola told him wretchedly. Now there was no secret. The whole deception had been pointless. She'd been a fool on every level.

'I did not know you were married,' said the doctor.

She shrugged. 'Another secret, if you like,' she replied. 'But I'm sure they're both safe in your hands.'

'Of course. If that is your wish.'

'Yes, it is. I'll tell you why.'

She might as well give him a reason for discretion. 'As soon as the weather reports look promising, I'm going to fly on another long-distance flight.'

'You are attempting to break a record?'

'Yes, if all goes well. But there are so many hazards, you know – weather, wind, trouble with the aircraft, dirt in the fuel, and now the news you've given me.'

'You're a healthy young woman,' the doctor told her. 'You should be quite all right. Sometimes in the morning you may feel a bit sick, but that passes. And the further you go into the pregnancy, which, from what you tell me, is only a matter of weeks old, the fitter you will feel. It's amazing the bloom that comes to the cheeks of women who are expecting a child.'

'Really?' said Carola without interest.

'Really,' the doctor assured her. 'But your secret is certainly safe with me. I wish you all luck and, when you return, if you wish to see me with your husband' – he stressed the word husband – 'I would be very happy to help you both in any way I can.'

He wrote a receipt, handed it back to her. She put it mechanically into her handbag, stood up. They shook hands.

'Good luck,' he said. 'Good luck.'

Carola went down the white-stoned steps of the house and stood for a moment in Harley Street. The she took the ring off her finger, threw it away into the gutter. She felt dazed, like a sleepwalker living in a mist of unreality. The breeze felt cool on her forehead. Was she feverish? Was a hot flush one of the symptoms of pregnancy? She had no idea; she really knew nothing about the subject.

She leaned for a moment on the lacquered black railing until her heart slowed and she felt steady. On both sides of the road, front doors displayed discreet, well-polished brass plates: gynaecologists, psychiatrists, surgeons. Other similar plates advertised private nursing homes. Somewhere, surely, in one of these rooms, behind drawn curtains, must be a man or a woman who could help her end this pregnancy. An abortion was illegal, but there must be ways round that. She had often read about film stars and stage actresses and society women who from time to time underwent operations for what was generally described as appendicitis, but which the knowing described in cruder terms.

But to obtain this kind of illegal service, you had to know important friends, and have a lot of money. The other option was to visit some old woman in a back street, who would give her some ghastly concoction to drink or, worse, prod at her with a metal knitting needle. That was not uncommon, and very dangerous. Girls died as a result. There was no cure for septicaemia, and no way out for her, either. She had to go on with this charade.

Perhaps she could have the baby abroad? Or she might have it adopted. It. She couldn't think of the embryo within her as a person, someone who would grow up, maybe have children themselves. She was starting a dynasty, and she wanted no part of it.

She climbed into her little car and drove back slowly to Lady Warren's town house in Grosvenor Square where she had been staying for the past few days, ready for her departure. She hadn't unpacked her overnight case since the first cancelled attempt to take off. She had already been vaccinated against smallpox and inoculated against typhoid and yellow fever. What a pity she could not be inoculated against the unwanted burden of childbirth!

Everything was ready: the essential tools and spares she had to take, including a second propeller – wooden blades could easily be damaged if she made a clumsy landing; a funnel with a fine gauze filter for refuelling; spare tins of oil; a supply of boiled sweets and thermos flasks; bottles of water for herself; and a revolver, strapped to the side of her seat.

She stopped outside Lady Warren's house. At once the chauffeuse, who had been watching from an upper window, came down the steps and opened her car door.

'I'll put it away in the mews for you, ma'am,' she said. 'Lady Warren is upstairs in the sitting room. Perhaps you would join her.'

Carola nodded, walked up the marble staircase, past the statues on each landing. The afternoon sun shone through tall stained-glass windows which threw blues, reds, greens, yellows on the carpets like a luminous mosaic. She went into her bedroom and through to her private bathroom. She washed her face, and then looked at herself carefully in the mirror. There was no change. She remembered the first time she had made love to Tom. Next day, she had also examined her face in the mirror to see whether her expression or appearance had altered after losing her virginity. There was nothing that she could see. Inside, maybe, and mentally, but not outwardly. She combed her hair, powdered her face, walked downstairs into the first-floor drawing room. Lady Warren was sitting on a settee, her feet resting on a stool, eating smoked salmon sandwiches.

'Where have you been?' she said. 'Been looking all over the bloody place for you.'

'I just went out for a drive round London.'

'You'll get enough sitting on your arse in that plane. What you want now is a bit of exercise, relax the muscles. Care for a swim?'

Lady Warren had a heated swimming pool in the basement; she swam twenty lengths every morning and every evening when she was in London. Carola had been doing the same. She liked the sensation of the warm water, and the echoes when they called to each other as though they were in a grotto or a deep cave. But not today; she didn't feel like swimming today.

'Thank you, no,' she said.

'Have a sandwich, then. Won't do you any harm. Might do you some good – put hair on your chest. You're looking a bit peaky. What is it, wrong time of the month?'

Carola shook her head. How she wished it was. She smiled weakly, sat down. Lady Warren poured tea from a silver teapot into a fragile cup of bone china.

'Day after tomorrow, if the weather doesn't play silly buggers, you'll be on your way. Although I hate the prospect of flying, I must say I wish I was coming with you, that the plane had two seats. Not that I could do much good. Can't read a bloody map. I could tinker with the engine, I suppose, but that's all.'

'You've done more than anyone else,' said Carola. 'You've backed me right from the beginning. Without you, there wouldn't be a trip.'

'Probably someone financed Marco Polo in the beginning,' Lady Warren replied. 'And this is the Marco Polo flight. Look what the papers are saying.'

She threw a copy of the *Evening Enquirer* at Carola. She caught it, read the main story, 'Miss Marco Polo flies at dawn'. Beneath the headline, a map traced the route taken by the thirteenth-century Venetian explorer, Marco Polo.

This week Carola Marsh, the 27-year-old aviatrix, takes off in her single-engined aircraft on a journey as remarkable as Marco Polo's. Whereas he took four years to reach China, she flies to Vienna, then Constantinople, on to Basra, Karachi, Bombay, Delhi, Calcutta, down to Akyab Island off the coast of Burma, and then up north, over the mountains to Chungking.

From Chungking, where will she fly? Somewhere beyond the imagination even of Marco Polo. Down south, to Australia, east to New Zealand, then across the Pacific to Los Angeles, from there to New York. Finally, she will cross the Atlantic and so be back to her starting point, Croydon Airport. The thoughts, the good wishes, the prayers of everyone in these islands take wing with her. May Lady Luck smile on this lady of the air.

Carola threw the paper down angrily. 'I thought it was agreed there would be no publicity in case anything goes wrong.'

'I know, but Tom said people in the aerodrome were openly talking about your record attempt. It was only a matter of time before the press got wind of it, so he said it would be better to put out the truth rather than have lots of rumours and half-truths flying about.'

'I wish he'd asked me first. Now, if there are any more delays or false starts, we alert other rivals to have a go and look fools ourselves.'

'Nothing will go wrong, Carola. Not this time.'

The reporter had probably never been in an aircraft, thought Carola, and had no idea what it was really like in a cramped cockpit with ice forming on the wings, on the windscreen, so that even in a flying suit you shivered at the thought of the freezing death that lay just on the far side of a sheet of thirty gauge aluminium.

She had looked down so often on an ocean rippled by unseen eddies of wind and the heaving currents of the deep. She had often wondered what strange creatures must lurk in that silent darkness, fathoms beneath the surface, what wrecked vessels, encrusted with shells, home to giant fish that swam in silence through the cabins of the dead. She tried to force such thoughts out of her mind, to concentrate on happier things – how soon she would reach her destination, the long hot bath and soft downy bed she would enjoy then. But she could only chase away these sombre imaginings when she left the sea behind her.

She did not feel like this when she flew over towns, cities, fields, hills, though even then she felt consumed by a cold feeling of total aloneness. She was an earth-bound creature in an unfamiliar medium, being drawn along through the ambient air by a spinning piece of wood. She was always afraid, and no one could reassure her, because there was no means of reassurance. You either did these things, or you did not. No one asked you to fly alone to try and break a record. You invited yourself to make the journey. So you should accept the risks and keep quiet or get out of the business.

'I think I'll just take a walk round the square,' she announced suddenly. 'And then I'm going to bed.'

'*Bed?* At this hour?'

'I'll be awake for days and nights on end soon. So the more sleep I can pack in now, like charging the battery, the better.'

'As you like,' said Lady Warren sulkily.

Chapter Twenty-One

The flight was due to start at five o'clock in the morning, an hour chosen so that Carola could fly as far as possible, even against a strong head wind, before dusk. To make a landing after dark on a strange landing field, possibly only lit by the headlights of parked cars, could be suicidal.

Lady Warren drove her to Croydon in her Rolls. Carola sat in silence. The weather was perfect, the aircraft had been checked and rechecked; there would be no cancellation this time. She had worked for months, years, for this moment, and now that it was almost upon her, she felt qualms of sickness and inadequacy. Was this due to her pregnancy or to her concern about the immensity of the task ahead? The journey on her own, of around thirty thousand miles, in a tiny one-engined plane, driving a wooden propeller, seemed an almost impossible undertaking. She must be mad to attempt it. But then probably people had said the same about Marco Polo and Columbus, and all the other travellers of the past, pioneers who had gone where no one had journeyed before them. And now, mad or not, she could not turn back.

Amy Johnson must have felt exactly the same sense of foreboding before she set off on her record-breaking flight to Australia, but she had not backed out. Apart from pride, Carola had another reason for going on.

There were not too many flights left to make in the sense of pioneering.

In the United States, Amelia Earhart, having earlier succeeded in becoming the first woman to fly the Atlantic, was now said to be about to attempt a round-the-world flight. Her aircraft, so Carola had read, would be far larger and more technically advanced than hers, with two engines, the latest radio and direction-finding equipment, and she would take a navigator with her. Carola was about to attempt the flight on her own.

By the time they reached Croydon and turned into the aerodrome, she was beginning to feel more cheerful, more confident. She would succeed, and then the publicity would eclipse anything that had gone before. And as a result she would advance the cause of women, and help British aviation and engineering to an unparalleled extent. As Lady Warren said, nothing would go wrong.

A few planes were already parked outside the hangars. Newspaper reporters and photographers, with huge cameras slung by leather straps over their shoulders, stood smoking at one side. The morning was cold and they wore overcoats and trilby hats and stamped their feet on the hard concrete. They came towards her as she got out of the car.

'A quote before you go, miss,' said one of them.

'What's it feel like?' asked another.

What did it feel like? she wondered. How could she put her feelings into a few quotable words? She wanted to say, I'd like to back out of it. I want to get rid of this baby, which I never wanted, which no one even knows I'm going to have, and I don't know what to do or say when the child arrives. I dare not tell Lady Warren. She might instantly withdraw her sponsorship. Then I'd be ruined financially, morally, every way. But when the birth occurs, I probably will be in any case.

'What's it like?' She repeated the question breezily.

'You should ask a bird what it feels like to set off on a long flight. After all, swallows fly purely by instinct from here to South Africa and back again. I'm only doing what birds do, and with a compass, a radio and the best engine in the world I have a lot of advantages, even over eagles.

'One day, and not too long from now, you'll think no more of flying from here to China or any of the points I'm going to visit in between than you do now of getting into your car and driving down here from Fleet Street. That's why I'm doing it – to prove it can be done. And that a woman can do it. Amy Johnson flew to Australia on her own. And I, God willing, will fly right round the world and see you all here on my return. Then I'll do my best to tell you what it was like.'

'You a rival to Amy Johnson, miss?'

'I'm a rival to no one. I wish her every success in all her flights, and I'm sure she'd wish the same to me. There's room for more than one, you know. Lots of men try this. Now it's time for a few more women to show the way ahead.'

She walked away from them towards the aircraft where Richard and Tom were talking together. They shared a liking for her and for engines. What would their feelings and reactions be if she told them she was pregnant by one of them but she didn't know which one?

As she came towards them, Richard gave her the thumbs-down.

'Bit of bad news,' he said.

'Oh no. What?'

'A petrol leak. It only wants a union soldering but it's going to hold us up for a bit.'

'Odd,' said Tom, 'but almost exactly the same thing happened to Amy Johnson on her flight to Australia. But that didn't stop her getting there. So don't worry. It'll only take an hour at most to fix.'

'I agree,' said Richard. 'And to make sure you have a

483

lucky flight, I've got a lucky totem for you.'

He took a small copper ring from his jacket pocket. 'It's a piece of exhaust pipe I took off years ago from that toy steam engine. Remember it? I kept it all these years as a sort of souvenir – I'm not sure why. I'd like you to fly with it – as though a bit of me is flying with you.'

'You're a dear,' said Carola, her eyes suddenly moist, and kissed him.

She went into the lounge and sat down. Someone brought her a cup of coffee. Tom came in.

'The plane's really a flying petrol tank, so keep her nose up and give her the gun as you take off. Once you're in the air, you'll be all right. It's getting up there that can be difficult with this load. And just remember everything I've taught you.'

He looked at her closely. Their faces were only a foot apart.

'Everything.' He repeated the word softly.

Carola smiled, staring into his eyes. He had such blue eyes, the colour of the sea with the sun on it. She liked him. Did she love him? She liked Richard. Did she love him? Did she love both? Or was love like petrol in the aircraft's tanks, there was only so much of it? You could only love so much. Could a woman love two men? Easily, she thought. But possibly in different ways.

The head mechanic came into the lounge.

'We've stopped the leak, Miss Marsh,' he reported. 'It was more a weep than a leak, nothing bad. But you'll be better without it. Ready when you are.'

'I'm ready now,' she told him.

She went into the Ladies, powdered her face and walked out to the plane.

'Look this way, please.'

'And to me.'

'Smile, now. Head up. Hold your goggles, and your flying helmet. That's it. A great shot.'

The instructions from the press photographers came thick and fast. She obeyed them mechanically. She needed their help. If she succeeded, she would be the first woman to make such a flight. As Tom had told her, the story would be worth a fortune. She'd be paid enough to be free from all money worries for ever if she was careful. She must not antagonise anybody. She had to be known as a smiler, a cheerful person, always willing to help. Nothing must ever be too much trouble for Carola Marsh.

Lady Warren took her by the hand. 'Take care, dear,' she said in an unusually husky voice. 'And come back safely now. There's only one of you.'

'And there's only one of you,' replied Carola.

'Most people are bloody glad of that,' retorted Lady Warren tartly. 'Now get up there. Show them what a girl can do.'

'I'll do my best,' she said.

'I know you will,' said Lady Warren.

Carola climbed up into the cockpit, slid the cowl forward, locked it. A mechanic waited by the propeller. She threw the switches. He put his weight on the horizontal blade. The propeller turned reluctantly, jerked back. He pulled it down again. This time the engine fired. Gouts of blue smoke blew out of the stubby exhaust. She let the oil warm, blipped the throttle slightly, checked the instruments, the controls, the ailerons, the rudder.

Through the side window in the cockpit she could see reporters holding their hats against the rush of air from the propeller. She saw Lady Warren, eyes screwed up against the blowing dust. Mechanics, spanners in hand, stood watching her. Did they wish they were making this flight? Carola wondered. Or were they just thankful they could stay at home?

She set the compasses. They had been set yesterday,

but she wanted to check them. She carried three. Originally, she had put in a spare one against the main one supplied by the makers in case it proved faulty, but then Tom pointed out a flaw in this proposal.

'If they both give different readings, how will you know which one is right?'

How, indeed. So she carried three. That would mean two against one or, hopefully, all three giving the same message. She saw the needle on the oil thermometer move slowly up the gauge, then raised her right hand in a thumbs-up. The mechanics pulled away the wheel chocks.

She gunned the engine. The aircraft began to trundle sluggishly across the oil-stained tarmac. She opened the throttle further.

She taxied downwind on the grass at the side of the runway and then turned to face the wind. Now she was on her own. She opened up the throttle. The plane felt so heavy she wondered if she would ever get it airborne. She remembered what she had to do, pull the joystick back as soon as possible. If the plane still did not respond and rise, she must throttle back at once, otherwise she would hit the trees at the far end of the airfield.

Back came the stick. The rumbling of the tyres on the ribbed concrete eased and then ceased. The aircraft bucked slightly to the left. She corrected it to the right and knew they were up. Up and away. Her flight had begun.

Carola suddenly realised she had been holding her breath, she did not know for how long. Now she started to breathe more easily. Far beneath her, she could see roads, thin as lengths of tape, a railway line with a train blowing out a frond of white steam, a river and fields, scattered houses. She headed for the English Channel. At last she was on her way. On her own.

★ ★ ★

Lady Warren stepped into her Rolls-Royce, opened the polished sandalwood box under the partition that divided the driver from the driven, took out a cheroot from the humidor, lit it.

'Where to, your ladyship?' the driver asked through the ivory speaking tube.

'Elvira's,' she said, and put the plug back into the tube.

They drove up through straggling suburbs to Gravesend on the River Thames. The huge car threaded its way slowly through streets of semi-detached and terraced houses, stopped on a corner. The driver jumped down, opened the rear door.

Lady Warren walked up a little path with a sooty privet hedge on either side, and beat on the front door. A middle-aged woman opened it. She wore a flowing black skirt that dusted the ground and a flowered bandanna round her hair. She had big spectacles with thick lenses like the bottoms of bottles. They magnified her eyes grotesquely, making them look like strange, pale fish seen through the glass of a goldfish bowl. This was Elvira, the fortune-teller Lady Warren consulted when she felt she needed comfort or reassurance or even advice.

'I haven't seen you for some time, your ladyship,' said Elvira.

She had a soft voice with a foreign accent. Lady Warren was not quite sure where she came from. It could be Romania or one of those Middle Eastern countries. She vaguely believed that people born there might possess stronger psychic abilities than people born in England.

'I haven't needed your services. That's why. But I do now.'

'Please come inside.'

Elvira led the way into a back room. A dusty window

looked out onto a minute garden, overgrown, uncared for. A roller stood near a garden shed. A cold frame had the lid off and weeds sprouted out. Elvira pulled the curtains. The two women sat down opposite each other in the dimness of a May morning with the sunlight excluded.

Apart from their two hard-backed wooden chairs, the only furniture was a small round table. On this, a crystal ball was covered by a cloth, as some people with a caged bird throw a cloth over the cage at night so the bird can sleep. Elvira removed the cloth.

'Now tell me how I can help you,' she said in a firmer voice than when she had first greeted her visitor. She felt in control. This Lady Warren might be rich and influential, but she needed her. In a sense she was in her power.

'I have seen a brave young woman fly off in an aircraft,' Lady Warren explained. 'She's going a long way. I want to know if she'll come back.'

'You mean Carola Marsh's flight? I read about that in the paper.'

'Yes. Well, what do you see in your crystal?'

'You must think of her first,' said Elvira. 'Put everything else out of your mind but her face. Have you anything that belonged to her?'

Lady Warren produced a small white handkerchief. 'I took this out of her luggage.'

'Now, *think*,' said Elvira. 'And hold that handkerchief very firmly in your right hand. Make a ball of it. Close your hand round it and I'll tell you what I see.'

For a moment, the two women sat in silence. Lady Warren shut her eyes so that she could focus her mind more readily. Elvira peered short-sightedly through her spectacles at the crystal ball.

'I do not know whether what I see is true or false. I can only tell you what is vouchsafed to me by my guide on the other side. You know that?'

'Of course I know that,' said Lady Warren testily. 'But what do you see?'

'I see an aircraft, silver, like a bird, flying south into the sun. I see the pilot wearing some kind of white suit.'

'Will she be all right?'

'She will not die on the flight, if that is what you mean.'

'Yes. It is. I'm glad to hear that. Very relieved. What else do you see?'

'I see someone else flying with her.'

'What do you mean, someone else? Who?'

'I cannot tell you. But there is more than one person in that plane.'

'There can't be. I saw her get in myself. It's a tiny plane. There's barely room for her, never mind anyone else.'

'I see two spirits, two souls.'

'Rubbish,' said Lady Warren firmly. 'There can't be. And there aren't.'

'I can only tell you what I see, Lady Warren. I do not know if it is true or false. But I see what I see. And I would be false to you and to myself if I told you otherwise.'

Lady Warren took a deep breath. She stood up. 'Thank you very much, Elvira. I appreciate your honesty. But this time you're wrong, quite wrong.' She opened her purse, took out a five pound note.

'I don't want your money, if you're not satisfied,' said Elvira.

'I want to give you this. You've never let me down. It's just that I can't understand what you say you see.'

Elvira nodded, putting the note in a pocket in her skirt.

'Sometimes,' she said seriously, 'I don't understand it myself.'

★ ★ ★

489

Carola found that flying over England it was relatively simple to keep on her course. Because she was flying so low, it was easier to look out and see the railway line or a road, a river, than to plot by map and compass. She had learned from Tom that whenever she was not quite sure of her direction or when she wanted to check exactly where she was, she could come down so low over a railway station that she could read its name on the platform and then check this against the map.

Crossing the English Channel presented no difficulties. Again she took Tom's rule-of-thumb advice and lined up her tailplane with the coastline, and kept straight on until the beaches of France lay beneath her, empty and inviting.

Her flying speed should have been around ninety miles an hour but, on Richard's advice, a special propeller had been fitted in case the standard propeller disintegrated in the different temperatures and weather conditions through which the plane would be flying, and constant running at high speed. This kept her flying speed down to around eighty miles an hour. Her first planned stop was Vienna, about nine hours ahead.

Originally, Richard had thought that an electric pump would be the easiest way to pump petrol from the rear tank to the standard tank, but this would have added to the weight and involved extra strain on a battery, already smaller than he would have liked, because of the need to keep down weight. To avoid this, a hand pump was installed instead, with a wooden handle, the sort used to pump up car tyres. When the petrol gauge for the standard tank dropped to a certain level, Carola had to start pumping to replenish it. There were essential air vents in both tanks, and the plunger of the pump was not a perfect fit, with the result that the smell of petrol hung in the compact cockpit like a foul, sickening miasma. Was it these fumes or her condition that made her feel so ill? She could not be sure.

From time to time she checked her instruments, more of a reflex action than a necessity. She had the compasses, a chronometer set on rubber blocks to absorb any vibration from the engine, an air speed indicator, a drift indicator, an altimeter, a marine sextant and a small bubble octant to provide an artificial horizon should she run into fog or darkness or thick cloud.

Part of the cockpit was taken up with a 50-watt radio transmitter locked on to Royal Air Force frequencies. She had a Morse key to send messages, earphones to receive them. The aerial was a wire, more than two hundred feet long, that she had to wind out by a handle like the reel on a fishing rod before the set could receive or send. A metal weight at its end kept the aerial taut and trailing behind the aircraft, out of the way of the rudder.

She wound this out once on the way to Vienna, just to see whether she could pick up any signals, but there was nothing but static. She wound it in again, watching the weight bob from side to side in the wind.

She landed at Vienna in the early evening, on schedule. Tom had written ahead to every aerodrome where she could expect to land, and for some in between in case she had to make an emergency landing. In his letters he had asked for facilities, explaining they would be paid for by banker's draft immediately the bill was telegraphed to him, and giving the address of local banks that would honour this arrangement.

The aerodrome staff were therefore expecting her. Mechanics checked the oil, filled up the petrol tanks and then wheeled the aircraft into a hangar. Carola spent the night in a local hotel, and in the morning had a hot bath and an Austrian breakfast of a poached egg in a glass bowl, with crisp bread and black coffee.

By eight o'clock she was again airborne. The second

leg to Constantinople was slightly longer, about eight hundred miles. She felt familiar aches in her back and legs from the cramped conditions of the cockpit. Fortunately the feeling of claustrophobia which she experienced in a closed cockpit had diminished, and she reckoned she had come to terms with being uncomfortable. The engine was running well, and the crackle of the open exhausts sounded healthy. From time to time she checked her position, for a strong head wind was blowing and she kept drifting to the left.

She had a thermos flask of coffee and two large bottles of aerated mineral water in a leather bag along with some sandwiches, a few apples and several packets of fruit gums. She sipped water and chewed the gums in an attempt to overcome the feeling of nausea brought on, she hoped, by the smell of petrol. Hours passed. Morning gave way to noon, then the sun went down the sky. It was early evening when she came in to land at San Stefano, outside Constantinople city.

The airfield was more primitive than she had expected. There were no lights to mark the perimeter, but the drivers of two cars on either side of the landing strip had heard engines in the sky and turned on their headlights. She came in by their light and made a clumsy three-point landing. As she climbed out of the aircraft, glad to stretch her legs and feel a fresh breeze on her face, two soldiers came out of the dusk towards her.

'Do you speak English?' she asked them.

They stood, staring at her, silhouetted against the glare of the headlamps, rifles slung over their shoulders. They had not expected a woman pilot. One soldier spat on the ground. A voice from the darkness behind them called, 'I speak English. Come here.'

Carola leaned back into the cockpit and found the wallet that contained the aircraft papers. The two soldiers escorted her, one on each side, to a hut. Inside, by a pumped naphtha light, sat the man who had called from the darkness, an officer in his late forties. His uniform was unbuttoned and he had not shaved that morning.

'What permission have you to land?' he asked her as she produced the papers.

'A letter about my arrival was sent here two weeks ago,' Carola told him.

'I know nothing about that. Where are you bound for?'

'India,' Carola replied.

There was no need to explain the whole itinerary here. The next stop was far enough.

'By what authority?'

'By my own authority. Here are the aircraft papers. You'll find them all in order, I'm sure.'

The officer thumbed through them. 'You have no permit to land in Turkey, or to fly from Turkey,' he told her.

'Perhaps you could give me one.'

'That is very difficult.'

'Who can supply it?'

'The head of the aircraft department of the government.'

'Could we speak to him on the telephone?'

'That is impossible.'

'Is there no deputy who could give this permission?'

'That might be arranged. Who can say? But you will have to stay here meanwhile.'

'I'm very happy to do that for tonight. But I need to go on tomorrow.'

'Who says you must fly tomorrow?'

'I need to get to India as quickly as I can.' Carola struggled to keep irritation and any hint of panic out of her voice. She must not antagonise this man. He had it in his power to impound the aircraft. Then she could be here for days, even weeks. This had happened to other fliers who had broken their journey in Turkey. Whether she stayed or left in the morning as planned was literally the will of Allah, as translated by the will of this officer. And such officiousness was not restricted to the Turks. She remembered that when Blériot had flown from France to England, the first flight across the English Channel, a policeman had run to meet him in the field near Dover where he had landed.

This was, of course, the first time a foreigner had ever arrived on British soil by air and the policeman was not quite sure what to do.

'You'll have to wait here, sir,' he said. 'Until the Customs officers arrive.' And this the pioneer airman had to do.

'There is a rest room here,' the officer told Carola. 'You can sleep.'

'But what about the permit?'

He shrugged his shoulders.

She took a photograph of herself from the wallet, signed it, handed it to him.

'For you,' she said, and smiled.

'You are kind,' the officer replied. 'I will try to assist you.'

She walked back to the aircraft. The officer and the two soldiers helped her to hammer pegs into the grass and tie ropes from them to the wings and tail in case a wind sprang up in the night and tipped the aircraft over.

She wrapped a cloth over the engine to prevent dust and sand blowing into the carburettor. Then she went into the rest room. One of the soldiers filled a tin bath with two buckets of hot water. After she bathed, she was given a meal of rice and kebab. She ate by the smoky light of a hurricane lamp. Moths beat their wings against its hot glass.

She was more tired than she realised, and still worried about the permission. She slept uneasily, now and then

494

starting up from her hard bed, hearing the whine of mosquitoes or one of the soldiers who slept next door hawking in his throat. At dawn, around half past four, she was up, washed in the bath water, dressed, and went out of the hut.

She had not expected to find anyone else awake. But to her surprise the officer was already standing outside, still unshaven, uniform still unbuttoned. He might never have been to bed. His face showed he had good news. He was smiling.

'I have the permit,' he said. 'You may fly when you wish.'

She did not ask how he had acquired the permit, for she suspected there was no permit; this was simply a ploy to give him importance. Not too many foreign aircraft would land on this airfield.

'Have you any fuel?' she asked him.

'Petrol? Of course. If you can pay.'

'I can pay.'

He shouted an order. The soldiers came shambling out of their hut. They went into another building and collected two drums of fuel. Carola produced a large funnel. The petrol was dirty; the filter on the funnel became clogged with grit and even the occasional twig as the petrol was poured.

When the tanks were filled, she explained to the officer how the engine had to be started by swinging the propeller. He ordered the biggest of the two soldiers to do this. After three attempts, the engine fired. Within minutes, she was airborne. As she gained height, the drumming in her ears from the engine, which yesterday had seemed so comforting, now sounded wearisome, a constant irritation she could do without. She was very tired from the strain of the flight, and she had what felt like slight indigestion – or could it be her pregnancy?

She flew south-east towards the Taurus Mountains.

She noticed how the tree-covered foothills quickly gave way to sparser vegetation higher up. The mountain peaks themselves were concealed by clouds, and Carola suddenly realised she had no idea how high they were. Could she fly over them? Had her engine the power to lift the aircraft sufficiently to clear them? She saw on the map that they were not marked for height – an astonishing omission. But then she realised she might well be the first person whose survival could depend on that information.

Carola began to climb. Seven thousand feet, eight thousand, ten thousand came up on the altimeter. She calculated she should go to twelve thousand feet. Surely that must clear them? But the engine began to cough just above ten thousand feet. The air was so cold and the mixture of petrol and air so weak that it could not keep firing constantly. The cockpit, totally unheated, was freezing. She felt she was in some kind of aerial tomb, flying into thick white cloud; at any moment she could hit the mountainside. She could die or, worse still, be fearfully injured and lie out there in the snow in agony without any hope of rescue. Despite the cold, she was sweating.

She stared at the altimeter. She would have to come down. She dropped to nine thousand feet and saw a railway line beneath her, and a train moving along it, trailing a long plume of smoke. She could follow the train, fly above it, and so hope it would guide her between the peaks, because no railway could be built so high that it reached over the mountains. Then suddenly the railway line disappeared into a tunnel. Once more she was flying blind. She could not go back. She dared not turn to left or right in case she flew into the side of the mountains. She had to go on.

She opened the throttle. The faster she was going, the quicker she would be over this range – or into it. Either way, since she could not influence her flight, speed would be a bonus. She sat, staring straight ahead, seeing nothing but the swirling mist, hearing the roar of the engine's open exhausts echoing from the rocks – how many feet below? Ten, twenty, a hundred?

Then suddenly the mist thinned. Streaks of vapour, like long strands of tufted wool, drifted past on either side and she was through. Far beneath her she could see the railway line and the long train racing ahead out of the tunnel.

Soon, she was coming down the sky to land in Aleppo. The evening air felt very warm here, as though she was standing near an open fire. She watched French mechanics check over the aircraft, then an army officer, apparently in control of the little airfield, showed her to a rest house. She had a bath, a meal of cold meat and bread, and slept soundly. Next morning, she was again airborne by eight o'clock. Her next stop was Basra, on the Shatt-el-Arab river which formed a natural frontier between Iraq and Persia.

She had been cold the previous day, but now the heat began to dry her skin. She was flying above the desert which seemed to reflect and amplify the heat. She touched the inside of the fuselage. The thin metal felt warm. She undid her flying suit, put on a pair of sunglasses against the eye-aching brilliance of the sun.

Far beneath her lay the desert, almost featureless, fissured here and there as though a giant hand had aimlessly gouged out valleys and ravines. From time to time she saw a caravan of camels, one behind the other, but otherwise the sands stretched to infinity, empty and desolate.

Currents of air began to play with the aircraft. From flying steadily at three thousand feet, the machine soared to five, then dropped to two. Carola realised, with mounting horror, that these winds were much stronger

497

than her engine. In this tiny metal and fabric shell, she felt as much in control as a walnut shell floating in an ocean.

She desperately tried to gain height, in the hope that the higher she flew, the weaker the hostile currents would become. Flying at full throttle and barely maintaining her height, she knew she was still far too low for safety. And then, as she struggled for control, the plane dipped and dived.

Her only chance of survival was to land and wait in the hope that the sandstorm abated. But where the devil was she? What was she landing on? Soft sand, dried mud, rock? She could not see beneath the cloud of sand and braced herself for a crash.

The wheels bounced, jumped, bounced as she landed. The plane lurched clumsily to the left. Part of the undercarriage had broken. Clouds of sand, whipped up by the spinning propeller, covered the windows. Carola throttled back as steadily and quickly as she could, fearful lest in her blindness she ran into a rock and the whole aircraft disintegrated.

The engine stopped so suddenly that she was flung forward against the windscreen. The unexpected blow to her forehead stunned her momentarily. She sagged, head down, while waves of pain and nausea washed over her. Gradually, consciousness returned. She put up one hand and touched her forehead; there was blood on her fingers, and even to move her head brought dagger thrusts of pain. But she had to move; she must somehow get out and wrap up the air intake to the engine against the driving sand. The wind flung shovelfuls of hot grit against the fuselage.

She clenched her teeth and heaved on the cockpit cover. It moved back reluctantly; sand had clogged the slides. Slowly, painfully, she climbed out into the storm. She closed her eyes against the driving cataract of grit, and fumbled for a foothold on the metal climb plates by the side of the engine. She held a square of cloth, and threw this over the engine, tied it on as best she could with tapes in each corner and climbed back into the cockpit.

Already, half an inch of hot sand covered the seat, the floor. Grit was everywhere, up her nose, in her eyes, her ears. She poured some water from one of the bottles onto a towel, wiped her face and hands. Then she sat back in the seat and waited, sweating in the metal cocoon.

The storm lasted for more than an hour, and then dropped as quickly as it had begun. She drank a beaker of water and climbed out for a second time. The wheels were covered with sand. One of the struts supporting the lefthand wheel had snapped. She stared at this for a moment, trying to force her numbed mind to produce a solution. Then she took out a roll of adhesive tape and various lengths of thin metal rod and laths of wood that she had brought with her for just such an emergency. But it was one thing to plan carrying out a repair in England and quite another to execute it in this arid wasteland that shimmered with heat.

Carola tied a wooden lath to one side of the undercarriage, a piece of metal to the other, and strapped them together with tape as though she was binding a broken bone into splints. This was not a proper engineering repair. She could imagine Richard's contempt, his caustic comments about it, but it was all she could do. Hopefully, it would be better than nothing.

She stood up, wiping perspiration and sand from her face. She had landed in a rolling expanse of desert, with sand dunes all around, unencroached by any footprint of man or animal. She could not see any vegetation, not a single tree, nothing but burning, baking sky and the naked sand trembling with heat as though a giant oven door had been opened. She did not know where she was, in what country, whether the area was inhabited or not, whether it contained wild animals. This was clearly not the time to stay and seek answers to any of these questions. The sooner she was up and away, the safer she would be.

She took out a small shovel and began to dig round the wheels, smoothing a path in front of each one. Then she put the shovel back inside the aircraft, removed the cover from the engine, set the controls, and swung the propeller. The engine fired on the second swing. She ran round the side of the aircraft, climbed up through the door, fighting a horrible fear that the plane might somehow run away, even take off without her, leaving her marooned to die alone. But it didn't. It couldn't, for the ailerons were down. But the feeling stayed with her as she locked the cockpit cover in position, checked her instruments, opened the throttle.

For a moment, the aircraft simply stood where it was. It trembled, shuddered, and then, as she was about to stop the engine and climb out and dig more sand out from in front of the wheels, it began to run forward slowly. Within minutes she was airborne.

Carola checked the instruments. She had made a complete turn as she landed without realising it. If she kept on flying in this direction she could be back where she started. Now she described a big arc in the sky and went on more slowly, for the first time fully realising the immensity of the task she had set herself, and its constant dangers. She was fighting not only the winds of heaven, but all manner of mechanical mishaps, and probably worst of all she was fighting herself. Her head ached where she had banged it, she felt sick and she was exhausted. Her eyelids felt like lead weights; she could hardly keep them open in the heat, and if she fell asleep, she would never wake up.

She reached Karachi at dusk. The RAF establishment

here had a hangar set up alongside a high metal tower like the one at Cardington, intended to moor the airships which would never now fly across the Empire. The commanding officer set a team of mechanics to fashion a new strut. They also checked the entire aircraft, changed the oil, washed out the petrol tanks in case sand had blown inside them. They then fitted new plugs, cleaned all the filters, and by eight o'clock the next morning she was again on her way.

Delhi came and went; then Calcutta and Rangoon. At all these places the British communities had heard of her flight and turned out in strength to welcome her and to speed her on her way. Local papers had carried wired reports from London of her progress. She was already a celebrity. They wanted to give dinners in her honour, to put her in an open car and drive through the streets with a band playing. She resisted all these well-intentioned diversions. She knew she had to press on or her resolve might weaken.

In Rangoon she stayed in the home of the local RAF commander. His wife realised the strain she was under and tried to persuade her to go straight to the house for a hot bath and a long night's rest before she started in the morning. She assured Carola that the aircraft would be serviced by the ground staff; her husband would person-ally supervise the work. Carola thanked her warmly, but insisted she personally checked everything. She felt she owed this to herself. Then, if anything went wrong, she would only have herself to blame.

Carola already felt more exhausted than she dared to admit. She had confidence in the aircraft, but faith in herself, in her own ability to keep awake and not make any mistakes in flight, was beginning to dwindle.

The constant drum of the engine, the vibration of the little aircraft, the sun in her eyes, the heat, the cold, the dust, the clouds, the smell of petrol, the worry of the leak springing up again, and constantly listening for any change in the sound of the engine that could foreshadow breakdown had wearied her and weakened her resolve.

She felt she needed a week in bed with no early morning calls, no more flying until she felt like flying. But that was an impossible dream. She had covered more than a third of her journey, but she was not yet halfway. And the toughest part would come now, over the Pegu Yomas mountain range in central Burma, over uncharted jungles and forests which no mapmaker had ever survived to survey, and above which, as far as she knew, no aircraft had ever flown.

At Chungking she would be nearly halfway home, and the problems that awaited her there. The thought depressed her. So far, she had felt she was flying away from the prospect of a totally unwanted birth. She sat in front of the dressing table in her bedroom, staring at her pale, tense face in the mirror. She felt overwhelmingly tired and alone. Oh, for a chance to talk to Tom or Richard and explain the terrible situation in which she found herself. She put her elbows on the dressing table, bowed her head and wept.

The commander's wife heard her and came in.

'Are you ill, child?' she asked gently.

Carola shook her head. 'No,' she said. 'I'm just so tired. I didn't realise what I was taking on. In London it seemed easy, just to keep on flying east, and all would be well.'

'It will be,' the older woman assured her.

Carola nodded. She could not bring herself to speak. How could she tell this kindly soul of the torment raging inside her? She did not mention her aching head in case the commander's wife insisted she told the station doctor. He might say she was medically unfit to continue; she could not risk this. She had to go on.

She had covered the bruises on her forehead with

powder, which partially concealed them. But she was far more concerned about any internal injuries than how she looked. Could she have cracked her skull? Was she slightly concussed? She swallowed four aspirins and went to bed.

When she awoke, she felt more cheerful, more confident. Sleep was all she needed, she assured herself. She made a very early start, half past five by her mother's watch. The commanding officer had warned her that later in the day, when it grew very hot, air currents could upset flying. With vivid memories of this above the desert, Carola hoped to be over the worst and most dangerous leg of her flight, above the jungle, before midday.

The Air Force turned out with a band to send her on her way. She waved to them through the side window of the cabin; then she was up, and they were all just tiny people, like toy soldiers with toy cars, the sun catching the polished brass of toy instruments.

She headed north, following the main road and railway up towards Mandalay, and then branched north-east. Beneath her lay stretches of flat green paddy fields and then the jungle. This stretched as far as she could see in every direction, dark green, sometimes black, with never a clearing between the densely packed trees.

Hills rose and fell away and only their peaks stood above the forests. There was something immensely awe-inspiring, even fearful, in the sight. What manner of wild beasts must roam there? she wondered. Could there be any human settlements? Would they ever be discovered? It was best not to think of these things. The answers could be depressing, and the last thing she needed now was to depress herself.

She was flying into a steadily increasing head wind. She climbed two thousand feet, hoping to lose it, but it stayed with her. She climbed to nine thousand feet and kept to this height. She could see for a distance of several miles, but nowhere could she see a break in the trees where she might land should she need to come down.

According to the map and her speed of eighty miles an hour, she had at least another three hours' flying before she would be clear of the jungle. Then there might be more paddy fields. But these, she knew, were all ridged with mud walls, about a foot high, to hold water after the monsoon and help the rice crops. If she crash-landed there she would be very lucky to survive, and even if she escaped unhurt, the walls would prevent her taking off again.

The wind changed. Carola felt the aircraft drift with it. She corrected the drift automatically, wound out the aerial for the radio. She had no message to send. She just hoped a message might come in, some word from some civilian or service station to reassure her, to tell her she was not alone, that others were down there, following her flight, wishing her well, checking on her position in case she needed their help.

Carola put on her earphones, turned the Bakelite tuning dials, but there was nothing but static, a great crackling in her ears, the voice of empty space.

She was frightened; that was the trouble. She had flown on too soon. She should have stayed for another day in Rangoon. But she knew if she had stayed for another day, she would have wanted to stay for a third day, and then a fourth, a fifth. She was losing her nerve. She had tried too much too soon, and this feeling of near panic was the result.

Maybe there was some drug a doctor could give her to restore her confidence. Perhaps in Chungking the British Embassy doctor could help her. She would tell him she was pregnant. He'd keep her secret. There was the Hippocratic Oath; doctors could always be trusted to stay silent. If she continued pregnant, she might have a seizure or a miscarriage or even die in the air. Could this be an excuse to have a legal abortion?

The thought took hold. She felt more cheerful, and then suddenly she heard a slight change of tone in the engine, a crackle, a splutter, before its familiar resonant drone returned. She checked the mixture. The lever had a habit of sliding in its quadrant. There was some play there. She should have taken it up. She had forgotten, or hadn't thought it important. Either way, she had done nothing about it.

But the mixture was set correctly. She checked oil pressure, oil temperature. Both were steady and well within the limits of safety. Then the oil pressure dropped slightly. The white needle fluttered like a frightened finger against its black dial. Could the oil pump be breaking down? Was a pipe blocked, the filter clogged? No. They couldn't be. They had all been checked at Rangoon. The engine kept faltering, missing, losing power. She blipped the throttle. The engine increased speed, but sluggishly, reluctantly, as though against its will, almost angrily. She reduced speed. Something was wrong. She'd have to come down. That meant she'd have to turn back, because there was nowhere to land here.

Back to Rangoon and swallow her pride? Well, at least she could have the fault diagnosed and repaired. After all, anyone could have a mechanical breakdown. This wasn't a human failure, a sign of her weakness or of feminine frailty. The makers of the aircraft were to blame, or maybe the mechanics who checked it out. Or maybe Richard's blower was all right for short flights, but not for a flight as long as this.

She turned round, began to head south. Now misfiring began. Gouts of thick black smoke blew out of the exhaust. The propeller stumbled, went on more quickly, slowed again. The engine was running lumpily, on five cylinders, not six. She'd never reach Rangoon like this.

She had to come down now, but where the devil could she land?

She began to lose height, not willingly, but because the plane was losing power, losing speed. She travelled in a wide circle, peering out of the side window, trying to find any open space where she could land.

Once she was on the ground, she could soon get the engine right; change the plugs, clean the jets. A couple of hours at most should see her airborne again. But how to get on the ground? She was losing height too rapidly for comfort. The aircraft dropped five hundred feet, then another three hundred, then two. She banked steeply, peering out at the dark and secret forests. Then in the distance, on the right, she saw a space she must have missed before. It appeared to have been hacked out of the jungle in the shape of a giant cross.

Carola came down low over this. Could she land here? She turned, flew the other way, came back for a second look. She'd have to; it was here or nowhere. But what the devil did this cross mean in the middle of the trees? No matter, it was providential. She turned into the wind and came in to land. The first time she was going too fast, and overshot the cross. She was losing confidence, making a fool of herself, making silly mistakes that even a learner pilot would never countenance. She came in again for the second time, and this time made a clumsy two-point landing. She taxied to the end of the cross and turned, meaning to come back. But then the engine cut completely. The plane rolled on for a few more yards and stopped.

She climbed out. It had been cool within the cocoon of the cockpit, but now the heat felt raw and damp, like a steam room turned up to full temperature. Sweat poured off her face and body. She ripped open her flying suit, stood for a moment, staring at the solid green walls that surrounded her. What trees are these? she wondered.

Teak? She had no idea. They seemed so close together she could not imagine even a small slim animal gliding between their huge, unfriendly trunks.

She moved stiffly, slowly, with a dry mouth, to look at the engine. She could see something wrong right away. A plug lead was loose. Worse, the porcelain insulator in the centre of the plug had burned right out. That was why it had been running on five cylinders. Instead of a sparking plug in the sixth there was an open hole. Well, that was not a difficult job to mend. A new plug and she'd be away again. She went back into the cockpit, took out the tool kit. Then something made her turn.

From the edge of the jungle that seemed so thick no human creature could live there, about twenty men were walking towards her. They wore *longgyis*, like skirts, of brightly coloured cloth wound round their bodies, the ends tucked in beneath a belt, and white shirts. Some carried sticks, others what she took to be swords. They kept walking towards her, all in step, not hurrying. There was something terrifying in their measured, steady pace.

Who were they? Could they be head-hunters? Would they kill her? They were not the sort of excited natives she had seen when landing in India. Then they had surrounded the plane with childlike enthusiasm at seeing the white man's bird come down from the sky.

These were men of a different stamp altogether. She found something immeasurably sinister in the deliberate way they walked. She took a step towards the cockpit to reach the pistol strapped to the side of her seat. Then she remembered. It only had six shots in the cylinder and there were three times as many men here. She couldn't shoot them all, and even if she could, more were probably waiting in the trees. She would have to face them.

They approached slowly. Their arms and bare legs

507

were tattooed with intricate blue patterns. They all had grave, sombre faces.

'I am English,' she said desperately. 'I am English. I do not mean to harm you. I come in peace.'

Could they understand the language? Somewhere in the plane's papers she had phrase books for all the countries over which she'd pass. But what country was this? What language did they speak? Burmese? Hindustani? Chinese? She had no idea.

They stopped about twenty feet away and then one, taller than the rest, holding a drawn sword in one hand, came towards her. He stopped a few feet from her and stood, staring at her. She stared back, feeling this could not be happening. It was a dream, one of the nightmares she had endured on the journey when she slept for a few hours in strange beds. She smelled petrol and burnt oil from the damaged sparking plug. No, she was not asleep. She was awake and alone and very probably about to die.

The man came on towards her, and then stood, facing her, barely a foot away. With a swift, graceful movement he raised the sword high above his head – and then brought it down so close to Carola's face, she could hear its fine edge hiss through the air. She did not move. If he was going to kill her, she could do nothing to stop him. She felt her headache return, beating heavily in her brain like a madman on a drum.

Abruptly the man threw his sword to one side. It fell on the hard ground with a clatter. Slowly, deliberately, he made the sign of the cross with his right hand. And then he spoke, unbelievably, in English.

'We have been expecting you for many years,' he said quietly. 'Why have you kept us waiting for so long?'

Chapter Twenty-Two

When Richard saw Carola's plane disappear over the rooftops beyond Croydon Airport, he drove back to his flat to ponder on his own future. At school, Mr Compton had stressed to him that before coming to any decision, it was always helpful to put down points for and against on a piece of paper.

Against him was the dismal fact that he was out of work. While Zimbro Cars might not prosper on their own, there was clearly no place for him in the organisation while his brother controlled it. And, looking back, he could not think of any major proposal he had made that had been acted upon. There had been small ones, such as hinging the doors from the front, so they could not swing open dangerously. But these improvements were little more than cosmetic suggestions.

The fact that he possessed a good engineering degree could count against him in the motor industry. As a matter of policy many British motor manufacturers refused to employ people with degrees. They considered such a qualification unnecessary. Graduates could be impractical theorists – ignoring the fact that German polytechnics had been awarding doctorates in engineering since the nineteenth century.

What had he on the positive side? Two ideas which he felt showed great possibilities, but because they would require large investments, he had not even bothered to suggest them to the Zimbro directors.

The first was a variation on the blower. Instead of having it driven by the car or aircraft engine, so causing a loss of power and an increase in petrol consumption, he had worked out a scheme to drive it by a fan set into the exhaust system. At present, exhaust gases just went out into the air. His idea would mean they could drive a blower with enormous advantages. A blown car engine of one-litre capacity could provide the performance of an unblown engine twice or even three times as large (and attracting two or three times the amount of tax). Initially, he called this an exhaust turbine blower, but the title sounded clumsy. Then he hit on a description he liked: turbo-charger.

The second idea was more complex, but of greater potential. He believed he could produce an engine, again like a turbine, which blew hot air out of a jet in the rear of an aircraft. The jet could propel it without any propeller, and was a modern adaptation of an invention by a Greek scientist, Hero, long before the time of Christ. Hero constructed a small boat in which he placed a boiler leading to a pipe in the stern. Steam under pressure from the boiler blew through this pipe into the water and pushed the little craft along. Truly, Richard thought, as Mr Compton had again said, 'Science is only a series of experiments – one leads to the other.'

He threw down his pencil, walked to the window, and stood looking out, wondering where Carola was now, how she was faring. He wished he could contact her, but that was impossible. She would be in touch as soon as she was able. He was about to turn away from the window and apply himself again to his private profit and loss account, when he saw a Rolls-Royce stop outside the house.

A footman leapt smartly from his seat beside the driver, opened the rear door. Sir James Mannering climbed out, looked up at the house, then marched to the front door. Richard went down to let him in.

'I was told you were here,' said Mannering without preamble. 'I understand your brother has dispensed with your services.'

'Yes, he has.'

'I thought it might be difficult for you to find another job of the same kind,' Mannering continued. 'So I decided to come and see you. It's possible I may be able to help you.'

Richard led him into the kitchen. 'I was just putting down the good and bad points of my situation,' he explained.

Mannering nodded and glanced at the sketches of the new ideas. 'Still drawing, I see.'

'Yes, still drawing.'

'And at some profit, I'm glad to tell you.' Mannering took an envelope from his pocket, handed it to Richard. 'My gallery sold five of your paintings last week at two hundred pounds apiece. After the gallery commission of thirty per cent, here's a cheque for seven hundred.'

'Amazing,' said Richard; he had temporarily forgotten that several of his pictures were in Mannering's gallery.

'If you keep on producing these paintings, Rowlands, their value will increase dramatically. More and more collectors will want them. One day you will be a rich man. But that is not the help I have in mind for you now. I have the highest admiration for your abilities as an inventive engineer. And I see from your sketches here you have some new ideas. Please explain them to me, remembering that I am not an engineer. If you can make me understand their complexities, I can explain them to others equally lacking in mechanical understanding.'

Richard told him about his two proposals.

Mannering questioned him closely about the availability of metal capable of withstanding the tremendous temperatures and pressures involved, about research costs and possible firms sufficiently advanced technically to construct prototypes.

'I will make you a proposition, Rowlands,' he said at last. 'I'd like to offer you a consultancy with Beechwood Gears. Then you need not concern yourself with your day-to-day problems, such as paying the rent or buying food. In addition, I will finance all the research you require for your future projects. I will also pay you a royalty on these two ideas for permission to exploit them commercially. You, in turn, will make over all rights in these devices to me personally, and also the rights in any other inventions or developments that may stem from them. I will patent them to keep at arm's length any possible competitors.'

'Your offer is very fair, Sir James,' Richard replied, 'but I'd like to make you a counter-proposal.'

Mannering smiled. How odd that people with inventive abilities, these artists, so often imagined they could make money. But they had a different sort of brain, a different approach and attitude. Well, he would hear the fellow out.

'Go ahead,' he said.

'As you know, my elder brother, Tobin, inherited the house and lands which my father originally mortgaged to your North London Loan and Mortgage Company. You released my mother of that heavy burden of debt, but my brother remortgaged it so that he could buy the majority shareholding in Zimbro Cars.'

Mannering nodded. He did not think it necessary to explain that this had been his idea. He assumed that Richard either knew or guessed this.

'Well?'

'He is not an engineer and he knows nothing about cars. He's not even interested in them. But he has never missed any opportunity to try and harm me, ever since

512

childhood, and as you know, one of his first decisions in control has been to fire me. What happens if Zimbro fails, as I believe it may?'

'I would then foreclose on your family home and sell it to the highest bidder. The terms of the agreement allow my company to do this if any mortgage repayments are a month overdue.'

'You have just offered me a royalty on my two designs, which could prove extremely valuable to you over the years. I propose that you do not pay me any royalty whatever. I am willing to waive all rights to the jet engine and what I call the turbo-charger, in return for you giving me the house where I was born and spent my childhood should my brother default.'

Mannering shook his head slowly. 'An interesting suggestion, Rowlands, but not really practical. That is a valuable property.'

'Nothing like so valuable as these two designs.'

'Then why are you prepared to sell yourself short?'

'Because I want the house, and this is the only chance I'm likely to get to acquire it.'

Mannering smiled. 'I can understand your feelings. They do you credit. I will consider the matter.'

Even as he spoke, he was thinking that this was like the original double-headed penny. If he foreclosed on the estate, he would probably find it difficult to find a buyer in a hurry. At his rate of interest, Tobin Rowlands would have paid him its value in four or five years. Soon it would owe him nothing. Mannering had made investigations into Tobin's lifestyle. He was drinking heavily; in Mannering's opinion he would not make old bones.

Like Richard, Mannering had no confidence that the Zimbro Car Company would survive and prosper under Tobin's control. Why should it? He had no aptitude for business or for making money; only for spending it, whittling away his capital. In fact, Mannering could easily put about rumours as to the company's financial stability – as he had done to Mrs Blake's broker – and so accelerate its demise. Tobin would then almost certainly come to him for a loan and he could take over the company for a fraction of its worth.

In addition, all profits made from marketing this young man's inventions would be his. He allowed himself an accountant's thin and bloodless smile.

'I think we can work something out, Rowlands,' he said. 'Yes, I think we can.'

Carola stared at the Burmese man in astonishment and disbelief. He stood threateningly, with his companions behind him holding *dahs*, long Burmese knives, and sticks. She took a pace back, leaned against the fuselage of the aircraft. The metal felt reassuringly hot to her hand, warm even through her thick overalls.

'I don't understand you,' she said weakly.

'I will explain,' he said. 'I speak English because I was taught by one of your missionaries. I am a Christian – of a kind.'

'But where am I?' Carola asked him. 'Where is this place? Who are these men with you? Why is the grass cut in the shape of a cross?'

'First, you must come out of the sun. It is too hot to talk here. Come into the shade, and I will tell you.'

'But I've got work to do,' Carola protested. 'I'm flying this aircraft from Rangoon to Chungking.'

'Rangoon I know,' he said. 'I was there as a boy. My father took me. Chungking. Where is that?'

She pointed vaguely towards the jungle, shimmering like a mirage in the heat. 'Over there. My engine, there's something wrong with it. But I can put it right in ten minutes. Will you help me?'

He shook his head.

'You have come to stay with us. It was prophesied you would come. Not that you would leave so soon.'

'Who prophesied it? *Please* help me. Tell me as I work.'

Carola turned, climbed onto the step set into the fuselage to reach for the tool kit in the cockpit. She had several spare sparking plugs. She could be up and away within minutes, as she said, even without this man's help – as long as he didn't hinder her. Then she felt his hand on her back, a gentle hand but firm. Slowly, his fingers gripped her overalls.

'No,' he said. 'These people here have waited a long time for you. So have I.'

'I could come back,' she said desperately. 'I assure you. But I must go now.'

'No,' he repeated more urgently, and tugged at the overalls, pulling her backwards. She jumped down onto the ground or she would have fallen. She realised she would have to go with him. She could not afford to antagonise him.

'All right,' she agreed reluctantly. 'For a short time.'

She followed the men over the stubbly grass of the clearing; it reminded her incongruously of an English field after harvest. Her overalls felt heavy and hot. She was perspiring and felt suddenly sick and weary with reaction to the heat, the disappointment and frustration of being forced to break her journey when she had been doing so well. The whole idiocy of trying to explain to someone who could not or would not understand how important it was for her to go on made her want to scream, to shout.

But then, she thought, trying desperately to rationalise and see some positive points in her situation, if she was unlucky in having engine failure, at least she was lucky in that she had made a safe landing. These people, whoever they were, appeared to be friendly. They would let her

515

go eventually, she was sure of that – or so she kept telling herself.

They reached the jungle and within two paces had left the bright sunshine behind them. They were now in a deep green world, where thick flat leaves and long, curving fronds filtered the sunlight. The air felt stale and damp from rotting vegetation; sweat poured off her as she tried to keep up with the leader. He and his companions walked quickly and silently. She became very conscious of the noise her own shoes made on the floor of dead leaves, while they moved without a sound.

They reached a small clearing where a number of *bashas*, bamboo huts on poles, had been built in a circle. Beneath the huts stood tethered goats. Chickens scratched in the earth. A few thin and scabby dogs lay watching them arrive with yellow, wary eyes. Several huts had fires burning outside them and women, wearing the traditional *longgyis* of vivid cloth, crouched round cooking pots. Some were smoking cheroots. The sight suddenly reminded Carola of Lady Warren, and despite her worry, she smiled. What would Lady Warren say if she could see her now?

Several children, who had been playing, now ran to be close to their mothers at the approach of a stranger. The man walked to a *basha* slightly apart from the rest, climbed up a primitive staircase of bamboo poles. It led to a verandah with a roof of slatted bamboo. A child was playing here with a set of wooden bricks painted different colours. A woman came out of a back room and spoke to the man sharply. She ignored Carola.

'My wife,' the man explained. 'She speaks little English. She will give you food. You will stay with us.'

Carola bowed to the woman. 'Thank you,' she said as politely as she could. Food was the last thing she wanted, but she must not risk offending anyone.

Two younger women brought out a wooden stool and a

small bamboo table. Carola sat down. The woman put a bowl of mangoes and a bowl of water on the table. Carola washed the mangoes in the water and ate them. They were soft and ripe and refreshing. She rinsed her hands and her lips in the water, wiped them on her handkerchief, and began to feel more cheerful.

'Now,' she said. 'Please tell me. Where am I? You are very kind and hospitable to a stranger, but I have very important work elsewhere. People are expecting me. Do not think me rude if I leave, but you must understand.'

He shook his head. 'You will not leave,' he said simply. 'It was prophesied that a saviour would come from the skies.'

'I am not a saviour,' she said. 'Look, I am English. I am a flier.'

He nodded. 'Sometimes we have seen flying machines like yours high up in the sky, going west or north. We never thought one would land.'

'Why have you cut a cross out of the jungle?'

'The cross is the sign of salvation,' he explained. 'Years ago, a missionary came here. He told me about a different god from the one I was brought up to worship. This new god had a son born on earth. But people did not believe this son was the Son of God, who said He could save them from their sins and give them life eternal.

'They did not believe Him, so they nailed Him on a cross, which has become the symbol of His faith and His teaching. The missionary told me that one day this man would return. He had ascended to heaven after He was crucified. So when He returns He must come down to earth from heaven. I was the only one who believed what the missionary said. I am the son of the head man in this village.'

'Is your wife Christian?'

'No. She is an Animist.'

'What do they believe in?'

'Spirits. Our ancestors come back and help us. Sometimes they may hinder us, much as they would if they were still alive. There are spirits of trees, mountains and rivers, spirits of earth and sky, even of animals. Animists worship these spirits by sacrifice or maybe by leaving a twig, a leaf, a flower at some sacred place. No one ever cuts down tall trees in this area, particularly banyan trees. Spirits live in big trees, and most banyans house at least one. If you look around this village, you will see stakes with the skulls of animals impaled on them. They are sacrifices or they mark a grave and have a special significance.'

'But Christ was a man,' said Carola earnestly. 'I'm a woman. I could not possibly have come from heaven. I am only a traveller, a voyager. Just as you travel on land or by canoe or sampan on the rivers, some people in the West travel in the air. I assure you, that is all I am. I am not important to you – or to anyone. Please let me go.'

Suddenly Carola felt sick. She ran to the edge of the balcony and vomited over the side. She came back flushed, perspiring, dizzy, and sat down.

'Forgive me,' she said weakly. 'I am not well.'

'I know that sickness,' he said. 'You are with child.'

Carola looked at him, shock at his understanding showing in her eyes.

'You see? You do not deny it. You have brought the child of Christ to be born again, as he was born of Mary, long ago.'

'You are wrong!' Carola shouted despairingly. 'I tell you, you're wrong. Totally wrong!'

And then reaction overcame her. She leaned over the table and wept bitterly.

The Government House teleprinter in Rangoon was kept in a small office on the first floor overlooking an ornamental lake. Above it, a ceiling fan beat the humid air with long, slow, deliberate strokes. The Anglo-Burmese operator sat reading a newspaper and picking his teeth with a sharpened sliver of bamboo. He was going off duty at five o'clock that afternoon. In Rangoon, the hours from one o'clock until five each afternoon were generally reserved for more pleasurable activities than work, but still someone had to be on duty, and the clerks took this unpopular shift in turns.

As he glanced at his watch, counting the minutes before his relief arrived, the teleprinter unexpectedly began to chatter. He stood up, watched the strip of paper move jerkily over the roller.

It was from the Air Attaché in Chungking.

NO SIGN YET OF CAROLA MARSH'S AIRCRAFT STOP ASSUMING SHE KEPT ORIGINAL TAKE-OFF TIME FOLLOWING AGREED COURSE SHE IS NOW TWO HOURS OVERDUE STOP HAVE YOU ANY NEWS QUERY MESSAGE ENDS

He tore off the length of paper and took it through to the Chief Clerk.

'No reply,' the Chief Clerk told him. 'The Air Force telephoned us after she had taken off from Mingaladon Airfield. Weather reports were all okay. She's probably run into a head wind and will arrive later. Anyhow, there's nothing at all we can do about it here.'

The tall Burmese, whose name was Laung San, arranged accommodation for Carola in his house. This was simply a part of a larger room, walled off by strips of slatted bamboo woven tightly. His wife and another woman made up a simple bed for her on the floor. Carola slept badly that first night, but finally weariness overcame worry. The sun was well up above the trees that ringed the compound when she awoke.

The same two women brought her a shallow bamboo bath. Carola washed, dried herself on a rough towel, ate a breakfast of mangoes, two small hard-boiled eggs, a cup of bitter tea without milk or sugar. She decided then, feeling rested, and sitting on the verandah watching the children play in the dust, that she must escape as soon as possible. Every day, every hour she stayed here was time wasted, and each delay could make it more difficult to leave. She might be put under guard or moved elsewhere; she had to go now, while she was still within walking distance of her aircraft.

She took off her mother's wristwatch, put it on the table, turned the figure of twelve towards the sun so that she could set the watch as a compass. North lay roughly over a hill, towards two peaks at an unknown distance beyond the trees. She should be heading roughly north-north-east for Chungking. Now at least she knew the direction she must take. When she was airborne she might not have time to set the compasses at once, but now she could just take off and head slightly to the right of the mountains.

She had no possessions, for she had not brought anything from the plane. She heard a loud banging of metal bowls and basins under the *basha*. A cooking fire had already been lit. Chickens were squawking and clucking at the smoke as she went down the steps, walked across the dusty centre of the village and towards her aircraft.

No one stopped her; she did not look back. She walked slowly, without any appearance of haste or flight, as if she was simply taking a morning stroll. Ahead of her, through the jungle and across the paddy, her aeroplane stood at the end of the cross-shaped runway. The morning sun was sending bright reflected messages from its polished metal. She paused for a moment to see whether anyone else was in sight, but the clearing appeared deserted.

Carola took a deep breath, closed her eyes to try and steady the beating of her heart, and then set out through the grass to the plane. As she reached it, she fought a panic instinct to climb up into it at once, and instead forced herself to walk round it. She had a horrible fear that someone might have set a booby-trap inside the cockpit, probably something primitive like a piece of bent bamboo that could discharge a dart, but she had no way of knowing until she was inside.

She put one foot into the inset step, heaved herself up into the cockpit. She sat on the hot leather seat for a moment, wishing that she was already airborne. Then she leaned behind the seats for the tool kit. Her fingers searched slowly, then frantically to touch the familiar box, but it was not there. Neither was the pistol that had been clipped to the side of the seat. Oh well, she couldn't blame the villagers for removing them. She probably would have done the same in their position. She glanced at the instruments. At least nothing had been moved here. Then some instinct made her run her hand behind the metal dashboard. All the wires and capillary tubes that led to the gauges and thermometers had been cut and were hanging loosely. The plane would never fly now without the most major overhaul, which was quite beyond her ability to undertake.

Carola sat for a minute, bewildered by her discovery, her mouth dry. She felt a constriction grow in her chest as though she was being bound by tightening steel bonds. She leaned back against the padded headrest and tried to weep, but she could only choke. Then she heard a noise, and opened her eyes. Laung San had climbed up on the inset step and stood looking at her. He shook his head sadly.

'You are our guest,' he said. 'I told you, you are

staying here. This will never fly again. You will never leave us. Now, come back where you belong.'

Carola screamed then, beating her fists on the dash, on the hot perspex windows.

'No! No! Let me go!' she cried. 'You've no right to do this! I've never harmed you! *Let me go!*'

He waited patiently until she stopped screaming and then leaned over into the cockpit and physically hauled her out.

Carola collapsed on the ground and lay, crumpled in a coil, near the left landing wheel. And then she saw with horror something she had not noticed before. Both tyres had been cut savagely. The tops of the tyres, out of the grass, seemed perfect, but underneath they had been slashed with knives. The grass had concealed this from her. Such damage would be impossible to repair anywhere. She knew now she would never be able to fly away. Never, never, never.

Lady Warren stretched out in her hammock, pushing herself gently from side to side with a long stick. Tom sat in a wicker chair beside her. A half empty bottle of whisky and a siphon of soda were on a table between them. From time to time he added more whisky to the drink already in his glass.

'Don't just sit there drinking,' said Lady Warren irritably. '*Do* something. Find out what's happening.'

'There's nothing more we can do,' he replied shortly. 'You know that quite well. At your suggestion I asked the editor of the *Enquirer* to alert his correspondents and stringers along the route to keep us informed of her progress, on the understanding that the newspaper has exclusive rights to her story at a bargain price. There has been nothing since she left Rangoon. She hasn't arrived in Chungking. In fact, she hasn't been seen anywhere. The paper cabled their stringers in Mandalay and

Bangkok, but neither had heard any report of an aircraft missing or crashed.'

'It's a week since we heard from Rangoon,' said Lady Warren, lighting a cheroot. 'There *must* be someone somewhere who has seen her come down. You can't just disappear in an aeroplane.'

'You can in Burma. Look at the map. It's all jungle under her flight path. No white person has ever crossed it on land. There are no roads, no tracks. She could be anywhere if she landed there.'

Lady Warren nodded reluctant agreement. 'What about sending out a search party? Why don't we use troops? I have contacts at the War Office. We must have at least one regiment in Burma. Probably more. I could give a subscription to some regimental charity if they would stir themselves.'

'Impossible,' Tom replied firmly. 'If Carola had strayed only a couple of degrees off course, that's fifty miles on the ground. Fifty miles, in one direction alone, to cut their way through the forest. It just can't be done.'

'So we just leave her.'

'What would you suggest, Tony?'

'I went to a clairvoyant after she took off. She has always been pretty reliable in the past. She said Carola would be all right. Up to a point, so I gathered.'

'Up to what point?'

Lady Warren shrugged. 'They can't be precise, these people. But Elvira was certain she would not die on the flight, would not be killed.'

'In that case,' said Tom, pouring himself more whisky, 'we have no need to worry. We just sit and wait and hope. Maybe you should see the clairvoyant again. She might have more news.'

'On the other hand, she might not. Sarcasm, I was taught at school, is the wit of fools. When I first met you, I thought you were just another rather dim Aussie. Then

523

you rose in my estimation. Now you're beginning to fall again. I'm not going to approach the spirit world a second time while we have people in this world who can help.'

'Who exactly do you have in mind?'

'The Air Minister. Let's start at the top. He must know *something*. Or if he doesn't, he must know someone who does, or who can be ordered to find out.'

'It would help if we could publicise her disappearance.'

'Not so. Just who would it help? Certainly not Carola. If we put out a news story that she's missing, it would only diminish her standing as a potential record breaker. If we knew she was quite safe, and over the halfway mark, say on the leg over the Pacific, I agree we could then release the news and describe all the terrible experiences she's been through. But not when we don't know a damned thing about where she is or what has happened to her.'

Carola made her second attempt to escape at dawn next day. Since she could not fly away, she would have to walk, and the longer she delayed, the more difficult it might be to leave. Her pregnancy would advance. She might fall ill and be unable to leave. She had best go now, while she felt fit, and try to reach some small town or village with a British resident or official who could help her.

At the back of her mind was also the growing fear that every day, every week wasted would make her pregnancy more difficult to keep secret. Laung San had already guessed she was pregnant. It was wisest to go now.

She decided to leave at dawn, because that would give her an hour or two's start on any pursuit Laung San might send after her. She could not leave at night because she was afraid of the dangers the jungle might hold. She had read somewhere that man-eating tigers and other predators sought their prey at night, then gorged themselves and slept through the daylight hours. And she would never find her way without a light or a guide. Since she was totally unarmed and on her own, to travel by day was really her only option.

She had never had any difficulty with early rising because she had made so many early flights from different airfields in England, and at four o'clock she was awake.

She found a track that led into the jungle. It was matted with creepers that tripped her in the gloom, but as the sun came up and shone down between the trees, she made better time. She regularly checked her bearings by her mother's watch, concerned in case she was walking in a circle. Her canvas shoes were not meant for walking any distance, and her feet began to blister and then to bleed. Dust rasped like sandpaper between her toes. She sat down and bathed them in what she thought was a stream, but then she realised that it was a narrow inlet from a shallow river fifty yards wide. As she stared, she saw two crocodile eyes looking up at her from the water, unwinking, assessing her. She quickly hobbled away. She sat down and dried her feet with her handkerchief, enjoying a moment of relief, feeling air cool between her toes before she put on her shoes again, and set off.

The jungle was thicker now, and the sun that shone through the lattice of leaves felt very hot. By noon she was exhausted, and had to stop and rest. She moved off the narrow path and lay down.

For a moment she felt relaxed, almost at ease, and then she felt sudden pinpricks in her feet, her legs, her hands. She sat up quickly. She was swarming with red ants, each half an inch long. Their bodies glistened like polished rubies. She had lain down near an anthill. She jumped up, tearing at them, trying to rub her clothes against her body to kill them as their tiny sharp claws dug painfully into her flesh.

She must keep moving. It was not safe to lie down. And now as she walked she suddenly and horribly became aware that others were walking on either side of her, keeping pace with her. She could not see anyone, but she sensed they were there. They did not seem to need a path as she needed one. The jungle was their home; it held no terrors for them, no pitfalls.

She hurried, and so did they. She still could not see them; only now and then she heard a faint crackle of bare feet on broken twigs and dried leaves.

Was her imagination playing tricks? Was she going mad? Her heart was beating very fast. She stopped and closed her eyes wearily; the chequered sunlight shone blood-red against her eyelids. She felt she could not go any further. She had no idea where she was, let alone where she was going. She sat down against a tree.

She must have slept, for when she awoke she saw bare brown feet, bare brown legs, standing round her in a circle. She looked up hesitantly. Several men surrounded her. Laung San looked down at her.

'You were foolish to try to escape,' he said gently. 'I told you, you will stay with us. Do not ever attempt to leave us again.'

The Air Minister liked to drink a mug of hot sweet cocoa at eleven o'clock precisely every morning. He sat now in his padded leather armchair in his office, blowing on the drink to cool it. He hated to be interrupted in this ritual, and frowned when his private secretary came into the room.

'Sorry to disturb you, Minister, but Lady Warren is waiting downstairs to see you.'

'I've told you, I can't see anyone,' the Minister told

him. He tested the heat of the cocoa by sipping a teaspoonful. 'I'm too busy. You deal with the matter, whatever it is she wants. She can be a pest, that woman.'

'I agree and so I think, Minister, it would be prudent if you could spare time to see her. She's a very determined person. I know you don't follow the financial news closely, sir, but she has just acquired a controlling interest in the *Enquirer* newspaper chain. It would be more advantageous to have that group on our side than not.'

'Clearly. I fully appreciate that. But what does she want to see me about?'

'She says a friend of hers is missing in a private plane on a flight overseas.'

'How can I possibly help with a private matter? Has she tried the Foreign Office? They look after our citizens overseas, not the Air Ministry.'

'I think there may be more in this than that. I would advise, Minister, that you give her just a few moments.'

'Oh well, if you insist. Have her shown up. But let me finish this first.'

He drank the cocoa quickly. It was hot and burned his tongue. He was therefore in an irritable frame of mind when Lady Warren was shown in.

She glanced at photographs of biplanes and bombers on the walls, at his elegant desk, the leather chairs, the burnished fireplace.

'It is good of you to see me at such short notice,' she said. 'And I assure you I won't take up much of your time.'

'It is always a pleasure to see you, Lady Warren. How can I help you?'

'A friend of mine, Carola Marsh, took off from Croydon in a single-seater aeroplane two weeks ago. She flew by way of Constantinople, Basra, Karachi, Calcutta and Rangoon. Royal Air Force personnel at our bases on her route gave her every help and co-operation. In due course, I will instruct the editors of the *Enquirer* group to praise their efficiency and helpfulness.

'From Rangoon she set off to fly on to Chungking, but she never arrived. I want to know what happened to her. Where the hell is she? Did she crash? Did she land in some remote place? Was she blown off course, and came down in Siam? Is she alive or dead? You have the facilities to find out, Minister. I do not. So I ask your help.'

The Air Minister nodded. A few puffs from the press could only be useful to him. He picked up his internal telephone, asked for any relevant information to be brought in at once. A young man came into the room carrying a buff folder which he laid on the Minister's desk. He opened it, glanced at the decoded telegrams inside.

'Here are all the details at each stop, as you say, Lady Warren, but nothing at all after Rangoon. Our Air Attaché in Chungking telexed Rangoon to report that Miss Marsh never arrived. There is nothing from our Air Attaché in Bangkok, so presumably she has not landed over the Siamese border.'

'What do you think has happened?' asked Lady Warren.

'She must have come down elsewhere, in the jungle. At this time of year, before the monsoon, air currents in that part of the world are hazardous and quite unpredictable. There is of course a good chance she has landed safely in a paddy field. In such a situation, friendly natives would go to the nearest British presence. A rescue party could then be sent out, but it might take time to reach Miss Marsh through the jungle.'

'Do you think it's likely that this is what happened?' asked Lady Warren.

The Air Minister shrugged. 'We can only hope,' he

said sanctimoniously. 'Hope and pray.'

Elsewhere in the Air Ministry, Sir James Mannering sat with a silver-topped cane between his knees in a room outside the office of the Principal Scientific Officer. The clerk had explained very apologetically that the officer concerned, a Cambridge professor on loan from his college, had been unavoidably delayed for the appointment because he was driving and a lorry had overturned, blocking the main Cambridge to London road.

Mannering nodded understandingly. He was free for the next two hours, and he might as well sit in this pleasant quiet room as elsewhere. And if he did not show annoyance, if he appeared sympathetic and full of understanding, the professor must warm to him and perhaps be more receptive to the proposition he had come to make.

He stretched his legs, fingered his beard, and thought how odd it was that, looking back, so many of his more successful negotiations with the government of one country or another had involved weapons that depended on speed. First had been the submarine, moving silently and swiftly beneath the surface of the sea to deliver an unexpected and lethal blow by torpedo.

Then came the device to allow a fighter pilot to fire bullets through the blades of a propeller without harming them. And now, from the mind of the designer who had worked out that complex device, he had another proposition: for an engine to power an aircraft without a propeller and make it fly far faster than any aircraft with one. The spirit of inventiveness, the speed of a projectile: these were two essential ingredients of every weapon, and he had brokered more than he could easily recall. The spirit and the speed; he liked the sound of the phrase.

The Principal Scientific Officer eventually arrived, breathless and flustered. He was older than Mannering had expected, and nearly bald, with wisps of hair he kept smoothing down across his scalp.

'My apologies, Sir James,' he began nervously. He knew how influential his visitor was, and how ruthless; a few harsh words from him could ruin his career.

'Say no more,' said Mannering magnanimously. 'I have been enjoying the relaxed atmosphere of this elegant room, something out of a more spacious age than ours. It is difficult for me to appreciate that this is one of the main dynamos of progress in our country's fight for air supremacy.'

'Quite so, quite so. I often feel that way myself, Sir James. Please come into my office.'

The professor sat down at his desk, took two keys from a gold chain at his waistcoat, unlocked two locks on a drawer. Then he took out a folder, glanced briefly at its contents.

'So, you have come to see me about your proposal for a new type of propulsion for aircraft,' he said.

Mannering nodded. 'I have. The original drawings and specifications have been in the possession of your office for some weeks. Apart from a formal acknowledgement, I have heard nothing further. So, knowing the amount of work you have on hand, I made an appointment to come and see you personally to discover your opinion.'

The professor closed the folder, put his elbows on it, and looked earnestly at his visitor. He did not like the man. He did not trust him. He had checked his background and decided with distaste that Mannering was one of too many originally stateless and rootless financiers who carried several passports and seemed to float about the world, offering – at a price – propositions for new weapons of war to any buyer, without regard to possible consequences.

How these men acquired these designs, he had no idea, but they did, and seemingly very easily. The professor personally believed that implements of mass destruction should only be manufactured in government factories. But when he voiced these opinions, he was sharply reminded that the only weapons of war ever designed and produced under such conditions in Britain had been the pike and the lance. Every other weapon had been the product of private enterprise, and often the most useful had been the most difficult to persuade governments to accept.

Mannering was a dangerous man, then, but his propositions had always been viable in the past, even if the British had not accepted them – until they saw them taken up by another and potentially hostile country. He must be treated with the greatest courtesy and circumspection. A word out of place, any hint of implied criticism could be disastrous.

'I am very glad you have made time to come and see me personally,' the professor began. 'I was intending to get in touch with you later this week. I was hoping to arrange for senior officers of Fighter Command to be present so that they could explain their views to you themselves.'

'Does that mean you are not in favour of the proposition?' asked Mannering quickly.

'On the contrary, sir, we are very much in favour of it, but the fact is that scientists all over the world, as with people of other creative abilities such as painters and writers, often reach similar conclusions at the same time, although they may be thousands of miles apart and not in contact with each other, may never even have heard of each other.'

Mannering inclined his head slightly to signify that he accepted the point.

'One of our serving officers, Flight Lieutenant Frank Whittle, a brilliant man of whom the Royal Air Force holds such a high opinion that they sponsored him at

Cambridge, put up a very similar proposition about what we may loosely call a jet engine some years ago. We took a keen interest in his invention. It has undergone initial tests that are most promising, and we are committed to his design. In these circumstances, I am sure you will understand that we could not possibly become involved with a competing project.'

Mannering shrugged his shoulders. These things did happen, he knew, but not often, and so far in his career never to him. However, in the past, when one buyer had lost interest or been unable to pay his price, he had always found another. What really mattered was that now he knew the idea was sound and not simply the dream of an inventive brain.

'I quite appreciate your situation, Professor,' he said casually, as though the decision was not of any personal importance to him. 'I have spent a great deal of my own money on research into this project, and I simply wished to offer it first to this country.'

'It is much appreciated, Sir James. And I am sure you will be very careful if you consider any other market. I most earnestly hope you will not offer it to Germany. The political climate between Germany and ourselves seems bleak at the moment, and worsening all the time.'

'I would not do business on this with Germany. Please rest assured on that point.' He didn't give a damn about the political relations between Britain and Germany, but the stories that were beginning to emerge about the treatment of Jews in Germany were another matter. Whatever else he'd managed to shed with regard to his background, he was still a Jew.

'Good. I may say in confidence that all my scientific colleagues and the Air Force officers consulted speak very highly of your invention.'

'Is it better than the one you are already working on?'

'I would not say that. Ours is in a more advanced state,

532

but your designer, Mr . . .' he opened the folder, glanced at the name on the front page, 'Rowlands, appears to be a person of very rare talent.'

'I share that view. Perhaps you could give me back the plans I left with you. I will then wish you good day and the very best of success with your own project.'

Thirty kilometres beyond Bordeaux, the main road divided left and right. Mannering's driver took the right fork, signposted to Langon. Within minutes the road narrowed and they were driving along a lane with high grass verges. On either side forests stretched thick and silent. The road was quite deserted.

'Slowly,' ordered Mannering from the back of the car. He did not wish to miss the hotel, which he had been informed was small, more a restaurant with rooms than an hotel. For this journey he had left his Rolls behind. Instead, he was in a small Hillman coupé. His driver did not wear livery, but a brown sports jacket and grey flannel trousers. They could be two men of indefinite age travelling abroad together, not a multi-millionaire and his chauffeur/bodyguard.

Above the beards of grass at the roadside, giant butterflies swooped and fluttered. There was an atmosphere of space and emptiness about the area that impressed Mannering, although he did not like it. He always feared that long grass could conceal enemies, waiting for him. He felt safer in crowded places where someone else's body could conceivably take a bullet or a knife meant for him.

They came into the village. Outside a blacksmith's shop on the left a huge horse waited patiently to be shod. Then came a bakery with a Citröen van being loaded with long bread rolls, and then the hotel.

His driver parked on a patch of ground beside the hotel terrace. In the shade of a trellis along which vines had been trained were half a dozen tables laid with red tablecloths. The scene had an agreeable ambience, like a living advertisement for a French wayside restaurant, miles in the country.

Mannering climbed out of the car, walked into the hotel. The entrance hall felt cool and sheltered after the heat of the open road.

'My name is James Miller,' he told the receptionist in French, and produced a passport in that name. He always chose pseudonyms with his own initials. Then if anyone distrusted him and searched his luggage they would find these initials on his silk shirts and handkerchiefs. 'You have two rooms booked in my name?'

'We do, monsieur.'

'Good. I am expecting to meet a gentleman from Saigon, Monsieur François Vallon.'

'He is already here, monsieur. Shall I send someone for your bags?'

'Thank you. My companion is outside with them. Please see he has a room close to mine.'

The clerk handed over a key with the number 18 engraved on a brass tag. A young girl in a white blouse and black skirt led him up a curved staircase to a long corridor. Number 18 was at the end. The room had double windows that opened inwards, and overlooked the main street.

All the windows in the houses opposite were shuttered to keep out the glare of the afternoon sun. In any new and unknown place, Mannering always had the fear that someone with a hidden camera might photograph him, but here the risk seemed slight. Even so, he drew the net curtains. Then he poured water from a jug into a metal bowl, washed his face and hands. He combed his hair and beard carefully, picked up his slim briefcase and went downstairs to find the man he had come to meet.

A youngish man in casual clothes was sitting in the far

corner of the lounge, reading an evening paper. On the wall above him hung heads of various animals with antlers and horns. Stuffed fish, mouths open as though still amazed they had been hooked, watched them with glass eyes from heavily varnished frames.

'James Miller!' cried the man, coming towards Mannering as though he was an old friend. They had, in fact, never met before. 'You are on time, as always.' He spoke in French.

'My dear fellow,' replied Mannering also in French. 'How wonderful to see you after all this time. Come outside. The sun is so agreeable after the English weather.'

The basic recognition phrases spoken and answered, they sat down at a table under the trellis. Vallon wore dark glasses. His face was sallow, unhealthy. Close to, he seemed no more Indo-Chinese than Mannering was English. Mannering instantly put him down as Japanese and wondered what his real name was, whether he was here on his own or had someone with him, watching them both. Mannering pushed the thought aside. He must be getting old to worry about such things. They never used to bother him so much in the past. But then the stakes were lower, and the dangers so very much less; and he was younger, much younger. The older one grew the more cautious one became.

'I understand from my people in London you have something of interest for my firm,' said Vallon.

'I hope so. We have done business in the past, if at one or two removes, with various mechanisms I trust your company found useful. This is something quite different. It is the most important design I have ever handled. In brief, it concerns an engine that can power an aircraft so that it flies without any propeller and at speeds far greater than any propeller aircraft has ever achieved.'

'Have you offered it to our British friends?'

535

'They are not interested.'

'They have tried it?'

'They have examined it.'

'Then why are they not interested if it is as revolutionary as you claim?'

'Simply because their company is working on a similar project of their own.'

'Is that far advanced?'

'No. Only in its early stages. You know how it always is with the English. So many committees and subcommittees to examine every step. It will be years before they have anything like this in actual production. I can assure you of that. I have, of course, patented my design in every country in the world.'

The younger man smiled. 'You think we would make use of it without paying?'

'Of course not,' Mannering assured him smoothly. 'But one has to protect oneself. You understand?'

'Of course. What is the price?'

'Two million American dollars. In Geneva.'

'And for this we get?'

'All working drawings, the entire plans. I have some blueprints and test reports here for you to show to your colleagues.'

'Thank you. I may have to keep them for some time. My principals do not live in France.'

'How long do you want them for?'

'I would say a month.'

'Agreed. Thirty days from today.' Mannering took out a diary, ringed the date.

'And then it may be necessary for you to meet my principals, Mr Miller.'

'I would be pleased to do so. Where?'

'Possibly Saigon. Or more likely Hong Kong.'

'That would not be a problem. I have an office there.'

'So. You are staying here for long, Mr Miller?'

'Just for this one night. I am travelling with a friend. We are going on to Paris. And you?'

'I also leave tomorrow. I have some business in Geneva. Then I go home. But now we have met after so long, let us enjoy our stay here. I find there is so little time to relax in my job.'

'I feel the same,' Mannering agreed.

After Carola's second attempt to escape was foiled, she realised she had to stay where she was for the simple and terrible reason that she had no choice.

She consoled herself with the thought that there must be a chance that some missionary or British official might visit this village, or maybe, although much more unlikely, a British army patrol on manoeuvres, or even perhaps some expedition intent on surveying a new route for a railway or a road.

Several weeks passed before she accepted just how faint any of these possibilities were. As far as she could tell, the village had no visitors at all. There was no navigable river near it, there were no proper roads, no way out – or in. She was a prisoner, locked in an unknown land.

More weeks passed before she could finally bring herself to admit that she had lost all hope of making a round-the-world flight. Someone else would do it, of course. Amelia Earhart had announced she would like to be first. Now no one was standing in her way.

At first, Carola spent her time brooding, churning in her mind for some miracle to release her. The locals treated her with courtesy, but coolness. Whatever impact the visiting missionary had made on Laung San, he had not made much on anyone else.

Laung San's father, the head man, lay ill and never left his *basha*. From the symptoms Laung San described to her, Carola thought that his father must be suffering from some form of cancer. He was thin and shrivelled, his hair had fallen out, so that he felt humiliated, and did not wish any of his people to see him in this condition. He had visited Rangoon on several occasions, however, and had no such aversion to Carola visiting him. She began to care for him. She bathed his emaciated body. She rubbed his back and buttocks with petrol from her aircraft to try and harden the skin against bed sores. She did what she could to lessen the pain and discomfort of being confined to bed in a hot bamboo hut.

As weeks became months, Carola began to help the women with the cooking and cleaning. She started to learn the language, and when she tried to speak it, and they laughed at her and corrected her pronunciation, she learned more.

Within six months Carola could speak Burmese and understand what others said. But to write it, with all the squiggles of the vernacular script, was beyond her and she never attempted to master this. Subconsciously, she felt that to do so would be to admit she might never get away.

As the time drew near for her to have her child, the women attended her. She was given a larger room in the house, and they brought small clothes, shirts and skirts they had made, and gave them to her.

She felt touched by their friendliness and concern, and in turn she told them that their menfolk should take any parts of the aircraft they might find useful. They were doing this in any case, without her permission, but at least this showed she wished to share her few possessions with them.

Now the clock from the dashboard ticked on a wooden shelf in her room. Elsewhere, pieces of the wing had been cut up with hacksaws from her tool kit to make scoops for rice. Pipes and tubes had been filed and bent and sharpened into fish hooks. Even the engine and blower were removed to become the bottom step on a bamboo ladder leading up to the verandah of the old chief's house.

Curiously, Carola felt none of the loneliness she had often felt in Lady Warren's house, being part of that establishment and yet not of it. Here, where she was really a prisoner, she also felt freer.

Her son was born at five o'clock on a Thursday. She knew it was Thursday because she had diligently marked off in her diary each day since her arrival. When she had finished one year, she intended to start another. This thought made her weep. How many more years would she spend incarcerated here, forgotten by everyone at home? A lifetime loomed ahead, each day dripping away in the heat, for no purpose whatever, nothing achieved.

Frequently, she remembered Winston Churchill at the Alcock and Brown lunch at the Savoy, explaining how a speck of dirt in the carburettor, a drop of oil on a plug could so easily have brought down their aircraft. How ironic to reflect that an equally simple failure had brought down hers!

The birth was much less painful and complex than Carola had imagined. Women of the village were with her and had explained what exercises they took, which herbs they infused into tea, which roots they boiled to chew against the pains of labour. Thursday's child has far to go, she thought, looking down at the pink, wrinkled baby in her arms. She hoped it was true. She hoped, against all probability, that one day he could travel to England – with her.

Chapter Twenty-Three

Lady Warren prided herself on never giving up easily, never retreating when advance of any kind was possible.

Although she received further negative reports about Carola's whereabouts from the Air Ministry and the Royal Air Force, she did not despair of discovering what had happened, and whether Carola was alive or dead. And if she was alive, she intended to use all her wealth and influence to rescue her.

The *Enquirer* newspaper chain maintained a full-time correspondent in Rangoon. Lady Warren instructed the editors that the man should be given unlimited expenses to discover what had happened to someone she always carefully described as a 'young friend'. But despite this, he could produce nothing more substantial than rumours that some Burmese somewhere had seen a plane come down. Exactly where, no one appeared able to say.

Lady Warren organised what she called a botanical expedition, starting from Mandalay, to go through the jungle in an attempt to find out what had happened. The expedition discovered several new plants and tubers, and some strange and hitherto unknown and unclassified orchids, but no sign whatever of Carola.

There was never any mention in the newspapers of a failed record attempt. The press coverage that Tom had organised on the day Carola flew from Croydon was soon forgotten as attention turned to the American flier,

Amelia Earhart. She made a number of record-breaking flights, and then set off on a highly publicised attempt to fly round the world. She took with her a male navigator, and they flew in a far more sophisticated aircraft than Carola's. It had two engines instead of one, and incorporated the latest radio and direction-finding equipment.

Even so, she did not succeed. Her aircraft disappeared in the Pacific. At once, the Americans launched a huge search operation. Various pearl divers and fishermen claimed they had seen an aircraft come down in the sea. Some said they had actually watched it land safely in shallow water off an island and seen a man and woman come ashore, both wearing trouser suits. Then they disappeared. It was generally thought that the Japanese, who were conducting various surveys of the area, must have assumed they were American spies and shot them.

For Lady Warren, used to success in all her enterprises, the years after Carola's disappearance were years of great and increasing depression. She felt old and impotent and bereft. She had never thought of herself as a motherly person, but now she admitted to herself that Carola had become like a daughter to her. She had cared deeply for her, perhaps even loved her. Lady Warren missed her more than she cared to admit to anyone. She also felt deep regret that she should have been so insistent that Carola must make the flight. This feeling of guilt, quite new to her, increased when she learned from Richard and Tom that Carola had not enjoyed flying, indeed it had terrified her.

'Why didn't she tell me?' Lady Warren asked.

'She saw flying as the only way she could escape from a life without any future,' Richard explained.

'But she was keen enough on flying at the beginning,' Lady Warren insisted. 'She told me so herself.'

'She was keen on the idea,' Richard corrected her. 'The prospect of soaring away from all her problems was very attractive. Reality proved rather different.'

Lady Warren's spirits were not raised by the outbreak of war. Tom had returned to Australia a year previously, taking with him her hundred thousand pounds. Initially, she heard from him from time to time: he was paying off his father's mortgage; things were looking up. But he was not a very good correspondent, and neither was she.

Then Tom returned to Britain, with many other Australians and New Zealanders of his age, to join up. He was too old to fly operationally, but he did find a job as a test pilot.

Two years after the war began, Lady Warren instructed her secretary to find the latest address for Richard. She had not been in touch with him for a long time. Why, she did not know. But then he had not kept in contact with her either. There was no reason why he should, of course, but in her mind she grouped Carola, Tom and Richard together as a kind of team. Tom Gardener, Carola Marsh, Richard Rowlands: different characters, totally disparate personalities, but of the same generation. She cared for them all in different ways.

To Richard's surprise, he had been re-engaged by the Zimbro Car Company shortly after his brother's marriage to Eleanor. He was given a job as a consultant on new products, which he combined with his existing consultancy with Beechwood Gears.

He guessed that Tobin really wanted to have him in this position so that he could shoot down any new proposition he might suggest. And, indeed, Tobin succeeded in doing this very successfully at first. The company, however, was less successful. Eleanor spent more and more time in the States. She admitted to herself, if to no one else, that her marriage to Tobin was disastrous. He had been in love with her money, not with her. And she was not really in love with him, probably never had been.

Tobin, for his part, found to his annoyance and concern that the North London Loan and Mortgage Company had a habit of sending inspectors to examine Zimbro's books. He found their visits as irksome as their interest. He felt that someone behind the company must be needling him – gunning for him, was the phrase he used. The North London Loan and Mortgage Company suggested from time to time that he should borrow more money, and he had done so to pay for new plant, but the interest on these sums became increasingly difficult to repay.

The war proved the temporary saving of Zimbro, as of so many other unsuccessful or moderately successful engineering and car manufacturing companies. Tobin was not in the country when war was declared in September 1939, for he had decided to visit his wife at their family home in Massachusetts the previous month. Passages back to England were difficult to obtain, and Tobin did not go to any great lengths to discover one. He felt it was wiser, and infinitely more comfortable, to keep away from blackouts and rationing and bombing, and the very real possibility of invasion. In his absence, Zimbro acquired new business and kept its creditors at bay. The company built gear boxes for army trucks, parts for aircraft fuselages, panels for tanks.

It was not difficult for Lady Warren's secretary to find Richard. He took her telephone call in his office.

'You haven't heard from me for a long time,' Lady Warren began.

'That makes it all the better to hear from you now,' he told her.

'Don't charm me. But come and see an old woman.'

'Where are you?'

'Where I've always been.'

'I have a little petrol,' he said, for petrol, like food, was strictly rationed. 'I'll be delighted to drive over and see you.'

'When? Are you free tonight?'

'I will make myself free,' he assured her.

So at seven that night Richard was sitting opposite Lady Warren in her study. She was smoking a cheroot, and offered one to him.

'No. Never,' he said.

'I'm glad. They're hard to get now. Come from Burma, you know. And there's not much coming out of there that's good news.'

'Nothing about Carola, certainly.'

'She's dead, poor girl. Must be. I just hope she died quickly. The idea of her crashing and being in pain for days, maybe even weeks, with broken legs or a broken back, in the jungle, is too horrible to contemplate. And I think about it all the time.'

'She was never very keen on flying.'

'So you have told me. I feel guilty about sending her off round the world on her own like that, but there it is. I did what I thought was best at the time. I didn't know she was afraid. She seemed to have enormous potential. I wanted her to realise it. So many people never have the chance. I gave her the chance, but perhaps it was the wrong one.'

She sat for a moment, puffing at her cheroot, looking at the fire. Lady Warren had aged more than her years, Richard thought. She was almost benign now. She pulled herself together with an obvious effort.

'I called you here to give you some bad news.'

'What about?'

'Tom. Tom Gardener.'

'I haven't heard from him for ages. He sent me a card when he arrived back in Australia, but nothing since. How is he?'

'He's dead.'

'How? When?'

'He came back here, you know, and tried to join up.'

'I didn't know. He didn't get in touch with me.'

Lady Warren drew on her cheroot. She had thought of explaining that she had given money to Tom, but decided against it. This would help neither of them, and might even antagonise Richard, for she had never given him money. He didn't look the sort of person who would care whether he had money or not, which was rare, she thought, very rare. But then he was a rare person; as Carola had been; as Tom had been. Three to start and now only one left. She sighed.

'Air crash,' she said brusquely, to hide her feelings. 'He was a test pilot. He was trying out some new and very fast fighter over Salisbury Plain and the engine cut out suddenly. He hadn't the chance to bail out. He was flying too low, anyhow.'

'Poor Tom. He was a good fellow.'

'No. You're wrong. He wasn't a good fellow. He was bad in many ways. But he knew what he wanted. Most people have no idea what they want, except they're envious when they see other people getting what they think they want, but he did, and he wasn't afraid to go for it. He reminded me of myself at his age.'

She suddenly smiled. 'Like me, he thought he would marry money. Sitting in this very room, he proposed marriage to me, you know.'

'*Tom* did?' Richard's amazement sounded in his voice.

Lady Warren nodded. 'I turned him down, needless to say. I'm old enough to have been his mother, though I'm damn glad I wasn't.'

Richard smiled.

'I have the address of his station in Australia,' he said. 'I expect his brother's living there. I think I'll write to him.'

'I'll be doing the same. As you grow old, and you have

children, so I'm told, you hope they'll achieve things you never achieved, but wanted. I never had children, but you three young people were children by proxy. I have lived through all your achievements and setbacks. I never showed what I felt because that's not my way, but I admired you all. Now, before I forget, I have something to give you.'

Lady Warren stood up, opened a small cupboard and took out Richard's toy steam engine.

'Carola gave it to me for safe keeping,' she explained. 'But as I don't think she'll be coming back, I feel I should hand it over to you. It is yours, after all.'

'Thank you.' Richard held the engine in his hands, reading the legend 'The Spirit and the Speed', seeing the copy of his birthmark that Carola had soldered on it – how long ago? It seemed a lifetime.

'Now,' said Lady Warren briskly, 'are you staying to dinner?'

'You haven't invited me.'

'Surely I don't have to invite a friend?'

'Then I'm staying,' said Richard, and leaning over in front of the fire, he kissed the old woman on the cheek.

On the Monday afternoon of the first week of December of that year, 1941, Sir James Mannering stood on the pavement overlooking Causeway Bay in Hong Kong, savouring the warm sun on his face, and the freedom of having escaped from wartime restrictions in London.

A handful of yachts of the Royal Hong Kong Yacht Club bobbed at anchor on the shallow swell, their long frail masts moving like pointers against the cloudless cobalt sky. Sunshine bathed the great buildings facing the bay. The scene here seemed infinitely peaceful, and somehow unreal, an illusion.

Mannering's office was in one of the buildings facing the bay. He always felt attracted by the sea, a constant

547

reminder of the enormous distance he had travelled since he had haunted the docks at Constantinople, touting for brothels. No one now, seeing him in his perfectly pressed linen suit, would ever imagine he had anything but a supremely aristocratic and sheltered background.

Gleaming American cars were being drive slowly past by immaculately uniformed chauffeurs, with rich Chinese and Japanese businessmen in the rear seats. Mannering wondered how they had all started. Were they all – were any – what they seemed?

As Chairman of People's Petroleum Products, Mannering had been given permission from the British War Cabinet to fly to Hong Kong from England, a hazardous undertaking, involving many stops to refuel and rest. The official reason for this long and dangerous journey was to acquire more oil tankers from shipowners in the East. German U-boats were sinking Allied tankers faster than they could be built, but in Hong Kong, so Mannering had assured the War Cabinet, his vast range of contacts would almost certainly be able to provide other ships laid up in swampy inlets.

His real aim, however, was less altruistic; as always, it was to advance his own interests and, after years of delay, conclude the sale of Richard Rowlands' design for a jet aircraft engine.

Following his meeting with François Vallon in France, he had heard nothing, and all attempts to discover where Vallon was now and how his plan to sell the designs to the Japanese was progressing, failed to produce any results whatever. Unaccountably, the man had simply disappeared.

Mannering had toyed with selling the design to the Americans, but they showed little interest. The Italians, like the Germans, he did not wish to approach, and when war broke out he could not do so safely even if he had wanted to. That left the Japanese as the only potential buyers in a world at war.

He knew they were building a huge modern air force. He also knew that Japan represented a grave potential threat to British possessions in the East. But British possessions were not Mannering's possessions, and if he did not sell to the Japanese, he could think of no other buyer who could pay his price.

He had mentioned the project to members of the Japanese Embassy he met at diplomatic parties, but while they expressed polite interest – and he could not explain the invention in detail for obvious reasons – he heard nothing further. Then, quite unexpectedly, he received a letter posted in England. The writer explained that a Mr Mojo wished to discuss the supply of tankers on an informal basis in the headquarters of People's Petroleum Products in Hong Kong. He gave a date and a time. There was no return address. The note was surprising in that it showed that Mr Mojo, whoever he might be, knew about Britain's shortage of tankers – and also because the envelope contained a second plain sheet of paper, without any heading or signature, on which were the words, in a different type, 'This will be a continuation of earlier discussions in Langon, France'.

Mannering assumed that the letter must have arrived in the diplomatic bag, and been posted to him by someone in the Japanese Embassy in London. That way, it would not be opened by the censor, as were all other letters arriving in Britain or going out from it. François Vallon must have passed on his documents to his Japanese principals after all, and now at last Mannering believed he could finalise the deal he had started in the lounge of a French inn years earlier.

He walked slowly along the road, sea on one side, buildings on the other, waiting for a break in the traffic. He crossed the road, went into the PPP building. A

Chinese lift attendant saluted him smartly, took him up to his office on the fifth floor.

Mannering's private secretary here was a Chinese, Mr Ching, a man of indefinite age, perhaps forty, perhaps fifty, one of many underlings who served him around the world and about whom he knew almost nothing. Ching had worked for him in Hong Kong for more than ten years; he was efficient, self-effacing and very loyal.

'We have just had a telex from Mr Mojo in Shanghai,' Ching told him now. 'He very much regrets he cannot keep the appointment he arranged with you.'

'Why not? I've flown halfway round the world to meet him.'

'He is delayed for personal reasons, sir.'

'Personal reasons should never interfere with serious business matters,' said Mannering sharply. 'Does he give another date? Or an address where we can contact him?'

'No, sir. But he says he hopes to arrange a meeting very soon. Here is the telex.'

Mannering read the short message.

'Well, I will just have to await his pleasure. But how did he know I had arrived? He never contacted me to confirm his appointment.'

Mr Ching shrugged. It was not for him to explain to his superior the delicate and complex network of rumour and gossip that surrounded every commercial deal in the East, or to suggest that Hong Kong was a nest of Japanese agents and spies.

Mannering sat down behind his desk. He felt instinctively that something was seriously wrong here, but what, he was not certain. The feeling that the appearance of peace and prosperity in Hong Kong might only be a façade returned more strongly.

'What do you think his reason was?' he asked Ching. After all, the man lived here; he was Oriental; he must understand the Oriental mind.

'The political situation here is very grave, sir, much worse than you may realise. I was surprised when you arrived here. Most Europeans are making plans to leave, if they have not already done so. Japan is about invade Hong Kong and possibly Singapore, and then declare war on the Allies.'

'Are you serious, Mr Ching?'

'Sadly, very much so, sir. Japan adopted the same course against Russia in the early years of the century. Attack first. Win the early battles. Then declare war.'

'But with what in mind now?'

'To seize British and Dutch colonies in the East. And possibly to humiliate the Americans in the Philippines at the same time.'

'But then why would Mr Mojo send me a message about being able to help the British with oil tankers?'

'Perhaps when he sent it he did not know what his government had in mind. Or . . .' Ching stopped speaking, as though too embarrassed to continue.

'Or what?' Mannering asked him, frowning.

'Or there was some other reason, sir.'

'Such as? Come on, man. Out with it.'

'I do not like to suggest this, sir, but maybe it would suit the Japanese very well to have you here if they do attack the colony. You could be a most valuable hostage.'

'You think that is the reason?'

'It is possible, sir.'

Mannering stroked his beard. Ching knew nothing whatever about the jet engine project; he might well be an alarmist, although he had always appeared quiet and sober. Mannering sought for less alarming reasons for being invited out here. Maybe the Japanese had already built a prototype of the engine. Certainly, they had had ample time to do so. Perhaps they wanted his opinion on something that might have given trouble. But he could not help them; he had no technical ability. His aim was simply to sell it. But if Ching was right, then he should abandon hope of collecting any money and leave while he could still go. In the past he had set many traps for others. He had the horrible feeling he could be about to fall into one himself unless he acted quickly.

'You think I should leave now?' he asked Ching.

'I do, sir. I have friends at the airfield and they tell me all aircraft are fully booked, with long waiting lists. All passenger liners are also full and most have already sailed. I am not alone in my belief of invasion being imminent.'

Mannering nodded. 'Get me the Governor on the phone,' he said brusquely, and then sat back to wait for the telephone to ring.

The Governor was engaged; an important American trade delegation had arrived and he was showing them round a local manufactory. Mannering spoke to a deputy.

'I hear rumours that the Japanese are casting envious eyes on Hong Kong,' he began bluntly. 'Is there anything in such rumours?'

The deputy did not wish to discuss such delicate matters over an open telephone line, but he had heard from London of Mannering's importance. His instructions were to help him in any way possible.

'That is a widespread belief, Sir James, I am sorry to say.'

'Could Hong Kong hold out against an invasion?' Mannering asked him.

'That naturally depends on the scale of the invasion,' the deputy replied cautiously.

This did not sound optimistic to Mannering; he recognised the delicate nuance of a diplomatic reply, when a cautious affirmative could actually mean a negative.

'I hope you are being unduly pessimistic,' he said.

'I hope so, too, Sir James.'

552

'I hear all air seats out of Hong Kong are booked for weeks ahead. It looks as though lots of people believe these rumours.'

'We hope to hold back a few seats for top priority passengers.'

'I see. Let us hope it will not be necessary to use them.'

'Quite so, Sir James.'

This conversation worried Mannering; he smelled danger and defeat in the air and did not like the smell. He called Ching back into the room.

'Tell me exactly how Hong Kong will be defended if the Japs do invade,' he said. 'In England, Hong Kong is described in the papers as a fortress.'

'Hong Kong is a paper fortress, Sir James. It is an island totally impossible to defend from a resolute attack. Consider the facts. The Japanese already occupy Hainan Island to the south-west and are in Indo-China to the west. To repulse them we have a line of pillboxes on the Kowloon Peninsula. The strength of this fortification can be gauged from its nickname here – the Gindrinkers' Line.

'Hong Kong garrison has six infantry battalions, two British, two Canadian, two Indian. There is one destroyer, HMS *Thracian*, three obsolete RAF Wilde-beeste aircraft and two Walrus amphibians. The defence plan is to hold any invaders on the mainland, while military stores there are evacuated to Hong Kong island.'

'And then?'

'Who can say? But if the south coast of England were totally in enemy hands and all defenders had withdrawn to the Isle of Wight, you would not give much for their chances, sir, would you?'

'It's as bad as that?'

'At least as bad, possibly worse, for the Japanese are not a merciful race. Are you by any chance familiar with the works of the Chinese writer, Sun Tzu, who wrote a treatise on war two thousand years ago?'

'No. I am not. What has that got to do with this situation?'

'In his classic *The Art of War*, Sun Tzu declares, "He who lacks foresight and underestimates his enemy will surely be captured by him." That is his relevance to our situation, Sir James.'

'I cannot believe we are so ill-equipped.'

'Belief, Sir James, is one thing. Facts are another,' said Ching grimly.

'But how do you know all these details? Aren't they supposed to be secret?'

'Nothing is secret in Hong Kong, least of all to the Japanese. They have a huge fifth column here – businessmen, servants, waiters, barbers. We are led to believe that the Japanese forces are badly equipped, poorly led. British military attachés in Tokyo have tried very hard to dispel such absurd illusions, but people prefer comfortable lies to unpleasant facts, Sir James.'

Just how unpleasant the facts could be, Mannering discovering at eight o'clock on the following Sunday morning. Twelve Japanese bombers, with an escort of thirty-six fighters, totally destroyed the five aircraft, plus civilian airliners parked at Kai Tak airfield. Japanese land forces then swept down through Kowloon and across the Gindrinkers' Line. In less than a week, the defenders withdrew to Hong Kong Island. Looting began as soon as they retreated. The ferries were crammed with terrified civilians. A bargeload of dynamite blew up accidentally to add to the chaos of retreat as dock installations and power stations were destroyed.

Terror now gripped Hong Kong. The end could at best be only days away; stories of Japanese atrocities multiplied.

It was unthinkable for Mannering to stay and yet

impossible for him to escape. All ships of any size had already sailed for Ceylon or Australia. Now, launches, motor yachts, small sailing boats, even sampans were carrying passengers who preferred to risk death at sea than certain imprisonment and possible torture and death on land.

The Japanese had already called on the Governor to surrender Hong Kong. He had refused, but the end now could only be hours away.

The irony of Mannering's situation compounded his concern. All his adult life he had peddled arms, guns, bombs to any nation with the will and funds to buy them. Now, for the first time, he realised he could be at the deadly receiving end of weapons he had sold. He had no hope of extracting money from Mr Mojo or anyone else. The imperative need was simply to escape and survive.

He had already withdrawn all his money, around two million American dollars, from local banks. He was well-placed to pay for his passage, but who could help him?

Ching had not been in the office for several days – not surprising in the chaos of the colony's imminent surrender. And of course this was the Christmas season, although in the present conditions this mattered little. Mannering tried to assure himself that he could reasonably expect good terms from the Japanese. After all, he had provided them with the present of a remarkable engine that would revolutionise aerial warfare. But would soldiers on the ground know this? Hardly. To them he would simply be another rich *taipan* to be robbed and shot.

Then, quite unexpectedly, Ching came into his office on Christmas morning, bowed deeply. 'Hong Kong will surrender within the hour,' he announced without any preamble.

'Can you get me out?' Mannering asked him bluntly.

'I have one suggestion, sir,' Ching replied. 'I have made provisional arrangements to leave myself. If you chose, we could leave together.'

'Where to?'

'Macau,' Ching replied. 'The Portuguese colony to the west. Portugal is neutral.'

'Won't the Japanese go there anyway?'

'They have no need to. It might suit the Japanese very well to leave Macau alone. It could become a valuable and neutral staging post for them. When we reach Macau, you could take ship to Lisbon and thence to England. I am unmarried and live on my own. I would be content to stay in Macau until the war is over.'

'But how can we get there?'

'By fishing boat. There is a big trade in dried fish between Hong Kong and Macau. These vessels cross each week under the control of one man. I have approached a fisherman and he is willing to let me travel as his assistant. For a price, of course. I think I could persuade him to take you as well. Again, for a price. You would have to keep under cover for the voyage, which would take a day and a half. Then I think all would be well. In Macau you would not be a charge on the Portuguese state. You would have sufficient funds of your own with you.'

'Organise it,' Mannering told him. 'At once. I will pay whatever it costs.'

Ching returned within the hour. 'I have engaged the fisherman, a Mr Li,' he reported. 'He is sailing this afternoon. I have offered him five hundred American dollars to take you, a huge sum to him. He has accepted.'

'Can I take anything with me?' asked Mannering.

Ching shook his head. 'You can buy whatever you need in Macau. Just bring your money.'

'Where do we pick up the boat?'

'Along the coast. And do not wear that suit, sir. It is

far too conspicuous. Come in your shirtsleeves and an old pair of trousers. And rub earth or boot polish on your face and hands. You must look like a tramp, not a *taipan*.'

Mannering wrapped his banknotes in an old newspaper, put this in a carrier bag. He put on his oldest clothes, deliberately tore his shirt, scuffed his handmade shoes, darkened his face and hands. Then the two men set out, walking in silence.

The roads were packed with Chinese pouring out of the city. About three miles along the coast, they reached a small promontory overlooking a coral beach. Here, a number of country boats, with sails made from thin flat strips of wood, their decks piled with dried fish, buzzing with flies, lay moored in the shallow water. Seagulls swarmed over rotting fish heads on the shore.

Chinese fishermen squatted on the beach, smoking and throwing dice. None looked up as they approached. Mannering wondered whether, as soon as they had gone, one of them would inform the Japanese. He hoped that he and Ching looked so wretched that they must obviously be considered vagrants, men of no importance.

Ching led the way to a shallow craft, moored fore and aft, about two feet from land. He jumped aboard. There was no cabin, only a flat roof made from a thatch of bamboo strips. Mannering followed him. The boat rocked violently under their weight. She seemed absurdly small, not much larger than a punt, with a narrow unpainted deck all round the centre hold filled with dried and strong-smelling fish.

A middle-aged Chinese, wearing a hat like a plate and smoking a cigarette made from a rolled-up leaf, sat in the stern. As his passengers, bent double, entered the bamboo shelter, he spat over the side. This, Mannering assumed, must be Mr Li.

Ching spoke to him roughly as to a very unimportant

inferior. The man nodded impassively, cast loose, dug a long bamboo pole into the clear water. The boat moved slowly out towards the open sea. Li ran forward, hoisted the sail. The wind filled this with a great clattering of wooden slats. Within minutes they were half a mile out from Hong Kong Island.

Mannering crawled to the front of the shelter and peered through a hole between slivers of bamboo. He was concerned they might be followed by a Japanese patrol boat, but the only other vessels he could see were fishing boats like theirs. He wondered whether any were also ferrying rich men to safety. They seemed, however, to be more intent on fishing near land. Soon, Li's boat was out on its own. So far, the escape had been extremely easy and straightforward.

The white buildings of Hong Kong, under a huge pall of black smoke from bombing and shelling, shrank steadily against the purple background of the hills, and then melted into merciful infinity. The sea was unexpectedly calm. Here and there, a flying fish would suddenly leap from the surface, flicker like a polished dagger blade, and then dive again beneath the waves. The war seemed a million miles away.

'It's safe to come out now, sir,' said Ching. He indicated the stern of the boat. Mannering climbed out from the shelter, relieved to be away from the stench of dried fish. He sat down by the side of the rudder. This was controlled by Li up in the bows by means of two long thin ropes that stretched along the decking, one on either side of the vessel.

'I have worked for your company for ten years,' Mr Ching told Mannering thoughtfully.

'I know, and be sure that I will see that your great service to me does not go unrewarded,' Mannering replied unctuously. He must give the fellow something for saving his life. What, he was not quite sure. But he noticed that for probably the first time in their association, Ching did not address him as 'sir'. There was probably no significance in this, but somehow it made Mannering feel uneasy. He was very susceptible to atmosphere and nuances of speech and behaviour, a sensitivity that had often contributed to his survival and his success.

'I regret that it has taken a time of great danger for you to make such a promise,' said Ching sadly. 'I have always been very loyal to you, and to your interests.'

'I am well aware of that. I propose promoting you to have charge of all PPP's offices east of Suez as soon as this war is over. And I will double your salary the moment we reach Macau. Backdated, of course, for twelve months.'

'Thank you. But I have sometimes heard you give very good advice to those who care to take it. You say that a man can only *earn* money by working for someone else. If he wants to *make* money, he must work for himself.'

'Quite so. That has always been my belief, words by which I personally have lived,' Mannering agreed.

'So I am sure you will understand why, after much thought, I have decided to follow your example, and be my own master.'

Mannering nodded approvingly. 'A very wise decision,' he agreed. Why was the fellow telling him this now, when they were miles out at sea? This was surely not the moment for a kind of Dale Carnegie self-help discussion?

'I am pleased you agree,' said Ching, 'for I am starting now. From this moment on.'

Then Mannering saw the snub nose of a revolver in Ching's right hand.

'What are you doing?' he asked, his voice hoarse with fear. The man must have become deranged. Was he on drugs? Mannering had heard that some Chinese were opium and cocaine addicts.

Ching did not reply. Instead, he fired twice.

Just for a moment, Mannering saw a tiny puff of cordite smoke. Then agony overcame him. Ching's features, the boat, the shimmering sea were suddenly blurred, fused together in a red mist of pain, as though he was seeing them through a diminishing glass, out of focus. He fell forward into the bottom of the boat.

At once, Ching's expert fingers removed his passport, his wallet, crocodile-skin cigar case, gold wristwatch. Then he heaved the body over the side. These waters were full of sharp-toothed hungry fish. They would eat the *taipan*, handmade shoes and all, within minutes.

Ching went up forward. Li gave no indication he had seen the shooting or heard the splash of the falling body. Ching threw him Mannering's wristwatch.

'A present for you,' he said shortly. Better give the peasant something to keep his mouth shut, and that watch would fetch more than the man could make in a twelvemonth.

Li inclined his head respectfully in gratitude.

'He was a red-bristled barbarian of the worst sort, that one,' Ching told him. 'He should have read the sayings of Sun Tzu on the art of war. "One who has few must prepare against the enemy; one who has many, makes the enemy prepare against him." '

Li nodded. 'It is as you say, sagacious one,' he agreed humbly.

'How soon do we reach Macau?'

'At dawn. There's a good wind behind us.'

Ching nodded his approval, walked back to the stern of the boat. He wanted to take a look in Mannering's bag to make sure it contained what he was certain it contained.

In the bows, Li rose to his feet. Still puffing his leaf

cigarette, watching Ching closely, he pulled one of the rudder ropes smartly. It rode up on Ching's left leg, rasping against his flesh. He bent down instinctively at the unexpected pain, thinking he must have been bitten by an insect. In bending he lost his balance and fell backwards into the sea with a great splash.

He surfaced quickly and swam rapidly towards the boat, but Li had tacked. The fishing boat was turning in a circle, away from him. Ching swam on strongly towards it, shouting to Li to stop. But instead the man kept changing course to catch the wind, as though he did not hear him. Presently, Ching wearied. He trod water and watched the fishing boat head for Macau without him.

From time to time, Li glanced back and saw Ching's head and shoulders bobbing above the water. He was crying out despairingly now and waved his arms for help he knew would never come, for who was there to hear on the empty, open sea? Gradually his cries became fainter and then diminished altogether. He sank slowly beneath the surface of the sea. One moment he was there, a murderer with two million dollars within his grasp. The next, it was as though he had never been.

Li waited until he was sure he would not surface again. Then he spat out his rolled-up cigarette and removed a nine-inch Havana from Mannering's cigar case. He sniffed at it appreciatively, bit off the blunt end, lit it with the care a great cigar demanded. Then he opened the carrier bag and examined its contents approvingly.

Ching was right to remember the words of the great Sun Tzu, he thought. But he had not chosen the saying dearest to Li's own heart. He spoke it aloud now, savouring its truth: 'In happiness at overcoming difficulties, people forget the danger of death.'

How very true, he thought contentedly, and guided his little boat on across the shining sea.

561

Chapter Twenty-Four

When Richard went into his office one Monday morning, two telegrams lay on his desk. One was from the Mannering Art Gallery in New York; he had totally forgotten they were holding an exhibition of his paintings. The message from the manager was short and cheering.

EVERY CANVAS SOLD STOP TWO HUNDRED THOU-
SAND DOLLARS CREDITED YOUR BANK ACCOUNT
HERE STOP PLEASE ADVISE WHEN WE MAY RECEIVE
FURTHER PAINTINGS REGARDS

That was amazing news. A fortune. And yet somehow it did not seem to Richard like real money, whereas the few hundred pounds a year he earned at his job with Zimbro and Beechwood was real money. This was something extra, an unexpected bonus, cream on top of the milk, froth on a pint of beer. He put the cable on one side, picked up the second. It was from Sir Bernard Warner, in a government department in London, the Security Co-ordination Section.

PLEASE TELEPHONE TO ARRANGE EARLY APPOINT-
MENT ON MATTER NATIONAL IMPORTANCE.

Sir Bernard Warner; a name from the past. He'd

been the Chief Constable, and a guest at his father's ball the night he left home – nearly thirty years ago now. Why should this man suddenly want to see him so urgently, after so long, and on a matter of national importance?

Richard discovered the reason on the following morning. Sir Bernard's office was a small drawing room in a Queen Anne house near St James's Park. Apart from sandbags around the front door and some protective tape on the windows, legacies from the days of bombing in 1940, there were no signs of war.

A neat fire burned in the grate. Sir Bernard offered him a black coffee and a seat on the other side of the fire. Richard took the coffee, sat down.

'We've only met briefly once before,' Warner began. 'You were in your early teens then and probably don't remember it.'

'I don't think we actually met,' Richard corrected him. 'But I remember you were at my father's house for that ball before the First World War.'

Sir Bernard nodded. 'I saw your mother from time to time after your father's death. She told me how well you were doing and how proud she was of you.'

'I didn't know that.'

'I owed your father a number of good turns, and after his death I felt guilty I didn't keep in closer touch with your mother. But when you've been friendly with the husband you somehow don't want to rush the widow, as it were. But at least I was able to help her.'

'In what way?'

'Now that most sadly she is also no longer with us, there's no point in keeping this a secret, but your father had taken out a most unwise and usurious mortgage. I was able to persuade the holder of the mortgage not to proceed with it.'

'You mean Sir James Mannering?'

Sir Bernard nodded, snipped the end of a cigar, lit it. 'Precisely.'

'He told me that he had done that.'

'So he did, my dear fellow. But on my suggestion.'

'You persuaded him in some way?'

'You could say that – in some way,' Sir Bernard admitted.

'He appears to have been taken in the bag in Hong Kong, so I read in the paper,' said Richard.

'Yes. I think he may not have survived. It may be that he tried to avoid being taken in the bag, but even so, when your number comes up, you can't avoid the reckoning.'

'So he's dead, is he?'

'We hear things from time to time from our people in Macau. Some Chinese boatman was seen spending a mint of money in the casino there soon after the Japs took Hong Kong. And he was offering a gold watch for sale. He did not realise that inside was Sir James Mannering's name. It had been a present from loyal employees of the North London Loan and Mortgage Company, the concern that held the mortgage on your home.

'Life is very strange, Rowlands. Often people run away from the consequences of their actions and then find, too late, that they're really just running towards them. Which brings me to the reason I have asked you to see me now. I need your help.

'As you'll have gathered, I'm involved in what I may loosely call security. I've been brought out of retirement and my involvement is not large, but still we deal with some quite vital matters. Sometimes these are things no one else wants to get involved with for various reasons. It's one of those matters that I want to talk to you about.'

He paused.

'Go on,' said Richard.

'You know that our scientists are working on a jet

engine. It's at a very advanced stage of development, but there have been all sorts of hold-ups, largely due to bureaucratic nonsense. We have reason to believe that the Germans also are developing such an engine, but they are still behind us. Until the other day, we didn't think the Japanese were even in the race.'

'And are they?'

'Judge for yourself.'

Sir Bernard crossed to his desk, took out a folder of photographs which he handed to Richard with a huge magnifying glass. The photographs had been taken from the air and were slightly out of focus; the reconnaissance plane had been travelling fast. The first showed a stretch of jungle containing what looked like a crashed aircraft. The next one featured the tip of an aircraft wing; the third, the engine, although it did not look like a normal aircraft engine. The next was a view from the rear, showing a blackened hole beneath the rudder. Others were taken from different angles.

'There's no propeller,' said Richard.

'Precisely.'

'But it's not a glider.'

'No. It's a Zero. You can tell that from the wing configuration and the tailplane and so on. Look at that hole in the front. That's the air intake for the jet. The hole in the back is the jet. Now, look all round the plane. There's no sign of an engine that's been flung out, and there would have been if this had been a stock Zero, because it carries a fourteen-cylinder radial engine – a fairly substantial lump of metal. Equally, there's no sign of anything resembling a propeller, or parts of one. In our people's view there was no propeller. This is a Japanese jet, and as such very dangerous indeed.'

'Where were these taken?'

'In Burma. About a hundred miles north-east of Rangoon. The Japanese have an air base there. They were probably trying it out over the jungle because if it can fly there, it can fly anywhere. There are so many eddies and hot-air currents and goodness knows what else in that part of the world.'

'What do you want me to do about this?'

'I want you to go out and examine it. We want to know exactly how far ahead of us they are – if they are.'

'But you have your own jet engine experts. Frank Whittle's team.'

'They're all working twenty hours a day on their own jet.'

'What makes you think I'm not busy?'

'I don't. But you're the only man I know personally who understands the jet, who actually put up to the Air Ministry his own design, through Mannering. The Ministry turned it down, of course, because they were already so involved with Whittle's jet.'

'What precisely do you want me to tell you?'

'Everything you can. Why did the plane come down? It wasn't shot down, so was it pilot error, bad flying conditions or engine trouble? I know we've got all sorts of troubles with seals and vanes standing up to the great heat and pressure and so on. The Japanese have probably got them, too. Only more so. And there's something else we'd like to know. Could you say whether this jet is based on your design?'

'I think so. If it is, do you think Mannering sold it to them?'

'That is a strong possibility. In the last war he arranged for the Germans to have details of that mechanism which enabled a fighter pilot to aim a machine-gun through his propeller blades.'

'He sold that directly to them? He was a traitor?'

'He was beaten to it by the Russians, to whom he'd originally hoped to sell it. But Lenin appropriated the plans and did his own deal with the Germans.'

'I had no idea.'

'Nor had we until after the war.'

'How would I get out to Burma?'

'There's a regular service of RAF Dakotas between this country and India, and on to Burma. It'll take you nearly a week, but it's the quickest way there is. When you get to Chittagong, that's our nearest big base, we'll get you into Burma by boat and Jeep. You will go?'

'Of course. If it's that important.'

'It is.'

'When do you want me to leave?'

'Five o'clock tomorrow morning.'

Richard's most lasting impression of his flight to the East was of extreme and constant discomfort. He had often seen Dakotas land and take off at airfields, but he had never flown in one. The aircraft was very noisy; its bare metal fuselage amplified the constant roar of the engines. There were no seats. He sat on a parachute pack braced against the wall of the plane which was heavily studded with rivets that dug painfully into his back. He had been primed with inoculations and injections against typhoid, smallpox, yellow fever and various other ailments of the East and his whole body ached.

He had also been provided with lightweight jungle-green battledress, army boots, a slouch hat, webbing belt, a Smith and Wesson revolver, a water bottle, a small pack containing a set of tools, a camera, and a rubber gas cape. This, he was told, would be useful if he had to sleep rough in the jungle. He also had with him a number of strong lightweight sacks, folded and tied together, for any pieces of the Zero's engine he was able to remove and bring back.

The Dakota came down to refuel in northern Africa; then in Basra. They flew to Karachi, then across India to Delhi and Calcutta. At Chittagong he spent the night in a transit camp. All he remembered of his stay here were the constant attacks by mosquitoes which bored their way through the army-issue mosquito net over his bed, and a sign he saw on the way to embark on a launch for the next stage of the journey: 'Good Health, Keep your bowels open. Good Security, Keep your mouth shut.'

The launch landed on the Arakan coast, and he was driven in an army Jeep to the headquarters of the British battalion nearest to the crashed plane. The Jeep bumped along a rough mule track, trailing a huge plume of amber dust. On either side lay paddy fields, dry and parched; this had been the most important rice-growing area in Burma before the war. Artillery guns were parked along the route under camouflage nets stuck with branches and leaves.

'How much further?' Richard asked the driver.

'Quite a few miles yet, sir,' the driver replied vaguely. 'Then this track ends and the jungle begins.' He took a handkerchief out of his pocket, tied it like a bandit's mask round his nose. 'I'd do the same if I were you, sir. It filters the dust a bit.'

He glanced curiously at Richard. Here was a man in his forties, clearly not military, but fitted out in battle-dress. Talked like a nob but didn't behave like one, and he wore no badges of rank. What on earth would bring a civilian to this dangerous and godforsaken part of the world?

Battalion HQ had been established on the edge of the jungle, where the track ended in a bare patch of trodden earth, about a hundred yards across. Several *bashas* of plaited bamboo had been built round the perimeter. Jeeps were parked beneath the trees. To Richard's eye, an air of casual disarray hung over the camp. Soldiers wore long denim trousers, boots and slouch hats but no shirts. Some had revolvers strapped to their belts; others rifles slung over their shoulders. The driver stopped outside a small *basha* with a crudely painted sign: 'Battalion HQ'. An officer came out to meet them.

'Are you Mr Rowlands?' he asked at once.

'The same. I feel like Stanley or Livingstone.'

The officer smiled. He explained he was the adjutant. He wore a faded khaki shirt with a captain's stars sewn on the epaulettes in cloth.

'The colonel's waiting to see you, sir.'

He took Richard into the *basha*. The colonel was a short, stubby man, with sandy hair and pale blue eyes. They shook hands.

'Any way we can help you, Mr Rowlands, please just ask. We've had a number of signals from Brigade, passed down from Division, about the vital nature of your visit but none explaining exactly what it is.'

'Then I must tell you, strictly for your ears only,' Richard replied. 'According to aerial photographs, the Japs have a plane that doesn't need a propeller – and it's not a glider.'

'Sounds bloody odd to me,' replied the colonel shortly.

Richard showed him copies of the reconnaissance photographs.

'You're right,' said the colonel, mystified. 'But how the hell does it fly?'

'That's one of the things I want to find out. How do I get there to examine it?'

'The only way is on your two feet, Mr Rowlands. How fit are you?'

'Not very, at least not by your standards here.'

'Then the march will probably take you three days. We've already mounted a guard on the plane in case the Japanese come in to move it. We're in radio contact with the section commander, a corporal. He reports Japanese patrols in the area, but the jungle's very thick, and so far they've not made contact. But if their patrols are indeed looking for the aircraft, it can't be too long before they find it.'

'How many men can you spare to come with me?'

'How many do you need?'

'I have to carry the engine back with me or at least some major parts of it if I can dismantle it.'

'You'd better take three more sections from the same platoon. About twenty-five men. Would they be enough?'

'Plenty. Well, I'm ready to go as soon as you like, Colonel.'

'It's too late to start today. You'd only get a few miles into the jungle before you'd have to hole up for the night. Then you'd need another day, and perhaps another night and maybe a third. Spend tonight here, and be off before dawn.'

'As you say. Where do I sleep?'

'The adjutant will show you. There's a *basha* to the right where we can put you up.'

Next day, before sun-up, Richard was on his way. The adjutant had detailed a batman to carry the tools, and advised Richard to soak his feet in a solution of potassium permanganate and water, to harden them. Otherwise, blisters from his first long march in jungle conditions could become crippling.

The adjutant also produced a Tommy gun for him and a belt with two ammunition pouches for extra magazines.

'Take orders from Mr Browne, the platoon commander, and do exactly what he says,' he advised Richard. 'He knows his job thoroughly, so if he says fight, fight. If he says run, run.'

'Like flying,' replied Richard. 'No arguments.'

'Absolutely. Out here it's a case of the quick or the dead.'

The men marched easily, knowing they had a long way to go. Two scouts were out in front, two behind the main

571

body, with Richard in the middle with a Burmese interpreter. Soon sweat was running down his forehead into his eyes. Heat and humidity bore down on him like a physical weight.

No one spoke as they marched, partly for reasons of security in case the enemy heard them, and partly because to speak meant they had to open their mouths, already dry from thirst.

Powdered earth lay thick on the jungle floor; this was the eve of the monsoon and the ground was hard and dry. From time to time they stopped while the platoon commander checked their position with compass and map. The foliage was very thick. Flies pestered them continually. Little stinging midges crept into the corners of their eyes, crawled up inside their nostrils as they breathed.

They had started on the hour and for each succeeding hour they marched for fifty minutes, then rested for ten, lying down in a wide circle, feet inwards, heads facing outwards, rifles and Tommy guns at the ready in case of attack.

That evening, they stopped near a river. They stripped off their clothes, bathed, and then sat naked for as long as possible before putting on their sweat-soaked clothes. Constant perspiring had brought out clusters of raw red spots on Richard's flesh; a sweat rash that stung painfully.

One man in each section now collected up rations of tinned soya beans and dehydrated onions and potatoes from each man's pack. He put the food in a pan, added water, and warmed up the meal over a fire, kept as small as possible in case flames or smoke gave away their position.

Dusk was very brief, only a matter of minutes, before darkness fell. They lay down on the hard, dusty earth, wrapping hands, faces and necks in strips of netting in an attempt to keep off the worst of the mosquitoes.

Richard slept fitfully, and was glad to wake an hour before dawn, when everyone stood to, weapons loaded, ready in case of attack.

The second day was virtually a repetition of the first, but by the morning of the third day the platoon commander reported that according to his map reading they must be within a few hundred yards of the crashed plane.

'We've made radio contact with the section we left up here,' Browne explained. 'The plane is down in a paddy field on the edge of the jungle. Do you want to examine it now?'

'The sooner the better, I think.'

'Do you need any men to go with you?'

'I'll examine it myself first. Give me thirty minutes on my own and then send me half a dozen men. As I dismantle the engine, I'll label the pieces and put them in the sacks I've brought along. If anything happens to me, please get the engine parts back to Battalion HQ.'

'Will do,' said Browne briskly. 'Follow me.'

He led Richard through the trees. The light gradually became brighter as they approached the end of that spread of jungle. Suddenly they were standing on the edge of a paddy field. The Zero's pilot had presumably made an attempt to land and just missed the tops of the trees in doing so. The aircraft's wings were still attached to the fuselage, but bent backwards. Its undercarriage had ploughed two long furrows in the dry earth. The rudder swung to and fro lazily in a slight breeze, reminding Richard of the wreckage of the R.101 near Beauvais.

'There's a bit of a pong around the plane, so the section commander says,' Browne explained. 'Pilot's still inside – must have been there for a week or ten days at least. They didn't want to touch him in case he's booby-trapped. So be very careful before you open the cockpit cover.'

'Thanks for the tip. But I don't think I'll need to disturb him.'

'I'll wait here, where I can keep an eye on things. Good luck.' Browne unslung his Tommy gun, crouched down in the undergrowth. On either side of him, Richard could see other men of the platoon, rifles at the ready. He took a deep breath and went forward on his own.

He walked slowly, wondering with each step whether enemy eyes were also watching him. He half expected to hear a burst of fire, but all stayed quiet.

As he approached the aircraft, he could see the dead pilot strapped in his seat, still wearing helmet and goggles. The top of the canopy had been partly pushed back as though he had hoped to jump out before the crash. Flies buzzed in a thick blue cloud round the opening. The wind changed and Richard breathed the foul stench of death and putrefaction. Through the blood-stained perspex window, he could see great, greedy worms crawl over the dead man's face. He looked away from the repulsive sight, walked on towards the nose of the aircraft.

Here, he paused. Across the paddy lay another patch of jungle, thick, dark, dangerous. But he could not see any movement in it, and no sign of anyone else watching him. The heat was intense; sweat poured off him as he swung the pack from his back, took out his camera and photographed the plane from the front, from both sides, from the rear. Then he selected half a dozen screwdrivers of different sizes, all joined by a thin wire in case he dropped one in the grass, and carefully began to unscrew the engine cover.

The shock of the crash had loosened the screw threads. He had been afraid that some might have jammed and he would have to spend time chiselling them out, but all turned easily. He lifted off one side of the canopy, then the other. There was no doubt that the power unit was a jet – it could hardly be anything else without a propeller. There was also no doubt that he had designed it. The Japanese had diligently copied everything, down to the smallest detail – including his birthmark. On one of the castings the initials M.P. were clearly visible.

'It's mine,' he said aloud, without meaning to speak, and looked around hurriedly in case someone had heard him. But the paddy field was empty, shimmering like a mirage under the burning heat of the overhead sun.

He searched for something else – the deliberate fault he had made in the design. Staring at it now, he remembered Sir James Mannering coming into his office at Beechwood Gears after visiting the Scientific Adviser at the Air Ministry.

'They don't want it,' Mannering had told him flatly. 'They're already ahead with their own jet. I'll have to sell it elsewhere.'

'Then let me have it back,' said Richard. 'I've thought of a modification I should do.'

Mannering pushed the folder of drawings across the table to him. 'Don't take too long,' he said sharply.

Richard redesigned one small part so that the jet would still work, but not for long, and never at full efficiency. He had heard too much about Mannering's earlier deals. Richard could not bear to think that his invention could ever be used against his own country.

Standing by the side of the wrecked plane, he knew that the Japanese had also copied this flaw. He beckoned to the lieutenant, watching from under the trees. Browne came towards Richard at the double.

'Everything all right, sir?' he asked.

'Yes. Please get your men out here and I'll start to dismantle it.'

575

'The corporal tells me he used to work in a garage back home.'

'Then he can take the other side, and I'll work on this one, and we'll be through in half the time.'

By late afternoon they had removed the parts he needed. Richard labelled each one, drawing a small sketch to show exactly where it fitted on the engine. Then he photographed each piece in case any went missing on the long journey back to England.

As darkness fell, they went back into the jungle and spent another uncomfortable night warding off mosquitoes.

In the morning, after stand-to, the lieutenant approached him.

'If you're ready, sir, I'd like to move off as soon as possible. I don't want to hang about here a moment longer than we have to. We're very close to the Japs and although we haven't seen a soul, it's quite likely that locals have seen us, or you working on the engine, and told the Japs.

'I put out a patrol last night and they brought in a Burmese who was lurking about. He seems friendly enough, but you never can be sure. Our interpreter says he reports a large group of Japs, at least a company, maybe more, less than a mile away. They may be on their way to dismantle the plane. I don't know. But if so, they could be here very soon. So the quicker we leave, the better.'

'Ready to go when you are,' Richard told him.

'One other thing, sir. As you're obviously concerned with Jap aircraft, I should tell you that this local says there's another plane down not half a mile from here.'

'What sort of plane? One of ours?'

'He doesn't know.'

'Do you think he's genuine or is this just a ruse to get us over there and into an ambush?'

'Difficult to say. We're quite near a village of some sort, according to our patrol, and the Japs may be hiding there. They do that sometimes. They'll take a few locals hostage and then send out one of their relatives with a story they think we'll fall for.'

'What's your opinion of this man? Do you trust him?'

'We held him here overnight and kept questioning him in case he altered his story, but he didn't. At a guess I'd say he was genuine.'

'Let me have a word with him,' said Richard.

The Burmese was very thin and small. He spoke rapidly and nervously, looking from Richard to the lieutenant, then at the platoon sergeant, the interpreter, and back again at Richard.

'He insists he doesn't know what sort of plane it is that's down,' the interpreter explained. 'And his story doesn't change. I'd trust him.'

'Even so, I think we'll leave it,' said Richard. 'It's more important to get this stuff back as soon as possible – that's what we're here for. And whatever plane he refers to, it's unlikely to have much scientific interest. We'll go whenever you're ready.'

As he turned away, Richard saw that one of the soldiers was having difficulty fitting a delicate part of the engine into its bag. As Richard turned to help him, the Burmese suddenly gave a cry of surprise, and pointed in astonishment to the M.P. mark on the metal – and on the back of Richard's hand. He spoke excitedly to the interpreter.

'He says that same mark is on the other plane's engine,' said the interpreter.

'Is he sure?' asked Richard, his voice suddenly hoarse.

'Positive, sir.'

'In that case,' Richard told Browne, 'I will go and see the aircraft. But on my own. If this is a trap, I'll be the

577

only one to suffer and you hightail it back to base with these bits and pieces.'

'I can't let you go alone, sir,' said the lieutenant. 'If anything went wrong, what do we do with all this stuff? No one knows where it's to go exactly. If you must stay and see this other plane – and I'm against it – take the platoon sergeant and the interpreter.'

Richard nodded agreement. 'Thank you. I promise you we'll be back as soon as we possibly can.'

The Burmese led them away through the jungle, puffing on a primitive, sharp-smelling cheroot. They reached a paddy field, crossed this into a clump of trees. Ahead of them was a flat area ringed by bamboo huts. Some dogs lay in the dust, watching them. Children playing a game of hopscotch ran to the shelter of their *bashas* at the sight of soldiers. The space was suddenly deserted. Only a few blue wisps of smoke from fires burning under cooking pots gave any indication that the area was inhabited.

The Burmese led the way to one hut and pointed to the door. Richard saw that it was made from a sheet of aluminium, once curved, now hammered flat. Paint, faded by years of heat and monsoon rain, had peeled and flaked away, but a few small patches still remained. The door had been part of an aircraft wing; he could see lines of rivet heads.

Outside another *basha*, an engine block, half buried in the hard, dry earth, formed the bottom step of a bamboo stairway leading up to a verandah. The Burmese pointed to this. Near the engine number, stamped into the metal, Richard recognised his sign. There was only one aircraft whose engine he had adapted in this way. It had powered Carola's plane.

Could her journey have ended here, in this desolate, scrubby patch of jungle? He paused, heart beating like a captive drum, looking down at the solid lump of metal, thinking of the vast distance it had travelled to this extraordinary destination.

'Does it mean anything to you, sir?' asked the sergeant. He was anxious to be away; he did not trust these villages. The *bashas* could be swarming with Japs. He had been caught like this before and the memory haunted him.

'It's beginning to,' said Richard grimly.

He looked up at the hut, then at the one next door, and then at each of the others in turn. None showed any signs of human life. Beneath them, chickens pecked in the dust; a tethered goat began to bleat.

Richard felt he could not simply return home without at least attempting to solve the mystery. Was Carola alive or dead? Surely someone here must know. He turned to the interpreter.

'Please let the local fellow go. And assure him we come in peace. Get him to shout that message out to the whole village.'

'And hurry,' added the platoon sergeant. 'I don't like the smell of this place. The Japs must have been here recently. That's why everyone's hiding, in case they come back. They can't risk being seen talking to us.'

The interpreter cupped his hands round his mouth and began to shout his message.

A few birds fluttered oily wings above the *bashas*, flew off, circled briefly and came back to perch on the roofs. One dog barked, another growled. Faces began to appear on the verandahs, watching them carefully, impassively.

On an impulse, Richard shouted 'Carola! *Carola!* It's me, Richard!' The platoon sergeant stared at him. Had this bloke gone mad? Richard was about to explain why he was calling when he saw Carola.

She was wearing a red and yellow *longgyi*. Her long dark hair hung down her back. She had come out of an upper room and stood, hands on the rail of the verandah, staring down at him. He raised his camera, photographed her with disbelief and astonishment on her face.

'It's me!' he shouted excitedly and raced across the clearing. He bounded up the steps to the verandah two at a time. Carola stood, not moving. At last she spoke.

'I can't believe it,' she said softly. 'Prove it. Show me I'm not dreaming.'

Richard kissed her fiercely, hungrily, holding her tightly as though he would never let her go. All around them now, people began to come out of their *bashas*, staring at them, chattering like starlings.

'It *is* you,' Carola said in amazement, drawing away, but still holding both his hands. She spoke carefully, as though English was not a language she often had the chance to use.

'How long have you been here?' Richard asked her, also unconsciously speaking slowly, as to a foreigner.

'Since I landed,' Carola replied.

'Were you injured?'

'No. I managed to come down safely. Then . . .' She paused as though reluctant to go on.

'You couldn't get away?'

'No. I tried. But it was impossible. You can see what the jungle's like. You must have come through it. But everyone has been very kind to me here. And they sheltered me when the Japanese soldiers came. They've been here twice. Once several months ago, and then this week. I would have been killed if anyone had told them about me. But no one did. As it was, the Japanese took away Laung San. We've not heard from him since.'

'Who is Laung San?'

As Carola began to explain, Richard heard a sudden movement behind him. A boy about ten, barefoot, wearing shorts and a shirt, had come out of one of the rooms and stood watching him with hostile eyes. His right hand rested on a *dah* stuck into his belt. He was obviously prepared to defend Carola from the unwanted attentions of a strange soldier.

Carola spoke urgently to him. Surprise and disbelief showed on the boy's face. Still staring at Richard, he put up a hand to brush away a fly that had settled on his nose. Richard's heart gave a great and sudden leap.

'Your hand,' he said, and held out his own right hand, palm downwards. The boy put his hand alongside it. Then he looked up at his mother, puzzled, and said something rapidly in Burmese. She took the boy's hand in hers, and smiled.

'What does he say?' Richard asked her.

'He says you both have the same mark on your hands, as on the engine. He wants to know why this is and who you are.'

'Can he speak English?'

'I've taught him, but he doesn't get much chance to speak it here, and I think he's a bit embarrassed in case you laugh at his attempts. You tell him. After all, you are his father.'

Chapter Twenty-Five

Richard stared at Carola, and then at the boy. His son. He dredged despairingly for words, found none.

'You live here?' he asked at last, and was immediately conscious of the question's absurdity. Looking at Carola, he could see that she was equally at a loss. They were both mentally and emotionally drained by the shock and surprise of meeting after so long. She who was lost had now been found; and he had found her. This basic fact was too important for either of them to assimilate.

Then Carola laughed, and her laughter broke the spell of silence and disbelief.

'*Of course* I live here. I've nowhere else to live.'

'So you've been in this village, this hut, ever since you crashed?'

'Yes. They cut the plane's tyres and tore out all the wires, so that put paid to me ever flying away. Then I tried to walk off through the jungle, but I was brought back. I would probably not have survived, so it was really lucky for me. But it didn't seem like it then.'

'So you've been here ever since as a prisoner?'

'I suppose I have, yes, though it hasn't felt like it. A missionary told Laung San that Christ went up to heaven but was going to return one day. He believed I was the fulfilment of that prophecy because I came down from the sky. I'm not sure he still believes that. Certainly he's never treated my son as if he's some kind of saviour, but

I couldn't persuade him to let us leave. None of the other locals are Christian. They simply accepted me for what I was, and am – an ordinary person.

'At first I hated it here and everyone around me, although they were all kind to me. And then gradually I grew to like the people. They're very simple, very loyal. I was touched by their kindness. They wanted to be friends. I learned to speak the language, and tried to teach English to anyone who wanted to learn. There's no sort of difference between us because I'm a European and they're Burmese. We get on well. I kept hoping, praying that a British official or trader, anyone, would come along one day and then I'd be all right. But when no one did arrive, I gradually gave up hope and tried to make the best of things. I had to. I had no other choice.'

'What about the plane's radio? Couldn't you get a message out on that?'

'No. I tried it once, but they'd smashed the valves. Eventually I came to accept the fact that I was here indefinitely, perhaps for ever. This was my life, all I had.'

'What made you come down here?'

'The engine started to misfire badly. I began to lose height very quickly. At first I couldn't see anywhere I could possibly land, then I saw a huge cross cut out of the paddy, so I aimed for that and made it just before the engine cut out altogether.

'I found that the centre of a sparking plug had blown out. I only needed to put in a new plug, a ten-minute job, and I would be on my way again. But I hadn't got ten minutes before men from the village came out and brought me here.'

'And you've lived here ever since, on your own?'

'Yes. I have a section of this *basha* with a bamboo division. My son – our son – has one part, I have the other. I saved the clock from the plane, by the way. It's inside the *basha*, still going well. Locals cut off the wings to make doors and so on, as you may have seen. Nothing was wasted. I've even still got the plane's papers.' Carola frowned, remembering something else. 'Tom Gardener,' she said. 'How is he?'

'I'm sorry to say he was killed, testing a new plane. He went back to Australia eventually but he didn't stay long. When war broke out he returned to England. He was too old to fly operationally, but he did good work as a test pilot.'

'He asked me to marry him once,' said Carola slowly. 'I wasn't sure, so I said no. I trusted him, you know, and I thought he must like me or he wouldn't have proposed. But just before I left he asked me to sign a contract about selling the story of my flight to newspapers or book publishers and so on. I was so taken up with the prospect of making the flight I simply couldn't bring myself to read all the legal jargon, so I just signed as he asked, put it in my bag and forgot about it. I've had plenty of time to read it since.'

'What does it contain?'

'Nothing at all to my advantage. I'd signed everything over to him. If I'd completed the flight I wouldn't have got a penny, and he'd have made a fortune. But there was nothing for him in the end, because I didn't succeed. What about Amelia Earhart, by the way? Before I left she was planning much the same flight. Did she make it?'

'No. She and her navigator disappeared over the Pacific.'

'So no woman's flown round the world yet?'

'No. You could still be the first. Except that after this war it's going to be a quite different world to fly round. These records won't count for as much as they did. And you probably won't get the permissions needed to fly over all the countries as easily as you could in the past.'

'I see. I knew from Laung San that Britain and the

585

United States were at war with Japan – and the Japs have been here, as I told you. But that's about all I do know. Why are you here? Are you in the army?'

'No. This is simply a uniform I was given. I was too young for the last war and apparently too old for this. I flew out from England to examine a Japanese plane that crashed near here.'

'I saw it come down, but I haven't gone near it. I was afraid the Japanese might have a guard on it and arrest me.'

'Well, a villager told the interpreter a second plane had come down, with my birthmark on the engine – you remember how you put the mark on my toy steam engine with solder? Anyway, I had to see for myself.'

Carola put her hand into a pocket in her *longgyi*, took out a small copper ring, very smooth, very well polished, and handed it to him.

Richard smiled. 'I gave this to you as a sort of totem just before you left Croydon,' he said, turning it over in his hand. 'It didn't bring you too much luck, though, did it?'

'Maybe it did. Maybe it brought you here.' She smiled happily and Richard smiled with her. 'And Lady Warren, how is she?'

'Very old and frail. You'll be able to cheer her up.'

'How?'

'Because you're coming back with me, now.'

Carola lowered her eyes. 'I don't know if I can leave.'

'What do you mean? Of course you can. I'll take you out by force if necessary.'

She shook her head. 'I've told you these people have been very kind to me. I can't just run out on them. If the Japs ever find out they hid me here, they're quite likely to kill them all as a warning to others.'

'That may or may not happen, but staying here puts them at even greater risk if the Japanese do return. You can't expect them to shelter you indefinitely. The locals have their lives to lead, as you have yours. Also, I love you,' Richard said simply. 'I've told you that before, but you didn't listen, you didn't care.'

'I did care. I just didn't know if I could love you,' Carola replied.

'Do you know now?'

'Yes.'

'And what's the answer?'

'Yes. I had a soft spot for Tom, I admit, in the curious way women often have towards rogues. I suppose we think we're going to reform them, though we never can, and we never do. But I don't think I need reform you, although I'd make you *much* tougher and harder. I think you've been cheated and bamboozled out of too many good ideas. If I'm around, I'll stop all that.'

'I'd like you to be around to stop all that. And for every other reason you can possibly think of.' He was still holding the copper ring. He lifted Carola's left hand and slipped it onto her third finger. 'Now we're officially engaged,' he said.

As Carola laughed and hugged him, a British soldier ran across the open space towards the sergeant who had been waiting at the bottom of the steps, silently cursing the delay.

'A Japanese patrol's just been sighted less than a mile off and coming this way, Sarge,' the soldier said, sweating and breathless. 'About twenty men.'

'Right,' said the sergeant briskly. 'We must get out of here now. These locals are bound to tell them we've been here. It's their lives at stake if they don't and the Japs find out.'

Richard turned towards Carola. 'You hear that?'

'I do. You'd better go.'

'I'm taking you both as well.'

'No,' she said firmly. 'I can't leave just like that. I

want to come with you, you must know that. But I can't just walk out on Laung San and not even say goodbye.'

'Then I'll stay here with you.'

'That's impossible, sir,' said the sergeant who had come up the steps. 'You'll never get back on your own. And if the Japs come here, you won't even have the chance to try and these villagers will pay the price.'

At that moment they all heard a sharp crack, like a circus whip being flicked.

'Mortar,' said the sergeant grimly. 'Come on. No more talking. We're going. *Now!*'

Richard seized Carola with one hand, his son with the other. They followed the sergeant, the interpreter and the soldier across the clearing, and into the jungle.

'I can't come with you!' Carola shouted. 'I can't!'

'Be quiet,' ordered the sergeant roughly. 'Sound carries like hell out here. Now follow me in single file. Boy first, lady in the middle, you behind, sir. Keep your Tommy gun cocked, but don't fire unless I give the order. They'll probably loose off a few rounds just to try and draw our fire and find out exactly where we are, because they may not be quite sure. If we fire back, they'll know – and that's the end for us.'

They started to move in single file deeper into the jungle. They found the platoon waiting, rifles unslung, Tommy guns at the ready.

'You stay with me,' the lieutenant told Richard. 'This woman and boy, who are they? Are they with us?'

'They're both English.'

'English? What are they doing here? Where have they come from? They're dressed as Burmese.'

'It's a long story. I can't go into it now. But they're coming back with us.'

'Did you see that other plane, sir?'

'Yes, that's part of the story. I'll tell you everything back at Battalion HQ.'

'Right. All of you lie down flat. Don't move and don't lift your heads if firing starts. Put your feet out with your heels on the ground. Heels stick up. And if you get shot in the heel you'll never walk away.'

They lay down on the ground as he ordered.

'This may be an advance patrol of a company or a battalion and we don't want to tangle with them if we can avoid it. So, no firing unless they're only feet away.'

Carola spoke rapidly in Burmese to her son.

'What's she saying?' asked Browne anxiously. 'You can trust her?'

'Of course.'

'She's his wife, sir,' the sergeant explained.

'His wife?' Browne repeated in amazement.

'Well, going to be, sir.'

'I'm only telling my son we're going to be all right – all of us,' Carola explained.

'Of course we are,' said Richard with a confidence he did not feel.

A loud hollow noise, unexpected as the cough of a hidden giant, drowned Carola's reply.

'Mortar again, and much nearer,' explained Browne grimly. 'Keep down on the ground and cover your ears.'

As he spoke, a shell exploded above them in the treetops. Richard glanced up. The phosphorus had set the branches ablaze. They flamed briefly and died. The air was suddenly sharp with the smell of burning wood, as though a dozen bonfires had been lit in English suburban gardens. Now, in the distance, they could hear shouting, screams of pain.

'Someone's hit,' said Browne tersely. 'Wait here.'

He moved away through the trees. Richard lay on his stomach, his gun trained on a small patch ahead of him, between thick, high trunks. As he watched, the legs of a man appeared in his sights. They moved slowly, cautiously. The legs wore light khaki trousers, puttees and

589

brown boots. These were unusual, because they had a separate part for the big toes, like thumbs on a pair of mittens. The legs came steadily on towards him. Within seconds the Japanese must see him. Richard set the Tommy gun to Single Shot, fired two rounds in quick succession. The legs collapsed.

A Japanese soldier, festooned with leather straps and belts for ammunition and a water bottle, lay dead only feet away. The whole forest now erupted with shouts and firing, the crack of mortars, the stuttering stammer of machine-guns. The lieutenant came running back through the forest, doubled up as men run under fire to present as small a target as possible. Then the firing stopped as suddenly as it had begun.

'One of our men's been killed,' he reported, 'and there are five dead Japs out there. Trouble is, the others aren't coming on as they usually do. That means there are probably a hell of a lot behind them and they're waiting for them to catch up. I'm going to take a section to try and find out what's happening. Wait here. Don't move. You'll only get lost if you go off on your own.'

Firing started again as he ran back into the jungle. Trees split with great peals like thunder when shells hit them. Then Carola screamed. A group of Japanese came running towards them through the trees in an extended line. Richard pushed the lever on his Tommy gun to Automatic and sprayed them with a magazine of cartridges. Five went down. Two ran to one side. A third stopped and fired from the shoulder with a machine-gun. Richard ripped out the empty magazine, slammed in a full one, fired again. The Japanese dropped. Richard turned to Carola, gripped her hand. As he did so, a single shot cracked and whistled past them harmlessly into a tree.

Richard suddenly felt Carola's hand pull out of his. She collapsed on the ground. He knelt down by her side.

The bullet must have ricocheted and grazed her temple and stunned her.

He felt her pulse, but there was no beat. He examined the graze more closely. It looked deeper than he had thought at first sight. He shook her, trying to revive her, but she did not respond. She had been killed by a one in a million chance.

As he knelt, stroking Carola's wrists desperately, still trying to coax life into her body, Browne came back through the jungle. He walked slowly and his face was white. He was sweating with pain. His left arm had been shot away below the elbow. He collapsed, moaning in agony.

'Right pocket,' he whispered weakly. 'Morphia.'

Richard felt in Browne's field dressing pocket, found a little phial of morphia, bit off the neck, dug the jagged edge into the young man's arm. Browne began to breathe heavily, then sighed and rolled over on one side, snoring. Richard took out his field dressing, bound up the stump of the arm to stop the bleeding. The sergeant came up.

'You all right, sir?'

'Yes.'

'Officer's copped it,' said the sergeant. 'We'll have to carry him back.'

Then he saw Carola lying on the ground.

'What's happened to her? Fainted, has she?'

'No. She's dead.'

'*Dead?* A goner?'

The boy crouched by Carola's side, weeping. He looked up at Richard with beseeching eyes. Richard put his arm round him, trying to comfort him.

'We'll have to go now if we're to have any chance of getting back before the Japs regroup,' said the sergeant.

Other members of the platoon were arriving. They lit cigarettes or drank greedily from water bottles. Two pulled some long branches from a tree, cut away the

591

smaller shoots with their bayonets and made a crude litter using creeper to tie the poles together.

'A burial party,' said the sergeant sharply. 'Six men to bury this lady here. She's English. And *hurry*!'

Half a dozen soldiers began to hack at the hard ground with entrenching tools and bayonets until they had scooped out a shallow grave. Richard and the sergeant laid Carola in it gently. He crossed her hands, closed her eyes. Her face was pale but composed. The only mark was the slight graze on her forehead, of a size and apparent insignificance most people would barely notice. Richard slipped the copper ring from her finger; he would keep it as carefully as she had kept it.

He felt numb, as though this must be happening to someone else, not to him. He wasn't involved in any way. It was all a dream. He had found Carola after so many years, and with her a son he did not even know existed. And now she was dead. The grief would come later, he knew. And it would never completely leave him. Every morning as he awoke he would remember this day, a greeting, then a goodbye. Every evening he would think of her here.

His pain, like Lieutenant Browne's, one mental, the other physical, was clouded temporarily, Browne's by morphia, his by shock. Later, they would both feel the full agony of their loss. Miserably, Richard wondered whose pain then would be the greater.

They set off along the jungle track, scouts out at front and rear, Richard and the boy in the centre, the sergeant by the side of the unconscious lieutenant tied to the litter with creeper. Every now and then they checked their position with the compass, cursing as the needle swung uselessly from one side to the other. As a result of some form of electric interference that no one understood, compasses could suddenly go mad in the jungle. Their needles would swing crazily, then, within ten paces, would give a true and steady reading.

They marched until dusk, spent that night by the side of the track, taking it in turns to sleep and stand guard. Late on the following afternoon they reached Battalion Headquarters. The lieutenant's wound was beginning to go septic. The effect of the morphia had long since worn off. He was now delirious. The boy had hardly spoken on the whole march, nor had he eaten. He had drunk only a little water from Richard's bottle, but he kept pace with them, head down, so that the men would not see his tears.

The adjutant was waiting for them outside his *basha*. 'I heard on the radio you ran into trouble,' he said.

'It ran into us,' Richard explained. 'The lieutenant's in a bad way.'

Medical orderlies carried Browne into a *basha* to examine his wound.

'Who's the Burmese boy?' asked the adjutant.

'He's not Burmese, he's English. He's my son.'

'Your *son*? Did you know he was up here?'

'No. I found him, with his mother. But she was killed. A Jap bullet ricocheted.'

'My God.' For a moment the adjutant wondered whether Richard's brief experience of war in the jungle had deranged him. How could he possibly have found his son, and presumably his wife, in some Burmese village? 'The Jeep's ready when you are,' he said, glad to be able to turn the conversation into a channel he understood.

'Then we'll leave now,' Richard told him.

He checked the parts they had removed from the engine. He did not know the names of the men who had carried them, sweating under their awkward weight.

'Thank you all,' he told them. 'I'm sorry to have been the cause of this trouble. But, believe me, you've done a more valuable job here than anyone can possibly imagine.'

'Glad to hear it,' said the sergeant heavily. 'How's the kid doing?' He turned to the boy. 'What's your name?'

'My mother told me I was a traveller, like Marco Polo. She named me Mark.'

'That your only name?'

'Mark Richard,' he said.

'An old English name, Richard,' said the sergeant.

'Yes,' the boy agreed solemnly. 'She named me after my father.'

For Richard, the journey home was a blurred kaleidoscope of activity. Somehow he and Mark reached Chittagong where Richard bought his son a shirt and some trousers, a pair of shoes and socks, and a sweater. The weather would be cold in England. His Burmese clothes were only suitable for a hot climate.

A Dakota then flew them back over India, Iraq, North Africa, up across the Bay of Biscay to land in the damp chill of an English spring.

'My mother promised I would come to England, one day,' Mark told Richard as the plane came in to land. 'She told me so much about it. She was always sure I'd get here one day. She had so much to show me, she said.'

'I will try and take her place,' Richard said gently. 'It will be difficult for both of us, but I will do my best. You and I will always remember her, Mark, and the things she said and did. So in that sense she'll live on in our minds and thoughts. You may go on to some new place, or we may meet some stranger, and we can both say whether or not she would have liked them. And at any time of decision, we will think what course she would have advised us to take. That way, she will always be with us. She was a very brave person, Mark. Some day I will tell you just how brave.'

They had no immigration formalities to pass through at Northolt airfield and a minimal Customs search. In a world at war, not too many strangers arrived in England, and those who did came on official business. When anyone asked who Mark was, Richard replied simply: my son. A courier waited with an RAF truck to collect the parts from the Zero. The driver dropped Richard and Mark at Richard's flat.

A mass of letters, bills, final demands lay behind the front door. Richard opened some of the letters. He was surprised to discover that nearly all were from buyers of his pictures. His prices were now among the highest of any artist in New York. He was a rich man – and this was only the beginning. Yet he felt no elation, no real pleasure in the news. It might all be happening to someone else with whom he had no contact. If Carola had been here, then everything would be different. But she was not here, and she never would be here.

Epilogue

Sometimes it seemed that the years between then and now crowded one on another with all the speed of those days flying from Burma to London in the Second World War. Time, Richard discovered, was like a concertina. It could stretch or shrink, and often he found difficulty in separating what had happened then from what was happening now.

Some memories still stood out clearly. One was seeing Lady Warren on his return. He was saddened by the sudden deterioration in her health and appearance; it reminded him of his mother's swift and final decline. People could stay much the same for years, ageing slightly but almost imperceptibly, just mellowing gently round the edges, and then suddenly they weren't middle-aged any longer. They weren't even old; they were very old. It was clear that her faculties were failing, like her eyesight.

'I have some news for you,' he told her.

'And what is that?'

'I found Carola,' he said.

'What do you mean, you found her?' She was sharp now, eyes narrowed, lips tight in her bloodless face.

He told her, explaining everything as gently as he could. Then he handed her the photograph he had taken of Carola, standing on the verandah of the *basha* that had been her home for so long.

'Where is she?'

'She died on the way back.'

He explained what had happened. Lady Warren nodded sadly, as though she had almost expected this. Elvira, the fortune-teller, had been quite right. Carola had not died on her outward flight. The journey home, however, had been something else.

'Did she ask about me?'

'Yes,' Richard replied. 'She asked especially about you.'

'She didn't blame me for the years she spent in the jungle, living like a native?'

'Why should she? It wasn't your fault, it wasn't anyone's fault. A sparking plug blew out of the engine. If that hadn't happened, something else might have.'

'And this was her home all that time? This bamboo hut?'

'Yes.'

'Poor Carola. I never imagined that could possibly happen. I thought that if she did come down safely, she would be well looked after, and then travel home.'

She was silent for a while. 'And you say there's a boy. Where is he now?'

'At home with me.'

'Whose son is he? Yours or that Australian's?'

'Mine.'

'How do you know? When I was a young girl, there was a saying up north: it's a wise child who knows his own father.'

'Possibly. But in this case, there's a birthmark, my family mark.' He turned over the back of his hand.

'Ah, I've often seen that. Didn't want to remark on it.'

'I have copied it on all my castings for engines. M.P. For Marco Polo. Carola was flying above the route he took about six hundred years before her.'

'I remember. What's the boy called?'

'Mark.'

'A good name.' She was silent again, thinking. Elvira had said she saw two people flying, not one. Again, she had been quite right, in a most unexpected way. Lady Warren looked at Richard. 'Well, as a father, how are you placed for money?' she asked him bluntly.

'For pretty well the first time in my life, I'm not short of it.'

'Not like that fellow Tom, then? He was always short of it. But how have you got so rich? Inventors don't usually make much money. It's the people who exploit them who make the millions.'

Richard explained about his paintings.

'I'm very glad to hear that,' she told him, her voice softening for the first time. 'Very glad indeed. I can tell you that if you'd said you were hard up I was going to give you some money. I haven't long to live, and there's no virtue in hanging on to what you can't take with you. Might as well enjoy the pleasure it gives other people. But as you don't want it, or don't need it, I'll put it into a trust for orphans of the war. Maybe to help the people in that village if the Japanese went back for them. And that man you told me about, Laung San, who was kind to Carola.

'There is a lot of kindness in the world, and in my life I think I've often looked, quite wrongly, for the other side in people. I had a harsh upbringing, Richard, and I never forgot it. More, I never let anyone else forget it, either. Now I think it's time to forget, to put bad memories out of my mind and only remember the good. I've enough money to see me out. I'd have given it all away if I'd thought it would bring Carola back.'

'You loved her,' said Richard gently.

She nodded. 'Yes. I didn't know that then. I didn't think I could love anyone. I didn't think I was capable of that sort of emotion. But when she didn't come back, I knew I was. And I prayed every day, though I've never been a religious woman, that she was all right. I went to see clairvoyants. Most told me nothing. But one, Elvira, told me she would live. She was honest. She could see some way beyond the mists of time and distance. But not all the way. I must see that she is rewarded, too. Honesty is about as rare as kindness.'

Her voice began to fade; it was time to go. Richard kissed her lightly on the forehead. She gripped his wrist firmly.

'Dear boy,' she said. 'It's some time since a man kissed me. You will probably be the last person ever to do so.'

In this Lady Warren was right. She died a month afterwards, but not before the Carola Marsh Children's Foundation was established.

There really wasn't much left after that, Richard often thought. It was as though his own life really ended when Carola died. He painted a great deal. His son grew up and married. Lady Warren had said once how parents lived through their children. This wasn't the case with Richard and Mark, but it most certainly was true of him and his grandson David.

While Mark had never shown much interest in engines or in art, or indeed any of the things that captivated Richard's mind, David did. He liked the steam engine. And he remarked on the sign that Carola, his grandmother, had soldered on it; his sign, their sign, the initials of the great journeyer.

Richard lay in bed, an old man thinking of the past. Faces drifted across his mind in a mist procession; people who had helped or hindered him. The doctor had been quite right in calling him a speculator; so were many of the other people in his life, probably most of them. Mr Compton, the schoolmaster, speculating on the help he could give a promising pupil; Tobin, now dead of alcoholism, who had speculated that a wealthy wife and a huge loan could make him rich; Mannering, who speculated on governments buying arms or selling concessions, but who ended up as someone else's speculation. Of them all, Carola had speculated the most. She had lost her freedom, eventually her life, in a gamble that, even if it had succeeded, would now only be a half-forgotten footnote in the long and turbulent history of flight.

As always, his thoughts, like his days, began and ended with her. If he hadn't met her, would his life have followed the same course? He had not married. He never had time for casual affairs, and as little inclination for them. He had spent his life with engines, drawings, paintings. They had not only been his mistresses, and his wife, they had been his life. Kipling had been quite right when he had written that he who travels the fastest travels alone, and Richard had travelled alone. It had often been a lonely journey but, looking back, he thought he would not have had it any other way, even if he had the chance. Or was he really just trying to convince himself?

If he had his time again he would have changed many things. For one, he would have been far more positive in his relationship with Carola. Similarly with Eleanor. With her backing, he could have built Zimbro Cars into a company of international renown. But again he had been far more concerned with the company than the girl, with inanimate things rather than flesh and blood. Perhaps he would not change that because he could not, even if he had his time again.

Richard had found his fulfilment, first in his inventions, then in his paintings. He was not concerned that others might make fortunes from jets or turbo-chargers or anything else he had designed. He enjoyed what to him was the much deeper satisfaction of having conceived them. They were the children of his mind.

Money had never meant much to him. And yet he had made a fortune from his pictures. Money now poured in, unexpected and unplanned. There was even talk that he should be given a knighthood for his services to art. He would rather have been honoured for his services to engineering, but engineers were rarely honoured.

Like Marco Polo, who started life as an unknown merchant and then found fame as a traveller, Richard had succeeded in a way he had never imagined.

As he lay, turning over in his mind the vicissitudes of chance and mischance, he heard small footsteps on the stairs. His grandson David came into the room, holding the steam engine.

'Did it work all right?' Richard asked him.

'Very well, Uncle Richard.' David scratched his nose and looked at his grandfather, trying to gauge his mood. 'I've had an idea,' he said at last. 'I was thinking, if I lightened the fly-wheel, if I shaved just a little bit of metal off all the way round, would that make the engine go faster?'

'Indeed. But don't take off too much, or it won't go at all.'

The boy put the engine back carefully under its glass case. From where Richard lay, he could see the lettering: 'The Spirit and the Speed' and the mark Carola had made on it. In the end, everything came back to her. And as far as Richard was concerned, it always would.

'Will you tell me about it one day?' David asked him, indicating the steam engine. 'You promised.'

'Yes,' agreed Richard gravely. 'I promised. I'll tell you all about it. One day.'